JANUARY REDEMPTION

R. LEANDA

WINTERSEED PRESS

This book is dedicated to my beautiful daughter, C.J. White

1985- 2016

1

Spring, New York, 2012

Janvier Reed barely existed anymore.

He walked into the café that cool spring morning as Jan Winters, the thirty-three-year-old owner of an escort service. No one connected to the escort service called him Janvier, and in New York, everyone he knew had a professional connection. In fact, he hadn't spoken to anyone he considered a friend in almost fifteen years.

Jan considered taking his regular table in the corner of the café, near the opening of the antique bookstore, but it was too pretty to sit inside. The new client he expected to meet was undoubtedly a one-timer who would probably rather not be out in the open, but Jan didn't care. The sun warmed the concrete, the pastries smelled sweet, and the old trans who ran the bookstore visually appraised an equally old hippy as she flipped through yellowed posters. Jan took a table on the sidewalk where he could watch the love story unfold inside the bookstore.

The city flowed in front of him. Usually, he felt claustrophobic with all the people, but it wasn't too bad that morning. He wasn't in a crush of people, or even in the shadow of a building. Sitting in the sun, he didn't inhale someone else's exhale.

Without asking for an order, the waitress brought him coffee and a bowl of peach ice cream. He asked about her son's grades in math. Jan was comfortable enough to let an echo of his childhood show. "I had a great tutor in high school." Talking about high school and Donny made him flush with embarrassment. Jan Winters never talked about his past, even to safe waitresses who were nice to him. Still, at the same time, it felt good. "Donny...all nose and ears, but he made me learn enough to stay on the football team. Maybe your boy should get a tutor."

An older man stomped up to the café, sat down, and snapped his fingers to get the waitress's attention. Jan sipped his coffee and scrutinized him. His services were far too expensive for anyone with a fifteen-dollar haircut and a department store suit. No, his new client was the late-thirties man in expensive jeans and good cotton dress shirt who strolled up to the café in a self-consciously casual way. The younger man was not what Jan expected, but there was no doubt that he, and not the rude older man, was the client.

The younger man was good looking. His dark hair had started turning gray but he looked like he was no more than forty. The gray hair contrasted with his dark eyebrows and his light blue eyes. Tall and well built, the client had a tan that came from living somewhere where skyscrapers didn't block the sun. He glanced around, obviously trying to look sophisticated and irritated. Instead, he looked a little lost. He almost headed for the finger-snapping old fart. Jan hooked his finger at the new client, and the guy reversed directions. Obediently, the client sat down across from him.

"Hi. Are you Winters?" Ah, sweet God, he had a southern accent.

The waitress, ignoring the finger snapping asshole, put coffee and a bowl of ice cream, the same order as Jan's, in front of the client. Before she stepped away, she also took a glance at those eyes which looked real, not like tinted contact lenses.

Jan gestured at the ice cream. "I'm Winters. It's still a little cool for ice cream, but I think you'll find it satisfying. They make their own here."

He waited for the client to try the ice cream or to say something. The man had contacted him via the website for Jan Winter's Inc. There was no real information on the website, not even the word "escort." Without a recommendation, the e-mail would go unanswered, but a regular client also contacted him saying that he had a cousin in town. Jan's assistant Alexia did a background check and arranged the meeting.

When a few seconds of uncomfortable silence passed, Jan took the reins. "You are Will Wilkerson, but you don't want to use your last name so let's pretend I don't already know it. So tell me, what do you have in mind?"

Will Wilkerson started to speak but stopped when the waitress passed too closely. Jan waited, sipping his coffee. There was enough chill left in the air to enhance the warmth of the drink. When the waitress moved away from the table, the client leaned towards him and whispered, "I've heard that you provide services with some very lovely women." He definitely had a southern accent.

Jan's voice held no trace of an accent. "I run an escort service. If you need a lovely young lady with impeccable table manners to accompany you while you visit our fair city, I can connect you with someone in about an hour." The ice cream tasted beyond good. He wondered if it was bad for his teeth to sip hot coffee and eat cold ice cream.

Obviously uncomfortable as hell, Will Wilkerson glanced around several times. Perhaps he was waiting for a moment of privacy or perhaps he was expecting the law to come down on them. Jan did not fear the police. He ran a clean service for wealthy patrons and the few times he had interacted with an official investigation, they found him cooperative and helpful. He even paid his taxes to the penny. Again, softly, he asked Will Wilkerson what he wanted.

The southern client leaned forward, almost whispering. "I know you're expensive. You were recommended…"

"I can provide a young lady, or a young man, who will escort you wherever you want to go. She or he will know what utensil to use for Lèvres rôties de vieille chèvre. If you want something memorable, I can set you up with a young man from New Zealand who has tattoos on his face, speaks with a combination British-Australian accent, and loves to show off his knowledge of world affairs."

The southern gentleman looked at him, and Jan looked right back. After a moment, Will Wilkerson's face relaxed, then slid into a good-natured smile. "Shee-it, you're playing with me."

"Yes, I am. Eat your ice cream and tell me what you want."

A well of homesickness opened inside Jan. He was used to the feeling, but the intensity surprised him. He barely paid attention to the city moving around them as he sat in the sunshine, ate his favorite ice cream, and listened to a nervous man speak. Jan's childhood home was full of green trees, warm days, and the same soft, rolling accent.

The nervous client looked him in the eye. "I'm looking for something memorable."

Jan spoke around the lump in his throat. "Maybe the grad student from New Zealand is an option for you." The client had a great, genuine smile. Good.

4

"I'm looking for women. Three or four of them. I understand you handle that situation really well."

That was disappointing to hear. The client who recommended Will Wilkerson was a cardiac surgeon and an arrogant jackass who paid to have several women adore him all at once. Jan didn't want the new client to be a jackass of any kind.

He took a sip of his coffee before he answered. "I can provide as much company as you want. However, with only one client, three or four women usually equal an awkward social situation. Besides being obscenely expensive, you have two women doing all the social part and two women trying not to show how bored they are. Are you looking to share the party with another client?"

Jan found himself sincerely hoping Will was not looking for a staged orgy. He didn't want the handsome, blue-eyed man to be disgusting enough to party with his cardiac surgeon cousin.

"Good God, no. No, just me."

Better. He liked Will Wilkerson. He even liked his foolish, repetitive name.

The guy, still leaning over the table and whispering, asked what Jan recommended.

"Two girls, supervised." Jan surprised himself again. He only 'supervised' with the billionaire, but he wanted to be there with Will Wilkerson. He wasn't interested in watching clients pant their way to a too-fast orgasm, but Will made him feel curious. He wondered if he'd volunteer to supervise if the guy had a New England accent instead of a southern one. It sounded like Carolina, but everything southern sounded like home to him.

Will Wilkerson looked surprised. "You're going to be there?"

Janvier shrugged in a non-committal way. "I can be."

The client frowned slightly. "Are you going to participate?"

"I'm the boss. That means no, and I don't have to be there."

Again, Wilkerson did that slight, thinking frown. "Okay. I

wouldn't mind that. There is one more thing. I want one girl who will, you understand, one who will...I guess the term is 'backdoor'—" A woman pushing a baby stroller walked by, and Will shut up. He leaned back and grabbed his coffee cup fast enough to slosh a little onto the table.

While Southern Charm struggled not to say he wanted a whore who'd play with his ass, Jan finished his ice cream and took the client's melting bowl. He wasn't wasting good peach ice cream.

"I have exactly the kind of company you're looking for." He took a pen out of his pocket and scribbled a number on a napkin. "This is the routing number for Jan Winter's Incorporated." He added three thousand on a whim. "Transfer fifteen thousand dollars."

"Fifteen thousand dollars for one night?" Wilkerson looked shocked, but Jan could tell it was fake. That amount was less than his cousin's orgies costs.

"A whole night? No. Fifteen thousand dollars for however long it takes you to finish. Don't wait to transfer the money. I have a slot open this evening."

Jan didn't expect to work that night, but he liked the guy. If Will Wilkerson made him wait too much, Jan might forget he liked him and only send the girls out.

Will hooked one of his eyebrows. "That sure is a lot of money."

"Yes. It is."

"That amount gets reported to the IRS."

"Yes, it does."

"The guy who told me about you said you ran a good operation. He's into this kind of thing and said you're a top pimp, worth the money."

Being called a pimp was nothing new, but he didn't like it coming from that homegrown boy. Evenly, he told him, "Call me a 'pimp' again, and you might as well put the money into bundled mortgage securities."

Will looked at him, confused and contrite. "I'm sorry. I didn't mean to offend you. I mean, you don't look anything like I thought. I figured I'd find someone a little sleazy or someone over the top. You look like someone who would have a wine tasting with a pro basketball game on in the background."

Jan corrected him. "College, not pro." He took a chance that the guy might make him for another Carolina boy. Without the slightest trace of an accent, he said "Tar Heels."

Will missed it. "Well, this Blue Devil will forgive you. If you don't like `pimp' and you don't look like a madam, what do you call yourself?"

"Wealthy."

If Wilkerson liked Duke, he probably came from North Carolina. He might even be from the Raleigh-Durham area. Jan told him what hotel and what time in a voice that meant the meeting was over. The guy didn't seem to be wearing contact lenses. His eyes really were that light blue color. Jan picked up his coffee and took a slow sip. "I'll see you then." He leaned back in his chair, still holding the coffee, and not showing the ache in his chest. He wanted Will to keep talking to him in that soft, slow drawl. The client looked hesitant, then nodded. He got up, and walked casually away with his hands in his pockets.

Jan stayed just long enough to finish his coffee. The waitress asked if he knew how to go about finding a math tutor for her son. He made several suggestions and dropped three twenties on the table instead of two because tutors were expensive. It took a dozen steps to be back in the shadow of a building, back in the crush of people. He called Alexia and set up the meeting for that evening, although he almost hated doing it. Jan didn't want Alexia to know about the Carolina man, which was ridiculous. Will Wilkerson was just another client.

7

Room 1117 was a two-room suite. The discreet, full service hotel only had a dozen suites. The rooms weren't large, but they were comfortable enough for people who were used to the best accommodations. Over the years, they'd used the room more times than Jan wanted to remember.

Will Wilkerson knocked on the door at two minutes before nine. Alexia opened the door and greeted him in a way that sounded like she was delighted with the way he looked and moved and everything about him.

His light blue eyes scanned both girls, but his attention kept wandering back to Jan. Alexia languidly slipped off his jacket and asked him what he was drinking.

The client did not appear to have heard her. "Wow, you're beautiful. Both of you. But...I mean...Winters, can I have a word with you?"

The girls gracefully took themselves into the bedroom.

"That dark eyed woman, she's gorgeous."

"Yes. Alexia. You're lucky to have her. Her time is very much in demand."

"What about you?"

Jan was disappointed. The client wanted him to leave. Why was he disappointed?

Will Wilkerson ran his hand through his graying hair. He didn't try to hide the fact that he was nervous. "You said 'supervised'. It occurred to me that maybe you didn't trust me. I mean, I transferred the money anyway, but are you really going to stay for this?"

"Yes." He didn't reassure the man that he trusted him. He didn't trust or not trust him. He wouldn't have taken him on as a client if he didn't have a basic level of trust, and he'd never seen a high-paid situation that Alexia couldn't handle by herself. Still, Jan said nothing, mostly because he wasn't sure why he was there.

Ever since he took over the business, he did the "supervised" thing with one client. The billionaire got whatever he wanted, even if all he wanted was Jan naked and watching. For the last four or five years, the voyeur sessions with the billionaire were the only time Jan professionally undressed.

But he wanted to be there that night. Jan had a real, and surprising, curiosity about Will Wilkerson. Frankly, that curiosity felt good. "Stay or leave. I don't do refunds."

The client surprised him. He put his hand on Jan's chest. It was a pat, but it lingered for a moment. "Okay. I'm in."

Even as they walked into the other room, he could feel Will Wilkerson's touch on his chest.

In the bedroom, Alexia gave the client a couple of conversational openers to see how much warm-up he needed. However, it was obvious that conversation was unnecessary. Jan took the upholstered chair near the window, and within a few minutes, the women had the client's clothes off. Alexia and the other girl slowly stripped each other, but Will couldn't seem to keep his focus on them. Even when the younger woman knelt in front of him, Will's attention kept drifting over to Jan.

"You're going sit there, fully dressed, and just watch us?"

Jan shrugged. "Would you feel more at ease if I took my clothes off?"

Will was hard and impressively large. "Yeah. It seems weird, otherwise." He grabbed the wardrobe to steady himself as the young woman worked him. She was going too fast. Alexia placed her hand on the girl's shoulder to stop her. It occurred to Jan that the girl must be nervous, working with Alexia and having him in the room. If he recalled, she was one of the college students whose name started with a vowel.

Jan stripped. He had an erection. Since he no longer worked with clients himself, he didn't bother with taking an erection aid anymore. Even though he was only thirty-three, a volunteer erection was rare, especially when he was awake.

Nude, Jan sat back down and let the women work. They led the client to the bed. Will was getting what he paid for, especially from Alexia. She set the languid pace. Alexia could read a client like a street sign and she took each step slowly, giving the other girl non-verbal clues.

Janvier had almost forgotten how genuine arousal felt. He kept his eyes on Will, afraid to look away because his erection might fail. Worse, if he looked away, Will might shift his attention to the women.

Will still watched him. He even gently pushed the girl out of the way when she tried to put her breasts in his face.

Alexia used her free hand to motion for the other girl to go into the other room. Looking confused, the college girl scooped up her clothes and left the room. Jan felt frantic as he turned his attention back to the man on the bed. Will still watched him, still moved with him.

Alexia did not stop her hand. "Jan, come here. It's okay, Jan. Come here."

She was right. Jan got up and went to the bed. Alexia stopped her hand, leaned close to Will, and whispered that Jan wanted him, that Jan was precious, take care of him, let him… She murmured words of need while she slipped a condom onto Jan. Will raised his head and kissed him.

He kissed him.

Jan's lips touched his and it was okay. It was okay to taste his mouth, to touch his tongue, to kiss him. He did not take his time. He did not go slowly.

Will's southern accent was in the words he moaned.

Seconds after Will came, Jan closed his eyes and let himself release. For a moment longer, he kept his eyes closed. He didn't want to see the post-ejaculation look on the client's face.

"Get off me."

Jan Winters rolled to the side of the bed and sat up. He didn't want to look at Will. He didn't want to see what the man was feeling. He didn't want to know what he was feeling either. From the bed, the man asked him if he was HIV negative.

Jan removed his condom. "I'm negative, but you're not likely to believe me." He threw the condom in the trashcan. "Look, I used a condom, okay? You're okay."

Will was lying with an arm over his eyes. "I let a pimp fuck me and I came like a freight train. How is this okay?"

Alexia, ignoring the client, handed Jan a damp washcloth. He stank. Jan wiped away the mess and threw the washcloth on the floor. He didn't want to shower in the room, so he put on his clothes, and even sat on the edge of the bed to put on his shoes. At least the client wasn't crying. He couldn't stand it when some ass cried after an orgasm. Without looking back, he marched into the outer room. Because Wilkerson was a one-time client, the women were already dressed and waiting for him. They fell in behind him as he left the room.

Jan parted from the women at the hotel's lobby. Alexia would take care of the rest of the night's business. Outside, it was a nice evening. He walked, letting himself follow familiar streets. He couldn't remember the last time he'd had an orgasm. Hell, he couldn't remember the last time he had sex that wasn't work related.

He crossed several streets, turned a few corners. The café and the bookstore were still open and filled with young urbanites. Jan looked through the window and realized that it might have been a good orgasm, he might have liked the guy, but it was still work related. It was all work related. He walked on, leaving the bookstore behind him. He ended up walking all the way back to his apartment, trying not to think of Will Wilkerson going back to the forested cities of the N.C. Piedmont.

Jan couldn't go back. He couldn't be Janvier Reed again.

A pimp, a whore. Jan never let Will Wilkerson hear Carolina

in his voice. He never let even a thread come out that said he was a southern boy, too, except when he slipped up and admitted he still followed the UNC sports team, but even that went right over the guy's head.

In a rolling accent, Will Wilkerson had said, "I let a pimp fuck me…"

The words echoed in Jan's ears as he walked into his apartment, stripped, and climbed into the shower. The shower in his apartment was large enough for two and that was a mistake. It was always drafty in there. Jan turned the water on hot and still shivered as he cleaned himself. He was negative, which was not unusual at his price range, but he knew that Will Wilkerson was still going to refrain from sex while he tested and retested. He'd make up some story with his girlfriend about being accidentally stuck with a needle in a trash can and needing to wear a condom until the tests came back, and he'd have trouble getting it up, at least for a while.

"I let a pimp fuck me…"

It wasn't the first time he'd heard the word "pimp." It was just a word. It shouldn't bother him. High end, but yeah, a pimp. A clean pimp, if there was such a thing. He was a sex worker who congratulated himself on his lack of disease.

Jan came out of the shower and looked around his bedroom. A king-sized bed stood in the middle of the room, lit by a series of discreetly placed lights. He'd never once had someone else in the bed. An interior decorator furnished his apartment in shades of white and black, and there was nothing so old school as a nightstand. The bathroom and linens stayed clean, the furniture wasn't dusty so Alexia must send a housekeeper, but he never saw a soul. He flopped down on the bed and listened to the lack of noise. The apartment building was secure, upscale, and the glass panels were thick enough to keep most of the street noise to a minimum.

He was surrounded by millions of people, yet all he heard was the ventilation system.

With wet, cold hair, Jan got up and went back into the living room. He didn't glance at the wall of glass that showed his naked body to the world, didn't even think about it as he hit a switch that caused indirect light to frame the ceiling. There were no end tables in his living room. Everything was glass, gray, or black. He should call some charity to take every god-damned thing out of the place.

The only item in the whole apartment that he could use as a nightstand was a gleaming onyx cube that was wired for something. Trailing the electric cord, he carried the heavy cube into his bedroom. He thumped it down next to the bed, not even curious about why the cube was electrified. He could see his reflection in the onyx-looking thing. He saw nothing but a rich pimp in a sterile apartment, looking for something he could put next to his bed to hold his gun.

———

It had taken two weeks, just two weeks, for Janvier Reed to go from a graduating high school student to a high-priced whore. Just two weeks during which Señor Rijos told him that he "had" to go get therapy, that he "had" to register for community college, and that he "had" to start planning for a future. Just two weeks during which he thought that Señor Rijos didn't understand what he was going through.

After Janvier's mother's suicide, a deep anger settled in and colored every thought that the teenager had. It wasn't fair, it wasn't right that his mother left him to fend for himself. He had no other biological relatives. Except for his friend, Nate Rijos, Janvier had no one. Nate's father took him in, but it wasn't the same. He was angry. Even small things, like having to be tutored or Donny's obvious crush on Nate seemed irritating or insignificant. The big thing was Nate leaving for college.

Janvier was angry about being alone. He couldn't stand the idea of living in the Rijos' spare room after Nate went away to college. He didn't want to even think about taking classes at the community college. When the so-called talent scout gave him a sketchy opportunity, Janvier took it. He was too angry to know better and too angry to understand that the Rijos family had given him a home. He was supposed to go work at Señor Rijos' restaurant with Nate, but he begged off with a 'stomach ache.' As soon as they'd left the small brick house, Janvier packed a bag and called the talent scout to pick him up.

The Woman met them at the airport in New York. Confused, he let the talent scout hand him over to her. Before they'd reached her apartment, she'd changed his name to "Jan" because she thought "Janvier" sounded like he wasn't Caucasian.

Two weeks after he'd arrived in New York, the Woman shook him awake. "Jan, wake up. Jan!"

He pretended to be asleep. It had been two weeks since he heard a rolling southern accent like his own, or since he had seen a lawn when he looked out a window.

Jan opened his eyes slowly. A little sunlight made it into the room, but he couldn't tell what time of day it was. The Woman's place was on the twentieth floor, and her bedroom windows faced another building. There was never any fucking light, even though it was June.

His stomach rolled in a dangerous way as he squinted up at her. The Woman leaned over him and the skin on her face fell forward. "Jan!"

"What?" His voice echoed inside his head.

"He's interested, Jan. He has the pictures and he's interested. Tomorrow night, you are going to meet one of the richest men in the world. Now get up. You need to spend the day at the gym getting the cut back on those muscles. Oh, sweet January, you might just have made it!"

"I told you, don't fucking call me January."

"And I told you to get up. Watch your language, too. Nothing vulgar! You're a southern gentleman, remember that."

He sat up. Next to him, the strange girl she called Alexia rolled over onto her stomach. Another young man slept on a couch over in the corner, naked and curled up, his back to the room. The skin around Janvier's mouth felt raw even though the Woman never let his mouth touch anything. Jan was more sellable as an "inexperienced southern boy." God, he felt nauseated. He barely made it into the bathroom before vomiting hard enough to work out his stomach muscles.

It would be okay. It would. He had the portfolio pictures, professionally done. The Woman said that her clients weren't interested in porn stars. They wanted clean, fresh young men and women. Janvier was completely over the idea that he was going to make commercials and model. He wasn't sure he ever believed it, even when he slipped away from North Carolina without telling Nate or Señor Rijos good-bye. They didn't understand how he felt, and they would have stopped him.

God, he wished they had.

He leaned over the sink, splashing his face with cold water. As he rinsed his mouth, the girl came into the bathroom, sniffed, and said "Oh, gross." She might have been eighteen, but he doubted it. "Leave me alone, Alexia." She ignored him and wiped the toilet seat with a towel before she sat on it.

Did he fuck her last night? He couldn't remember. The Woman was keeping him wrapped in cellophane. He vaguely remembered Alexia sucking on him. Or maybe it was that other boy. He remembered the Woman telling him not to touch either of them. "No previous experience! Just lay back and enjoy, Jan."

He was sure he came, but he wasn't sure there was any

enjoyment. He didn't like the idea of some anonymous guy doing him or even getting head from the weird, too-young girl. "How old are you, Alexia?"

She wiped and flushed. "Eighteen." Naked, she crossed her arms and looked at him with huge, dark eyes. "Why?"

"I wanted to know if I'm sleeping with a kid for the amusement of others."

The girl's face changed with her voice. She spoke with an unfamiliar accent. "Don't worry, Jan. I don't exist." She smiled, which was a weirdly cold thing on her pretty face. "You and that other boy, you don't have families, yes? Nobody to look for poor orphaned you, but you have birth certificates, some way of proving you're eighteen. You exist. Me? No. No birth certificate, no visa, no documents. Nothing. Poor me, yes? When my father sold me, I think I had twelve years. That was maybe two-three years ago."

She was the same age as Donny Ravaterra, but unlike him, there was no child in her eyes. Nothing warm at all. He tried not to jerk away as she patted him on the arm. Her accent was gone. "I can't prove that I'm eighteen, but no one can prove that I'm not. Feel better? She thinks she can sell you for major money, and she told me to keep you happy. That's all. If you need to throw up again, don't flush. I'm getting in the shower."

"Alexia, we can call someone, someone to help you…"

She laughed in a way that was almost happy. "Silly. I get tons of money from men who want to help me. It usually takes about an hour to rescue me completely."

He didn't throw up again. He closed the lid on the toilet and listened to her sing in the shower. She sang a popular love song, but it was flat, tuneless.

Was Nate even looking for him? His friend swore he wouldn't tell his dad about the talent scout, the one that said Janvier was perfect for modeling. Even if Janvier went back, he had no one to go home to. Señor Rijos wouldn't want him around once Nate left for school. And Janvier couldn't get into the same college because his grades were bad and he didn't have any money. And it was all too late anyway.

The smell of Alexia's perfumed shampoo combined with the lingering vomit smell. He would do this. The Woman would find clients and pay the hell out of him. In a year, he'd have enough to go home. They didn't have to know how he made the money.

Janvier would go home rich and tell Nate stories of runways in Milan and Brazil. "God, they love me in Japan!" He would claim to be tired of it, and homesick. He'd have enough to rent a small place near the college where Nate was going. Maybe they could be roommates. Maybe he wouldn't have to accept a single dime from Señor Rijos for college or anything else. He could pay Nate's father back for his mother's funeral. Put up a real headstone for his mom, not a flat stone that the cemetery people could easily mow over. Nate and his father would understand. When he went home, he'd lie but it would be okay.

Alexia stuck her head out of the curtain. "Jan, hand me the razor on the sink. Hey, isn't 'Jan' a girl's name? Or is it one of those swings-both-ways names?" He picked up a slightly used disposable razor from the sink. It trembled in his hand.

The Woman said that his inexperience was important. What if he couldn't do it? What if it was too much? What if it hurt? What if he could do it and what if Nate found him after he started prostituting?

He handed Alexia the disposable razor. He was disposable too. If he couldn't handle what they wanted from him and if he couldn't go home, there was always an exit available. He could do what his mother did. One year. He could stand it for one year.

———

IT WAS ALL a long time ago. Inside his closet, the thirty-three-year-old pimp fished the Colt.45 out of a built-in drawer. He'd been in New York fifteen years now. He had a wealthy owner who gave him an education and a lucrative business. He had the respect of everyone in the sex trade. It was ridiculous that a man with a Carolina accent affected him so deeply that he couldn't control his emotions.

But he couldn't. Feelings welled up inside him until he felt like a wet volcano. The whore named Jan sat on his bed, checked to make sure the gun was loaded, and took the safety off. For a full minute, he pointed the gun at his temple. Then he slid it down until the barrel pointed at his mouth. He slid the barrel along his tongue. The metal tasted right.

The volcanic pressure inside him subsided a little. Running the side of his thumb against the trigger, he realized he had an option. He could get up in the morning and be a successful pimp because he could always come back to his cold apartment, sit on his bed, and put the gun in his mouth again. The tensions drained away. Janvier took the gun out of his mouth and placed it on the onyx cube. He sat for a minute staring at the gun.

It did make him feel better having it there. Now he could sleep.

2

AFTER A CHARITY DINNER IN RALEIGH, Perry Ravaterra held his wife's nude body against his and felt her breathing start to go soft and deep. She was falling asleep, and he needed to tell her something. For some reason, he badly needed to tell her how he felt.

"Paige, tonight was fantastic. I'm so proud of the way you handled yourself around all those contributors. You were the most elegant woman in the room, and you knew what you were doing."

Her breathing changed. She was still awake, so he whispered into her hair. "And you were sincere. You meant it when you thanked people."

She rolled over and wrapped her arm over his chest. "Yes, I'm absolutely sincere. We raised a lot of money tonight and for a very good cause."

Perry wasn't saying what he wanted to say. What he needed to say. "You handled yourself perfectly. I wouldn't be surprised if you ended up as chairperson of that little charity someday."

He immediately caught himself. He'd worked with enough women to know that the word 'little' was used to diminish their work. Frustrated, he tried to dig out of the 'little' hole. "I was impressed tonight. You were the most beautiful woman in the room, and you knew so much. I mean it. Paige, you knew what you were doing."

His words hadn't impressed his wife. In fact, Perry felt her stiffen up.

"Damn it, Paige. I'm trying to say that I am proud to be your husband and that I love you very much."

"I suspect that's true on some level. I love you, too."

Perry hated that response. He wanted to push her away. He wanted to grab her close. But he did find the words to say what he felt. "You used to be so much in love with me. I miss you. I miss us."

In the dark, his wife sighed. It was the same, exasperated sigh that she used when the children were being bad or when Uncle Cal sloshed beer on her coffee table. She propped herself on one elbow.

"Perry, you're being needy. You want me to tell you that I love you despite it all? Fine. I do. Why don't you believe that my lack of enthusiasm is just the cooling off period that comes with a long marriage and three kids?"

"I know, Paige. I'm trying to explain how I feel about you. I love you and I miss the way we used to be. Honey, I have to tell you, I'm not even seeing anyone anymore."

"Yes, dear. I figured that out when you rented the small condo to an elderly gentleman instead of keeping your latest girlfriend in there. But there will be someone else at some point."

He failed to keep the exasperation out of his voice. "Please! Would you listen to me?" He ran his hand along her side and felt her tuck in her tummy.

That self-conscious movement had nothing to do with

impressing him. Her words were cold. "I've loved you all along and I still love you. That probably won't ever change. But every time you tell me that my 'little' charity work makes you proud of me, I think about how your 'little' affairs make me ashamed of both of us. Perry, I'm tired. I had a long day, an adrenaline filled evening, and some pretty good sex with my husband, so please can we just go to sleep?"

She rolled away from him and went to sleep. Perry stared at the ceiling for a long, long time wondering when he'd become so needy where his wife was concerned.

Maybe it was because she wasn't needy with him anymore.

The next morning, Perry had breakfast with his daughters while Paige dressed, and the whole family went off to start their day. Perry kissed his wife and his girls good-bye as they climbed into Paige's Mercedes. He got into his car, but he just sat there and watched Paige drive away. He'd forgotten to ask her what she was doing that day. He'd meant to, especially after the conversation last night. Perry meant to start taking an interest. Damn it. Damn it!

He'd try again tonight or tomorrow morning. He might forget how to pay attention to his wife, but Perry knew how to pay attention to his work. His best client's wife was in the hospital. He knew exactly which hospital to go to in an area that was full of hospitals.

An hour later, Perry stood in the hospital gift shop and debated about which bouquet of flowers to choose for his client's wife, but the attractive woman nodding off behind the cash register was more interesting. Blond and maybe in her late twenties, she perched upon a stool as her eyes drifted closed. In her hand, a crosswords booklet started to fall. Her chin tipped back for a second before she jerked awake and caught him looking at her. Her nametag read J. Cooper, Gift Shop Manager.

"Oh, I'm sorry!" She looked at the booklet in her hand and

obviously had no idea what she was about to do with it. The booklet dropped on the counter top as she hopped off the stool. Perhaps the crosswords were sticky because she wiped her hands on her wrinkled, linen pants which fit tightly over a nice pair of hips.

Perry put on his best sympathetic smile. "I understand sleep deprivation. One of my kids was particularly good at keeping everybody awake until she was about three years old. She seemed to like Tuesday nights, for some reason."

J. Cooper smiled politely. "I don't have kids, but I do have a second job. It's temporary, I hope." For a flicker of a moment, he saw her visually assess him. She did not wear a wedding band. He did.

Perry used his left hand to indicate the flowers in a glass front cooler. "The youthful wife of my biggest client recently had a particularly nasty surgery on one of her Achilles' tendons. Her life on the tennis court is in serious jeopardy. Which arrangement would you suggest?"

Moving with a slight wiggle, J. Cooper joined him at the flower cooler. Her head didn't reach his chin, but she was curvy and in good shape. He preferred taller women, but petite worked for her. He also preferred women who shared the same decade as he did, but the tiny woman was cute and maybe she wasn't that young. Up close, she could have been in her thirties.

She looked up at him with wide eyes. "If your client's wife is a woman who appreciates artistic design and the spending of serious money, I would suggest this one." She indicated a flower creation that had deep purple spikes and one odd looking orange flower.

"Good God, what is that?"

"Does it matter?" J. Cooper smiled up at him. She flirted with him despite his wedding band. Perry didn't intend for the tingle of attraction to go anywhere, but he pushed it to see how she would react. He leaned a little too close and looked her in the eye.

"I'll take it."

J. Cooper blushed and turned towards the cooler. Nice. She wasn't slutty, but she wasn't innocent. She was somewhere in between. Letting her get the flowers out of the glass case, Perry removed his credit card from his wallet. He handed it to her along with a business card that clearly had his cell phone number printed below his name.

J. Cooper, gift store manager, was purely business when she thanked "Dr. Ravaterra."

Even though his father and his sister were not associated with the small hospital, he felt a little uncomfortable with the reference to doctors named Ravaterra. He shook his head. "I'm not in a field of work that involves the word 'doctor.'"

She held up his business card in an "I know" way, but gave a small wave of her hand to indicate their surroundings. "Professional hazard. Around here, it is usually best to go around calling everyone 'doctor.'"

A grandmotherly woman came in the shop. She hurried directly towards the register, urgency all over her face. "You got any of those crystal bracelets the kids like? The faddish interlocking ones?"

Perry thanked J. Cooper for her help and left the shop. He stopped at a wall map. The hospital was a small, local branch for one of the bigger hospitals but still managed to be a maze. He did figure out that orthopedics was a few floors up. Holding the weird flower arrangement with one arm, he made a call while waiting for the elevator. Uncle Cal answered, but the call dropped as soon as Perry got on the elevator. Annoyed, he got off on the fourth floor and redialed the number.

Cal answered immediately. "Hey, Perry, are you playing hang-up games with your shiny, high-tech phone?"

"Sure, Uncle Cal. Forgive me long enough to do me a favor, okay?"

"I live to do you favors, Perry. It makes my whole day sunny."

"Ah, well, Sunshine, you're going to like this one. I need information on a young woman named J. Cooper. She manages the gift shop at the S Street Hospital." Perry wasn't sure this was a good idea, but it probably wasn't a bad one, either.

Cal snorted into the phone. "What'd you do, give her a tickle in the panties without finding out her first name?"

"I haven't tickled anything yet. I doubt J. Cooper is particularly easy and she's a little young for me. I want to find out how young, and if she's as nice as she seems."

Cal's voice became level. "Since when do you like nice girls?"

Maybe it wasn't a good idea. Still, his uncle needed a little attention from him and this seemed harmless enough. Besides, the petite woman was interesting. "I don't like a nice girl yet. I just want a little information."

His uncle had a warning tone that irritated the hell out of Perry. "A nice girl will want to stay a nice girl. She wants love with her sex."

Perry went through some doors into a corridor that had patient rooms. A woman in a wheelchair had a propped-up leg covered in gauze. It looked like her ankle area was in bad shape. Perry looked away when he realized the spot on the gauze was a seepage stain.

At least he found himself in the part of the hospital that dealt with damaged ankles. Maybe his client's wife wasn't that far away. On the phone, Cal still warned him about the evils of nice girls.

Perry could live without the lecture from his hard-luck uncle. "Uncle Cal, you're sounding like an old woman."

"Do old women lecture on the dangers of nice girls?"

He saw his client in the hospital hallway, halfway down the

corridor. Despite the plastic surgery and the hair transplants, the man looked every single one of his sixty-one years. "I'll talk to you later, Uncle Cal. I have to go give a friend's wife some artsy flower thing."

Perry ended the call and grinned at his client, who looked askew at the flower arrangement. "What can I say? The flower shop woman was pretty as hell. How did Ashlee's surgery go?"

3

———————

2013

IN THE BANQUET HALL, Donny Ravaterra tried not to listen to the diners tease his father about the old days. An almost-naturally blond woman walked slowly past the table. Half the pediatricians watched her, including his father, but she watched Donny. In the twenty-four hours since Donny and his father arrived at the pediatric conference, two prostitutes had approached him, once right in front of his father. One of them called him "cutie." The other one purred the word "tall" as if height was the most desirable thing in the world.

Despite his thick, ashy hair and his large hazel eyes, Donny knew that he was ugly enough to make hookers look at him and see dollar signs. He was tall, but so skinny that his clothes always seemed baggy. Even his tailored suit seemed to slide towards one shoulder or the other. His Adam's apple stuck out as far as his chin, and his nose was a potato-shaped monument to his face.

Given his clownish features, most people thought his ears stuck out, but they were actually normal ears. Donny's most embarrassingly remarkable feature was his smile. Lopsided and large, his smile scrunched up his left eye.

Having hookers approach him didn't help. All Donny wanted was to go home, read his baby girl a bedtime story, and spend the rest of the evening grading papers. The drive between the convention center and his condo in Chapel Hill wasn't more than a few hours, but his father seemed to be enjoying the weekend, so Donny would stick it out.

He'd come to the conference to keep his father company. Donny wasn't a medical doctor, just a PhD, but he understood much of what he'd heard. So far, he'd sat through lectures on early diagnosis for mental disorders, pediatric treatment for allergies, and the medical consequences of children exposed to herpes simplex at birth.

It was far more information than the single father wanted to know.

By now, Madeline would be in her footie pajamas and her bedtime diaper. It was the first time he'd ever left her for the weekend. She was staying with his brother and his family. Perry's daughters adored Madeline, and his wife doted on her. His baby would be fine without him.

Donny's father and his pediatrician cronies enjoyed a lively dinner talking about the old days and what a dog his father used to be. He laughed with the rest. "Please don't tell me that y'all are cleaning these little stories up because I'm here." Donny loved his serially-married father, but he was also glad that his dad had hidden most of his philandering when Donny and his sisters were growing up.

After the main course was over, he decided to do all of them a favor and stop being a drag on the conversation. A pretty brunette walked by the table and headed out to the lobby. Donny patted his father's arm and said, "Excuse me." He got up and followed the woman out of the restaurant, ignoring the sounds of appreciation from his father's half-drunk friends. For about a second, Donny wondered if his father would set them straight, but it didn't matter whether he did or didn't.

He glanced in at the bar as he headed for the elevator, and a familiar face caught his eye and he stopped. A Hispanic man sat at the bar. Donny knew that man. He knew his name was Nate and that he was thirty-three years old. He knew that strong profile, the way the man's body moved, and he knew that his eyes were dark enough to reflect light. After fifteen years, Natanael Rijos was still the best-looking man Donny had ever seen. Nate glanced at him, and he saw the recognition on the man's face.

Donny moved over to the bar and self-consciously stopped his lopsided smile before it became too big. "Hi, Nate. Any chance that you remember me?"

"Yeah. I definitely do. Damn, it's good to see you!" Nate smiled a perfectly even smile, showing perfectly even teeth. He indicated the bar stool next to him. Donny slid onto the seat and damned if it didn't wobble so he had to catch his balance. Nate reached out and steadied him. "Here, move over on this side."

He switched bar stools. Of course, Nate remembered him. Ugly was as memorable as beautiful. Back in high school, Donny had tutored Nate's best friend for six months. The ex-football player might not remember his name. Seating himself on the un-wobbly bar stool, Donny wondered how to remind him. He didn't need to.

"So, Donato Ravaterra, what are you drinking?" Nate signaled for the bartender.

Donny didn't know what to say to that. His older brother drank a specific scotch and ginger ale, but there was a special name for that and if Donny sipped a scotch, his nose and ears would be red for the rest of the evening. His dad drank gin and tonic, but that might be too old school. He should just order a beer, but the kind the nerds club drank in college was probably some awful brand. A couple of name brands came to mind, but he didn't know if they were any good or not.

"Gin and tonic, please." Of course, the bartender asked for ID. Irrationally, Donny felt himself blush as he pulled his license out. At thirty, he shouldn't blush. Maybe the dim lighting would keep Nate from noticing his embarrassment.

A brunette pediatrician walked out of the almost empty bar, her fanny swaying with each step. Nate watched her and Donny's heart gave an unpleasant, jealous squeeze. He almost missed Nate asking, "So, what brings you to the lovely Convention Center? What have you been doing for the last fifteen years? Are you a restaurant owner or a pediatrician?"

"Me? No. I'm at the university. I just started there." Donny suppressed the desire to brag about his academic career, although Nate seemed like he really wanted to know. God, even in the dim light of the bar, Nate's eyes still sparkled. "I came with my dad. He's the pediatrician, remember? What about you?"

"I'm here with my dad, too."

Donny forgot there was a convention of restaurant owners meeting at the other end of the hotel. "Oh, did you go into the restaurant business with your father? In Raleigh? I mean, do you work there?" Jesus! He told himself to shut-up. "Is that what you do now? In Raleigh?" Could he leap any harder at the chance that he and Nate were both living in the same area again?

Nate nodded, but said, "No. Dad still has the restaurant in Raleigh, but I'm a paramedic in Chapel Hill."

God. Nate did live in the area. Not only in the area, but right in Chapel Hill. "I'm in Chapel Hill too." He'd said that already, hadn't he? "I teach."

Nate let his eyes slip over Donny's face before he said, "You're young to be a professor, but you always were smart."

Donny nodded yes, he was young. He didn't bother to explain the difference between adjunct and tenure tract. "So how did you become a paramedic?"

"I did a couple of tours as a medic and when I came back, it seemed the best way to go. It suits me, like I'll bet teaching suits you. You were good with Janvier, back in high school."

"Thanks. Janvier, wow. I haven't heard that name in a long time. What did he end up doing?"

Right before Nate's and Janvier's graduation, Donny spent as much time as possible with the two football players, trying to make every blissful moment last. He knew that a self-proclaimed talent scout wanted Janvier, the quarterback, to become a model and an actor. Everyone knew it was a scam, so Donny didn't give it much thought. Back then, the looming graduation of the seniors just about killed fifteen-year-old Donny because he couldn't stand the idea that he wouldn't see Nate and Janvier again. He liked Janvier, but he adored Nate.

From time to time, Donny still thought about the football players. Now the adult and still-handsome Nate sat on a bar stool and said something horrible.

"Janvier left right after graduation. There wasn't anything Dad and I could do because he was eighteen. He just disappeared. We went up to New York the first break I had from school but Janvier was gone. We hired a private detective, but the only thing we found out was that the `talent scout' that took him had a record for pimping, prostitution, procurement…"

"Oh, God no. What about Janvier? What happened to him?"

"Gone."

Donny put his hand on Nate's arm. He didn't mean to.

Nate didn't pull his arm away. "Janvier sent me a postcard on my twenty-first birthday, so we know he was still alive then. There was a New York postmark, but no return address. My dad even hired another private detective, but we have nothing. After a few years, I guess I decided that he was dead, you know? But a couple of years back, my father got a cashier's check and a note that said Janvier wanted to pay him back for his mother's funeral. And I got another card from him on my thirtieth birthday. Same postmark."

"Do you still look for him?"

"Yeah. We still do internet searches and stuff like that but these days, we don't talk about it much."

The bartender asked if Nate wanted a refill. He nodded and looked at Donny's almost untouched gin and tonic. "You still like that sweet soda?" He told the bartender to bring him another beer and to bring Donny a Dr. Pepper.

"I can't believe you remember what kind of soda I drink."

The corners of Nate's eyes crinkled in a way that showed his age and said, "Of course I remember. I remember you, Donny, the gentle boy who was my first male crush."

Donny forgot how to breathe. He assumed Nate meant that Donny was the first guy to have a crush on him, not the other way around. Before he could think of an appropriate way to ask for clarification, his phone went off in his pocket. It was his brother's ring tone. Oh, God. The timing was so incredibly bad. "I have to take this, Nate." He pulled the phone out of his pocket and almost dropped it. "I have a baby at home."

He turned away from Nate but didn't get off the stool as he talked to his little girl. He could hear Paige telling Madeline to give him a kiss on the phone. She made a noise that might have been a kiss. He had no choice. He had to kiss back.

"Sorry." Donny hung up the phone.

"How old?"

"Madeline is almost one. She just started walking." He pulled a picture up on the phone. It showed a baby with honey-blond hair and large, hazel eyes.

"Wow. She looks like you."

"Well, no, she's pretty. But she takes after my family. My sisters are pretty."

"If I recall, they were pretty and smart, like you. And you had a much older brother who was already through college."

Donny couldn't believe how much Nate remembered about his family.

"Does your baby girl come with a wife?"

"No. Never. Madeline's mother is not in the picture. She's doing a long stint in prison. She thought smuggling drugs was a good way to earn a living while pregnant." Donny reined himself in. He usually did not explain his fall into fatherhood. "We were never a real couple, not really. Anyway, I have full custody. What about you? Do you have any kids?"

Nate shook his head no. "No wife, no partner, and no kids. Donny, my dad's about to walk in, but I'd like to see you again." Nate watched an older man walk into the bar. The older man nodded to Donny and sat down on the wobbly bar stool. It didn't wobble.

"Donny Ravaterra, this is my father, Eduardo Rijos. I don't remember if you two ever met when we were in high school. Dad, Donny tutored Janvier during senior year."

"Of course." Obviously, the restaurateur didn't remember Donny. The older man agreed that it was a small world and said that he'd be ready to go in a minute. However, he needed to use the restroom first, so he politely excused himself.

As soon as Mr. Rijos walked out of sight, Nate sighed heavily. "I'm going to have to meet the daughter of another restaurant owner. I guarantee she'll be pretty, call me Natanael instead of Nate, and will not consider raising the children as anything but Catholic. Can I see your phone for a minute?"

Donny hoped he knew what Nate was about to do. He handed his phone to him.

Nate made a call on Donny's phone. The phone in Nate's

pocket rang twice before he disconnected the call. "Now you have my number, Donny. Give me two hours and call me, okay?"

Nate put a few bills on the bar, too much for a couple of beers and an untouched gin and tonic. Donny started to protest, but Nate waved him silent. "Let me buy you your gin and your Dr. Pepper, Donny. Call me?"

"Sure." Oh dear God, the look on Nate's face was so…sincere!

Two hours. It was eight o'clock. Donny went and found his father. The doctors were all standing up and heading for the door. Donny cut his father from the herd.

"Dad, you'll never guess who I ran into. Nate Rijos. He was the football player I was so in love with in high school, remember? We're going to meet later." Donny grinned so big that his left eye closed completely.

4

December, 2014

Jan's eyes opened in the dark room. He was curled on his left side and hot in the perfectly climate controlled bedroom, but he made no move to kick away any covers. It wasn't allowed. The billionaire, who still snored lightly beside him, became chilled easily, which was why the room was seventy-eight degrees and why the blankets stayed on. Jan wasn't supposed to be awake before the billionaire. He had no idea what time it was, but he stayed on his side, nude and sweating, and waited.

Alexia had not been asked to spend the night. The old man moved in his sleep, reaching for him. Jan stared at nothing and vaguely wondered who the old man slept with when he was not in New York. Just the touch of Jan's skin made the old man settle back into deep sleep. Perhaps he had the equivalent of Jan and Alexia in the cities he frequented.

Sex hardly ever happened anymore, but it had the night

before. Jan 'watched' while Alexia and a couple of others made the old man's erectile aids work. Jan had to take one also to make his erection work until the billionaire was finished. Jan's job was to make sure the sex and sleep went well.

Next to him, the old man abruptly twitched awake. It had to be four a.m. Jan didn't move, but slowed his breathing down to mimic sleep as the billionaire spooned against him, murmering, "You're awake. Hmmm. And you are sweating."

It was a relief to breath normally. Jan didn't even consider complaining about the room's temperature "Yes. I had a bad dream. Something about falling."

The billionaire made a "Tsk-tsk" sound. "No bad dreams when you're with me, Jan. Only sweetness and affection are allowed in this bed. I have a surprise for you this morning." He gave Jan a full body hug before getting up.

Jan did not want a surprise. He did not want anything. Nothing pleased him anymore. With a head full of fuzzy nothing, he got up and sat in his breakfast chair with the lambswool blanket draped over him. As sweaty as he was, he vaguely wondered if the valet would have the gray blanket cleaned.

A servant dressed in black silk was asking him if he was okay. "Yes." He looked around the room quickly. The billionaire was still getting dressed, so it was okay to speak to her. "I'm fine."

She looked at him quizzically. "You were staring into nothing, Jan-kun."

"Yes ma'am. I'm just sleepy."

It was happening to him more and more. He was fine, then he'd blank out. Jan took a deep breath and smiled as she set the breakfast table with the billionaire's homemade mug. Right on cue, the billionaire entered the room, sat down, and sipped his coffee.

"Ah, Jan. My retirement has changed so many things. Now, when I get up in the morning, I still make people meet me at the office, only now it is any office I choose. This morning, I am meeting with a group of historians who are interested in some scrolls I own. Oh, you didn't know about those? I think you should join me this morning. Yes, I will delay the meeting to give you time to shower and dress. I think you'll find it amusing how polite needy people are when they have to be in their offices at five in the morning and are kept waiting until six."

Jan nodded. Had he just agreed to go with him or agreed that needy people are polite?

He had a meeting with Alexia about hiring a new girl, but it wouldn't be until later, and she'd wait if he was late. He sipped his coffee from an antique china cup. It was so thin that he felt like he could nibble the rim. What the hell did the billionaire just say about traveling?

"I'm no longer worried about your reluctance to get a passport because you've lived in New York for almost half your life. By now, you are over your fear of leaving the country or that your little adoptive Mexican family will find you. And if they do, so what? You can't still care about them. You are successful and wealthy, certainly by their modest standards. We'll get you that passport, put a manager into the business and you and Alexia will retire, like me."

Jan said nothing and tried to stare at the fog that was circling his vision.

"Jan!" The billionaire squeezed his hand. "The world! I'm going to show you the ancient world. You know how I feel about antiquity, even before I became an antique." The old man's face formed an oval of wrinkles as he smiled hugely. Jan watched the expression with detachment. The billionaire's dark eyes all but disappeared in the folds of his flesh, but the small dots of light showed he looked directly into Jan's eyes. He spoke in an admonishing tone. "You are less than delighted, Jan. Believe me, if I thought you truly liked your life, I'd not take you away, but you don't care about little whores and rich men, do you? No. It's always been you, me, and Alexia and that will continue." His eyes still on Jan, he reached for his blue, handmade mug. "I've spent my life looking at the treasures of the ancient world, and now I'm going to show them to Alexia and you. Ruins so massive that you will feel insignificant when you look on them. Ha!" The old man wagged a finger at him. "I suspect you never realized that I enjoy feeling insignificant, did you? Ha, that's my boy. Look at that smile."

Jan was smiling. He touched his own face to confirm it.

The billionaire was true to his word. He waited while Jan showered and changed. Jan hurried, absently wondering how he felt about being 'retired' with the old man. He was right that Jan didn't care about the escort service. He wondered if he'd learn to care about traveling. He wondered if he was odd because he had no wanderlust. He had no passions at all.

Jan didn't enjoy the transaction with the scrolls. They walked into a modern building and into a sterile meeting room. Wall-to-ceiling windows that looked out at the pre-dawn lights on the street below. He paid little attention to the men who were in the room. They ranged from a stooped, gray haired scholar who looked dismissively at Janvier from beneath a tangle of eyebrows, to a young man who had a perpetual blush and barely contained his excitement. The only woman in the room was a fiftyish theologian dressed in a somber black suit. She seemed to study the billionaire from behind thick, utilitarian glasses.

The room smelled slightly of cleaner and wool. Apparently, the billionaire had teased the historians and the theologian with the ancient scrolls for several weeks. The old man and Jan entered the room and immediately the billionaire offered the ancient scrolls for free in exchange for favors the learned men couldn't produce.

The scrolls were not with them, but Jan could tell from the

discussion that they were priceless and that the scholars were trying to find a way to make the exchange reasonable, but the old man simply toyed with them. After about an hour, Jan saw tears in the eyes of the stooped old anthropologist. Without thinking, Jan blurted out, "Give them the scrolls."

The billionaire looked at him with an unreadable light in his eyes. "Jan, are you offering to purchase the scrolls for this school?"

The fog that was around the edges of Jan's mind cleared. "They are priceless and you don't want money for them."

"Jan, there is no such thing as priceless. Gentlemen..." The billionaire turned to the collected buyers. "This morning, I told this young man something that upset him. Something he does not want to do. However, I want him to do it. So Jan, will you accompany me in exchange for this and other donations of charity? Will you be the reason that the colleges and museums of the world generously receive the better parts my collections?"

"Give them the scrolls. I'm late." He was late for something, but he never left the billionaire before he was dismissed. "Alexia needs me." He couldn't meet the billionaire's eye.

"Of course, dear boy. But don't tell her the big surprise. Leave that for me."

Jan walked out of the school, ignoring the collection of scholars, and ignoring the billionaire's limo. He tried to hail a taxi but walked blocks before he could find one. The sun was up, the city was awake, and the taxi drove through wave after wave of traffic and people. The December sunlight was cold and the fog had rolled back into his brain.

It should have taken at least twenty minutes to reach the building where he had a two-room office, but he had no idea how long it took. He paid the fare and probably over-tipped. When he stepped onto the curb, movement caught his eye and made him look up. A wreath with a tinsel candle in the middle of it decorated the building's facade. It was placed between his office's windows and swayed slightly in a cold breeze.

He took the stairs to his office. He had two simple rooms in a moderately priced building. Other than the billionaire, his clients were not interested in socializing with him or coming to his office. If any clients asked to meet him, he'd tell them to go to the coffee shop. He met the escorts there and did the payroll and taxes. Jan didn't give a damn what the employees thought. The clean, plain rooms met his standards and no one else's.

In his office, Alexia interviewed a new girl. He walked in without speaking and went to the windows. He saw the girl start to say something and saw Alexia put her finger to her lips. Hush.

The ugly, shiny wreath was not visible from his window. Somehow, that was important.

Alexia sat behind a stark desk that held a simple computer screen. Jan reached down and tapped on the screen to see what his assistant already had on hand about the girl. College student, twenty-two, health check good, and a code that meant the girl was sexually experienced and ready to go professional.

Without looking at her, he wondered if he should ask her some questions, but he couldn't focus. He wasn't supposed to tell Alexia the surprise retirement. Jan thought that Alexia liked running the escort service. She might even love it.

He checked the computer to see what Alexia had already gone over. The logs for the previous night, money in, escorts paid, were much as they always were. He spotted the place where Alexia skimmed some money, but he didn't care. He'd never cared.

He looked the girl in the eye and spoke by rote. "I pay my escorts well. Be good at this and you will have enough money to pay your way through college without bankrupting your parents. Do exactly what you're told to do and I'll pay the hell out of you.

Decide that you are smarter than Alexia or me, even once, and you're out."

Jan was ready to leave. In fact, he needed to get out of the building and into the air, but Alexia spoke. "Mr. Winter needs to see what you look like."

He didn't want to inspect her or anyone else. "Don't bother." Alexia would have already taken care of the details. The new one would be waxed, bleached, and whatever she needed done would be done. If she had an episiotomy scar or some other flaw, Alexia would have noted it on the computer and he did not want to know that much about the girl. He wanted to go home and put the gun into his mouth until he calmed down. If he pulled the trigger, would Alexia still be here running the business?

Yes.

"No. I've changed my mind. I don't want you here."

Alexia looked at him with genuine surprise. Janvier shook his head at the girl. "Go away, take student loans, bankrupt your parents, just go home. Get out of here." He got up and left, leaving the door open.

The seasonally low sunlight didn't clear the buildings. He didn't remember how far he walked or when he sat down, but at some point he managed to find sunshine. He sat on a bench in a park and watched an old woman, who sat on an opposite bench reading a yellowed paperback.

The old woman looked clean and careless. Wisps of her thin hair floated from under a hand knitted cap. Her face was doughy but unlined, and she wore a shapeless, practical coat. The only unusual thing about her outfit was a lightweight scarf. The wheat colored scarf looked like nubby raw silk. It looked too expensive for her outfit and too lightweight for the weather.

He wasn't entirely sure she was real or if she had materialized out of the white noise in his head. No other sounds reached him, even though the city seemed to move as usual, all around him. She seemed to float in and out of his line of vision.

Jan Winters knew he was breaking down. He'd crawled inside the white noise and was losing time now. He needed his gun. He needed to pull the trigger. He didn't move.

The sun was gone. He hadn't noticed when the clouds took over the sky or when the breeze had developed a hard edge. The old woman's feet barely touched the ground. She wore cheap, sturdy shoes. Her book was in her lap and she watched him.

"Son, are you okay?"

He must have blanked again because the book-reading woman abruptly stood next to him. She smelled like lemon furniture polish. Gently, she put a hand on his shoulder. The skin on her hands was thin and finely wrinkled. He could see the metacarpals. It was freezing and she should have had on gloves. He placed his hand over hers, warming it.

She did not pull away from his touch. When she spoke, she had a faint southern accent. "It's starting to snow. I'm sorry to startle you, dear, but you seem kind of out of it. Are you okay?"

A fat flake of white landed on her scarf and melted immediately.

Jan opened his mouth and, for the first time in years, he heard his own southern accent come back. "No ma'am. I'm not okay, but I do appreciate you asking." He stood up, wondering at the slow drawl of his voice. "I saw your book. You've read it a lot. May I ask what book it is?"

"It's a little story by Mark Twain about someone arrogant who couldn't be more out of place, but has great compassion for the downtrodden. It doesn't end well, but the protagonist does find some happiness. He ends up married to a local and has a baby named 'Hello Central'."

"*Connecticut Yankee in King Arthur's Court?*"

Her eyes turned into happy slits. One eye was slightly

drooping. "Yay you!" Above the scarf, she showed a single dimple. "Now, young man, walk an old woman across the street and get me out of this weather. Are you a reader professionally or do you just love it?"

Jan strolled with her to the street, where she pushed the crosswalk button. "Neither, ma'am." He couldn't believe how thick his accent sounded. "It was the baby named 'Hello Central.' I remember that from high school. The book is sarcastic, isn't it?"

"It is." She patted his arm. "And it's political but I like the story." They crossed and walked a few yards to a slightly seedy hotel. Janvier held the door open for her.

"Is there anything I can do for you, ma'am?" He didn't know why he was asking other than it felt good. "I'm rich. I have money."

"Well, aren't you sweet, young man, but I have plenty of what I need, so I don't need a thing. I didn't catch your name. Is there anything I can do for you?"

"Ma'am, my name is Janvier."

"Janvier. That's a lovely name and it suits you. I'm sure your mother loved you a great deal to have given you such a good name. I'm Rebecca." She took off her scarf, and he bent his head down so she could drape it around his neck. "Now go home and be happy, Janvier."

He watched her enter the building and before she faded away, the old woman spoke to him once more. "Take the help you need because it's time for you to go home."

He took one step. Two. He tasted gun metal in his mouth. Janvier almost ran down the sidewalk to the bank. A soft dusting of snow covered the Christmas decorations. Janvier made some financial arrangements and retrieved his birth certificate from his safety deposit box. He then used a computer at a library to find what he needed. If he went straight back to North Carolina, the billionaire would try to get to him or his family. He needed to protect himself because if he didn't make the billionaire understand, the next time Janvier put a gun in his mouth, he would pull the trigger.

He didn't want to die. He wanted his life back.

After handling his finances, he got on a plane. Janvier stared at the clouds outside his window and wondered if Alexia would go through his apartment or if she would have someone else clean it out. He hadn't taken so much as a toothbrush with him. As the safety belt sign came on to indicate they were near BWI airport, he wondered if Alexia would see the loaded gun on the nightstand. Would she understand? Whether she saw it or not, it was more likely that a hired mover would stick the gun into his waistband and cover it with his shirt.

By that evening, he had admitted himself into a quiet mental hospital in Maryland. It surprised him that he felt guilty when he signed himself in as Janvier Reed, but that was who he was, who he needed to be again.

5

Good ol' Uncle Cal spent the week repairing an old metal bench and, even though it looked great under the magnolia tree in his front yard, he didn't want to be the kind of sixty-something man that spent his time puttering around junk stores looking for yard art.

It was a good bench, though. It was cast iron with flowers in the arms and across the back. He'd show it to Perry next time his nephew came over. Cal tested the paint on the metal bench before plunking himself down. It was nice under the magnolia tree. The bench was big enough for two, sort of. It would be a tight two. He admired the view of his house. Cal kept the place nice although the front door was a little faded. It could use some paint. He'd go to the hardware store that afternoon to get some paint the same shade of dark brown. After all, he had plenty of time on his hands with his nephew acting like he was the husband of the year.

A neighbor walked by, but the bench wasn't facing the street, so Cal ignored the greeting. His neighbors used to look down on him because he didn't work, but now that he was in his sixties, he was 'retired.' It wasn't like there were jobs all over the place for ex-cons, and besides, he worked for his nephew as a private assistant. He did lots of stuff for Perry, although lately it was all boring as hell, like driving the Dummy twin around and looking for the kind of patio furniture that Perry's wife wanted. He really missed the good old days when Perry needed Cal to keep tabs on a girlfriend or two.

His phone rang while Cal stared at the front of his house. Most people would put the heavy bench facing out so they could stare at the street, but he liked it better facing the front door.

The phone purred with Perry's ringtone. Cal answered almost breathlessly.

"Uncle Cal. Are you okay? You sound out of breath."

"I redid a metal bench and just hauled it out of the house to put under the big tree."

"Hey, I bet it looks great there. Listen, I was calling to cancel watching the game Thursday night. Two of the girls are in a school play and that's a must-attend. Do you want to come?"

With a lump in his throat, Cal said, "Sure." He didn't want to go to any kiddie play. He wanted to watch the game with Perry and ignore his nephew's family. Perry chatted a few minutes, telling Cal about the evening before when the oldest girl twisted her ankle.

"She's okay, it's just a slight sprain, but we ended up in the emergency room of the S Street Hospital, and I excused myself to go to the gift shop to buy her a little present. Guess who still works there?"

J. Cooper, aka Honey Butt. Julie Cooper, gift shop trinket. A slow smile spread across Cal's face as he sat in that dappled sunlight. His nephew sounded amused as he said that the young woman remembered him. "It's been a couple of years, and I'm still not interested in starting that girlfriend stuff up again, but it was nice to be remembered."

Cal immediately felt his heart race a little. Obviously, Perry only needed a push in the right direction to get his love life going again. Perry's secret life was far more interesting than refinishing benches. Cal agreed to meet them at the girls' school on Thursday and didn't say a word to Perry about sweet Honey Butt.

The fun stuff was going to start again. Cal was sure of it. He had to check Honey Butt out to make sure she still was a good pick for his nephew. As soon as he hung up, he hauled himself off the bench and hurried into the house to get his keys and his housebreaking tools.

Obviously, the girl had Perry's attention or he wouldn't have gone into the gift shop looking for her. It wouldn't take much to tip his nephew in the right direction, and then Cal could do the things he really enjoyed, like making sure the girl didn't have a boyfriend on the side and making sure she knew that she was bought and paid for.

Cal looked up Julie Cooper's address again and drove over to the apartment that she shared with roommates. After two years, he wasn't even sure she still lived there, but her name was on the mailbox. Cal had checked her out back when Perry first met her, but he hadn't gone to the point of going inside the apartment because Perry insisted he wasn't going to get a new girlfriend and because at the time, Honey Butt had a fatal flaw. She was newly separated from a penniless husband. That made the situation too complicated.

But that was two years ago.

The apartments where Honey Butt lived were cheap. Not welfare crappy, but not one extra dime had been spent on the landscaping. The apartments were tucked back into the woods with very little lawn. That was good for privacy even if the parking lot was nothing but a big rectangle. Cal's car was nondescript. He parked it slightly away from the building. It was two o'clock on a weekday afternoon and there were very few cars in the parking lot.

Perry always told him not to do anything that would get good ol' Uncle Cal sent back to jail, but Cal wanted all the information possible on the girl. Besides, Perry didn't know how good his uncle was at this kind of thing. He didn't worry too much about walking in. Cal was in his sixties and wore a suit. The latex gloves he wore over his hands just made him look more official. If someone was inside, all he would have to do is flash his fake badge and no one would call 911.

The lock was a joke and the deadbolt hadn't been thrown. As soon as he got the front door opened, he knew why no one bothered with the dead bolt. No self-respecting thief would try to find anything worth stealing in that trash-can of an apartment.

The closed, smeary shades let in enough sunlight to show the dirty dishes and take-out containers that covered the coffee table. The smell of ingrained dirt assaulted Cal's senses. He almost backed out until he saw the junk mail that was piled on a dusty side table. He might as well make sure she still lived there. Thankful for his gloves, Cal pushed the junk mail around with only two fingers. Half of it slid to the floor, but he saw Honey Butt's name on several items. She still lived there.

Just to be safe, he pulled one of those paper masks out of his pocket and slid the loops over his ears. The mask didn't stop the grubby smell.

But Honey Butt was still a plum worth picking. Cal needed his nephew to play the game again, and Perry liked the little blond with the curvy butt. He quickly checked out the kitchen. Hell, no. The sink was empty of dirty dishes, but every inch of the counter-top was covered in grocery bags, canisters, and kitchen crap. It had to be dirty under all that clutter.

A tabby cat walked down the hallway towards the bathroom, and Cal followed it. If he had a pet, it would be a cat because they were clean animals. He wouldn't make it shit in a litter box, either. The cat would go outside. His landlord-brother told him he could have one but that Cal needed to get the shots and get it fixed and everything. His brother might own Cal's house, but Cal didn't like it when he said he would "allow" the cat, so Cal never got one.

The cat rubbed against his leg and looked up at him with amazing green eyes. It made a soft "ro-ow" sound. Cal pointed a finger at the cat's nose, and it rubbed its cheek against the finger. He liked that. The cat rubbed a few more times, but then scooted into the bathroom. It probably needed to do its business.

Poor cat. He'd be willing to bet the litter box was filthy.

He opened the first bedroom door. It had a path to the bed, but the discarded medical scrubs were at least a size 2X, so the wearer wasn't Honey Butt. Cal closed the door, thankful that he had on gloves. He wouldn't touch someone who slept in the middle of her own swamp, even if she offered it for free. God knows what kind of germs were in there.

The second room wasn't bad. The unmade bed had reasonably clean sheets and only a few clothes thrown carelessly on the floor. A pair of pajamas with little hearts on them were on top of an open dresser drawer. Better still, there was mail on the dresser addressed to "Julie Cooper." This was Honey Butt's room.

The mail was bills, including a statement from a lawyer's office that showed her record of payment. Honey Butt was an idiot. She didn't have kids, so the divorce could have been rubber-stamped. To run up that much in legal fees, they must have decided to fight it out and pay for the right to blame and insult each other. Honey Butt still owed nine thousand dollars for that little mess and she was way behind on the payments. That would be pocket change to Perry. Damn, other than the messiness, she was perfect.

Cal didn't see anything in the room except Julie Cooper's laptop. Since she had roommates, it would be password protected. That was fine because he knew what he'd find out. That she flirted online? Or messed around in a dating service? Who gave a shit what she looked for in a man?

Honey Butt was perfect, but she'd need somewhere to live besides here. He couldn't see Perry picking his way across that living room to get to the back bedroom. But Perry had rented out his little love nest to some aging professor, so the small condo wasn't available. The important thing was there were no pieces of men's clothing anywhere, no framed photos, nothing to indicate that Honey Butt had a boyfriend. And flannel pajamas with little hearts were almost virginal. Just to make sure, Cal pulled back the covers and looked at the sheets. She wasn't seeing anyone, at least not in the apartment.

When Cal left the room, he remembered to close the door behind him to block the semi-clean room from the rest of the filth. In the hallway, the cat followed him as he walked past the bathroom door.

He picked up the cat and petted it with his gloved hands. Poor thing shouldn't have to live like that. "Do you want to come home with me? I have a nice fenced backyard."

In his arms, the green-eyed cat purred. That vibration felt great. He took the animal with him, locking the front door behind him. The cat was fine until they reached the parking lot. As soon as they left the building, the damned cat freaked out and started hissing and scratching at him, tearing his latex glove with one of its claws. Swearing, Cal threw the cat away from him. It raced into the woods next to the parking lot.

He looked at a scratch on his thumb. God damned cat didn't know what was good for it. Without looking back, he got into his car and opened a disinfecting wipe. Hopefully it cleaned his thumb enough until he got home and could put alcohol and a bandage on it. God only knew what was in that cat's claws. He thought of the litter box and felt sick to his stomach.

6

2013

JANVIER'S THERAPIST'S office wasn't a large room, but it had two floor-to-ceiling windows that let in a lot of light and had a view of treetops. It was February and the light had a gray hue to it, but it was still nice to look out at the frost-covered bare branches.

Dr. Hein looked at him over the top of her glasses. He liked her. She managed to combine professionalism with genuine warmth, even though he'd told her how he'd left Nate and his father. He'd told her about the billionaire, New York, and elaborated on the prostitution when she asked him for more information. She'd seen him angry, grieving, but mostly she'd seen him ashamed. He'd even told her about the gun and how it became his coping mechanism.

His new coping mechanism was the wheat colored scarf that the old woman gave him that day in the park. During his stay in the hospital, he wore it constantly.

Peeking over her glasses, Dr. Hein said, "I'd like to explore a little more about your mother's death, Janvier. Details. Memories. Do you feel up to talking about her?"

No. He nodded anyway. "It was summer…"

Outside, the bare branches scratched at the sky, but in his head, it was the summer between their junior and senior year in high school. The night before, the seventeen-year-olds managed to drink until even Nate had thrown up. Janvier barely remembered coming back to Nate's house, checking in with Señor Rijos, and collapsing on Nate's bed.

That morning, Señor Rijos stepped over his teenaged son, who had passed out on the floor. With a hard yank, Nate's father opened the blinds above the bed, letting shards of July sunlight slice into the room. Janvier and Nate were halfway between drunk and hung over, and the sunlight hurt like hell. Señor Rijos probably knew this, of course. In Spanish, he said, "Get up, boys. It's time for Mass. Janvier, are you okay?"

Janvier blinked rapidly, translating in his head. Oh God. No. He was a long way from okay. "Sí." Act sober. Speak Spanish. He told himself to sit up and not to pass out. "Oui." Janvier spoke French at home. For a moment, he couldn't untangle the two languages. "Sí. I'm fine, but I'm not Catholic."

"This morning you are. Wear the same suit as last time. It's in the closet. Let's go, gentlemen. There's no reason to be late."

Dizzy and moving slowly, the seventeen-year-old boys survived getting dressed and riding in the car for the eleven-mile drive. They sat in a pew that seemed to move slightly. At one point, Nate nodded off while kneeling, so Janvier nudged him awake. The service was in Spanish, but he spoke it well enough to know how slowly the priest crawled through the readings. On and off, he'd come to Mass since he was a little red-headed boy, so it drew no attention that he stayed in the pew when Nate and his father lined up to take communion.

For two hung-over teenagers, Mass was hell on earth.

The ride home wasn't much easier, either. Señor Rijos wasn't about to let them ride home in hung-over silence.

"In a month, you two are going to start your last year of high school. You both need to start acting with responsibility. Janvier, have you decided which colleges you might want to attend?"

Janvier's grades and his mother's money were both mediocre, and Señor Rijos knew it. "It depends. I'm still hoping to get a football scholarship." His head hurt too much to think about how unlikely it was that football would pay for his education, even if he was the quarterback.

Señor Rijos chatted about different ways to pay for college on the drive home. Janvier, and occasionally Nate, made the correct responses to the verbal torture. He almost missed it when Nate's father said, "And, of course, I'll help financially if it comes to that. Do you want me to drop you off at your house or take you back to ours to get your clothes?"

Did he just offer to help pay for college? "Uh, thank you sir, I appreciate...if you wouldn't mind taking me home. I'll come get my clothes later and bring the suit back. Thank you." Nate caught his eye and shrugged. Janvier knew that to his friend, his dad offering financial help was no big deal.

Only two blocks from Nate's house, Señor Rijos pulled up to the curb. Janvier climbed out of the car, waved goodbye, and tried not to look like he was dizzy as he walked across the short lawn to the house.

As the Rijos' car pulled away, Janvier realized something was wrong. His mother's car was in the carport, but the house seemed too still. He walked to the driveway and picked up the Sunday paper. It wasn't unusual for his mother to sleep late on Sunday, but it wasn't morning anymore and the house felt wrong. He carried the paper to the carport door, vaguely wondering what time it was. Fortunately, the side door was unlocked. He thought his key chain was in the pocket of his jeans, somewhere on Nate's bathroom floor. He swung the carport door open carefully. If he opened it too fast, it hit the dining room table.

"Mom?"

The living room was dark because of the closed curtains, but a couple of lights were still on. As Janvier walked by, he switched off the good lamp. "Mom?" The hall light was on, too.

He smelled her bowels before he pushed her door open. She lay on top of the covers with a thin trail of dried vomit across her cheek. Her ivory colored skin looked too smooth and one eye was slightly open. He barely touched her cheek. Under the tips of his fingers, her flesh felt cold, unreal.

On the nightstand, a litter of pill bottles were next to an envelope with his name written in her handwriting. He was a kid. He didn't want her to explain it to him. He didn't want to understand why.

Without touching the note, he left the house and walked the two blocks to Nate's. There, seventeen-year-old Janvier sat down on the front step, unable to go any further.

———

"NATE and his dad took me in…."

It was going to snow. The bare treetops outside his therapist's window looked so damned good against that low sky. Janvier rubbed the edge of the wheat-colored scarf against his lips, feeling the rough/smooth silk. He remembered to move the scarf before he started talking again, but he wished the therapist would let him mumble into the fabric.

"I know that I want to go back to North Carolina, that I want to go to what I consider home, but my mother was all the family I had. Nate was my best friend from high school, but he must be mad because of the way I left, if he thinks about me at all. It must be different now. It has to be…not home anymore."

Dr. Hein looked at him over the edge of her glasses as if she had all the answers. She didn't. For a couple of months, she had looked at him over the edge of her glasses and slowly, as he wore holes in the scarf, she let him find the questions for himself.

He stayed in the hospital while the leaves outside her window budded out in the spring and grew lush in the summer. Ten months after checking himself into the hospital, Janvier checked himself out. The leaves had turned into fall colors. He was not as medicated as his doctor wanted, but they both felt he was mostly ready. The "mostly" part was a little terrifying.

Janvier paid the cab driver and walked out of the cold, drizzling day and into the BWI terminal, already fingering his wheat colored scarf. He clutched a small leather bag that held a change of clothes, his prescriptions, and a few toiletries including a disposable razor blade. His hair was still shaggy, but he'd shaved the ten-month-old beard off the night before. About twenty feet into the terminal, sweat broke out across his body and he came to a stop. He was about to get on an airplane and fly to North Carolina.

Home. What the hell was he doing? He was not ready. It was too important and maybe he was going to screw everything up for the second time in his life. A surge of people came up behind him and that got him moving forwards again. Janvier got in the security line feeling completely alone and terrified.

Why hadn't he let the doctor get in touch with Nate? Why had he refused stronger medications? Why did he think he could handle it if Nate didn't want to see him, or was disgusted, or politely awkward?

People pulled suitcases, pushed wheelchairs, and held children close to their legs. Cold-sounding muted electronic noises floated down from various speakers. A kid squealed behind him, making him jump.

Janvier had searched on the internet for Nate and had his current address, but it wasn't enough information. He had hired a private investigator to find out more, but he still didn't feel ready.

No.

He was ready to go home, or to find out that he couldn't go home. He couldn't remember the last time he felt so afraid. Janvier put his bag on the conveyor belt and started to slip off his leather loafers. He didn't have any keys or change in his pocket and wasn't wearing a belt, but he put his new wallet with his new driver's license and bank cards into the little plastic tray before walking through the metal detector. It struck him as odd that no one was going to stop him. He didn't know why, but it felt like someone should stop him. Calmly, Janvier collected his bag and wallet while the TSA officer met his eye and gave him a polite nod. He politely nodded back.

All it would have taken was a phone call to find out if Nate would accept him, but he hadn't done that. He was going home cold and that was hard enough, but it was what he needed to do. Nate didn't owe him a thing. He still had a life if Nate rejected him. Janvier could go anywhere and start over.

It was bad enough that he had worked in the sex trade. He had been a whore who had put other people in the same position when he became a pimp. How many young men and women had he sold? He didn't forgive himself, not really. Why would anyone else forgive him?

He'd been over that a million times with his therapist.

Grabbing his small bag, he slipped his shoes back on and looked at the overhead board. His flight to RDU was on time. He had spent ten months in the hospital trying to forgive himself. If

Señor Rijos or Nate rejected him, he'd survive. He'd move on. He could handle it.

Maybe. But he couldn't handle not finding out. He had to know.

From the corner of his eyes, he saw a slight, older man staring at him. For a second, he thought it was the billionaire.

He had spoken to the doctor at length about the billionaire but refused to use his name. She knew who he was because the billionaire had no problem tracking him down. There was no running away from the man. The billionaire called the hospital often and even showed up once. Janvier refused to see him or speak to him, although he did authorize the release of some medical information to the billionaire.

Of course, it wasn't the billionaire standing there, staring at him. An older woman came out of the restroom and the old man gave her a rolling suitcase. Hers had a flower print. His didn't.

Janvier had given the information to the billionaire for two reasons. The first was because if the old man wanted it, he'd get it, even if he had to break a few laws. The second was that maybe the old man would leave him alone if he understood that the escort Jan Winters died with a gun in his mouth. The human wreck that was Janvier Reed wanted to live.

Watching the elderly couple make their way down the concourse, Janvier knew that giving the billionaire his mental health information was the right idea. It seemed to have worked. The old man told Janvier's doctor that he only wanted the best for him. The old man probably saw suicidal tendencies as weakness. It might have even disgusted him enough to turn his back on Janvier. He hoped so.

Glancing at the gate directions, he started walking in the opposite direction from the elderly couple. While in the hospital, Janvier had hired a private detective to find out what he could about Nate Rijos. The private detective told him that Nate, a paramedic, had married Donny Ravaterra a little more than a year before. As a kid, he figured that Donny was probably gay, but Nate? Still, the idea that they were together made Janvier happy as hell. That seemed so right. God, how could he know what was right for Nate? He hadn't seen him in so damned long.

People kept moving around him. A heavy woman bumped into him and apologized profusely. A young couple scrutinized their tickets to make sure they had aisle seats. A teenager slept on a molded, plastic seat. A little boy announced loudly that he had to go potty.

Inside his head, Janvier said all the right things to himself, but he couldn't quite get his hands to quit shaking. Aw, God damn it. Turn around. Go back to the hospital until he was ready. He was not ready. He had plenty of money. He could go back and tell Dr. Hein he needed more time.

Or he could start his life.

All Janvier had to do was go to North Carolina, be honest with Nate and his father about what he had been doing for the last half of his life, and find out about Nate and Donny. Smile, and ignore how uncomfortable they were around him. Then he could move on.

He had the resources to do anything. He'd left New York with over fourteen million dollars. It was not a limitless fortune, but it was enough to let him figure out where he belonged. Maybe next, he'd go see the Grand Canyon. That sounded good, although he thought maybe he wanted to go somewhere where people spoke with a soft, slow drawl. He didn't want to go anywhere crowded. And he didn't want anywhere that was loud or rich or…grabby.

Maybe he could go find a place on the Mississippi or on the Gulf in Louisiana. He could get a place on the water, somewhere where life was slow and where he didn't owe anyone an explanation.

He reached his gate and found a seat that looked at a wall.

Three hours until he was home. One hour left at the gate. One-hour flight time. One hour to get a car and drive to Chapel Hill.

That was another worry. Janvier barely knew how to drive. They had worked with him at the hospital, practicing in the parking lot and on the surrounding rural roads, but that wasn't the same thing. Thinking about driving from the airport in Raleigh to Chapel Hill made him sweat, but he reminded himself that both places were off Route 40 and his phone had GPS. The rental car probably did, too.

God, he had to drive an unfamiliar car. He could take a taxi, but a car gave him control over when he could leave. Or if. He needed that control.

"Excuse me." A young woman flopped into the seat next to his. "Hi. Are you on this flight?"

He opened his mouth to say "yes" but words weren't working, so he shook his head. He jumped up and went to the ticket agent at the gate, both to escape the young woman and to have something to do. He stood in line, although he already had his boarding pass. His face felt naked. Janvier wished he hadn't shaved off the beard. Standing behind a heavy woman with fashionably clashing clothes, he kept rubbing the scarf on his clean-shaven jaw. It was all he could do to keep from pulling the scarf over his mouth as he waited his turn.

With a slightly trembling hand, he showed his boarding pass. "I'd like to upgrade to first class please. In fact, if there are two available, I'd like to get both seats." Spending ten months in a private mental health hospital had only set Janvier back a few hundred thousand. He could afford to fly quietly.

"I'm sorry, this is a shuttle jet. There is no first class and I'm afraid we're booked solid."

The flight left on time. Janvier was crammed into a seat

between a window and a teenager who wiggled to the beat of whatever was blasting into his eardrums until Janvier politely threatened him with bodily harm. He was too miserable to worry about the kid's mother glowering at him. Janvier stared out the window and thought about Nate and home every minute of the hour-long flight.

About halfway there, the cloudscape gave away to clear air. He could see the patchwork of fields and sweeps of forests as they started their descent into the piedmont area. Next to him, the kid saw him fingering his scarf and asked him if he was "like gay or something." Ignoring the brat, Janvier tucked the scarf's ends into his jacket and let his jaw sink down into the folds. His hair fell across his eyes and it felt good. Shaving had been a bad idea.

The flight was so short that the fasten seat belt sign stayed lit. Once it landed, Janvier was the last one off the plane. He should have called Nate, or maybe Nate's father, Señor Rijos. He should have called them the minute he got to New York, eighteen years ago.

When he walked out of the terminal, the air was immediately familiar. It had the right smell, the right humidity, it even felt right. For a moment, he stood there, letting the slight breeze touch his bare face. He was home.

The rental car was a mid-sized gray sedan. Mounds of chrysanthemums decorated the car rental place. As it was warmer in North Carolina, he threw his jacket in the passenger seat with his meager little bag but kept the scarf wrapped around his neck.

It took him about ten minutes before he managed to maneuver the rental car out of the lot, but Janvier had the hang of driving the car by the time he was away from the airport. He realized he was going too slowly when he merged onto the highway, so he stomped the accelerator. Fortunately, the truck he cut off was already braking. Once he was firmly established in the slow lane, he pried his left hand off the steering wheel long enough to lower a window and let in some cool air. The truck passed him.

His hair blew into his eyes and he was sweating, but he wasn't about to look away from the road to work the window again. He drove about ten miles under the speed limit and noticed that even though there were new roads, the drive was also familiar. As he passed the Route 70 exit for Raleigh, he calmed down. He knew where he was. His old neighborhood was off that exit. So was Señor Rijos' restaurant. He risked glancing at the exit as he passed. It helped. He was still scared as hell, but it was so good to see an exit that he knew. A small sound escaped his throat as he realized he'd veered a little into the other lane.

The familiar exit disappeared behind him, and he drove on. Janvier ordered himself to enjoy the mild October weather. Enjoy the forests that grew on both sides of the highway. The trees still had more green leaves than gold and orange ones, but they were wonderful just the same. Because of the trees, the cities of the Triangle were barely visible. Hell, Raleigh, Durham and Chapel Hill had grown large enough to blend together, but they had politely tucked their suburbs into graceful woodlands.

The private detective had said that Donny's condo was "nice, the best one there." Janvier wasn't sure what that meant, but the detective had also said that he thought Donny might have family money. Nate owned a modest duplex in Chapel Hill but lived with Donny in a renovated textile warehouse next to a lake. Their unit was once the office of the fieldstone building.

Janvier's GPS told him what he already knew. He took the exit and, at the red light, wiped his hands on his jeans. A homeless man eyed his open window. He wore a red vest and held up a sign. "Please help. Truly homeless. God Bless."

Janvier's heart thudded in his chest. He would have given the man some money, but the light was green and pulling over was too scary. It was hard enough making the turn and staying in his lane without running over the poor guy. In a short amount of time, the GPS told him to turn onto a street. Between trees, he saw the glitter of the lake. It took no time to find the street. Or the building. He even found three empty spots and parked in the center one. He looked when he got out and yeah, the wheels of the rental car were on the painted line. Maybe he should re-park, but he probably wouldn't do it any better.

Pulling the scarf over his chin, Janvier walked halfway across the parking lot before he realized that the condo was right in front of him, up a stone flight of stairs. He stopped.

Janvier couldn't do this. It was too important. Nate was all he had.

What made him think he could do this? Nate had to suspect what he'd become in New York. What made him think he'd survive the look on his friend's face? Eighteen years ago, they were kids, teenagers. Nate had a child now, Donny's little girl. Nate wasn't going to let a whore, a pimp, get anywhere near her.

He couldn't do it. He'd lose his good memories of Nate. He couldn't.

Janvier turned around.

Nate crossed the parking lot, coming towards him. He was walking with a tall, skinny man who held a little girl's hand.

God, he was the same. Older, but the same. Janvier put his hand to the scarf and pulled it down so it wasn't covering his chin. He watched recognition dawn on Nate. His old friend covered the space between them with his hands out. He grabbed Janvier's shirt, his arm. Nate pulled Janvier to him, he held him, and Janvier couldn't help it when he tried to breathe and sobbed instead.

7

ON OCTOBER ELEVENTH, Perry was at his middle daughter's soccer game. The girl's team was undistinguished, but by halftime they were only losing by four points. Perry hoped for a late season thunderstorm that would end the game early while the score was still reasonably close. However, the afternoon was cloud-free. The referee blew his whistle, and his non-athletic daughter ran out to her fullback position. She watched like a hawk as the other team's center dribbled the ball straight towards her. As the tougher girl approached, Beth politely let her go by and ran next to her towards the goal, just in case she happened to fumble the ball or something.

His phone rang. It was Uncle Cal. He ignored the call even though his uncle had called a couple of hours earlier. That morning, Perry had gone to the small condo to meet the tenant's son. The elderly professor who rented the furnished condo died in his sleep, and the gentleman's son was moving his possessions out. It helped that the small condo was furnished. Perry helped pack up the personal items, gave his sincere condolences to the son, locked up the condo, and came to his middle daughter's game.

He felt bad about the tenant. The professor seemed like a nice man, and he was a soft-spoken, tidy person. Perry assumed he'd quietly buy a new mattress and box springs and re-list the condo without mentioning it to his wife or his uncle. His wife would say nothing but would assume that he was going to find another girlfriend. His uncle would irritate him endlessly, trying to get him to find a new girlfriend.

Perry's wife called out encouragement to the middle school soccer players. Paige paid no attention when his phone rang. This time, he barely glanced at the caller's number before bringing it to his ear. No name was on his screen, but Perry had enough business ties that he always answered anyway

"Hello?" He turned away from the knot of parents. It wasn't unusual to see him take business calls any time of day or night. Talking on the cell phone didn't even warrant a glance from his wife, but his youngest girl was bored out of her mind and slipped her hand into his. She wandered away with him.

"Hi. Mr. Ravaterra. Perry. This is Julie Cooper. I'm the woman that…You talked to me at the gift shop when your daughter twisted her ankle?"

Inside, he smiled at the memory of the tiny, curvaceous woman. Outside, he showed nothing.

His youngest girl was eight and a ballerina. He held his hand over her head, and she pirouetted. "Yes, I remember." There was silence on the other end of the line. Perry pushed a little bit. "I'm delighted to hear from you." He was delighted. It shamed him to realize how much he liked hearing from her. A plane went overhead, a ref blew a whistle, there was noise all around, but Perry thought he could hear the nervousness in her voice when she asked if this was a bad time to call.

His little girl spun again, digging the toe of her sneakers into the grass. "Perhaps."

Julie Cooper hesitated. "Can I talk to you later?"

"Sure. In person or on the phone?"

She was so hesitant, her words tripped over themselves. "I just…I don't have any plans this weekend and I thought maybe I could meet you somewhere, later, you know."

"Yes. I'd be happy to schedule that."

"Well, I'm at work now, but I get off at five. Is tonight okay?"

"It would have to be early." He wasn't blatant about Saturday night dates, but he could easily tell his girls that he had a business dinner with an out-of-town client. "I could meet you for dinner, say at…" He almost said Nate's father's restaurant. It was a damn good establishment with excellent food and a great staff. But since Nate and his father were estranged, and Nate was married to Perry's brother…well, maybe the restaurant was not the best place for Perry to take a date. He started to say a different restaurant, but Julie interrupted.

"Can you pick me up?"

He assumed that she'd want the first date to be a meet-me thing. "Of course. If you could give me the address?"

She nervously rattled off her address. "I mean, normally I do first dates meeting someone at the restaurant, but my car is in the shop."

"I'm sorry to hear that. Is seven o'clock good?"

"That would be great. Someone can hear you, right? I mean, you sound…"

"That's absolutely correct."

His daughter put her feet in an impossible position and did a graceful squat that he recognized as a demi-plié.

There was nothing on the other end of the phone for a second. Then Julie, almost too quietly to hear, said, "Just dinner, okay?"

"I agree. I'll see you then."

His little girl stopped dancing and leaned against him, looking up at an airplane with her lovely hazel eyes. "That plane is landing, isn't it?"

Perry slipped his phone back into his pocket and looked up. The shuttle was low enough that he thought it was a Delta flight. "Yep. The airport is right over there." A gust of wind billowed his daughter's dress around her stocking-covered legs. It was a little late in the season for a sun dress, but she loved them and wore a cotton sweater over the top. His little ballerina shivered dramatically and hugged herself, even though she had to be warm enough in her over-protective layers of clothes.

Perry stroked her hair. "What do you say, kiddo? Do you want to go get a lousy cup of hot chocolate at the snack bar? They have a donation jar there for people who want to pay a bribe to the referees to make your sister's team hurry up and lose so we can go home."

His eight-year-old informed him that the snack bar served hot chocolate in Styrofoam cups and those were bad for the environment. "Besides, I don't think we need to pay the referee. The team sucks."

Perry refrained from saying he agreed. They went back to watch the rest of the game for the thirty-four more minutes it took to lose. Afterwards, he gave his bookish, not-athletic, middle daughter a hard hug. "Good game, Beth! You did some serious blocking out there."

She wasn't even sweaty.

8

DONNY DIDN'T KNOW what to do about Madeline. She was four and a sponge when it came to listening to grown-ups' conversations. He didn't know if he should whisk her out of the room, or the condo, and let Nate and Janvier catch up, or if the long-lost man was okay around small children, or what the hell he should do.

Glancing occasionally at Madeline, Nate and Janvier spoke in rapid Spanish. Donny understood enough to gather some spectacular broad strokes, but not enough to keep up. Fortunately, Madeline spoke no Spanish beyond the simple words Nate had taught her.

The person in front of Donny was a stranger and, from what Donny could make out, a whore. A pimp. He had been in a psychiatric hospital. And now he was sitting just a few feet away from Donny's little girl. What in the hell was he supposed to do about that?

"Daddy, why did that man cry?"

Janvier sat on the couch, talking softly with Nate. He still looked a little red-eyed, but he wasn't wiping his eyes. He had himself under control, but Madeline couldn't understand that. She'd never seen an adult sob and she didn't get this at all.

"He's happy to see us, Honey. He's an old friend of ours and he's very happy to see us." Crap, he didn't know what to tell Madeline about the way Nate kept grabbing Janvier's arm. His husband sat on the coffee table, knee to knee and kept one hand on Janvier as if he expected him to disappear.

Jesus. Janvier Reed.

His hair was more brown than red now and long enough to skim his shoulders while Nate rattled on that yes, they'd married and no, his father didn't approve. He thought that Nate switched to French at one point. Did Nate speak French? Janvier messed with a scarf, sometimes pulling it up to cover his chin, but Donny could see a tan line that indicated the recent shaving of a beard.

"Daddy, what's that man's name?"

Nate blurted "He's your Uncle Janvier!"

Donny quickly corrected him. "His name is Mr. Reed. It's your resting time. Let's get you to bed."

Janvier pulled his scarf down and tilted his head a little. "Bye, little girl." Donny wanted more information before those two got to know each other, but he probably shouldn't worry. Not yet, at least.

Jesus! Janvier Reed.

His old friend met his eye for a minute. There was such a look of struggle in Janvier's eyes that it gave Donny's heart a serious tug. "Come on, Madeline. Nap."

She nodded as if the world was an orderly place where strange men came with an eventual, logical explanation. "Is that man going to be here when I get up?"

Nate answered. "Yes, honey, he is."

Donny let the computer play classical music softly in her room. Usually, he didn't want her to get used to background music, but it would also help Madeline not to overhear the grownups. He intended to ask Janvier questions in English, and he did not want her to hear the answers.

For the last three years, Donny had been expecting some woman to show up at the door, insisting that Nate belonged to her in some way. His husband never flirted with anyone male or female, but he was so damned good-looking that Donny just assumed it had to happen. Nate always looked bewildered when Donny's jealous streak showed. Bewildered was how Donny felt when Janvier just showed up. He was not jealous, but he was completely bewildered. He put cuddle toys on Madeline's bed, kissed his little girl "good-nap," and went out to the hallway. The back bedrooms were down a long hallway that ended in a patio overlooking the lake. He could hear Nate and Janvier talking, but he couldn't make out what they were saying. Good.

Donny truly was glad to see Janvier, but there was no way he was going to let a prostitute and a pimp around his daughter. Some things are just unacceptable. Not that he thought Janvier would expose her to anything, but it was just not right.

But there was no way Nate was going to turn his back on the man he'd always thought of as his brother. Nate's father hadn't spoken to him in two years, not since the day they told him that they were moving in together. Six months after living with each other, they went to Vermont and made it legal. Donny's father was the best man and all three of Donny's siblings were the maids/men of honor, but Nate's father was conspicuously missing. And now the brother-like Janvier was back and Donny had no idea what to do about all this.

Janvier looked up, his eyes shining through his hair. "Your little girl, she can't hear me now, can she?"

Donny shook his head.

"Good," He looked at Nate, sitting right in front of him on the coffee table. "Because I've spent the last eighteen years terrified that you, all of you, would find out what I was. I'm so sorry, Nate, Donny. I'm so, so sorry for leaving, for what I've done, and even for showing up out of the blue. I'm so fucking sorry."

Nate grabbed Janvier and hugged him hard. "You're home now. That's all that counts."

Donny stood in the doorway to the hall and felt the same thing. Then didn't. Then did.

9

PERRY AND JULIE hit it off and made easy conversation from the moment he picked her up to the moment their entrées came. She looked at him with sparkling eyes and an open expression. Obviously, Julie Cooper liked him. That was good. He liked her, too. She surprised him by not wanting to go to the expensive restaurant where he'd made reservations.

"I have on a second-hand little black dress and shoes where the left heel might stay attached for the rest of the night. Can't we go to that steak place over there?"

"They're very loud. I don't want to yell at you over our dinners."

She bubbled. "Okay, I know a quiet place. How do you feel about Chinese food?"

Perry loved Asian cooking but hated Chinese fast food. "I'm okay with that if they're easy on the onion." It wasn't the night for being picky.

He parked his understated sedan in a parking lot full of overstated pick-up trucks, but at least he could leave his coat and tie in the car. She had a lightweight jacket on and once they were inside, he made sure that she knew she looked stunning in her second-hand dress.

She apparently did not have any secrets. While they waited for their entrées, Julie chatted about how messy her roommates were. "Two normal-messy types and one hoarder. The living room and kitchen keep getting worse because no one wants to pick up after someone else. The only thing we have in common is the cat. Was. She doesn't have a name, it's just Tabby. We all love her but we can't find her. She must have gotten out of the apartment, and poor thing, she's not used to being outside. We've been checking the pound and put lost-cat posters everywhere. Oh, the steamed dumplings taste better than they look, don't they?"

He had to admit, they were good.

She dipped each dumpling into soy sauce and ate them with two bites. "Anyway, the hoarder roommate says that as far as she knew, Tabby is at least ten years old. We all chipped in and took care of her, though, because she's a love. Good Lord, I'm prattling on about my roommate's cat."

"I'm sorry she's lost."

"I am, too. I like her but I've found myself checking the adoptable cats at the pound already. I found three or four others I wouldn't mind having. You don't think that's the first sign of becoming a crazy cat lady, do you?"

Perry nodded. "Absolutely. It's a clear warning signal. If you find yourself wearing a pea-green, hand-knitted hat and buying kitty litter in bulk, you should start to worry. This chicken is good. I'm glad you suggested this place."

She flashed a smile at him. "You know what, Perry? I like you. I don't even know if you have a cat, or if you sit up nights knitting pea-green hats. I mean, bulk kitty litter is a general assumption for a cat lady, but a pea-green, hand-knitted hat is a specific detail. How many green hats and various cats do you have?"

"I like you too, and I have zero cats, a faded green ball cap, and a golden retriever who is elderly. For the last fourteen years, my wife has sworn that she only tolerates the shedding dog because of the children, but she gives him his medicine, takes him for long walks, and keeps telling him that it isn't time yet."

Julie studied him for a moment. "She sounds nice."

Perry tore his attention away from the perfectly seasoned chicken dish. "I'm happily married and I intend to stay that way, Julie. I hope it's enough to let you enjoy your dinner, maybe kiss me goodnight when I take you home, and hopefully go out with me again."

Several emotions showed clearly on her face, including a strangely out-of-place look of resignation. She looked him in the eye, as if she could tell if he was lying. "Does your wife know? About you taking me to dinner and all?"

"I don't give her details, but we understand each other."

Perry didn't have trouble steering her back into the happy, chatty Julie on a date. "Before you decide I'm a horrible husband who sits up nights knitting pea-green hats, tell me a little about yourself. Where are you from, because that accent isn't from around here." It didn't take too much nudging to get her talking about her divorce. Perry listened to it all, with sympathy that was real at times.

He drove her home at nine-thirty. She seemed disappointed that the evening was over, and he was, too. He parked near her building, walked around the car to do the archaic open-the-door thing, but she was already out, holding one broken shoe in her hand. "Look at this. I guess the evening is over. My coach turned back into a pumpkin."

He kissed her. Again. She was short, but she was soft and warm and oh God, it was hard to let her go.

10

Holding Madeline's hand, Donny walked into his father's house just as his family was about to leave. His dressed-up little girl ran to Tessie, his sister, giving her granddaddy a small hug on the way. Donny felt comparatively scruffy in his jeans and t-shirt. "Morning, everyone. Madeline wants to go to church with y'all. And Dad, I need to talk to you about something important."

His sister and Madeline cooed over each other's outfits. His dad's trophy wife dryly looked at Donny's jeans and said, "Are you two talking about something important on the way to church?"

"Um, no. And it is important, Dad…please?"

His deacon dad immediately said, "Why don't you lovely ladies go on and I'll catch up with you."

Tessie looked enormously relieved. "Oh good, because I was afraid you were going to make us late. I sing in the choir so I should go early. Dad does stuff too. Dad? You aren't supposed to be late."

The new wife looked daggers at his father.

His dad shrugged. "I'm sure they can adjust. You ladies go on." He acted like he was going to kiss his wife but thought better of it. The latest wife, his father's fourth, had a fast temper. Donny figured she wouldn't last long. Tessie and Madeline had to scramble to follow her to the car. He heard his sister yelling that the new wife was going to the wrong car. Her Lexus didn't have the car seat in it. The big car did.

Inside, his dad took off his jacket and loosened his tie. "You know, I don't even wear a tie to the office anymore, but she likes the way I look dressed up. She's willing to go to church with me if I look the way she wants me to look, so I put on a tie and a suit. I do look sharp, though, don't I?"

Donny admitted that his father was a fine-looking man. "Especially when you've trimmed up that mess of a beard."

"What's going on, Donny? You haven't accidentally had another jailhouse baby or decided Nate was looking at some pretty woman again, have you?"

"No, but my news might be on the same level as the baby thing. A former male prostitute and high-end pimp got out of a mental institution yesterday and spent the night on my couch. He's broken Nate's heart and scared the shit out of me and I do not know what to do."

His father scratched at his neatly trimmed beard. "Say that again using less colorful words."

"Janvier Reed, Nate's old missing friend."

"Ah, Jesus."

"He came home yesterday afternoon. To my home, to Nate." He explained to his father how Janvier had spent the last eighteen years. "Apparently, last Christmas, he became suicidal. He's been in some hospital outside of Baltimore for about ten months. As soon as Nate laid eyes on him, he didn't hesitate. I'm glad he's back and safe, but I'm hesitating like crazy."

"Wow." His father went towards the kitchen. The downstairs

of his house had an open set-up with the kitchen in the center. Every direction led to the kitchen. "Do you believe him?"

"Why would he make up being a prostitute?"

"Did he say 'escort' or 'prostitute'? They don't necessarily mean the same thing."

"I think he used both."

"What about the 'high end' thing. Is that you or him?"

"Him. But he didn't brag about anything. He didn't go on and on about where he'd been or who he'd seen. He said 'high end' and mentioned a few things about it, including…Okay, this is weird, but Janvier has great teeth, Dad. I mean, they look like he's had good dental care. If he was not high-end, he wouldn't have teeth that look like that. I mean, if he was on the street or something, Nate would still take him back, and I'd still want to help him out but I don't think that was the case."

They reached the kitchen. His dad indicated that Donny should sit at the stool next to the countertop. It was a slab of granite that swept the impressive length of the kitchen and matched the countertops and even the hearth on the fireplace in the living area. It was a lot of granite.

His father stood near the stovetop as if he was about to start a massive cooking project. "Okay. For now, assume he's being honest. Wow. Donny, you've been a great kid all along, but when you have 'something important,' it usually messes up my whole day. Still, while this is interesting, it isn't on the same level as getting you a lawyer to get your newborn daughter out of jail."

Donny pulled a piece of paper out of his pocket. "Janvier's kind of messed up, Dad, but he's being honest. Maybe too honest. He says I can have access to his medical records if I want them and he gave me this." He handed his father a piece of printer paper.

His dad nodded. "I suspect he's deeply messed up. The medical records thing is unusual and yes, you do want them. If nothing else, the records will give validity to his story and it will decide the degree to which you are going to accept him. I take it this is a list of his prescriptions. And diagnosis. Wow. He isn't keeping secrets, is he?"

"He said he didn't want to come home with secrets. He also said that he might have to take anti-depressants the rest of his life."

"At least he's willing to entertain the possibility that he'll need them for a while. The ones he's on now are reasonable. Is this his psychiatrist? I've heard of this hospital. It's expensive."

"Yeah, I looked it up. And down here is a list of doctors in this area that they recommended."

"Well, he's being impressively up-front with you, Donny. Besides his teeth, how's his overall health?"

"Good, I think."

"Any legal problems from the prostitution thing?"

"No, I asked him about that. He said that he was more ethical than the woman who came before him and probably more ethical than the woman who came after him. I told him I wasn't sure what that meant, so he said that he ran it clean, right down to paying his taxes."

"What about drugs, alcohol? Do you want some coffee?"

"No, I mean, sure, I'll take a cup. I don't think Janvier has drug or alcohol addiction. I asked him about that, too. He said he never got too far into it and no one lasted long at that level if they didn't keep themselves in control. We were together all evening. Janvier didn't ask for a beer, but took one when Nate offered it. I saw no craving, nothing like that. I'm sure if I asked him for a urine sample, he'd pee in the nearest clean container. Dad, he was amazingly open with me, except he never gave details about his work. I'm not talking about the nasty-who-did-what stuff either. He'd tell me anything about himself, but nothing but broad sweeps about what he did."

"I expect that has something to do with the legal-trouble end of it. Prostitution is illegal. He'd probably find trouble by discussing anything too specific and if he was high-end, I expect he dealt with some important people. It isn't a good idea to talk too much about them. Hand me that pen, would you?"

His father circled one of the doctors' names and crossed another one off the list. He then tore that part off the paper and handed it back to Donny, while pocketing the half of the paper that had Janvier's prescriptions and diagnosis written down. "Donny, do you know how to use one of these coffee makers?"

Donny looked at the circled doctor and then at the appliance his Dad indicated. "Is that a coffeemaker? No, I don't have a clue how to use it. Dad, what do I do about Janvier? He's sleeping on my couch." Donny paused for a minute, trying to get his thoughts into something that made sense. "I mean, I want to help him. He needs us to accept him so badly and I feel horrible that I am having reservations, but…God, I couldn't be happier that he's back and Nate, he's ecstatic."

His husband had stayed up until all hours talking to Janvier. "He asked Janvier to go see his dad. Just like that. He wants him to go tomorrow morning because the restaurant is closed on Mondays so Señor Rijos will be home. I couldn't believe it, but you should have seen the expression on Nate's face."

Donny was nervous about Janvier seeing Nate's father. It could go so wrong. "Nate badly wants Janvier to go. His own father won't speak to him because he's gay, but according to Nate, he might accept Janvier because he's 'repentant.' I don't get that. I mean, I guess that Nate's father will want to know that Janvier's alive, but what will it do to him if Señor Rijos rejects him?"

"What will it do to Nate or Janvier?"

"Both!"

His dad pulled his tie all the way off and dropped it on the immaculate counter-top. "Unfortunately, I've never met Nate's father. Or maybe that's fortunate. I'd probably tell him that he's a real moron for cutting Nate off. Still, was Janvier close to Nate's father?"

"Yeah. Janvier even lived with them after his mother committed suicide."

"Damn. I'd forgotten about that. It explains a lot, doesn't it? Do you realize that all three of you don't have mothers?"

"I'm aware of that."

His dad stroked his beard in a way that meant he was doing some heavy thinking. "It's not the first time I've worried about Janvier, you know. I worried about many things when you were a tender fourteen-year-old and started tutoring those almost-grown jocks. Back then, I worried about you as much as you worry about Madeline. Did you know that I sat Janvier down and talked to him, explained to him that you were only fourteen and that the football players were far more mature than you?"

"You didn't, did you? Wow, I'm embarrassed for the teenaged-me. Well, Janvier and Nate didn't give me a beer or a joint, not even once."

"They never offered to introduce you to whatever girl had all the experience?"

"No, Dad. Truth is, I loved hanging around them, but it was usually just the tutoring. We're a long way off topic."

"No, baby boy. We're not off topic. I still worry about you. I still want to sit Janvier down and have a talk with him, and maybe I'll get that chance. He was your friend once. Try to remember that. I know that right now, Nate would probably freak out if you tried to get Janvier back out of your life."

"I'd have to pry Nate's fingers off him to get Janvier out the door."

"And if you insisted, how would Nate react?"

"He'd go with him."

"Permanently?" His father gave him a long look.

"No. But I can't ask that."

"You can, but you shouldn't."

"So I should relax, keep an eye on things and don't worry about him sleeping on my couch?"

"Well, I'm thinking about that little bone of contention between you and Nate, right? His place?"

Nate owned the left side of a small duplex in Chapel Hill. He had moved in with Donny because the duplex was a slightly run-down one-bedroom, and the stone condo Donny bought from Perry was, well, nice. The stone condo was also mortgage free, so it was easy for Nate to keep making the payments on his little house. He was going to sell it, but the mortgage was almost more than the tiny duplex was worth. He was going to rent it, but the one time he let another EMT stay in it, the guy didn't take care of it.

To Donny, keeping the empty place was tantamount to keeping one foot out the door, but Nate didn't like it when Donny was insecure. His husband probably didn't rent the place out to prove a point, but for whatever reason, the furnished duplex was empty. There was no better place to keep your old, iffy friend than in a duplex, especially since it was a short drive from your own house.

His father took a resealed bag of coffee beans out of the refrigerator. They had the name of the local organic market stamped on the side. "This thing grinds the beans first. I wish like hell she'd just buy regular coffee and a regular coffee maker." His dad dumped the entire contents of the bag into a space on the top of the coffee maker. About a quarter of a cup worth of the beans spilled all over the counter. Donny hopped off the bar stool and helped scoop the spilled ones back into the bag.

Apparently, his dad didn't think the ones on the floor counted. With his foot, Donny scooted them under the edge of the cabinets. He also noticed that several beans were blending in to the pattern on the granite.

His dad pushed a button that didn't do anything. He tried another one. For a minute, a horrendous grinding noise took over the conversation. "Good, I was afraid I'd put the beans into the water container, but I think this thing is hard wired into the plumbing. I take it that Janvier is broke and needs a place to stay until he's on his feet?"

"Oh, hell no. Unless he's a terrific liar, he came away with some serious money."

"Well, that explains the hospital in Maryland." His father pushed buttons until a green light came on.

Donny felt more relaxed than he had since yesterday afternoon. His dad had a way of accepting everything he had to, looking at it up and down, and declaring what was wrong and right about it all.

"Nate told Madeline to call him 'Uncle Janvier.' I had a panicked moment, wondering if 'uncle' was too familiar, but 'Janvier' is pretty much an impossible name for a four-year-old with a southern accent. She seems to prefer to call him nothing." Donny, feeling guilty about the coffee beans on the floor, took the last paper towel off the holder. He dampened the towel and used it to wipe the beans off the floor.

"Son, are you going to check him out, or did you come over here so I would check him out?"

Donny nodded. "Yes." He folded up the bean paper towel and began looking for the hidden trashcan.

His dad pulled open a cabinet that revealed the garbage bin. "Okay. And if he gives you those medical files, I'd like to see them." His pediatrician father crossed his arms and frowned at the coffee maker. "I don't think I was supposed to put a filter in that. It would get ground up with the beans, wouldn't it? Why isn't coffee coming out?"

Donny didn't see a carafe. "Where does the coffee go when it comes out?"

"Oh, hell!" His father shoved a mug under the spout. Nothing happened.

"Dad, do you think this is going to be okay? Not the coffee maker. I think that's broken. I mean this thing with Janvier."

"Son, consider your Uncle Cal."

"What about him?"

"My brother. My little brother. Do you think that I haven't had the same agonies about him being around you kids when you were little? Especially with Perry. He never gave a damn about you and the twins, but Perry? He wants to be Perry's father. Think about it. Cal's an ex-con who deserved the jail time. Let me back up. When I was first in med school, your uncle Cal was dating Perry's mother. You know that, right?"

Donny was vaguely aware of the story. "Yeah, he wanted to marry her, and he stole that ring from your parents' next door neighbor to give it to her."

His father stopped messing with the coffee maker to look Donny in the eye. "The next-door neighbor was a kind elderly woman and our parents made us do chores for her to earn our allowance. I mean, Mom's family had all the money in the world but we still had to earn our pocket money. Our parents wanted us to be responsible people. I understood that, but Cal thought it was unfair.

"Cal went over there and found the old dear had died on the kitchen floor. Instead of calling for help, he took the diamond off her finger and left her there. He drove Selma out to the lake and asked her to marry him. My stupid brother, who'd been in trouble on and off since he was twelve, didn't realize that he'd fallen in love with a woman who was bound and determined to marry a doctor."

Donny had never heard his father talk about his uncle this

way. He kept quiet, despite what the coffee maker was doing, and listened.

His dad had his back to the coffee machine. "To say the least, she refused Cal's proposal, but he didn't take no for an answer. He broke her finger in two places putting that ring on her."

Donny knew the story, but not like this.

"Anyway, your Uncle Cal wasn't a kid anymore. That was the first time he went to jail. She seduced me, but I can't blame her, not entirely. I was ridiculously easy to seduce even though I shouldn't have touched her. It would be easy to blame Selma because she intended to get pregnant, but there's no getting around the fact that I slept with the woman my little brother loved. I regret that so deeply, even though I don't regret Perry. I've loved him every single minute of his life."

Donny softly said, "The coffee maker is leaking hot water. Were you worried about Cal being around Perry?"

His father turned around, and unplugged the machine. "I was extremely worried. Our parents died right before he got out of jail. I was all he had left and they'd left all the money to me and to Perry. Cal had no choice but to forgive me for Selma. And he was my brother so I had no choice but to be responsible for him, but I drew the line at letting him see Perry. I absolutely refused.

"He showed up on a weekend when Perry was with me. He was three years old and we were out in the little front yard, playing. That's when I saw Cal watching us from the other side of the fence. Cal's whole face lit up. He came into the yard, so happy he had tears in his eyes. All he said was 'Hi sweet boy, I'm your Uncle Cal'."

Donny never thought of his uncle as having heartbreak or breaking someone's fingers. He hardly ever thought of him at all except as the farting uncle who was at every holiday dinner. Opening cabinets, Donny pulled out a roll of paper towels from the utility closet and gave them to his father, who used the whole roll to dab at the water on the counter-top. "Back then, there was no right answer. You tell me. In hindsight, did I do the right thing?"

Donny took a second roll of paper towels. They were going to need it, too. "Dad, I wish I could say yes, you did the right thing, but the honest answer would be 'I don't know.' I suppose that's true for Janvier, too."

"I always knew you were smart, Donny."

"Janvier doesn't know anything about children. He teased Madeline about being an alien from outer space. My gut says Janvier's a good man."

Donny thought Janvier was a way, way better man than Uncle Cal, but he didn't say that part out loud.

His father threw the dripping roll of paper towels into the trash. "Ah, baby boy, you have a good gut. Try to enjoy the fact that your old friend is home, but keep your eyes open and get him off your couch. I think we broke the coffee maker. Actually, you broke it. Kimberly spends every Sunday morning angry because she has to go to church.

Today, I promise it will be worse, and I'd rather she was mad at you. I want our marriage to work and a broken coffee maker could be a deal breaker to her. This divorce thing is getting ridiculous."

Something strange occurred to Donny. "Dad, do you love her?"

"Yeah. I do.

11

JANVIER ALREADY KNEW that the house he grew up in was gone, sacrificed to the widening of the main road, but he drove past slowly anyway. His mother had rented the house when he was four years old. All that was left of the little rental was a highway fence overgrown with trees. He couldn't even tell where the building had been without orienting himself with landmarks. Janvier turned right at a new traffic light, swinging out a little too far and scaring a jogger. As he held up his hand in apology, he realized with a rush that he was back in familiar territory. The neighborhood was still there. A few blocks down, he turned again and was on Señor Rijos's street. Most of the small brick houses looked cared for and well maintained. Janvier pulled up to the Rijos house and parked the car almost close to the curb. Driving was getting easier. Parking wasn't easy at all.

Two hours earlier, he'd purchased the dark suit to compliment the scarf. He'd chosen the tie for the same reason. He'd held dozens up to the scarf while they hemmed the suit pants. Getting out of the car, he finger-combed his shaggy hair.

The suit and tie were good, the shirt perfect, and even his new shoes had a shine. He ran his hand over the wheat colored scarf that he wore around his neck. Fingering the scarf still helped when he was a little nervous.

As a kid, he could have run up to the side door and gone on in, making sure not to let it slam behind him, but his childhood was long gone. He stopped to look at the house and yard before knocking. There wasn't a basketball hoop next to the driveway anymore, but mums still bloomed in the flowerbed next to the front steps. The big tree, which was not as large as he remembered, was covered with red and gold leaves. So was the ground. Nate and he were ten years old the year they were supposed to rake up the leaves and put them in bags, but one of them decided to burn the pile instead and almost set the tree on fire. They ended up doing many punishment chores that fall, including digging out the grass for the flowerbed. Nate's father worked them hard enough to make his point. Janvier had never burned another pile of leaves, and he doubted Nate had either. There probably weren't still scorch marks going up the trunk. Walking around a large, white sedan, he went to the carport door instead of the front door.

He couldn't just open it. He even put his hand on the knob, but he couldn't turn it. It felt wrong. It also felt wrong to knock. He'd never knocked on that door, even when he was a kid. So many years were gone. He owed Sr. Rijos an explanation for every one of those years.

The knob slipped out of his fingers as the door opened. Señor Rijos' remaining hair was white and cut close to the scalp. Other than that, Nate's father looked the same.

"Hola, Señor Rijos. Es bueno verle."

Emotions played across the older man's face. With visible effort, he controlled himself. "Hola, Janvier." He stepped aside and let him in.

Walking past the dining room table, Janvier took in the familiar house. Much of the furniture was the same, though the plaid couch was gone and the curtains were now shades. He turned in a slow circle in the living room. Down the hall were three bedrooms and one bathroom. Nate's plump mother, eternally twenty-five years old, still smiled from an oil painting over the mantle. The artist had given her a slight glowing halo.

Speaking in Spanish, Señor Rijos said, "Janvier, it is wonderful to see you. Are you back to live or is it just a visit so we'd stop mourning you?"

"Señor Rijos, I am so sorry about everything—leaving, Nate, everything," he answered, also in Spanish.

"If you are apologizing to me for disappearing, then I'll need a little more. If you are apologizing for the rift between my son and me, then that apology does not belong to you. If you are apologizing about what I assume you were doing all these years, then that is between you and God."

"You were right about what I was doing in New York. Lo lamento mucho."

"You sent two postcards to my son so we would know you weren't dead. And not a word since."

"Sir, I was ashamed. I still am." Janvier nodded, his chin touching his scarf. He reached up to touch the scarf with his fingers but made his hand stop.

The two men faced each other in the small living room with the new shades and the old painting of Nate's mother. Señor Rijos was fighting emotion again. With an expression full of grief, he clinched his fists.

"I took you in after your mother died and then I lost you. I felt so much guilt for failing to protect you."

"No, Sir, please. I was angry, and I struck out in that anger. I didn't choose to be protected. There was nothing you could have done."

"I put pressure on you. To go to school. To get therapy. I put too much pressure on you."

Janvier fingered the scarf. "No, no. You wanted me to have a future. After Nate left for school, I thought I couldn't belong here, in this house. It doesn't make sense, but at the time it did. I know now that you only wanted the best for me. Maybe I knew that then, but I believed I couldn't come home. I was an ashamed boy, and I thought…I couldn't."

"You are home now for good?"

He nodded. It felt like a promise, and it felt good. Señor Rijos stepped in and put his arms around Janvier, giving him a brief hug. It was unexpected and almost made tears well up in Janvier's eyes.

Blinking and looking away, Señor Rijos stepped back. "Did you find my son? Are you with him now?"

"Sí." He wanted to plead Nate's case, tell him what a good man Donny was, beg Señor Rijos to return to his son, but he didn't. "I've stayed with them the last two nights."

Nate's father repeated "Them" in a flat tone. He sat down in his usual chair, an overstuffed leather recliner. The chair was new, but it was the same brown leather recliner. "Sit down, Janvier."

He did after he glanced down the hallway. Janvier's mother died a month before he started his senior year in high school. From where he was, he could see the closed door that had been his bedroom for a year. The twin bed with the navy-blue cord bedspread probably wasn't still there.

He sat, letting the senior man lead the conversation.

Señor Rijos wiped his eyes. "Are you going to tell me how I should not turn my back on my child, how I should accept him the way he is?"

"That would be my hope."

Señor Rijos finally smiled a little, but it was a sad smile. "Is he happy?"

"Nate misses you terribly but yes, he loves Donny and he's happy."

"I miss him, too. My heart couldn't be more badly broken, but I cannot pretend to accept this life he has chosen."

"Sir," He hadn't expected it to be this hard. "Sir, he loves Donny. And there's a little girl, she's only this big…" He held out his hand to show him how tall Madeline was, but Mr. Rijos shook his head.

"No peudo, Janvier. You know how much I love my son. I'd give my life for him. Please understand the strength of my conviction when I say that I can't condone this relationship, this life that he has chosen." He held up a hand to stop Janvier from interrupting. "No, I cannot even passively condone it and if you only want to try to persuade me, then I'm afraid this visit is over. Otherwise, I'd like to know a little bit about you. Are you completely finished with whatever you did before?"

"Sí." God, he felt sick at the rift between father and son.

Señor Rijos looked hard at him. "Janvier, if you are truly repentant and finished with the life you have been leading, then there are a few things I want to know because I truly want to find a way back to you."

"I am finished with that life, Sir and I am…" Janvier's head filled with useless words and impossible explanations. "I think perhaps you used the best word. I am repentant, so repentant. Whatever you need to know, I will tell you. Anything at all." He stopped himself from touching his scarf. Señor Rijos was going to forgive him. He hadn't realized that he'd expected something different.

Nate's father was struggling. "You did things, I assume, with men."

"Sí."

"My son. You and my son…"

"No, never. We have always been like brothers."

"Gracias a Dios. Janvier, this next question is important, but I will love you as a son no matter what. Are you healthy?"

"Sí."

In his mind, he saw the Woman as she told him that he had to stay clean and negative. She cupped his face and told him not to worry. She wouldn't waste her best boy on a millionaire who wanted to ride bareback when she had a billionaire who also wanted that. She instructed him to let the billionaire do whatever he wanted. Everyone else had to wear a condom.

"I'm fine."

Señor Rijos let a flicker of relief show.

"I must know one sordid detail, Janvier. Did you ever deal with children or anyone helpless?"

"No." A memory was triggered. He remembered the Woman's apartment and a very young Alexia. She sang without emotion in the shower. Guilt washed over him. Guilt he was sure that Señor Rijos could see.

Señor Rijos asked him about the law. Janvier tried to keep his voice calm as explained again that the police didn't interfere with the escort services "Our clients were powerful men, Sir. As long as we didn't mess with under-aged children or try to blackmail any of our clients, law enforcement left us alone."

The morality of the business obviously failed to impress Señor Rijos. He managed to convey a lot in the way he leaned back in his chair. Sitting on the couch, Janvier leaned forward and confessed his guilt. "When I was eighteen, there was a girl, Alexia, who was only fifteen. She worked with me from the time I arrived in New York. After a few years, I ran the business with her help. I never put anyone underage in, but I did put people, mostly women, into the business. I'm guilty of so much, but they came to me. I never forced or even led anyone into the business, but I know that's a poor defense."

"Why did you stop? Did something happen?"

"No. No, I fell apart. I felt alone for a long time, and I couldn't stand it anymore. I felt I didn't want to exist anymore."

"Did you harm yourself?"

"Not quite, but I was going to. Instead, I checked myself into a mental health hospital for several months. It's a place that pretends to be a refuge, sort of a spa with psychiatrists on staff, but it's really a mental institution. I was there for the better part of a year."

"Did they help you?"

"Sí."

Señor Rijos ran his hand over his head. "Dios mío, help this boy. Janvier, how do you feel now?"

"I'm still broken in many ways, but I'm not alone. I have Nate and that means more than I have words to say. I was so afraid when I came back that he'd reject me, but he didn't. He took me in immediately."

"Good. I'm happy to hear that, Janvier."

"Sir...did you keep my things?"

"Your sport trophies and such are packed up in the attic. Your letterman's jacket is in your mother's cedar chest in your bedroom along with her keepsakes."

Unexpected relief rushed through Janvier, but he contained it. "Thank you."

"I would never give away your mother's things, Janvier. Or yours."

He couldn't speak. He hadn't realized how important it was that Sr. Rijos still had his mother's things. Without asking permission, he stood and walked slowly down the hallway, opening the shut door.

When Janvier moved in after his mother's death, Señor Rijos bought furniture and gave Janvier his own room. His twin bed was still there, but the navy bedspread had faded to a shade more purple than blue. At the foot of the bed was the cedar chest. It was his mother's one good piece of furniture. Kneeling on the floor, he thumbed the catch and opened the chest. The letterman jacket lay on top. He moved it over and looked at the neatly folded dresses. Janvier knew there were three dresses, one lace tablecloth, one wool sweater, and a matching fake pearl necklace and earrings. Señor Rijos selected these things for Janvier. He did not save her socks or her curtains or her worn coat, only her best things.

"Is the letter still at the bottom?" Señor Rijos had put his mother's unread suicide note at the bottom of the chest when he first packed it.

"Yes. Of course."

Janvier still had not read the note, but he knew that the police and presumably Señor Rijos had. He imagined it with the envelope curled up, waiting at the bottom of the chest. He did not lift the clothes to look. Instead, he put his hand on the dress on top. It was her favorite. The dress was the ugliest color of green, but his mother had felt so pretty when she wore it.

"Oh, God."

Peripherally, he saw Nate's father sit on the bed. Briefly, Señor Rijos smoothed his hair, saying nothing as Janvier pulled the dress out of the chest. "I think, Sir, if it's okay, I'll take this dress with me."

"No, Janvier. Not yet. When you are completely settled, you let me know and I'll give you her things. Before then, I think they are safe here."

He started to argue, but Señor Rijos cut him off. "You are sitting on the floor holding that dress like a small child clutches a blanket. I'm going to be a parent and say that you are not ready to have something so valuable. Leave these things with me. I'll refold it."

Janvier relinquished the dress. Before he stood up, he took off his scarf. "A kind woman gave me this. She said she knew my mother loved me because of the name she chose for me." As he folded the scarf into the chest and stood up, he asked, "Did you like my mother?"

Señor Rijos had the dress laid out on the bed and folded it as if it was made of silk, not a cotton/poly blend. "I didn't like or dislike her. She was your mother. She was nice, but a little silly, always speaking in French as if being Canadian was a big deal." He layered the discarded tissue paper between the folds.

"Nate and I used to pretend that the two of you would get married and then we could be brothers."

"Your mother would never have married a brown man and I have been married since I was nineteen to Natanael's mother. Her death did not change that."

Needing a minute, Janvier excused himself and ducked into the bathroom. The long, narrow room looked as it always had. Spare and neat. It smelled like a freshly ironed shirt. The toilet now looked small and too round, and the low tub was still harvest gold. The sliding glass door was past the point where it would ever look good, but it was clean. He still remembered banging on the bathroom door, telling Nate to hurry up because he needed to take a crap. He also remembered Nate's father explaining to him what constituted vulgar language.

When Janvier came out of the bathroom, Señor Rijos was back in the living room. The bedroom door was open, but Janvier did not revisit the room. Instead, he took the offered glass of iced tea and resumed his seat on the couch.

Señor Rijos leaned back in his chair, but this time he seemed more relaxed. "I was going to ask you if you needed a job in the restaurant, but you apparently have enough money to pay for a private hospital. I take it that you weren't too broken to make some money?"

"I am a wealthy man but it might be fun to have my old job back. I remember how to bus tables."

"You have tainted money."

"Sí, I suppose it is."

"That wasn't a question. It is tainted money, Janvier. Give it all to Catholic charities, move back into your old room, and I'll promote you at the restaurant. Maybe it isn't too late to teach you how to chop vegetables."

Part of Janvier wanted to say yes. "Sir, thank you, but I haven't even made a sandwich in years. I think I'll keep some of my money and I'm going to move into Nate's old place."

Señor Rijos gave a small frown. "Since he no longer needs to pretend to live there, I'm surprised he hasn't sold it or rented it out. Is his relationship with Donato secure?"

"Sí, it is very secure."

"So why hasn't he rented it out?"

"He just did. To me."

"You're going to pay him with your tainted money."

"I suppose so. He didn't say anything about money, but I'll ask Donny."

"Is he as accepting as Natanael?"

Donny's face appeared in his mind with his sweet, dopey expression and intelligent eyes. "No, Sir. Donny is a careful man and a good father. He is hesitant about me but seems willing to give me a chance."

"You like him?"

For the first time since he arrived at the house, Janvier gave a big, honest smile. "Oh, yeah. He's great. He's Donny. He always has somebody hugging on him. I think it's because he's so skinny or maybe it is just because he's Donny."

Señor Rijos shook his head, but he didn't look upset. Janvier hoped he wanted his son to be with someone as unique as Donny, but it was impossible to read Nate's father that closely. Señor Rijos stood, and Janvier followed his lead.

"As happy as I am to see you, Janvier, I am afraid I must get ready for work now. The restaurant is closed but I'm catering a business dinner tonight. I expect to see you at the restaurant tomorrow afternoon for an early dinner, three o'clock. We're going to discuss how much of your tainted money you are going to clean via Catholic charities. Will you be there?"

"Yes Sir, I will. Let me give you my phone number." He rooted around in his pocket and came up with the receipt for the suit. Senior Rijos handed him a pen and he scribbled down the number.

Nate's father walked him out, pointing out how the scorched tree was dropping its leaves at an alarming rate.

"Sir, if you need any help with gardening or maintenance..." Janvier waved his hand to take in the house and yard. "Anything at all, you call me."

Eduardo Rijos put his hand on Janvier's shoulder. He didn't remember that Nate's father was shorter than he was. It surprised him that Señor Rijos had to look up.

"Please, Janvier. Take care of my son. Look after him."

Janvier, surprised, said, "Of course," but Sr. Rijos shook his head. It was obvious that he couldn't speak for a moment, so Janvier waited.

"When you two were boys, my Nate, he would run from this thing to that thing, happy all the time. You were the one who thought about things, the one who would figure out how to make things work, how to stay out of trouble at school, remember? When Nate's car broke down and you two told me that you had an SAT prep class after school, I let you take my car, remember that?"

Janvier grinned and blushed a little bit at the same time. "Sí."

"And then you came back and told me that you were driving it, not Nate, and you hit a 'no parking' sign."

"I don't know about that sign, but I remember girls named Lizzie and...Jessica."

"That day you told me a lie. Natanael would never let you drive. He always drove. What happened to that car?"

"Sir, I'm not about to answer that question." Janvier remembered a muddy field, the girls who wanted to prove their love, and the fact that he drove because Nate was too stoned. Janvier managed to hit the only skinny little tree in the field.

"You were the one who took care of the messes, Janvier. Maybe you don't see this as a mess, but I feel better now that you're back, for your sake and for Natanael's. Please. Look after my son."

"Of course I will. Always. I promise."

They headed towards the car while Sr. Rijos looked at the receipt with the phone number written on it. He stopped in mid-step and asked Janvier why he paid so much for the suit.

"To impress you, Sir."

"You could spend this much for a suit and you couldn't spend fifteen dollars for a haircut? And why did you park in the middle of the road?"

12

PERRY STOOD in the middle of the small, furnished condo when his mother called from Sweden to ask if he had plans for Thanksgiving. She planned to fly back to the states to see him and the grandchildren. And Paige, of course. His mom was thinking of redecorating and really wanted to get some of his wife's ideas.

He motioned to Julie to go look around while he talked to his mother. The last thing he needed was to have his girlfriend say something that his mother might overhear. Julie almost skipped back to the bedroom.

Since the family holiday dinners were always at his house, Perry did have plans for Thanksgiving, which involved his father and his Uncle Cal. His mother knew that. "How about we do our own Thanksgiving dinner the Saturday afterwards?…No, I'm afraid I'm too busy to plan a European trip at the moment, so it is great that you're coming here. The girls will love seeing you. Has Paige posted their pictures lately? Can you believe that my baby girl just turned eighteen? I keep thinking about how small she was when she was born. Four pounds, two ounces...Me? No. I was never an infant." He smiled deeply at the chatter on the other end of the phone. Perry was fond of his mother, once he scratched his way through all the childhood problems. "Okay, Mom. I'll see you then. Love you, too."

As he pocketed his phone, Julie popped her head around the bedroom door. "Hey, the mattress is new. You said your tenant died. It wasn't in here, was it?"

The tenant was a nice old man. Perry didn't want him to become a gruesome image in Julie's imagination, so he lied. "No, he stroked out in the hospital. I always buy a new mattress after a lease." That was true. Perry didn't like sleeping in someone else's bed.

Julie wandered into the living room again. Perry found the couch uncomfortable, but she sat down and put her feet on the floor. "This couch is perfect."

He didn't agree but was pleased that she fit. "The whole apartment is Julie-sized."

She looked up from the low couch. "Perry, this place is great, but I can't afford it. I mean, I wish I could, but even with two jobs I couldn't come close to the rent."

He folded himself up and sat next to her. "I'm not asking you to pay me any rent, Julie. We've been over this."

She leaned against him with her head on his shoulder. "I know. But it's bad enough that I'm sleeping with a married man...to let him pay me with free rent...that's someplace I don't want to go."

"Honey, I told you. I'm not rich, but I'm comfortable. I would be happy to contribute to such a worthy cause as getting you out of debt. And frankly, it's probably cheaper than paying for hotel rooms because I don't like your messy roommates. By the way, I'm not going to ever step a foot into your current apartment again."

She wiggled slightly. "That isn't me, you know that, right? I'm cleaner than that."

He nodded. She'd better keep the condo cleaner than the apartment. He'd gone into her apartment once, and he'd come right back out again. He understood when she said that she wasn't about to start picking up after the other roommates, but damn.

Perry liked her. She seemed clean to him. Her clothes didn't have that smell, and she didn't throw her stuff all over the hotel rooms. When he was with her, he felt this odd relief wash over him. She looked at him like she adored him and she made love like he fascinated her. It made him cringe to think he was that needy, that he wanted to be adored, but it did explain why they were in the condo in slightly less than a month.

"Honey, this is to my advantage as well as yours. I'm usually available in the evenings. Your second job is from six to nine. I'm not paying you. I'm making it possible to quit the second job so I can be with you."

She climbed up on his lap and looked at him as if he was the most wonderful man in the world just as his phone rang again. It was Donny's ring tone.

Nose to nose, he said, "I have to take this. Why don't you find some sheets for that new mattress?" She scrambled off, and he answered the phone while getting off that uncomfortable couch. "Hey, Donny."

"Hi, Perry." His brother took a deep breath before speaking. "I see your car in the parking lot. Are you at the little condo?"

"Yep. You need something?"

Of course, his brother did not offer to come over. He never barged in on Perry in the little condo. "I need a favor from you. A couple of them. Can you recommend a good real estate attorney, commercial property inspectors, and anyone involved in selling and buying commercial real estate?"

"Are you thinking of doing some high-dollar investing, Baby Brother?"

"No, I'm a nerdy college professor, not a professional risk taker, but I have a friend. Do you remember when I tutored the high-school's quarterback when I was a teenager?"

"Sure, isn't that where you met Nate?"

"Yeah, but Nate wasn't the quarterback. His friend Janvier was. Do you remember that?"

"Vaguely. I remember Nate's name should have had an accent and there was a guy with a ridiculously accented name He died, didn't he?"

"No, his mother did. His name is Janvier Reed. He's Nate's best friend. He lived with him the last year of high school after his mother died. Then he moved away, but he's back and he wants to buy some commercial property here in Chapel Hill. I thought you'd be a good contact for that."

"I would, but does he have any experience in this sort of thing? I swear I thought you said that the guy was dead. What's he been doing?"

"No, very much alive and here, and he's been looking at a bunch of commercial properties in the area and I thought maybe you could help him out because you have connections."

"Okay." It was four in the afternoon. Perry was intending to have dinner with Julie and make it home in time to watch a little television with his girls, but Donny sounded almost nervous. "Where and when?"

"Can you come over for dinner? Nate's going to grill something on the patio." The patio overlooked the lake. Julie couldn't see any part of Donny's condo from the small condo, which only overlooked the parking lot.

"Does Nate have any real beer in the fridge or only the swill that he thinks is beer?"

"No. It's all swill."

"Okay. What time?"

"Six?"

"Do you have an idea which properties the guy is looking at?"

"No. Janvier's only been back a couple of weeks. He's been driving around, looking at a bunch of different ones."

"Interesting. Okay, I'll see you then."

"Great. Bye, Perry."

He hung up, vaguely curious about what was going on in his brother's house.

Julie was halfway under the mattress, trying to pull the plastic out. Perry thought she did have a sweet, sweet ass. "Hey, Honey. Do you want to come out of there for a minute?" He held the mattress to keep it from squishing her as she backed out, a large piece of plastic wrap in her hand. God, she was cute.

"Julie, I'm sorry, but something has come up. I'm going to have dinner with my brother and I have to spend the time looking up some guy named January. That's one of the things about moving into here that you need to consider. You know I've done this before. I've moved girlfriends in here." Crap. Even though he'd mentioned it before, he could tell from the look on her face that she hadn't heard him.

"Yeah, I know, Perry. That's kind of why I don't want to move in here."

"I know, Sweetie. Look, I'm trying like hell not to spin this in a way that makes me look good. I want you to decide with all the facts. Complete honesty. One of the things you need to know is that my brother lives in this complex, in the unit that has the stone steps going up. Did you notice them? He's a good guy who will leave you alone and there is no way you can have anything to do with him or his family. That's important to me, Julie."

He had to listen to her talk about how she didn't want to be another notch on his bedpost, another name in his string of girls, another kept woman. It took him almost an additional hour to make her feel like she was different than the others, without actually saying that she was different than the others. The funny part was that Julie was different. Any other woman, he'd tell her to stay away from his brother or forget it. He was being soft with Julie and he didn't know why.

Somehow, they went from telling each other that they were special to showing each other how they felt. Perry didn't make it to his brother's until six-thirty, and his hair was still wet from the shower when he let himself in the door.

"Madeline! I need some sugar!" His tiny niece flew towards him, dressed in a metallic looking coverall. He scooped her up and tried to rub his stubble-covered chin on her ticklish neck, but she had retracted her head into her shell. "You're a Turtle, you know that?"

He held the giggling girl as she pointed across the room. "No, I'm in my Halloween costume! Uncle says I'm an alien from outer space, so I picked this one."

"Oh, my mistake. Turtles and aliens look alike."

Who was this "uncle"?

One-and-only real Uncle Perry looked where his niece pointed. There was a slightly amused man looking at them with his head tilted.

Perry held Madeline against him. "Gimme a bear hug." She wrapped her skinny arms around his neck and squeezed while he inspected the fake "Uncle."

Where Nate left broken hearts wherever he went, his friend was quietly handsome. He stood tall, comfortably straight, but without military rigidness. His hair was ragged but clean, and his clothes were simple but well made. The guy's expression was softly neutral. Perry couldn't tell if the man was dull or sharp.

"Hi. I'm Donny's brother, Perry Ravaterra. You must be Janvier Reed." Perry didn't need two hands to hold Madeline. There was no meat on her four-year-old bones, so he put out his hand. Reed had a perfect handshake, and he held Perry's eye comfortably.

By the time the handshake was over, Perry would have bet money on the fact the man wasn't dull. He was also curious to find out what else he was.

13

JANVIER DROVE to his first therapy session the next morning and didn't hit anything in the parking lot. He liked the new doctor but missed the big windows in the Baltimore psychologist's office. The Raleigh office had regular windows. The new doctor already knew his background and was prepared. He had the feeling she wanted an extra hour or two, but Janvier had an appointment with Señor Rijos. He managed to get the new car from the doctor's office to the restaurant without incident. The car felt too wide as he turned into the customer parking area. He didn't want to have his first accident in the parking lot of Nate's father's restaurant.

Donny had picked out the sedan for him. The car helped him drive by telling him when someone was in his blind spot or if he was too close to someone. So far, in the restaurant's parking lot, the car was silent as he drove to the side lot where the pavement turned into gravel. He parked with the driver's side wheels on gravel and the passenger side wheels on asphalt. No one would park too close to him there. It was where Nate parked when they were teenagers and worked as busboys.

He got out of the car, feeling nostalgic. From where he parked, he couldn't see behind the restaurant, but he knew there was a reserved parking spot next to the kitchen door for Señor Rijos. The restaurant was named after Nate's late mother, Angelica.

He had a vivid flash of himself as a small boy, scrambling out of the backseat of whatever sedan Nate's father was driving, and racing into the kitchen. The boys tried not to be too loud or too bumping-into-stuff. Janvier wondered if he still knew anyone who worked there.

He didn't go to the kitchen. Again, he wasn't sure what he was supposed to do, so he went to the restaurant's front door. As he entered, he pushed the hair out of his eyes, straightened his tie and jacket, and said "hello" to the attractive woman who greeted him.

"Janvier! My God, it's true, you have come home."

It was Smyth. She'd been a waitress seventeen years before. Now, judging from the way she was dressed, she was the Maître d' of Angelica's.

"He's set up at the chef's table. We were all so happy when he said you were back, but why did you go? You broke his heart, you know." She held up one finger, scolding him, but linked her arm through his and led him into the dining room. Smyth was shorter than he remembered, and her dark hair was now silvery-white. The slight clean smell that rose from her brought back a rush of memories.

"I…um…"

"No, don't say a thing, it's none of my business or Eduardo would have told me. I'm thrilled because he's thrilled, so it must be a good thing that you're back."

Arms linked, they walked through the restaurant. The dining rooms were closed, but he heard murmuring from the bar area. The décor had changed slightly. The artwork on the walls was now watercolors instead of floral prints. The clean linen tablecloths were the same, but the tables were spaced farther apart. The pewter bud vases were gone. Tea candles now sat unlit in cut-glass holders.

He could see Nate, eight years old, crawling under the tables at the restaurant in the morning. The two little boys were armed with bud vases. The necks of the little vases were exactly barrel shaped, so they made excellent guns. Janvier slid out from behind a potted plant, but he wasn't careful enough. "BANG!" Nate pointed his bud vase and shot him dead.

Smyth walked him all the way back and seated him at a linen covered table set in the middle of the kitchen. There was no tea light, but one of the old bud vases was in the middle of the table, a daisy blooming from the middle.

Janvier had some confused feelings about Señor Rijos, but Nate was firm. He wanted to know how his father was doing. "Besides, it would break Dad's heart if you didn't go."

Señor Rijos sat down at the table, a bottle of wine in his hand. "Have you been thinking about how you are going to clean up your money via Catholic Charities?"

Janvier couldn't help it. He grinned when he said, "Sir, I'm still not Catholic." How many times had he said that when he was a kid?

The elder man waved away this information as unimportant. "The point is to prove your repentance, not to convert to the true Christian religion. That can come later. Why are you fiddling with that vase?"

"Nate and I used to play with these, remember?"

"Sí. You played guns."

One of the chefs served plates of lamb stew over couscous.

The smell made Janvier's mouth water. "Still serving cuisine from everywhere?"

"Only if it is excellent." Señor Rijos bowed his head, and Janvier did as well. "Dios nos da un nuevo comienzo and let us know deep appreciation of all we've been given."

Janvier agreed with the blessing, especially the part about new beginnings. The stew was as good as it smelled. He made himself eat slowly and converse just as carefully. In Spanish, he asked, "I need to bring home a report on how you are doing. Nate wants to know if you've found cholesterol medication that does not make your joints hurt."

"Please tell him I am well and taking all the proper medications designed to keep me that way. Things are still good with him?"

Janvier nodded. "You know I think the world of Donny. Nate and he are very much in love with each other."

Señor Rijos did not glance around to make sure no one heard him. He did not look uncomfortable or upset. Perhaps it was because they spoke in Spanish, although it was unlikely that none of the staff could understand them. Probably with respect, the kitchen staff didn't look as if they listened to the conversation.

Almost wearily, Señor Rijos nodded. "Janvier, I do not question that Natanael loves him, but I cannot condone the relationship."

Janvier quietly said, "I've done so much worse. So much."

"Sí, son, I expect that is true. I understand you left home because you felt an illogical rage that only a child can know, and there were people who saw that you were vulnerable and took advantage. No, do not interrupt. Yes, you have blame and responsibility for your own decisions, but so do the people who took you. The life you had gave you unbearable pain, and you have suffered to come back to a moral life. Janvier, that *is* atonement. Repentance. It is different than the choices that my son made."

"The life I had damaged me. Nate and Donny are not damaging each other. I envy them and wonder if I'm even capable of loving anyone romantically. I tell you this, however. If I loved someone, gender will be the last of my considerations."

Señor Rijos leaned over his untouched stew. "Janvier, promise me something. If you find yourself reaching towards a man, do it because you love him. If I must shun you too, then I want to know that you're as happy as my son is with Donny Ravaterra."

Janvier was stunned. "Sir?"

Señor Rijos only shrugged. "Did you think I was a complete monster? God always has a plan and I hope that Natanael's relationship is part of that plan. Why are you putting that flower in your wine glass?"

"Because I'm going to take the vase home with me." Janvier poured the water from the pewter bud vase into the glass as well. "Sir, I'd love to hear Madeline call you 'Abuelo.' Please, consider changing your mind. It would be worth it."

"Perhaps someday, Janvier. Perhaps someday you'll convert to Catholicism. Don't put that bud vase in your pocket dripping like that. Here, wrap it in a napkin. What are you going to do with that thing?"

"Play guns."

14

THANKSGIVING

DONNY THOUGHT that maybe the invitation to Thanksgiving dinner with the Ravaterras would cause Janvier to get his hair cut, but it didn't. When they pulled up in front of Nate's old place, Janvier came bounding out to the car, neatly dressed in his suit with his hair flying around his shoulders. He'd ensconced himself in the backseat with Madeline, happy as hell to be going to Thanksgiving dinner at Perry's house.

Going only ten miles over the speed limit, Nate drove the minivan on the short interstate hop between Chapel Hill and Raleigh. Donny wondered if Janvier knew that he had had a problem with his family because of him. Perry knew all about Janvier now. Donny still didn't know where Perry got the name 'Jan Winters'. He told Donny that he would be willing to work with Janvier on real estate purchases anytime, but he didn't want

Janvier at his house. Perry did not want the ex-pimp anywhere near his wife or his daughters.

Donny understood, but didn't. He understood that Janvier had a nasty past, but it wasn't like he was going to walk in somewhere and start spouting dirty stories, and being an ex-sex worker didn't make him a pedophile or a danger of any kind. In fact, Janvier was a good guy, but Perry didn't see it that way. It didn't matter. Nate said he wasn't about to leave Janvier alone on a holiday. He'd even gone so far to declare that if Janvier couldn't go, he wouldn't go.

"We'll cook turkey here and you can go have dinner with your family as they hover over their females, protecting them from Janvier, the hideously dangerous nice guy. Maybe we should keep Madeline away from him, too!"

The family drama took about two days to play out and now they were in his minivan on the way to Perry's. As far as Donny knew, no one told Janvier anything. Nate didn't want Janvier to feel unacceptable.

Perry relented about the dinner, but Donny wasn't sure that was a good thing either. He'd never seen his brother forced to do anything before. He told Donny, "Go ahead and bring your reformed bad-ass friend with you, but not one word about all this to Paige or the girls. I don't want my eighteen-year-old daughter to even glance at the man with curiosity." There was no way his eighteen-year-old niece wasn't going to check Janvier out. Sarah Grace checked out every single good-looking man she met.

So the 'reformed bad-ass' was in the backseat looking like a happy kid.

They were almost there. A sigh popped out of Donny, and he put his hand on Nate's arm. Nate held his hand until he had to make the sharp right turn onto Perry's property.

15

Janvier looked forward to meeting all the people in Donny's family. He'd met Perry, of course, and briefly met Donny's father when he turned over his medical and therapy records. The pediatrician seemed like a gentle, intelligent man. Donny said that about fifteen people would attend the dinner, including children.

Fifteen people, all in one family.

Madeline showed him how to play "itsy bitsy spider." He splayed out his fingers and sang with her, but he felt a wave of anxiety wash over him. It left a slight film of sweat on his skin. Still, he itsy-bitsy spider-ed.

He was surprised when the invitation to dinner came. Janvier had no illusions about what Donny's father and brother must think of him. They'd been polite to his face, but he was sure they didn't want him around their families. Donny must have done some serious arm-twisting. Janvier was going to refuse, but it seemed like it would cause problems for Nate, so he went along.

They turned into a driveway, and Janvier just said "Oh." At first, he saw a flat stone façade, built into a hill. Then his eyes focused, and the rest of the house flowed up the hill and swept down the ravine. He thought it was the best damned house he'd ever seen.

Madeline whispered. "Don't be scared of Uncle Perry's house. It isn't too bad inside."

"Okay, I won't."

Perry Ravaterra stood on the front steps, his hands in his pockets and his expression easy. Janvier liked Perry in a slightly guarded way. He had a friendly face with something razor-sharp behind that easy grin.

Madeline ran up to Perry, hands out, and he obliged by picking her up and kissing her several times.

"Hey, Janvier, I'm glad you've joined us. Madeline, Granddaddy is inside. Better go give him a hug, but be careful. His beard looks extra scratchy." She wiggled down and ran inside the house. Donny and Perry brother-hugged.

Perry raised an eyebrow to Nate. "I saw some bottled piss in the refrigerator, so I'm pretty sure Paige bought some of your brand of beer."

"Your wife is a miracle of grace, Perry."

Janvier said honestly, "I know you're an architect, but oh… This house is a masterpiece." The front of the house soared up, a cliff formed out of the landscape. One side curved, following a natural rock formation.

"Yeah. I worked on the drawings all through college and built it about eight years ago."

Donny disappeared into the foyer, following his little girl, while Perry asked, "How'd it go with the office building? Did you put in an offer to buy?"

"Yes, in fact, the office building on West Easton and a strip mall on Carroll Street."

Perry's expression shifted slightly. "That's in the triangulated area you showed me. One of these days, you're going to have to tell me where you were educated."

Perry knew about him. Janvier was sure of it.

Nate literally pushed them through the front door and into the house. "Business another day, Gentlemen. Turkey and football today."

They stepped into a foyer that was the perfect size for the house. There were a few good antiques mixed with an unexplainable abstract expressionist piece. Janvier thought the eighteenth-century altar and church pew were Perry's style. He wondered who had decided to put the orange artwork over the altar. It didn't work, but Janvier had plain tastes. He decided that he had no opinion about the abstract piece.

A poised woman slipped into the foyer. Perry put his hand on the small of her back. "This is my wife, Paige. Sweetheart, this is the old friend of Nate's and Donny's, Janvier Reed."

Paige Ravaterra was a study in money well spent. She wore her hair pulled back from her face and her clothes were richly plain. She also looked like the sort of person whose taste in art would be more refined than the orange glob artwork.

She smiled, showing flawless teeth. "Perry, you've mangled the pronunciation of his name. Is JZhan-vee-yay the correct way to say it?"

"Yes, although it all depends on the accent."

"Of course. Please come in. Was your mother French or Creole?"

"She was from Quebec. It's a pleasure to meet you." He said all the right things to Paige about her house as he followed them through the building. Obviously proud of her husband, she pointed out the architectural details. Perry's persona was in every angle of the building, in the walls, and in the floors. If Paige Ravaterra put her personality into the house, Janvier had no idea where she'd hidden it.

In the final room, the smell of cooking and of wood burning softened the atmosphere. The room was a relief because it was simply a big, open space filled with practical looking furniture. Kitchen noises came from an alcove on one end. Glass doors opened onto a regular old deck opposite a snapping fire inside a large stone fireplace. The room was also full of people who turned and stared at him.

That was not difficult for him. Janvier presented himself well. He knew how to do that. Children to elderly, he looked each person in the eye as he was introduced, memorizing their names and collecting first impressions. Perry had cold eyes as he introduced his three daughters. One was still a little girl, one an adolescent, and one was a teenager named Sarah Grace.

He told Donny's father that he was delighted to see him again and he was. He liked the pediatrician. He thought that the new Mrs. Ravaterra, the doctor's wife, was probably an interesting mix of intelligence and perhaps temper. She had far more frown lines than smile lines.

Nate introduced him to Donny's uncle, an older man who stood with his feet slightly apart and his chin thrust out. "Uncle Cal" simply nodded and ignored Janvier's outstretched hand. Janvier didn't think the uncle knew about him. The older man simply wasn't interested. He only glanced at Janvier before wandering towards what Janvier assumed was the bathroom.

Donny directed him towards two thin, thirty-ish women. "I'm sure you remember my sisters, Tessie, and this is Amy, minus the big glasses."

They were identical twins, but different enough to tell them apart. Their hair was streaked blond and their contacts were subtly blue. The women were about five-foot-five, but they couldn't weigh more than hundred and fifteen pounds each. One of them smiled curiously at him, tipping her head slightly. The other one gave him a huge, lopsided grin and blushed. They were not beautiful women, arguably not even pretty women, but they had something extremely appealing about them. He smiled back, delighted.

The one who tipped her head said, "Hi, I'm Tessie. I remember you from football." Janvier remembered that Tessie had a childhood accident that left her mentally challenged.

The lopsided smiling one said "Hi, Janvier. I don't suppose you remember me, but I went to school with you and Nate, a year behind you. My father told me that you moved back here from New York?" She awkwardly stuck her hand out. "Oh, I'm Amy. Amy Ravaterra."

Janvier grabbed her hand, giving it a slight squeeze more than shaking it. "Naturally I remember you. You're two years younger than I am, but like Donny, you skipped a year." He hoped Donny didn't mind that he presented the information like his own. "Donny says you're a family practice doctor now and engaged to be married. He's a lucky man."

Just like Donny always did, Amy stopped her smile before it got too big. The blush that rose from her neck intensified. "God, what a sweet thing to say. Now I remember why I had such a crush on you in high school. I did, but I shouldn't tell you that. Tessie preferred Nate."

Nate stood nearby and joined the conversation by slipping his arm around Tessie's waist. "Yeah, this is my girl. Do you know that the whole Ravaterra clan would come to the football games? Tessie always liked me better than you."

Tessie nodded, very seriously. "Yeah, I was for you and Amy was for Jon.i.ve..." She stumbled over his name.

Madeline ducked into the conversation, pushing Nate's arm off Tessie's waist. "Uncle's name is really hard to say. You have to practice."

Tessie carefully avoided saying his name. "You need a haircut."

He pushed a lock off his forehead. "Yes, I do. I've been meaning to get around to that."

Tessie offered her services. "I can cut it for you if you want. I work at a hair salon. I'm not supposed to cut hair. I didn't get a license, but I'm really good at it."

Janvier knew there was a reason that he hadn't cut his hair yet. He was waiting for her upturned, untroubled face. "I'd like that."

She said, "Okay," and walked away.

Amy put her hand on his arm, "Um, she's probably going to go get her scissors out of dad's car. I have a feeling she means she'd cut your hair right now."

The older Dr. Ravaterra laughed out loud. "Good. Janvier's walking around like a reject from the sixties. But don't worry about it. Tessie is very good. She cuts everyone's hair."

Perry and his wife came into the conversation. Paige, slightly distressed, interjected, "Yes, but she cuts our hair at the salon, not in my house. Perry, help me."

"Sure, Honey, I'll be happy to help." Perry handed Nate a bottle of beer. "Janvier, your hair looks like shit. Let Tessie cut it."

Tessie stood in the entrance with a leather kit in one hand and a large, blue apron in the other. Perry's wife, looking like she was pushing irritation down as far as it could go, simply said, "Out on the deck. The caterer said dinner is in thirty minutes. Amy, is Will going to make it in time?"

Uncle Cal came out of the bathroom. The older man briefly took in the situation, curled his lip and walked off, wine glass in hand. Even though Donny had never said a bad thing about the man, Nate once said about him, "He's a leech. Sucker on one end and an asshole on the other. He's done time, mostly for being mean and stupid."

Nate's impression of Donny's uncle was good enough for Janvier. He followed Tessie out to the deck and took a seat on the chair she indicated. Amy caught his eye. She seemed delighted that he was going to let Tessie cut his hair. The children played with a large dog in the backyard. Good-humored adults drifted in and out of the deck, to watch the haircut and to check on the children. Nate roared in dismay at the way one of Perry's daughters awkwardly caught a football. He ran into the yard to correct the mistake.

The day was cool, almost cold, and the sun had that clean sharpness that comes on some fall days. Janvier felt good as he sat and let Tessie fit the apron around his neck. Her touch felt good. The day felt good…easy, relaxed. No one was tense there. No one was judging him. Even Paige Ravaterra, with a house full of caterers and in-laws, accepted a glass of wine and joined Amy and Donny, leaning on the side of the deck and arguing about how Janvier's hair should be styled.

As Tessie sprayed water onto his hair, Donny and Paige agreed that he should have a short, clean professional look. Perry's wife asked, "You recently bought an office building. You want to be taken seriously when you meet all your tenants, don't you?"

Tessie fingered his hair. She had gentle fingers. "I like it long, but you know, shorter and shaped up. Maybe you should pull it back in a ponytail and keep it sort of slicked back. That's sexy."

It was bizarre hearing that innocent woman say anything was sexy. "You can cut my hair anyway you want, Tessie."

Paige tipped her head, considering Tessie's idea, but Donny was adamant. "No, he's starting a new professional life. He needs a clean haircut. Like Perry's."

Janvier kept his head still. "I'm going to pay a ton of money for those buildings. My professional life is going to begin if I show up with a purple Mohawk and with a rose between my teeth."

Amy, the doctor twin, giggled. "Screw professional. I vote for sexy." He loved the way she giggled. Smart and sweet, she was a female Donny, and Janvier felt a strong tug inside him. She met his eye again and blushed.

Completely serious, Tessie asked, "You're a handsome man. Do you want a sexy haircut?"

"If you think I'm handsome, then yes I do."

Janvier let the hand mirror dangle between his legs. He had not been physically near a woman in a long time, and it felt pleasant to have Tessie standing close enough to smell the gentle scents coming from her skin and to feel her fingers in his hair. He kept glancing at Amy as well. Standing in the sun, she chatted so easily to Donny and Paige.

Nate wandered back up on the deck. "Paige, your middle daughter might go out for J.V. football. Don't let her. She seriously cannot catch a ball. Damn, Janvier. I'd forgotten what a gorgeous mess you are."

Perry came back out onto the deck again with the grumpy-looking uncle. Janvier caught the way the old man sneered at Nate. Madeline, running across the deck, brushed against the uncle's leg. Janvier noticed that Madeline recoiled a little, and he noticed that the uncle brushed off his leg as the little girl ran down the stairs into the yard. He didn't know or care what the guy's problem was, but Janvier's guard was now up. The hateful old man said something about the stupidity of getting a free haircut on the back deck and went back inside.

Perry looked at Janvier with his head tipped, judging the haircut. "I don't know if I'd call it sexy, but it looks better than it did. Hey, Tessie. If I grow my hair longer, can I have that style too?"

"No. Your hair would be too curly if it got long." Tessie was apparently finished. She finger fluffed his hair, which still felt long. "Let it dry by itself in the mornings and do this with your fingers. If you want to put it back, make sure it's dry first. Go ahead. Look."

Janvier held up the mirror. His hair fell around his face. He looked sexy. "Tessie, this is a really good cut. You're amazing."

She took the towel off him and whisked his neck. He kept his head down, letting her get his neck even though he was sure he'd feel itchy the rest of the day. Tessie told him that this cut was free. "But the next time, you come to where I work, okay? I cut everybody's in the family's hair. Hi, Will."

Janvier looked up and saw Will Wilkerson, the client that he'd fucked three years earlier. The color ran out of Will's face. He looked sick, but at least he managed to look away from Janvier.

Damn it. Damn it!

Amy stepped over to Will Wilkerson and tiptoed up to kiss him on the cheek. "Hi, honey. We weren't sure you were going to make it in time."

God damn it. Why did that man have to show up? Janvier kept his face a blank mask. It was far better than Will Wilkerson was managing to do.

Amy mumbled something to Will, asking him if he was okay. He nodded and gave her a squeeze. The man was obviously trying to pull himself together. "It was a long drive. I think maybe I'd better visit a restroom." He turned and walked back into the house. Amy, looking confused, followed him.

God damn it. It was a simple thing. He was going to have a holiday meal with a real family. It was just a simple thing. People had Thanksgiving dinner all the time without running into former clients. His voice level, Janvier told Tessie that he loved his haircut and asked her for the location of her salon. He tried to make sure his face still looked like he was having a good time.

The memory whispered, "I let a pimp fuck me…I let a pimp…"

God damn it!

Paige allowed that the longer, sexy cut looked good on him. Perry asked him a few questions about the purchase of the buildings. Nate threw the football and was right about the middle girl's lack of athletic ability.

All Janvier had to do was get through the day.

Tessie told him to make sure he had a trim before Christmas. "We get so busy at Christmastime, but I still want to make sure your hair looks right. Come on, I'll show you where the bathroom is. We can wash our hands before dinner because I think it's soon now."

Apparently, Will Wilkerson had disappeared into the bathroom, but Janvier couldn't think of how to get out of following Tessie, so he fell in behind her. He couldn't think of how to get out of dinner. He couldn't think at all, and that scared him.

Amy stood outside the bathroom door as it opened, and the prematurely gray Will stepped out. Janvier and Will stood a few feet apart. They met each other's eye while Amy formally introduced them. "Will, this is Janvier Reed. He's an old friend of Donny and Nate's. We all went to high school together. Janvier, this is my fiancé, Will Wilkerson."

They did not extend their hands. Janvier gave the obligatory "It's a pleasure to meet you," but it seemed ridiculous to add anything else. Behind him, he heard Perry's wife ushering in children to get their hands washed.

Feeling foolish, he washed his hands with Tessie before releasing the bathroom to the children. Sweat broke out across his body, but Janvier patted Madeline on the head as he walked by the little girl.

All he had to do was get through the dinner. He badly wanted to tell Will that he'd never tell a client's name and that included his. Maybe at some point, he'd get the chance. Or not. If he got through the dinner, he would never have to see Will Wilkerson again.

He followed Tessie to the dining room. Female and male, everyone stood behind the chairs, waiting for Paige to sit, except the uncle. That old man was already seated and sniffing a full glass of wine. Tessie accidentally bumped into his chair, and the scowl that flicked across the uncle's face told Janvier volumes.

As distracted as he was, Janvier filed away the information. Back when he was Jan Winters, there were potential clients he turned away just because he didn't trust them. Uncle Cal would fall into that category.

He was thinking like a pimp again. Minutes after meeting Will, he'd sized Cal up as an unreliable client. God damn it. He was just a man at a Thanksgiving dinner—a real, holiday dinner.

Dr. Ravaterra came in and gave Janvier a smack on the shoulder. "Hey, I thought you were going to get a haircut? Tessie, you need to try again, sweetie. It's still pretty long."

"Dad, it's shaped up and nice for him."

The dining room looked great. The long, shaker-style table looked perfect with old, cut-work linens and simple, ivory china. Janvier would complement Paige at the first opportunity. She obviously took the role of hostess seriously.

This nice family had a pimp sitting with them. Janvier might be willing to avoid the extended family, but God damn it, he wasn't going to walk away from Nate, Donny, and Madeline. Not because he fucked some client. Hell no. Nate was his family. He had a right to a family too, didn't he?

A right? No. He didn't have a right to anyone.

To one side, a smaller table was set. It had three place settings, one with a pink, plastic cup.

Nate touched his arm. "You okay?"

Janvier motioned to the small table. "Do you know I've never seen one of those before?"

Nate looked confused. "One of what?"

"A kids' table."

"Damn, man. That's sad."

Janvier agreed, trying to sound good-natured. He stood behind his seat and didn't meet Will or Amy's eyes as they came in. Paige Ravaterra placed her father-in-law on one end of the table and her husband on the other. She sat to one side of Perry and had Janvier to her left. Mercifully, Amy and Will were much further down the table.

The elder Dr. Ravaterra carved the turkey. He received good-natured suggestions from up and down the table. Even the three girls at the kids' table chimed in. With much laughter, the doctor enlisted Perry's oldest daughter to finish carving.

After the turkey was properly mangled, they held hands as Dr. Ravaterra said grace. Food and conversation went around the table.

Janvier's mind calmed as he made polite conversation. Occasionally, he glanced down the table. Amy was midway down on his side, but Will was opposite and about two thirds of the way down. It looked like Will was making polite conversation as well.

Will Wilkerson looked in his direction, and there was a full second of eye contact. Will didn't look upset. He might have done an eyebrow wiggle, sort of a what-the-hell gesture, but the moment was over before Janvier could tell. Maybe it was going to be okay. It wasn't as if he was going to tell anyone what happened with Will. He'd told his psychologist about the billionaire but hadn't used his name. Beyond that, he had not identified a single client since he left the business.

He almost missed it when Paige Ravaterra said the billionaire's name. Snapping his attention back to her, Janvier mentally re-ran what he'd heard of the conversation. She talked about doing charity work and fundraising. There was brightness to Paige's eyes and a flush to her cheeks as she talked about her work. "Of course, I am dying with curiosity about the photograph."

Perry had a fake polite smile on his face. "Where did you see that picture, Paige?"

What picture? Of the billionaire? Oh please, no.

Paige waved her hand dismissively. "On your desk, Perry. Janvier, did you meet him through a business connection or do you know him personally?"

God damn it. God, please!

Perry stepped in. With the fake smile and eyes like a hawk, he said, "Dear, please don't put Janvier on the spot. I apologize for that, Reed. What you know about real estate is rather impressive and when you said you hadn't gone to college, I did a little research. I printed out a photo taken at the opening of some event. It looks out of context, Paige. He wasn't getting out of the same limo. I suspect he was holding the car door, weren't you?"

"Oh." Paige looked disappointed. "You don't know him?"

He wasn't going to give her any information, but he also wasn't going to lie. "I didn't say that. Why don't you tell me about your charity work."

Paige, obviously letting go of the billionaire question, brightly chattered about several charities. She seemed knowledgeable, so he asked her how she became a professional fundraiser. Her eyes shone with pride. "Oh, I'm not a professional. It's simply something I enjoy."

He made small talk with various members of the family. The food and wine was excellent. He ate and drank mechanically and glanced back down the table again. Will Wilkerson's hair was grayer now. He'd obviously spent time outdoors and had smile-wrinkles tanned into his face. Will chatted with Donny and seemed relaxed, but it was hard to tell. Blue eyes occasionally looked at him. Janvier dabbed his napkin to his mouth. It felt as though he had a bead line of sweat above his lip.

Paige conversed with several individual members of the family without having to lean over her plate or raise her voice. She even made a point of complimenting the uncle on his shirt. It looked new. The uncle didn't have much to say. His food had his attention. Twice, the irritating man pointed out problems. He told Paige he wished she had cooked the sweet potatoes because whoever cooked them didn't know a thing about southern cuisine. He also had an opinion about the gravy.

"Don't know why anyone thinks that the organ meat should end up in the gravy. This stuff is disgusting."

At that point, Janvier solidly did not like Cal Ravaterra.

Paige caught him glancing down the table. "Will comes from an old tobacco family," she informed him. "They've diversified now, of course. They have farm holdings all over the Carolinas, especially down east. Lots of pork, soy, that sort of thing."

"That sounds like he spends a lot of time traveling."

Perry answered. "Will's car drives itself by now, but there's a good living to be made from farm products, and Will is hands-on. None of this rich boy crap, even if he didn't exactly go to public schools. Right, Will?"

Will Wilkerson smiled down the table. "Depends. Am I agreeing with you or with Paige?" Perry pointed his fork at himself. Will announced, "Whatever it is, Janvier, don't believe him. Paige is a truly golden lady, but Perry will spread any old rumor just to get a laugh."

Will Wilkerson seemed to have his composure back.

An unsmiling Amy looked at her fiancée round-eyes. A slight frown line marked her eyebrows. She looked pensive.

Damn it, damn it, damn it.

The cranberries weren't canned. They were perfect. Shit, why was he fixating on the damned cranberries?

Perry casually asked him a question. "So, Janvier, do you know my sister's fiancée?"

Damn it!

"We were introduced next to your bathroom when we washed up for dinner. Paige, let me know the next time you do a fundraiser. I'm comfortable and would be happy to contribute."

Perry's face smiled. His eyes didn't.

16

DINNER OVER, Perry let himself be ushered into the family room. The game was about to start. As always, his dad made a production out of stealing Perry's recliner, and his daughters dumped a bag of old toys on the floor behind one of the couches. The rest of the family sorted themselves into chairs. It tickled Perry to see his girls playing Barbie with Madeline. His little niece shrieked with happiness at the ragged supply of dolls. When he didn't see Will, Perry scanned around the room. To his surprise, he found he wasn't looking for Amy; instead, he looked for Janvier Reed. Perry could swear something more was going on there. He'd kept his eyes on the former prostitute all evening.

Something was going on. Whatever it was might not involve Janvier, who stood next to Tessie listening while Perry's mentally challenged little sister explained something.

He really was listening, too. He wasn't humoring her.

The same private detective that he'd hired to check out Janvier Reed was now going to check out Will. Perry wanted to know why they kept glancing at each other during dinner. Maybe

Reed was telling the truth when he said that he just met him. Maybe not.

Perry wished he hadn't left that photograph on his desk. Chances were that once Janvier settled in, he would grow apart from Donny and Nate. Chances were equally good that Perry would have to do something to distance his family from the reformed pimp. The last thing he needed was Paige contacting him for a charitable donation or Will turning out to be an old...

Shit. Maybe Will was an old client.

His wife slipped her arm through his. Perry leaned down and kissed her on the top of her head. "Nice dinner, honey."

He saw Will out of the corner of his eye. His future brother-in-law appeared in the doorway and motioned Janvier to follow him.

Perry wanted to follow them, to listen at the door, but he couldn't get away. He'd deal with it when his family didn't surround him. Instead, he plopped down on one of the couches.

"Scoot over, Donny. Dad's in my chair."

There was conversation all around him, but Perry felt comfortable that no one was listening to him when he asked Donny to tell him why he got a "fragile vibe" from Janvier.

He was wrong. His uncle heard him.

Cal gave a disgusted grunt. "Fragile? Frenchie with the stupid hair?" He held up a limp wrist. "This is how he's fragile. No offense."

Donny and Perry both ignored Uncle Cal.

17

JANVIER FOLLOWED Will Wilkerson down the hall. Glancing around, Will slipped into a side room off the foyer and held the door for Janvier. As soon as he was in the room, Will softly closed the door.

The window let in some light, but the day was sliding into evening. They were in a home office, and Janvier wondered if this was where Perry left the picture of him with the billionaire.

Janvier waited, saying nothing. Will raked his fingers through his hair and rubbed the back of his neck. "Winters, I don't want you to say anything about me, but if you do, you do. I need to know if the Ravaterras know who you are."

Janvier waited a full two seconds before answering. "I'm not 'Winters.' That's over. By Perry's request, I haven't shared my past with anyone in this family besides Donny and Nate. Dr. Ravaterra and Perry also know all about me."

"Not Amy?"

Despite the shakiness inside of him, Janvier kept his shoulders squared and his voice even. For the first time since he'd come home, he missed the threadbare scarf. Instead, he touched his hand to his chin. "Will, I'm not going to say anything about you. I've never said a client's name and I'm not going to start now. My name is Janvier Reed. Jan Winters was my pseudonym and it is over." He spoke without a southern accent. Damn. It was the first time in almost a year that he'd heard his voice sound like that.

Will leaned against the desk. He had to look up at Janvier. "You seem pretty tight with Donny and Nate. Have you really been completely honest with them?"

Janvier nodded. He tried not to diminish the anxiety attack that was coming on. The light was bad in the room. Maybe Will would miss the slight sheen of sweat on his face.

"I came home. I grew up here, with Nate."

Janvier counted to ten again slowly, trying to control himself even though sweat rolled down his back. "Last year, I came unglued. I had depression so deep that I was completely messed up. What I needed was a chance at getting my life back, so I checked into a hospital for a while."

Damn it. Janvier squeezed his eyes shut and told himself to stop talking. This was none of Wilkerson's business.

"Did it help?"

"Yes. Coming home helped more."

He opened his eyes to find Will looking painfully at him. "I knew you recognized me, but you had to have a fair number of clients. Still, do you remember what we did?"

"Yes." Janvier remembered how badly he'd wanted Will. He remembered Will saying, "I let a pimp fuck me…" He remembered that afterwards he'd put the gun in his mouth for the first time.

Will Wilkerson said the most amazing, horrible thing. "I told Amy about it."

Surprise must have shown on his face because Will immediately told him that he wasn't seeing Amy when he was in

New York. "I didn't even know her then. I told her after we started getting serious, a kind of no-secrets thing. You, that night, you were the biggest…excitement I've ever had and I told her about it."

"Does she know it was me?"

Will shook his head. "Not yet."

God! Sweet Amy blushing when she said that she voted for a sexy haircut. The idea that Amy knew about that night tore the breath out of his lungs.

"Did you tell her that it wasn't what you paid for?"

Obviously surprised, Will shook his head. "I told her I was attracted to you. Jesus, Janvier. Are you okay?"

Janvier shrugged. "I haven't been okay in a long time, Will. That's why I left New York." There was a slight accent. Just a hint.

After knocking lightly, Amy stuck her head in hesitantly. Will, unbelievably, said, "Sweetheart, please come in."

"Hi…Will, is everything okay? What is going on?"

Will straightened up and put his arms around her. Janvier felt a pang of undefined jealousy. Will and Amy fit together.

"Honey, you remember me telling you about the guy in New York with the escort service? This is him. Janvier is Jan Winters. He used to be, anyway."

"Oh." That was all she said, just the one exhaled, two-letter word. Her face, her sweet face, showed a kaleidoscope of emotions, but she just said "oh" again. She looked surprised, mostly. Confused. And something he couldn't quite understand. He couldn't read her expression. It was too much that she knew about him. Amy knew he'd been with Will. Amy knew everything. He closed his eyes, but then rubbed his hand over them as if he was tired, not overwhelmed, as Will told her that he'd been in a hospital for depression before he came home.

"My past isn't a secret, but of course I won't say anything

about Will." God, he sounded so calm. She was a doctor. She had to know his heart was racing, and that he had too much air in his lungs. Janvier was embarrassed. He was losing it in front of them. He closed his eyes and forced himself to watch his breathing, to stand up straight. "Okay. Look. Obviously, I'm having a hard time with this. I'm ashamed of who I was and what I did."

Will tried to say some right-thing, but Janvier stopped them. "Please, I don't want this to touch Nate or Donny. Will, first I need you to understand that I will never tell anyone what happened with you in New York. I need you to promise me the same thing. I don't ever want Donny to look at me like I hurt a member of his family."

Will rubbed the back of his neck. "I don't know that `hurt' is the word I used, but yeah, Janvier. What happened with us isn't something I want to discuss with anyone but Amy."

It was a huge relief to hear him say that, but Janvier also knew that people end up talking about all kinds of things. Eventually, he might have to explain Will.

And was he lying by omission by not telling Donny and Nate about fucking Will.

Will was going to be Donny's brother-in-law. He already referred to himself that way.

Janvier put his hand over his chin. "I need you to understand that I'm not going to be there every time you turn around. Nate is my family, of course, which includes Donny, too. But there is no reason to think that means I'll be here for Christmas dinners or birthday parties or whatever. I will do everything I can to avoid you so you don't have to feel like this again."

Will and Amy looked at each other. Will fell all over his own words. "I appreciate your understanding, and I appreciate you not telling anyone about this, but I'm not sure that isn't overkill. I mean…"

Janvier felt better. His breathing was coming easier. The crushing embarrassment was easing.

Amy looked like she was trying to make her face match her words. "Obviously, Will and I have a lot to talk about. I don't know about the avoiding thing. Let's just relax, okay?" She didn't look relaxed. She looked like a professional doctor who had to pretend that the patient wasn't disgusting. Her voice cool but gentle, she said, "Nothing has happened here that is overwhelming. It's only surprising."

Janvier nodded. "Unfortunately, I'm overwhelmed. I'm sorry, Amy. Please know that. About all of it. I'm very sorry."

Will looked concerned again. What kind of man went from being horrified to being concerned? Janvier had a feeling that compassion was probably hard-wired into Will in a way that he'd never understand.

Amy asked him what he needed right now.

"I need my car here and an escape route that won't leave Nate wondering what happened."

"I can't make your car appear." Will smiled. The lines radiated around his eyes, and it looked like a real smile. "I'd offer you my car, but I heard horror stories over dinner about how you drive like an old woman."

Amy told him to hush. "Look, I'm kind of confused about how I feel about all this, but so what? I mean, this is all bizarre in a big way."

For a moment, she said nothing else. Then she put her hand on Janvier's arm, her incredibly warm hand, and said, "Come on, Janvier. Let's go watch football and not do anything weird like running away before the caterers feed us pie. It shouldn't be too hard. After all, you used to play football. You understand why men wearing padding like to run into each other. It makes a noise, you know. When they line up then run into each other, their helmets make a horrible 'clack' sound."

"It's the shoulder pads that make the noise."

He let her lead him out of the room, and they walked back into the great room together. Paige was holding sway over a dessert table that hadn't been there before they went into the office. "There you are. What kind of pie do you want?"

Nate, still speaking softly because Madeline was asleep on his lap, told him to sit down. "The game is starting."

With a huge piece of pumpkin pie in his hand, Janvier climbed onto the middle section of the couch to sit next to Nate. Janvier pulled Madeline's feet onto his lap, and she wiggled a little in her sleep. One side of her generous mouth lifted as she clutched a naked, scraggly-haired doll to her. Janvier hadn't realized before how much the little girl looked like her aunts.

Amy and Will sat together on chairs behind the recliner. When the kick-off happened, Janvier wasn't watching. He was thinking about the undecipherable "Oh" expression on Amy's face when she found out about him. He abruptly knew what that look was.

Fascination.

18

IT WASN'T ENOUGH. The football game lasted forever and by the time he was back in the duplex, Janvier was in a full-blown anxiety attack. Somehow, the Ravaterras were going to find out about Will, and Janvier's life was going to implode again. It had to happen.

He stepped out of the tub, reached for the towel, and buried his face in the terrycloth. He kept seeing Will's face. He put his wet back against the wall and slid down to the floor, holding the towel against his mouth. Naked and wet, he curled up on the tiles of Nate's old bathroom. Oh, God. The ease he'd felt with Will and Amy disappeared. The anxiety came crashing back on him an hour after he was back in the apartment.

It was never going to be over.

Amy, that sweet woman with the lopsided grin and the fascinated eyes knew what he did, what he was. A whore. There was no escape, no way not to be a whore and a pimp. He shouldn't have come back. If he'd gone anywhere else, he could have started over. He walked right into the Ravaterra house. Sat down at that table, ate the food, and acted as if he wasn't a whore, but half the people there knew. They looked at him. They knew.

He had given his medical records to Donny and Dr. Ravaterra to show them that he wasn't a danger to anyone, but it wasn't enough. It showed them too much. They now knew how naked he was. Everyone knew. Even the billionaire knew. The old man had refused to leave him alone in the hospital until Janvier had insisted his doctor tell the old man the truth.

Paige Ravaterra had said the billionaire's name that night, her eyes shining and her expression delighted. She didn't know about Janvier. She obviously did not know he was a whore. If she'd known, she wouldn't have allowed him to sit at her family dinner table. Shame physically washed through his body. He curled harder against the floor.

He knew what would happen. At least, when he was in New York, he was judged by what he was. A good whore. He was so good that he was the billionaire's personal favorite. Now he was slinking into normal homes, begging for acceptance as Janvier Reed. He'd tried to bring Janvier Reed back to life, only to find that the boy he used to be died when he left home.

———

THREE WEEKS after he had arrived in New York, the Woman took him to a private party at a penthouse. Jan knew the billionaire had seen his picture and was expecting him. The older man expected Jan to be inexperienced. The Woman gave him a pill to take the edge off but warned him to stay sober. "He doesn't want a drunk. He wants you.

Alexia went with them. As they walked to the car, the girl dropped back a little so the Woman wouldn't hear her. In a singsong whisper, she taunted Jan. "It's gonna hurt, ohhhh. It's going to hurt so much."

If the billionaire liked him, Jan's take for the night was going to be a thousand dollars. That much money was nothing in New York, but he thought it would go a long way when he went home. He pushed Alexia away, and she giggled as she climbed into the car.

The evening was a little cool, but half of the partiers were on the rooftop balcony where a heated pool glittered with underwater lights. For an hour, the Woman introduced him to several men. While he filed their faces and names away in his memory, he made conversation aimed at them. "Yes, I'm a southern boy. Where are you from? What do you do?"

He lost track of Alexia but always had one eye on the Woman. She pointed out the billionaire and told him that man counted more than all the others put together. "I'll introduce you in a few minutes. Do you remember what I told you? If he wants you to, you will kneel in front of him. You have to be gentle."

"I remember." He felt like gagging.

"I doubt that's what he'll want, not for the first time anyway. Don't worry about knowing what to do. He's paying for your first time, but don't screw this up, Jan. I saw him look at you. This could be gold."

When he finally shook the billionaire's hand, he received a polite but distant response. After a minute, the man turned away and the Woman led Jan by the arm to the bar. "Get yourself a drink, sweet boy. Only one, though. I think tonight is going so well!"

Jan didn't want a drink. His stomach was a little unsettled, probably because he was nervous about what she implied. Frankly, the lack of reaction from the rich man was a relief.

It was a cool evening, but there was a full moon and New York City rolled away from the railing as far as he could see.

The swimming pool was the only bright spot on the patio. Several women swam nude, backlit in the water. By two a.m., only a handful of people remained. The billionaire had apparently forgotten him, and he couldn't be happier about that. Maybe he'd made a big mistake. Maybe he should call Señor Rijos and see if Nate's father could send him a plane ticket home.

The Woman told him to stop looking bored. "Go have a swim. Do you need another pill?"

He shook his head and knew it wasn't over. It was harder to swim in tepid water than he would have expected. It sapped his energy in a short amount of time. He turned, kicking off the deep end of the small pool, and had a glimpse of the billionaire standing at the bar watching him. Only two strokes took him to the end where he could stand comfortably. Steam came off his upper body, swirling up as he caught his breath.

The old man was undressing. There was no one else around.

Jan didn't know what he was supposed to do, so he kept still and watched through the light fog coming off the heated water. The billionaire climbed down the ladder near him. He gestured for Jan to come over, and he obeyed. Jan held still while the older man ran his hands over him, cupping his genitals. The billionaire eventually turned him and told him to grab the ladder and lift his legs.

God, it hurt so much. He held onto the ladder and water went in his mouth. A light shone through the water right in front of him. He saw a thin line of blood curl between his legs and float upwards. The raw hurt, the sick pressure, please…

Alexia jumped in, splashing him. Jan couldn't stand the pain, couldn't take it, but it didn't stop. He looked down, looking at an underwater light highlighting his penis floating in a slight red mist.

The girl was beside him. Oh, God. He wanted the man to let

go of him and take her. Take Alexia. She knew how to do this, so please, please, please!

She came around to the ladder. Holding on, she put her face near his. Intensely, Alexia watched him. When he tried to look away, she took his face in her hands and kissed him lightly.

It made the billionaire come. Seeing her kiss Janvier like that made the old man come and it was over. Alexia helped the billionaire get to the ladder. Janvier crouched in the water, lit up from below, and tried to hide.

————

HE COULDN'T HIDE in Raleigh either. He couldn't change anything. They all knew how he'd spent those years. They all knew that he put other young people in the same damned situation.

No. He never put an innocent. He didn't push anyone into something that they didn't understand. Each one understood, or they didn't come through that door.

Fuck that. No one forced him in that pool. He went voluntarily.

He couldn't lie about the whores he sent out, either. Plenty of them were traumatized, although some truly enjoyed the work. It was a job. The traumatized ones collected their pay and didn't come back. He was responsible. Janvier was responsible for every single moment of his pathetic, justifying life.

Three years ago, Will said, "I let a pimp fuck me and I came like a freight train. How is this okay?"

It wasn't okay. None of the Ravaterras would ever look at him without images playing in their minds. There couldn't be any acceptance.

Janvier kicked at the toilet and the cabinet. The cabinet made a satisfying "boom" noise. He could reach every damned thing in the bathroom. The tub was right there. Toilet. Sink. He shoved the dirty clothes hamper. It fell over and dumped the clothes he wore to Thanksgiving dinner.

He reached over and opened the cabinet under the sink. Inside was a shoebox of toiletries Nate had left behind. When he had run out of deodorant, he'd taken out Nate's half-used, cologne-drenched stick. When he accidentally dropped his comb in the toilet, he fished it out, threw it away, and got the small black comb out of the shoebox. Little by little, he was using up Nate's old stuff. He'd never used the razor, but he knew it was there.

He took it out of the shoebox.

It was an old-fashioned double-edged razor in a screwed-on base. Javier dropped the razor into the tub. Kneeling over the side of the bathtub, he put the rubber stopper in and turned the water on as hot as he could stand it. He watched as the water covered the bottom of the tub, coming up over the razor's handle and finally the head. Three inches of water. Eight. The tub half full. A ghost of steam came off the surface.

He eased himself into the hot bath, making his skin redden. The water level went up almost to the overflow drain. He let it fill to capacity before turning off the water. Maybe it would be easier to clean up. Much of the mess would go down the drain. For the same reason, he jerked the shower curtain closed, letting the mildewed hem trail in the water. If blood squirted, it wouldn't go all over the bathroom.

If he cut his neck, it would go faster, but if he held his wrists under the water when he cut, maybe the blood wouldn't splatter. Maybe it would stay in the water.

He didn't worry about a mess when he used to sit with a gun in his mouth, but in New York he didn't care about who found him or who would have to clean it up. Now he couldn't think about that. He needed to do it, to get it over with and not think about that.

Janvier reached under his leg and picked the razor up from the bottom of the tub. The top unscrewed, and it yawned open to reveal the double-edged razor that had flecks of rust on it. He wondered if Nate had ever shaved with it.

Even knowing what he'd done, Nate had not flinched away from him. Not once. He was happy as hell to have him back.

He let the blade drop out of the razor. It sank into the water, coming to a rest on his thigh. Janvier dropped the empty holder back into the water. As he moved, the razor slid off his thigh. He watched with detached curiosity to see if it would cut him. It didn't. It slid harmlessly along his skin, coming to a rest under his genitals. When he plucked it up, he nicked his finger. It was a small cut, just enough to send a thread of blood in the water.

Who would clean up the mess? Re-grout the bathroom? Nate?

Who would find him?

He couldn't think about that. He had to make the shame stop. It was too much to handle. He didn't want to handle it anymore. He just wanted it to stop.

Nate would inherit everything. He'd know that Janvier loved him like a brother. He had to know that.

Janvier never read his mother's suicide note. Even though he knew she loved him, he never wanted to read the words she thought would justify her death.

Nate loved Janvier. Señor Rijos loved him. This would hurt them as much as it had hurt him when his mother died. He'd always felt she'd done it to him. Nate would feel that way, too. Would that be his legacy? The pale skin, the half-closed eyes… would that be the face Nate would see? And Janvier wasn't leaving a note. He'd never read his mother's note. He didn't want to feel the sympathy it might bring up in him. She'd left him. He didn't want to understand.

Nate wouldn't understand either.

A small helpless noise tried to come out of his throat, but with massive effort he kept the cry down, kept it inside him. He could finish this, but only if he didn't think about the pain it would cause other people. He couldn't think about Nate. He had to think about making his own pain stop. Not pain. Agony.

His suicide would cause Nate and Señor Rijos agony.

Tomorrow, Nate would call him. He would call and when he didn't get an answer, he might come over. Even if he didn't, Janvier was supposed to meet with the lawyer about the real estate. When he didn't show up, the guy would call Perry and Perry would call Nate.

No matter what, Nate would let himself into the townhouse. He'd find his body. Janvier's face would be pale, almost ivory. One eye would be slightly open.

He pulled back the curtain and threw the razor blade away from him. It bounced off the mirror and landed in the sink. He sat in the cooling water until his phone rang in the other room.

It rang a familiar ringtone four times until it went to message. Nate's ringtone.

He had to get out of the tub, call Nate back, and tell him that he couldn't stay in North Carolina. He'd tell him that he loved him like a brother, but he had to go away. He'd tried to be open about his past, but it wasn't working. He'd tell Nate that he needed to find somewhere where he could be Janvier Reed and not have something screwed-up associated with that name. Once, maybe twice a year, Nate and Donny could come stay with him. He'd take them to dinner, show them the small-town sights, and they could talk about how big Madeline was getting.

His legs shook, but they held him. Janvier dried himself off and noticed in the mirror that there was a smear of blood on his cheek and several spots on the towel. He washed his face and the cut finger, splashing the razor blade in the sink. Before he called Nate back, he picked up the blade and, taking it into the bedroom, put it carefully on the nightstand next to the pewter bud vase. His finger was barely bleeding, but he still held toilet paper against it.

Somewhere else. Anywhere else. He didn't have to carry his past with him like a dirty stain. He could start over. He could tell Nate that he was wrong to think that he could live with people knowing about his past. Obviously, he couldn't. Nate answered on the second ring. "Hey, Janvier. How's your haircut? Still feeling sexy?"

It took a second to reply. "My hair is wet and dripping into my eyes. Does that make me sexy?"

"You're God's gift to anything that moves. Speaking of which, Donny thinks that maybe something was going on with Will and Amy tonight and you were talking to them. Was there?"

"Yeah. I met Will before, but I think it's okay. We talked. And I'd like to let it go."

"Okay and wow. Small world."

"Fucking claustrophobic."

"Hey, I have to work tomorrow, but late shift. What time's your lawyer thing?"

"Eleven."

"Want to do the gym in the morning?"

"Yeah."

Janvier was exhausted. If he moved away, he'd be alone again. He didn't want to be alone. He could not be alone.

He fell asleep with the bud vase in his mouth.

19

In the week since Thanksgiving, Perry barely had time to see Julie, but she'd been understanding and spent most of the holiday weekend working. Their schedules finally meshed and he was there, but she hollered at him to stay in the living room because she wanted to make an appearance.

Julie came into the living room saying, "Ta Da! What do you think?"

The silky black dress fit her perfectly, and some professional had put her hair into a tumbling down upsweep. "I think you look fantastic, but this is overkill for the steak place."

Julie shook her head and grabbed her purse. "I've heard things about a restaurant called Angelica's. Sweetie, I went ahead and made a reservation. I know that means driving to Raleigh, back here and then back to Raleigh when you go home, but Angelica's is supposed to be really good."

"You're right. I don't want to do the driving." He also was not taking his girlfriend to Nate's father's restaurant. "What name did you use for the reservation?"

"Ravaterra, why?"

Shit. He struggled not to snap at her. "Honey, why don't you give me a call before you make reservations in a place like that?"

"Is it too expensive?"

Not for him, but it was for her. "My name wouldn't be appreciated by the owner."

"Why? What happened?"

"Nothing. And I'd like to keep it that way."

From where he stood in the tiny condo, he could see through the open door of the bedroom and he could see a neatly made bed. The rug showed vacuum marks.

"Sure, but Perry, this is a new dress, shoes, everything. I got my first paycheck where I didn't have to set aside rent, so I took off work early and splurged. Look, these shoes cost more than fifty dollars."

Perry thought she was going to put every extra dime into paying off her lawyer. At least that's what she said she was going to do when she moved into the condo and quit her second job. "You do look nice. I tell you what. Why don't we go to the little Mexican restaurant out on Route 50? We're over-dressed, but we can pretend we just got back from some fancy afternoon gala." The image of his wife popped into his mind. Paige had some charity gala-thing the day before.

Julie looked like she was going to pout, but she stopped. "I tell you what, Perry. I'll go slumming at the Mexican restaurant if you promise not to be angry at what else I did today."

He was already angry. "What's that?"

"I went by the pound today, you know, looking for Tabby? They didn't have her, but I saw the cutest little dog. They think he's a Chihuahua mixed with a Pomeranian and he's adorable. I filled out adoption papers."

She was acting like a teenaged girl. He had to remind himself that he liked Julie, that they were new together so she just needed to know his priorities. He told himself to deal with one issue at a time and not to lose his temper. "Sweetie, I hope I'm important to you, that you bought that dress and did your hair up to impress me, not to impress the restaurant."

Julie touched her hair. "Sure."

"I don't want pets here in the condo. Ever. Tabby was one thing because she was your cat before. But that's it. No little dogs, okay? And Julie, the condo looks great. I want you to know how much I appreciate that."

She stuck her chin out in a defiant, adolescent way. "I'm all dressed up for you, and you're looking for dust. Come on, Perry!"

"You're all dressed up in clothes you can't afford." A bubble of real anger came out of him, but if she was going to act like a teenager, he was going to treat her like one. "I know it's been a long time since you've been able to buy anything nice, but you need to return that dress and those shoes and send the money to your God-damned lawyer. Got it?"

He didn't want to deal with her temper, and he didn't have to. She was his whore, not his wife. Perry turned around and left the condo, surprising his family when he was on time for dinner in his nice, clean house with his tidy children and his wife whose shoes cost some unknown amount of money, but then again Paige wasn't paying off a divorce lawyer.

In the dining room, he gave his ancient golden retriever a back scratch that made the dog's hind leg tremble and made dog fur fly.

Good dog.

20

AFTER THE CLOSING, Janvier worked all week on the properties, but it didn't feel as if he'd accomplished very much. He moved into the office that the previous owner had occupied and searched through the ancient computer files, but he couldn't discover the name of the landscaping company that put up worn-out, ugly Christmas decorations all over the strip mall. The same company had apparently made the office building festive with tired, plastic wreaths that hung on every single exterior door. Janvier's first order of business was to remove them. It took a while to figure out where the dumpsters were, but the exhausted wreaths soon joined the rest of the trash.

The second pressing matter was to figure out where the smell was coming from near the rooms that comprised his office. His cramped space was the result of a divided four-room complex. He was beginning to suspect the smell was coming from the ancient upholstery in his office. He sniffed around. While the chairs smelled like stale cigarettes, they didn't smell like garbage and farts. The smell came and went. It wasn't in his office.

Someone only identified as a "consultant" occupied the two other rooms across the hall. Janvier stepped out into the hallway and sniffed. Drawing close to the door, he realized what it was.

He smelled an inner-city alleyway. Piss, shit, and old trash. It was the middle of December, and a big fly crawled along the doorframe. A chorus of dogs yipping answered his knock. The fly buzzed up to the ceiling. The little dogs sounded frantic as a doughy-faced guy stuck his head out. "Yeah?" The odor was stronger with the door open.

"I'm Janvier Reed, the new owner of the building. May I come in?"

"No, it'd upset my dogs."

"Sir, there is a distinct smell of garbage coming from this office. I'd like to inspect the place."

The consultant danced, trying to keep the dogs from getting around his feet. "You gotta give me forty-eight hours' notice before you can come in."

"Consider this your notice. Get it cleaned up. I'm coming in on Wednesday. Besides, I do believe that every lease in this place has a no-pets rule. Stop bringing them immediately." He had no idea what the man's lease said, but it wasn't okay to let the dogs foul the place.

One of the dogs, a miniature dachshund, zipped out and lunged at Janvier's ankle. He jumped back before he realized the thing was gray haired and almost toothless. He stepped on his own foot trying not to kick the dog. When the consultant retrieved the dachshund, he let the other two dogs out. A little black poof of hair ran immediately to Janvier's office door and lifted his leg.

"Jesus, clean that up, too. And you're evicted."

The consultant started whining, but Janvier walked away. The shit smell clung to him as he dialed Perry Ravaterra's personal phone number. Janvier might know that buying the two properties was a good business idea, but he also knew that he had no idea how to manage them.

Perry happened to know someone who had plenty of experience and could start immediately. "And don't kid yourself about Ms. Nancy Chopper. It's a question of whether she approves of you, not the other way around."

It took less than two hours for the woman to find Janvier. She was an elderly, African American woman with iron-gray hair. Her head was pitched forward on a curved spine and her hands looked like gnarled tree roots, but she looked him square in the eye and shook his hand firmly.

She said that Perry called her and maybe she could work with him. She was bored and wanted a challenge, and Perry told her that Janvier would certainly fit the bill. She looked hard at Janvier for about a second, told him what her salary and her benefits were, and told him that her first order of business was to find out where the dickens that smell was coming from.

He told her and said that he'd told the man he was evicted. Turned out, Ms. Nancy knew how to make that happen, but he had to keep it legal. Even though the woman announced her intention to work for him, Janvier thought it might be better to ask her a few questions.

"Perry Ravaterra sent you, so he must think highly of your abilities."

"He does."

"You have experience with commercial properties?"

"Yes. Thirty-five years' worth. Is that enough?"

"Yes, ma'am. Do you think you can teach me to deal with commercial properties?"

"Ravaterra says you're smart and that you will probably learn quickly. We'll see. I'll need a credit card to get a new computer system and some decent furniture."

"Yes, ma'am." He handed her his credit card.

"Personal account? No. Let's go set up a business account and then you can go around and introduce yourself to your tenants. Be polite but keep an eye on what they're doing and how they're doing it. You're a good-looking man. Don't do anything that could be construed as flirting, but be friendly. Make notes, especially if you come across anyone else whose leased space smells like a baby's diaper. Do you have a notebook?"

Janvier reached over and opened the drawer on the rickety old desk. There was a small spiral notebook left over from the previous tenant.

His new office manager said, "Lame. Let's go."

By lunch, Ms. Nancy was off shopping with his new credit card, and he was making the rounds with a small electronic notebook.

Most of the tenants in the office building were in and without exception were cleaner than the dog tenant. They also proved friendly and willing to talk to Janvier about whatever problems they were having.

The insurance agent in one of the smallest units was a chubby, cute redhead about his age. She looked like she had been formed with an ice-cream scoop. She asked him out, although she said she didn't usually date men with that much auburn in their hair. "One redhead is plenty and I get to be that one."

Janvier figured his office manager probably would say that he had a policy against dating tenants, but it didn't matter. The idea of going on a date was not something he was ready to do. He was a little worried that it might not be anything he ever wanted to do. He said that he was "not able to say yes, damn it." The cute redhead called him "Sugar" and told him that if he became available, don't forget where he could find her.

The strip mall didn't go as well. The parking lot was almost full. He parked as far away from the buildings and the press of other cars as he could go, which made the walk to the stores annoying because he got to see all the thread-bare, tired Christmas decorations dangling from the light posts. He already knew the parking lot and the lighting were in good shape. The neighborhood was middle-class. Why did the landscape company use cracked plastic four-foot candles surrounded by faded green tinsel wreaths? The drooping things didn't even light up. They just dangled from the light poles. And why were they up right after Thanksgiving?

He intended to go first into the Megasmall Toy Store that occupied the space built for a grocery store but came to a halt outside the building. The parking lot in front of the store was full, and he could see through the glass front that the place was crammed with shoppers. The store didn't use Christmas decorations. They simply loaded up the front of the store with Christmas items for sale. He stepped slowly up to the sidewalk in front of the store. Janvier could see through the glass as a woman sorted through a bin of stuffed reindeers. She had a look of intensity on her face that disturbed him. He'd call and set up an appointment with the managers. Megasmall Toys was his biggest retail tenant, so that would be more professional anyway.

The owner of the small Christian bookstore seemed happy to meet him and promised to pray for his success. The manager wasn't in at Fashion Flair, and there was a wall of women clawing through bins at the bead-and-craft store. He took telephone numbers and continued down the line of ten smaller establishments stopping long enough to have a sandwich at the deli with the owner of the franchise. With a thick accent, the deli owner expressed concern over the legitimacy of his next-door-neighbor, a massage parlor.

The massage parlor was the end unit which didn't open until later in the afternoon. It was reasonable to assume massage parlors were legit, but Janvier's background made him instantly suspicious. Most of the glass storefront was spray painted with fake snow, so he went to the locked door and looked inside. The only piece of furniture he saw was a desk off to one side. They'd tacked up shoddy walls, subdividing the place. He stood outside the store and thought that they'd better be legit. This was his property, and he wasn't having any of that old shit happening.

Walking back to the car, Janvier felt good. He'd just felt proprietary towards a piece of real estate. When he walked back into the office building, the smelly consultant was waiting for him.

"Listen, I called my lawyer. He told me that there's a protocol you gotta follow and that self-eviction is illegal and if I stop bringing my dogs with me, then…"

Janvier walked past him into his office. In the outer room, Ms. Nancy poured herself a cup of coffee out of a brand-new coffee maker set up on a folding table in the middle of the room. A computer was on the table as well. All the old furniture was gone and some good ol' boy was writing something up on a clipboard. From the amount of paint on his clothes, Janvier assumed the offices were getting a sprucing-up. Good. He introduced himself and asked a question. The painter assured him that he wouldn't get the faintest whiff of old ashtrays after they finished.

Ms. Nancy sat at a second card table. It was set up with a computer and a folding chair. "I'm transferring the leases to your system. The laws of eviction are up on your new computer, next to the coffeemaker. Stinky across the hall is in material violation of his lease. We can't strong arm him, but he doesn't get a grace period either. The only way this is going to end up in court is when he cleans the mess up and gets rid of the dogs and we evict him anyway." She took a sip of coffee. "Oh, this is good. You were right about this brand. You can use any of the white mugs. The red one is mine."

"Do we have a printer?"

She pointed to a small device on her table.

Ten minutes later, Janvier put a real-looking notice on the consultant's door. It was an appointment with a veterinarian for the euthanasia of three dogs. Of course, there was no appointment. It occurred to Janvier the notice would probably constitute what Ms. Nancy called 'strong-arming,' but he didn't care.

By the end of the day, the tenant was gone and the carpet people were in to measure his office. He told them to go ahead and pull the carpet out of the rooms across the hall. Ms. Nancy told him that she'd have the painters do that office as well.

Janvier passed by the cute redhead's insurance agency as she was locking up for the day. She flashed a smile at him and said, "Hey, I saw the carpet store's van out there earlier. How do I get the landlord to pay for new carpet for me?"

He shrugged his shoulders. "You could try letting your dog pee all over the old carpet but you'd probably still have to pay for the new one yourself."

She dimpled up. "Aw, Sugar, can't I just date the owner?"

Maybe he should try dating. She had to be fun. "No, it wouldn't work. You're so cute, you'd cost me a fortune in carpet."

She wiggled at him. "Yeah, but I'll make sure you were completely covered for collision, collision, collision."

He told her that she was going to get him into trouble and headed for his car. As he drove to the gym, he caught himself smiling several times. This was the way regular people lived. They went to work. They got credit cards for their office managers, and they flirted with cute insurance agents.

In the weight room, Nate, who'd had the day off, was warming up. "Did you see Dad yesterday?"

"Yeah. Nate, are you sure this is okay with you? I mean, I love your dad. He's the closest thing I've ever had to a father, but he isn't mine. He thinks I'm repentant so it's okay that I was a whore, but it's not okay for you to love Donny."

"According to Dad's faith, I can love Donny all I want to, but no sex. I like having sex with Donny and intend to keep doing it. Janvier, you're over-thinking the dinners with my dad. Keep going to the restaurant. Ask him if he's taking his vitamins and has he had his yearly physical." Nate put the weights down and wiped his face with the edge of his t-shirt. "It's weird, hearing you call yourself a 'whore.' All that escort stuff is surreal to me. I haven't even wrapped my head around the idea that you're a millionaire."

"Yeah, well. The whore thing hardly ever leads to the millionaire thing. I guess I was weirdly lucky. I think you should add some weight tonight. If you build up those biceps, maybe Donny will look past your obvious character flaws and agree to that sex thing."

Nate gave him a middle-finger salute. "It doesn't take much to get Donny to agree to sex and I'm not the one living the celibate life. Seriously, you're a millionaire living like a monk in my old place. Have you had one single date over there?"

"No, but there's a cute redhead that asked me out today."

He told him about the insurance agent. Nate didn't get why Janvier didn't want to go on a date. "I mean, I know you did all that escort stuff, but you still had to…. Janvier, you haven't been on a real date since high school? Just a simple date?"

Janvier picked up the twenty-five-pound hand weights. "No, I dated for a living. Nate, I don't like talking about that shit, but…I gave Donny and his dad my medical records. Did Donny not talk to you about what was in there about the whole celibate thing?"

Nate looked surprised. "No. He didn't. He said that he thought you were okay to be around and that you really needed acceptance."

"He didn't tell you that I'm kind of impotent?"

Nate ran his fingers through his sweaty hair. "Shit. What did they do to you, Janvier?"

"Made a whore out of me."

"Are you okay? The impotence isn't physical?"

"No, it's not a physical issue. And I think it's getting better."

Nate picked up his weights again. "So why can't you go out with cute redheads even if you have to be a gentleman?"

He didn't have an answer for that. "I don't know," was the best he could do, but Nate seemed to understand and let the subject go. They worked out, not bringing up fathers again until they showered and were about to leave. Nate talked about how he hoped the elder Dr. Ravaterra got his hint about wanting UNC tickets for Christmas.

"Football, basketball, anything. It's unholy how well connected he is when it comes to tickets. He might even cough up some March Madness. Stand close to me at Christmas, Janvier. The doc will give me at least two tickets and I promise you, Donny does not want to go."

Janvier, who could afford to buy Nate all the tickets he wanted, agreed. He'd like to go some games. It would be fun, but he was determined to avoid the Ravaterras. Also, he wasn't going to stand close to Nate during Christmas. Still, he didn't need to deal with that yet. At the moment, all he had to deal with was the fact that Nate could bench press more weight than he could, every damned time.

By eight o'clock, he sat naked on the edge of his bed in the duplex. He was tired but felt like he'd had a good day. It was too early to go to bed, but he didn't want to watch TV because he was still enjoying the way the day felt. He didn't want to lose that in the canned laughter of sitcoms or the drama of cop shows. But it was early and he had nothing to do, so he might as well see if anything was on. As he reached for the remote, he noticed that while the pewter bud vase still sat on the nightstand, the razor blade was gone. Janvier checked the carpet around the nightstand and under the bed. He didn't want to step barefooted on the rusty, double bladed razor.

It was gone. He didn't remember seeing it lately, not since Nate and Donny had come by a couple of days earlier. He bet that Donny took it because he hadn't taken the pewter bud vase. Nate knew the history of the vase. Donny didn't. He had no idea that it was a gun.

Janvier put the barrel shaped vase into his mouth. He closed his eyes and tasted the metal.

But it felt like a bud vase, not a gun. He put it back on the nightstand and pulled on a clean t-shirt and boxers. Then, screw it, he went to bed even though it was too early and even though he hadn't locked the front door and even though there was still a light on in the bathroom.

The sheets were cool against his legs. He didn't want to date the flirty insurance agent. Without triggering a feeling of shame, Amy floated in front of him. He let himself daydream a little. She was a female version of Donny and he could easily marry that sweet woman. He'd be a Ravaterra then, just like Nate.

Will. He could easily also see himself with Will, but that would break Amy's heart and he'd hate that. He'd hate that the Ravaterras would turn their backs on him if he messed with Amy and Will. Janvier would never, never hurt Amy.

Will. Easy going. Blue eyes and a warm accent.

He'd only met Amy once and he'd almost killed himself afterwards. Janvier's fingers groped his nightstand until he found the bud vase. He didn't put it in his mouth, only held onto it.

Amy with the fascinated eyes. And Will, who was so open that he'd told Amy about him. Janvier fell asleep, thinking of both of them and how he'd like to be part of their family.

At four o'clock the next morning, he woke up with an erection.

21

AT NOON ON FRIDAY, Paige came out of her dressing room and let Perry know exactly how many minutes remained before they had to leave the house. She reminded him not to bring up the "Nate" element when they were in the restaurant. "After all, we don't want to antagonize anyone by mentioning that the owner's estranged son is our brother-in-law."

"I don't have our family tree printed anywhere on my suit, Paige. By the way, you look great."

"Thank you, dear." She checked herself in one of the mirrors again and tucked in an imaginary hair. That was as close to a show of nerves as Paige would allow.

Perry felt uneasy but not for the same reasons as his wife. The billionaire's invitation to lunch came out of the blue. Among several other real estate types, the invitation came because the billionaire was looking at getting into the medical research field and wanted to acquire some property. The combination of money and real estate people didn't surprise him. The strange part was the luncheon invitations included their spouses and were mailed to the house, where Paige saw it first.

It was not the usual protocol, to say the least. Perry thought the whole thing was suspect and would have declined, but Paige wouldn't hear of it. She'd demanded that they go, probably because she could make a name for herself at one of her little charities if she could snare the billionaire as a benefactor, although pitching for a charity was not something Paige would do at a business lunch. It would be unprofessional.

He watched her smooth her smooth dress. "Dear, he probably won't be there. He'll send an associate."

Disagreeing, Paige shook her head. "He has already turned over most of his companies to his children and grandchildren. This may be the way he amuses himself in retirement. If that's the case, he'll be there."

The 'amuses himself' aspect was what bothered Perry. "I'm not even sure why we were included." Architects came in after the land speculation, not before.

"Dear, you undersell yourself. I'm sure they know who you are and what you can do."

Perry felt certain the old man knew there was a connection between the Ravaterra family and Janvier, his former boy-toy, but he couldn't think of a way to get Paige uninterested in going to the dinner.

All Perry had to do was take his beautiful wife and go to dinner at Angelica's. He had to listen to why the representative's boss thought he wanted more medical buildings in an area that had them on every corner. It was just a coincidence that the old man thought it was a good idea right after Janvier bought two buildings, and both had vacant properties next to them that had been for sale for a long time.

"We leave in seven minutes, Perry. Noon on Friday equals rush hour traffic."

He didn't comment on the fact that Paige had never worked and had extremely limited experience dealing with commuter traffic. He knew that wealthy people expected everyone to be on time. Perry also knew that if they didn't leave the moment Paige chose, she'd worry all the way to the restaurant.

His wife put on minuscule earrings. Her jewelry was so understated, Perry wondered why she bothered, but she did look fantastic. The deep blue dress wasn't dressy at all, but cut too well to be office attire. Her hair and figure and shoes all worked together to make her a striking woman. He put his hand on the small of her back. She smelled faintly of something clean and light. "You look beautiful, absolutely perfect."

She thanked him, told him he looked good too, and told him again that she'd met the billionaire once at a benefit, but that she didn't expect him to remember her. "Still, it's important for anyone in my position to keep the lines of communication open."

"Honey, he isn't going to be there." Perry felt disgust at the idea of meeting the billionaire, probably because of Janvier.

His wife arched an eyebrow. "Try not to look so bored, Perry. Even if it is a representative, I'm sure he or she is an important person who could make a real difference to this area. Networking is a huge part of business. It's who you know, and…"

Damn, he hated it when she got like that. "Go check the kids, Paige. You can lecture me all you want in the car on the ride over."

She paused at the bedroom door. "Do you remember when you printed out that picture of Janvier holding the car door?"

Perry nodded, wondering where she was going.

"You said that Janvier was holding the car door, but he wasn't. It looked like he had just come out of the car. And he didn't answer when I asked him. I wonder if we should tell Janvier about this lunch."

"No, we shouldn't. And we shouldn't mention it to anyone at

the dinner, either. It's like not mentioning Nate to his father. Let's mind our own business and our own business is architecture. That's all."

"You've done business with Janvier, haven't you? I liked him quite a bit. Are you sure we shouldn't bring him up to speed on a certain rich man who happens to be in town?"

"Absolutely not. Honey, there are things you probably should know about Janvier, things I should have told you, and I apologize for that. Let me explain it on the way over, and if you're as disgusted as I am about Janvier and that old man, then we can turn around, even in the parking lot of Angelica's, and get some Chinese food take-out."

He did explain it but found she was surprisingly sympathetic. She agreed that Janvier's past should be a "need to know" situation, but she was not off-put.

In Angelica's parking lot, she sighed heavily and said, "Turn off the car, Perry. I won't be late going in. Oh, stop looking at me like that. Now that I know what's going on, it's gone from an interesting lunch to a very interesting lunch. Besides, I always impress my husband at functions like this. Come watch me impress you."

She did.

22

ON FRIDAY, Donny's classes were over by noon. He usually had office hours and graded papers until four-thirty, but he was caught up on his work and decided to call it a day by three-thirty. Madeline wouldn't like being picked up early, but she couldn't tell time yet. Since the day was bright and cold, the entire preschool would be out on the playground. Like all four-year-olds, Madeline loved the playground. He parked in front of the daycare and walked around to the pick-up area.

Except for Madeline, the playground was full of bundled up kids that were actively climbing and shrieking. His little girl sat on the time-out bench, her blue eyes transformed into furious, glittering slits. She bolted off the time-out bench as soon as she saw him. Madeline started yelling about how he was too late picking her up and she was, "waiting and waiting and that FREAK-Head Sophie said that…"

The preschool teacher said Madeline had been a real stinker all day. She didn't say those exact words, but that was the idea.

The teacher added, "She barely ate any lunch. I think she might be coming down with something."

Madeline had to apologize to Sophie before she could leave. It didn't improve her attitude. All the way home, she whined about her coat being too puffy. A block from home, she sneezed violently and started screaming because she had snot on her mouth. Then she gagged.

"Madeline, stop it. You're going to make yourself throw-up."

She threw up. He turned into their parking space as her hysteria hit a high note.

Fortunately, most of the vomit went on her puffy coat and the car seat. He took her out of the car, told her to hold onto his pants leg, and started unfastening the cover to the car seat. It was a pain in the butt trying to get the washable fabric cover off, but if he left it in the car, it would be hours until Nate came home and he could get back down to the parking lot. He wistfully eyed Nate's empty parking spot. Nate had worked bad shifts since last Friday and wouldn't be home for almost four more hours. He spent every morning working out with Janvier, whether Donny had a class or not, and worked until eight at night. Donny was starting to take it personally.

"Daddy, my throw up is dripping!"

"Madeline, please stay right there. Stand here, Baby, one hand on my leg." A car went by, looking to park further down the lot. Still, he made sure Madeline had a firm grip on his pants. Obviously, he was going to have to have his pants cleaned. If more vomit was in the car, he'd find it later. She let go of his pants leg and gave her smeary face a deep rub with her coat sleeve.

"Okay, Madeline, give me your hand. Come on, we're going upstairs."

She crossed her messy arms across her pink-puffy-coat chest and refused. "I can't. I just can't walk."

Oh baby girl, give your daddy a break. Well, his lightweight jacket was washable. Donny picked up his child, vomit coat and all. With his free hand, he carried the wadded-up car seat cover.

"Daddy, you didn't lock the car. It didn't go beep-beep."

"I'll get it later." He carried her up the stone steps and set her down outside the front door. He let her push the button to make the car go "Beep-beep" and made a mental note to disinfect the key fob along with everything else.

Donny carried her into the main bathroom and stripped her down. He put Madeline's clothes, her puffy coat, his jacket, and the car seat cover into the washing machine and set it on pre-rinse. There weren't any chunks in the vomit, so it would probably be okay. Maybe he wouldn't have to wash her hair. It seemed vomit-free at first glance. Nate wouldn't wash it anymore. He said that if Donny didn't want Madeline to have a cute, short haircut, then Donny could wash her hair. Detangling was always an ordeal.

She had vomit in her hair. It wasn't much, but he couldn't ignore it.

"Put the toys you want in the tub, Honey." He tested the bath water and let her choose a handful of toys from the bath selection. The Barbie that Sarah Grace had given her at Thanksgiving was in the mix. Madeline adored her cousins. The half-bald Barbie with a ponytail was a genuine treasure.

"Let's get you washed up before you play. I don't know if it's a good idea to get your Barbie wet." They probably mildewed on the inside or something. The cut-off sock dress looked like a cinched sleeping bag on the skinny doll. It was the cuff of a man's athletic sock, with most of the foot part cut off. "Where did you get that sock?"

"It's not a sock, Daddy! It's her dress! And Barbie needs a bath, that's why I put her there. Sarah Grace saved this Barbie because it was her best-est one, but then she gived it to me and I promised to take good care of it."

The little girl who was too miserable to walk now carefully removed the sock dress. It didn't look like one of theirs, but he didn't keep a mental inventory of socks. "Did you get that sock out of my bedroom?"

"No. Uncle had it on his foot. He cutted it for me with my green scissors."

"Uh-huh, let's give the dress a little wash, too." Now the doll's belt made sense. Madeline didn't have black hair elastics and Janvier did. He was also weird enough to do something like cutting off his socks so Barbie could have a dress.

Madeline washed her doll and her doll's dress while Donny washed her. She started shivering in the bathtub before he rinsed the shampoo out of her long hair. "Daddy, the water feels cold."

Crap. Her cheeks were as pink as they could be. She was getting a fever. Donny blessed the stars for his pediatrician father. "In a minute, let's get the phone and call Granddaddy, okay? See if he wants to stop by on the way home."

Her feet went into the fuzzy pajamas first. Arms were next. He'd have to undress her completely to let her go potty, but she was happy for now. At least, she was happy enough for a sick, cranky four-year-old.

After wrapping the Barbie in a hand-towel, Madeline wanted him to carry her. He obliged her while calling his dad. After the beep, he said, "Hi, Dad. Madeline is sick- vomiting and fever. If you're not in a hurry to get home tonight, could you stop by?"

The doorbell rang as he hung up. Still holding Madeline, who still held the Barbie, he answered the door. He probably should have put her down. It was chilly out and she was still feverish with damp hair, but she had on her fuzzy pajamas.

A gorgeous, dark-haired woman stood on the landing. Slender, with cream colored skin, she had doe eyes and was dressed in a way that stopped short of being provocative. No coat covered the soft, peach colored sweater.

Cold air was coming in and his child had a fever. He wanted to shut the door.

She looked surprised to see Donny and then purred, "I'm sorry. I think I have the wrong place. I was looking for Natanael Rijos?"

Donny clutched Madeline to him. "Can I help you with something?"

The woman looked slightly amused as she looked Donny up and down. "Oh, a child and everything. No, no message. I just wanted to see the man that he abandoned me for." She did a finger wiggle at his child.

Abandon? Did Nate 'abandon' the flawless woman? Donny mentally beseeched God as he shifted Madeline a little. "Why don't you give me your name and I'll be happy to tell him you were here."

"No. I don't think so. Bye, little one." Her amazing, dark eyes looked deeply at him before she turned and walked lightly down the steps.

Donny calmly closed the door. He didn't chase peach-sweater woman into the parking lot, didn't scream at her to come back and explain herself. With hollow insides, he asked Madeline if she wanted some ginger ale. She said yes, and he forgot to give her the soda. She had to ask.

Nate abandoned her? They'd been together over three years, and Nate wasn't involved with anyone when they started dating. If he abandoned anyone, then he had to have done it within the last three years. No. There had to be another explanation. He was letting his imagination run him into a ditch of doubt. Peach sweater probably thought Nate was good looking and was only trying to make trouble to see if she could pry him loose. Of course, she thought he was good looking. Everyone did. Nate was gorgeous.

He handed Madeline the ginger ale in a drinking glass instead of a plastic cup. She set the towel wrapped Barbie on a chair, and her feverish eyes looked wild as she grabbed the breakable drinking vessel. "Oh shit. No. Madeline, wait. Let me put it into your cup."

"Daddy, you said 'shit.' It's a bad word."

It even flashed in his mind that this might be one of Perry's small condo girlfriends. Maybe Perry abandoned her. But Donny saw the old girlfriends in the parking lot, and he would have remembered Peach-Sweater. He thought maybe Perry's new one was a petite blond. Besides, the woman asked for Nate by name.

"Daddy! Why did you say 'shit?' We don't say that word."

He poured the soda into a pink plastic cup. It would be flatter now, but wasn't that better for her stomach anyway? "I'm sorry. I shouldn't have said that word. Don't gulp, Madeline. You'll get sick again."

Who was she and how did she know Nate's address? None of their friends would give out their address without checking with him first. No one at the station would give it out, no matter how her breasts swelled over her bra.

And she'd asked for "Natanael." Only his father called him that. But Señor Rijos would not play some game with his son.

He was letting it circle around. All he had to do was relax and when Nate came home, they'd talk it over.

Madeline carefully rewrapped Barbie in her towel.

While Donny finished the laundry, Madeline kept the soda down. She allowed as how she could manage some "little noodle chicken noodle soup" but not if it had "chunks" in it. Donny picked the chunks of chicken out while the salty soup cooked. She ate it. She threw it up. Most of the vomit went into the toilet. Some went on Barbie's towel.

He comforted Madeline, cleaned up the toilet, and threw the towel away. His Dad stopped by and yes, Madeline was sick. The pediatrician checked her, dosed her, and then settled her in front of the TV with a cartoon movie while he "talked to Daddy about boring stuff like how much medicine to give you." He stroked her hair and held up a clump that had a big tangle in it. "And maybe when you feel better, we can get Aunt Tessie to give you a little haircut. Okay?"

"Okay, Granddaddy. A lady came over today. She was pretty, but not as pretty as Aunt Tessie."

Donny followed his Dad into the kitchen, where he barely gave him time to sit down at the kitchen table. The story about the peach sweater woman popped out of Donny, like a verbal burp coming to the surface. "I mean, she wasn't flashing flesh, but a woman doesn't wear something like that to go to the grocery store, you know?"

His Dad looked surprised for a second. "You've told me you have a jealous streak, but this is the first time I've seen it. Huh. Does Nate screw around?"

There it was. "No. Dad, no."

His Dad wasn't going to let him get away with that. "No, or you hope not?"

"No."

"Then give him the benefit of the doubt. Wait until he comes home and ask him."

"Dad, what if I'm wrong? I mean, basically, Nate's bi-sexual."

"So? He's with you, and you managed to father a baby."

"But what if he is, you know, just looking? Not doing anything, but looking and flirting? I mean, that woman, her guns were loaded. Eventually flirting turns into something else, you know?"

"Donny, there are a lot of good-looking women out there. There's just one you and that's who Nate chose."

"But she said she was 'abandoned' and what the hell does that mean?"

His father put his hands over Donny's. "Neither of us knows the answer to that question. But, son, I don't think he's messing around. He's not the type and he loves you. So, when does he get home?"

"Little more than an hour."

"Then let's see if we can take an hour to get Madeline to bed, then I'll clear on out of here. Any more than an hour and Kimberly will think I'm having an affair, too. It's hard to live with someone who's always suspicious, and frankly, I have no right to ask for trust. I have a feeling Nate does have that right. Ask him. If he didn't do anything, then accept that answer. Please be careful not to mess up a good relationship with jealousy."

He didn't ask if his father was having an affair again. He couldn't care less about his father cheating, and that indifference shamed him a little.

Sprawled out on the recliner, his dad held Madeline in his lap. His father read to her from a stack of books. Donny stretched out on the couch. He tried hard to be quiet and calm, but he kept thinking about the woman at the door and the way that fucking sweater draped over her breasts. She said she'd been abandoned. Why?

His father had cheated on most of his wives and earned the lack of trust. He was a horrible husband, and Perry was just like him. But Nate wasn't like that. As far as Donny knew, his father and mother loved each other. Donny quietly held the idea that if his mother hadn't died, Perry would have been different and his father would be an ideal husband. He was too good of a man to do otherwise.

Donny had no memory of his mother. The day she died, ten-year-old Perry came home from school to find newborn Donny screaming in his crib. Toddler Tessie was unconscious at the bottom of the staircase, next to their dead mother. Two decades later, Donny had listened to the 9-1-1 tape. Perry's voice was still recognizable, even though he was a just a boy.

"My step-mom's dead. She's all twisted up! One of my sisters is hurt. I can't tell which one she is, but she's only little, please! Please! Get Dad, send someone!"

The operator tried to calm the boy, but the panic in Perry's voice didn't change. "I can hear the new baby, but I don't see the other twin. I don't know where she is. Get my dad! Send someone! Please!"

Of course, Donny had no memory of that day. Now, as an adult, he felt helplessly protective of the ten-year-old Perry. He knew that the first one on the scene had been a uniformed officer. The policeman found Perry on their parents' bed, one toddler clutching him while he held a newborn and a bloody, second toddler. He was shivering violently but trying to calm the babies. He had one hand pressed onto Tessie's damaged head, even though the blood was dry and Tessie wasn't conscious.

Poor Tessie. Donny was just glad she hadn't died in the fall.

He yawned hard and listened to his father read a book to Madeline—something about a snowman surprising a traffic cop.

After his mother's death, Donny's father fooled around, both during his next two marriages and in between them. If Donny's mother had lived, would his dad still have fooled around? Maybe not. If she'd lived, would Perry?

Yes.

Perry's wife didn't live with suspicion. Paige knew her husband had affairs. They'd never discussed it, so he had no idea if it was okay with her or not. Could Donny do that? Turn a blind eye for the sake of his marriage? For Nate?

Yes. It made him sick to think about it though. Nate wasn't

cheating on him. Nothing about their lives would change just because a beautiful woman in a peach colored sweater came to their door.

His dad had a way of reading that sounded soft and toneless. It was great at making children relax.

Before Donny, Nate had dated many gorgeous women. Beautiful people tended to date beautiful people. Donny did not qualify as attractive. The best he could do was to be sweet looking in a clownish sort of way.

His father's voice undulated softly. Donny was going to have to remember to do that when he read to Madeline. It rose and fell in a rhythm.

He woke up when he heard his father talking quietly to Nate. "She said you abandoned her." Thank God, Nate was finally home. Donny sat up and looked around. His father must have put Madeline to bed. "Talk to him, son." He left, giving Donny a kiss on top of his head.

Nate sat on the coffee table and, without a word, grabbed Donny's face and kissed him hard. "I love you. I have no idea who that woman was. I never abandoned anyone. I have not cheated on you and I will not cheat on you ever, Donny. Okay?"

Donny felt the blood rush to his face, and he knew his nose had just turned bright red and it was embarrassing as hell. Even worse were the words that came out of his mouth.

"If you say so."

23

ON SATURDAY MORNING, Janvier had breakfast at Angelica's. Señor Rijos suggested breakfast because for the rest of December, the restaurant would be too busy. "I want to spend my time with you, not having to jump up every two minutes." In the closed restaurant, five or six employees did prep work. Señor Rijos and Janvier ended up taking a table in the calm of the dining room. The tablecloth on their table was white lace and old. Janvier asked him where it came from.

"It belonged to Natanael's mother. We used it in our first apartment. The table was so small, but the lace made her feel like we were elegant. My wife came from humble beginnings and thought I was high class. She tried hard to change herself, to become something I never wanted her to be. I loved the way she was. Awkward at times, prone to second guessing herself…that was my Angelica. But she always saw the good side to everything. Natanael and I were truly blessed to have her in our lives."

"Nate's like that. Not the awkward part, that's pure Donny, but Nate sees the good side."

"Sí. He does."

Smyth poured their coffee for them. She overheard the last part and looked at Señor Rijos with such warmth that Janvier wondered, for the first time, if something else was going on. Señor Rijos stood and pulled another chair to the table. "Smyth, sit down a moment. I wish to explain our arrangement to Janvier." He held the chair for her.

Janvier's curiosity was peaked, but he was disappointed. There was no confession of romance with the married Smyth. What Señor Rijos explained was that Smyth owned a third of the restaurant and, over the next six years, would buy enough to own over half. "At that point, I shall retire and she will send me nice checks. If I should die, she will buy the restaurant at a reduced price from my heirs."

"From Nate." Janvier hoped that he hadn't cut Nate out of his will.

"Yes, of course. Three quarters to him, one to you. And I want you to know that I wrote that will over a decade ago. I thought perhaps the probate lawyers could find you."

Smyth stood up. "If you two are going to rehash old business, then I have work to do." She touched Señor Rijos's shoulder with a light gesture. It could go either way.

They had banana bread, thin slices of salty ham, eggs the way Janvier liked them, and small bowls of fruit. Janvier took a bite of the bread and smiled. "You made this yourself."

Señor Rijos nodded. "The rest was put together by a talented young chef that I'm torturing by making her work the lunch shift. I have an excellent staff right now and Smyth can run things as well as I can. She knows what she's doing, so I'm going to leave for Mexico on the twenty-third. I want to be home for Celebrations de la Víspera de Navidad."

It seemed strange that Nate's father called Mexico "home." Señor Rijos was one of seven Rijos children. In his boyhood,

Nate and Señor Rijos went to Mexico every year for Christmas, leaving on Christmas Eve and coming home in time for New Year's Eve because the restaurant was always booked solid. The year after his mother died, Janvier went with them.

"They are all happy you are alive, by the way." Señor Rijos chatted about his extended family for a while. His niece Marianna was the same age as Janvier and Nate. She worked for a major airline and had three boys, each one more rambunctious than the one before.

"I remember Tia Teresa's daughters from the trip we took our senior year. You wouldn't believe what Mariana wanted to give me for Christmas."

"That's my niece you are talking about. Oh, I need to give this to you." He pulled out three receipts from various Catholic charities that added up to a half a million dollars. "Be sure to keep these for your taxes."

He had electronic receipts, but Janvier pocketed the pieces of paper. "I know."

"Humor me. In my mind, you are perpetually a child, not someone who pays taxes. Do you have plenty of your money left after buying those buildings?"

"I'm still comfortable and the idea is that the buildings will generate more money. I think I can manage to kick up a nice donation again next year."

"You're not going to clean all the money up at once?"

"No, sir. I'm not."

Señor Rijos told him that he expected to see him at the restaurant for breakfast on the twenty-third. "My plane does not leave until mid-afternoon and I have a small present for you. I also have a request for a specific gift from you. Even though I cannot be there, I want you to attend Mass on Christmas Eve."

Janvier could not help but smile as he tried his childhood excuse. "Sir, I am not Catholic."

"On Christmas Eve, you are. Take my son with you."

"Sí. If I must go, then you bet he has to go, too."

"Donny and his brother don't look as Italian as their name sounds. Are they Catholic?"

"No, sir. I think the family has been in this country enough generations to be diluted. Their dad goes to a protestant church, but I don't know which one. How do you know Donny's brother?"

"He comes in with business dinners. After Natanael 'came out,' or whatever the term is for moving in with Donny, Smyth pointed out the name on Perry Ravaterra's credit card. I resisted the urge to increase his bill but only because his wife seems like a lovely person. They were back in yesterday for a lunch with a wealthy man."

Señor Rijos took the last bite of his fruit before mentioning the billionaire's name. Janvier's fork froze in mid-air. A crumb fell in slow motion towards the edge of his plate. He watched it miss the china and land on the dead wife's lace tablecloth.

Senior Rijos may or may not have noticed the drip. "I knew the Ravaterras had some money, but I didn't realize he ran in that man's circles. Janvier, is something wrong?"

"No Sir. I apologize, but I'm afraid I just dropped a crumb on the tablecloth." Janvier made himself pay attention and chatted easily for the rest of the meal. Acting calm, he excused himself as soon as possible and made it as far as the parking lot before his phone rang. He had an irrational fear that it was the billionaire even though the ring tone was Nate's.

Was the billionaire still in town? Why was he there? Janvier needed to call Perry. Why was the old man in Raleigh? Why was he meeting with Perry?

He answered the phone.

Nate sounded agitated. "Hey. I'm on my way to the gym. Want to join me?"

"I thought you were going to spend the morning with Donny and Madeline. Don't you have to work second shift again tonight?" His hand shook when he pointed the key-fob thing at his car to unlock it.

On the phone, Nate growled. "Yeah, well. Plans change. Donny and I aren't seeing eye-to-eye right now and Madeline is sick, so life at the gym seems better."

Shit. "How sick is the baby and what are you and Donny fighting over?"

"Madeline is okay. She just has a stomach bug. I wouldn't leave if she was really sick."

"You are leaving when she's a little sick. I know it's none of my business, but screw it. What are you and Donny fighting over?"

"Some hot woman showed up at the door yesterday evening while I was at work, said I had abandoned her and she wanted to see the guy I'd left her for. Apparently, she was incredible looking and Donny flipped out about the whole thing, right down to the peach colored sweater she wore."

Oh no. No, no, no. If the billionaire was in town, it was likely that Alexia was, too. One of his gifts to Alexia was a peach colored alpaca sweater with a few perfect-pearl buttons on the collar. Janvier bought it because it was the same color as peach ice cream. "Can you describe her?"

"Donny said that she had doe eyes, she was beautiful, and he kept going back to the sweater thing."

"Nate, I think this one is my problem. There's this guy in town—please, turn around and go home. I'll meet you there. Shit. Poor Donny."

"Poor Donny? Fuck that. Poor me. I've just spent a whole night telling him that I didn't do anything."

"Nate, you don't know Alexia. Poor Donny now does. Go home, I'm on my way."

Before he got the car in reverse, the phone rang again. This time it was Perry. Janvier answered with, "Let me guess, you and Paige had lunch with a wealthy man that you know I know."

"Yeah, Janvier. I'm doing you a favor here, so don't snap at me."

"Sorry. I'm trying to deal with the idea that he's here in town."

"Actually, I don't think he's still here. I think he flew out right after the luncheon."

Relief spread through Janvier, just knowing he was gone. "Perry, did he have a woman named Alexia Iacio with him?"

"Yes. Lovely woman. I assume she's an associate of yours?"

"I think she showed up at Donny and Nate's, looking for me. She caused problems. Do me a favor and give me a heads-up if that man or Alexia comes back to town, okay?"

"Listen, Reed. Consider this your heads-up. Your old sugar daddy is looking to buy the land adjacent to your buildings. Whatever mess your love life is in, I'd appreciate it if you'd leave my brother and me completely the fuck out of it. Got it?"

Shit, shit, shit! "I got it and I agree. I'll take care of it, Perry." His foot on the brake, the car in reverse, he sat in the parking lot of Angelica's and worried. Alexia felt abandoned?

Then it hit him.

He was the one consistent person in Alexia's life. In the early days, the billionaire would have tossed her aside except for her connection to Janvier. He'd left New York without a word to her. He'd abandoned her. She'd called several times at the hospital, but he refused to talk to her. He'd refused contact with anyone, including the billionaire. Shit. He'd not even thought about her before. He never gave Alexia credit for having any kind of emotional need. God, he had all kinds of emotional needs, including guilt.

"Janvier."

Señor Rijos was outside his car. It was cold, and he wasn't wearing a coat. Janvier lowered his window. "Sir?"

"Are you okay? Why are you sitting here?"

"Oh, sorry. I took two phone calls. Talking while driving is difficult so I waited until I was finished."

Señor Rijos didn't look terribly convinced. "That's not a bad idea, especially for a new driver. I'll see you soon and if you need anything, call."

For the first time, Janvier didn't pay attention to his driving. He went from Raleigh to Chapel Hill without sweating and clutching the wheel. Instead, he worried about what he'd said to Perry. He had to take care of the billionaire's intrusion into his life.

How? At his exit, he slammed his fist on the car's dash. Damn it, he felt helpless.

24

DONNY LET Madeline break the rules since she was sick. She could watch TV in the middle of the day. She could watch less-than-educational cartoons and she could do all of it on Daddy's and Nate's big bed, but she had to get out of bed if she wanted to sip at her electrolyte water.

She wanted Gatorade instead. Nate gave it to her without reinforcing the get-off-the-bed rule. It irritated Donny, but it kept her from demanding again an explanation of why she couldn't see Uncle.

Nate came home minutes after stomping off. For a few minutes, Donny had a flicker of hope that Nate wanted to try to tell him that he'd done nothing and that he loved him. Donny was ready to stop being such a jealous ass, but he needed Nate to tell him, just one more time. Instead, his husband said Janvier was on his way over, and that he was somehow responsible for the peach-sweater woman.

Once Madeline was ensconced in the bedroom, Donny sat on the couch and listened to Janvier explain who Peach Sweater was.

who she is, and I'll deal with it. Give us a few minutes, Janvier."

Janvier walked hesitantly out of the room, and Donny sat down next to Nate, took his hand and looked him in the eye. "Nate, I want you to stay here with Madeline while I go home with Janvier."

"Why?"

"Because our helpless little boy has had a rough day. I took a double-edged razor off his nightstand not long ago. I'm going to go search your old place for a gun or a bottle of pills that aren't his anti-depressants. No, don't look like that. I don't think he's in trouble, but I want to make sure."

"I'm coming, too."

"No. It would embarrass him if you were there, but he'll let me. The two of you go to the gym and work out until someone has a hernia, okay?"

Nate put his head in his hands. Stood up. Sat down again and put his arms around Donny. "I love you. I love you so God-damned much."

Donny nodded. "I love you too," although at the moment, he wasn't sure that he even liked Janvier. Or maybe he did.

Janvier drove them back to his house. He was becoming an adequate driver. As he parked in front of the duplex, he told Donny that he didn't need to search the apartment.

"I'll tell you what I have in there. I bought an antique straight razor off an internet store. I was looking at the razors, thinking that I was killing time, and this one was cool looking so I bought it. And I know that isn't exactly true and yes, I will tell my therapist."

From the passenger seat, Donny looked at him. Janvier turned the car off, put his hand on the door handle, and tossed his hair out of his eyes. "I should have already told the doctor. I didn't. I will."

"Yeah. You will. At your next appointment."

Once they were at the duplex, Donny went straight to the bedroom, took the antique razor off the nightstand, and resisted the urge to open the thing. It was heavier than he thought, but he put it in his pocket with the intention of throwing it into the dumpster when they left. Maybe. The razor had a horn handle that was appealing in a bad-ass sort of way. Janvier watched him but didn't say anything when Donny put the closed razor in his pocket. In the bathroom, Donny checked the bottle of anti-depressants. According to the date, Janvier should have about six left. He opened the bottle and checked. There were six left.

Janvier leaned against the doorframe and said, "I'm good about taking them. It's been an emotional landslide coming home and I need them."

Donny searched the rest of the apartment while he made small talk. He mentioned that Amy and Will lived a half mile or so down the road. "It's across that patch of woods on the other side of Route 54. Hold the mattress up so I can see under it. Why did you look like that when I said something about my sister?"

Janvier lifted the mattress, bending over and holding it so Donny could see there was nothing under there. The awkward position made Janvier's voice a little strained. "Because I inappropriately think she's wonderful."

Donny didn't ask why that was inappropriate. His sister was off limits. As his friend lowered the mattress, he kissed Janvier on top of his head. "No."

25

Instead of going to the gym, Nate stayed home with Donny, and Janvier's therapist had a cancelation so Janvier could see him right away. He'd already told the Raleigh doctor everything, but this time, realizing that the billionaire and Alexia might still be in town, he knew that all he'd told the doctor was the outline of his life. Janvier walked into the therapist's office and went to the windows, adjusting the blinds. He stared at the parking lot three floors below. He touched his collar where the scarf used to be.

"After my mother killed herself, I was so damn angry that I was chewing myself up. I resented Señor Rijos for trying to force me to make plans and to be okay. I wasn't okay. I was the kid whose mother had killed herself. Somehow going to New York was me showing the world that I didn't need taking care of and that I didn't need help. But when I got there, I was so ashamed. I wanted to go home, but I was so damned ashamed. I kept thinking that if I could get some money together, I could go home and be independent and somehow that would make it okay." He watched as a delivery truck made a complicated K turn in the parking lot. It didn't go well.

God, he wished he was telling the therapist all this while sitting in a small café that made peach ice cream. He would feel so much more in control. He needed control.

"The billionaire owned me. At first, the Woman was still my pimp, but the billionaire became fond of me and Alexia, and he basically bought us. We always worked together with him whenever he was in town, and he was often in town. I looked out the windows in the penthouse more times than I can remember. The edge of the pool was visible from the bedroom window. I hated that pool."

———

THE TWENTY-SEVEN-YEAR-OLD WHORE named Jan Winters slid out of the bed in the billionaire's New York penthouse. Alexia was still asleep, a small lump in the absurdly large bed. Only a spray of dark hair was visible on her pillow.

Jan been the billionaire's favorite for nine years, and was required to stay at the penthouse whenever the billionaire was in New York. He rarely was required to perform sexually anymore, but the old man still wanted him there, supervising.

Jan didn't care. He was well paid. He didn't feel even slightly jealous of Alexia's continued active participation. Jan was a trained bed-warmer, and his sexual response was completely unneeded. His job was to try not to look bored as he watched, and then get the other young man out the door.

It was just before dawn, and Jan knew he should get the blanket and sit on the side of the bed, the way the billionaire liked to find him. That morning, however, he didn't. Naked, Jan stared out the windows and listened to the muted sounds of the billionaire dressing in the next room. The city's pre-dawn lights glowed softly, as if they were tired of sparkling. His most important client rarely slept more than a few hours a night and kept early hours. Over the last nine years, the insomnia seemed worse.

Whenever he was in New York, the billionaire wanted Jan to stay in bed until the coffee was served. It pleased the client to have Jan, wrapped in a specific blanket, joining him for a mug of coffee. Alexia was to stay asleep. Folded on a chair near the window was a gray, lamb's wool blanket. It didn't matter if it was December or August, the blanket was always there.

Electric lights spread out like stars below the windows, but the skyline to the east had the faintest halo of pink light. Maybe if the billionaire cut him loose, he'd reignite the desire to go home. It was painful to even contemplate the possibility, but he couldn't help it.

Jan watched his breath lightly fog the glass. He could never go home, even if the old man let him go. Still, his bank account had over fifty thousand dollars in it. That was enough to go anywhere and start over. He saw his own reflection wince when he thought of going without permission. The subject had come up with the billionaire before. Jan understood that if he went back to North Carolina, the billionaire could make sure that Nate and Señor Rijos knew what a whore he was. He had photographs and videos to back that threat up. Once, the old man had implied that Jan would find himself addicted to some impossible-to-get drug if he tried anything that had not been approved. Unless the billionaire gave his permission, there was no going home or anywhere else. There was nothing to go home to anyway. He might have become a member of Nate's small family if he'd stayed, but not now.

The valet came briefly into the room and turned on a few lights, but Janvier did what he was supposed to do. He didn't look at or acknowledge the man. Instead, he watched the lamplight reflected in the window.

Before he left the room, the valet soundlessly waited for Jan to sit on the bed again. When he didn't, the servant draped the thin wool blanket around him and tugged it, letting one shoulder slip free, like always. The valet barely made a reflection on the glass. A moment later, Jan heard the billionaire re-enter the room.

Without looking, he knew the cut and color of the old man's suit. He knew how the billionaire's hair product smelled, that he had a close shave, and that his only piece of jewelry was a watch. Janvier watched his own reflection as he changed his facial expression into one of muddled sleepiness. "Morning."

The billionaire kissed him on his exposed shoulder. "Good morning, Jan. I am afraid we must take a few minutes to discuss something. Are you awake enough?"

Jan nodded. There was a feeling inside him that he couldn't quite define. It was both nervousness and excitement. The butler set the breakfast table in the corner of the room. From the window, Jan could see the glow from the lighted rooftop swimming pool.

The billionaire wore a suit that disguised the way age had thickened his middle and thinned out his arms and legs. Clutching his blanket around him, Jan followed the billionaire to the breakfast tray. The old man picked up a coffee mug that didn't match the rest of the china. It was a simple blue mug that Alexia made for him one Christmas. She'd pressed her lips into the clay when it was still soft, and the resulting smear almost looked like a lip print. Jan knew that the mug was available to the billionaire every morning no matter where he woke up.

There was a time when the old man wanted Jan to travel with him all over the world, but Jan consistently refused to get a passport or even a driver's license. The only time he used his real name was for taxes, but he didn't think that the IRS could give Señor Rijos his information.

"Sit down, Jan."

Jan sat, tucking the blanket around him.

"Starting today, I've arranged several tutors for you. They are mostly economics and business professors, either retired or active. The lessons will be both general and specific. You are not to ask any of the teachers' names or anything personal about them and, of course, they will reciprocate and simply call you Jan. There will be no record of these classes, but I expect you to excel, to learn everything they teach you. The lessons are to last from two to seven, Monday through Thursday, here in the penthouse. You will live here. Your personal belongings will be delivered this morning and your little apartment is paid for so Alexia can afford to live there alone. I am leaving for several months but will leave a staff here to take care of you. You will use these next few months to learn as much as you can. Perhaps you should have Alexia take the classes with you. That's up to you."

Jan reached for the billionaire's homemade mug, taking it instead of his own thin porcelain cup. It made a flicker of a smile cross the old man's face. Jan took several swallows, drinking half the mug before he managed to control the way the room pressed in around him. Dead calm, he asked, "Why?"

"Because I wish for you to be educated. I will try to make it back to see you when I can. Of course, I expect you and Alexia to make yourselves available to me. And to keep a lookout for the type of young people I enjoy." Finding the billionaire younger escorts was the Woman's job. Jan realized what the billionaire was about to do right before the older man opened his mouth. He fought to keep his face from showing the wave of nervous nausea that gripped him.

"The Woman has become an inconvenient buffer between us. I am inordinately fond of you, so I have made a few business changes. As of about ten o'clock today, you own the escort service. Several corporations will continue to own fifty-one percent, but you own the rest. I know how you are about using your own name, so it appears on the business license only briefly. It's legal and deeply hidden."

Questions tumbled in Jan's head. He should have realized the billionaire would find a way to keep him.

"I've even had the business renamed Jan Winter's. You've earned it, Jan. I know you'll do a good job because you've always had the kind of emotional control that a top pimp needs. Don't let anyone call you that, though. Rise above it."

He had to ask the next question. "Why not Alexia, too?"

The billionaire shrugged. "She's too young, Jan. You're not much better, but she's very much a whore. You are different."

Jan let out his breath in a way that sounded like a hiss. "Back at the beginning, did you know how old she was?"

"Dear, don't be naive. Listen carefully and learn because you need to understand a few things. I could pretend that I didn't know how old she was, and that you were the one who let a teenaged girl be a whore. And that is true. You are as much to blame for Alexia as I am, or anyone else in her loveless life."

The older man paused while that sank in.

"Think about it, Jan. You've been photographed with me dozens of times because you were a legal adult. Alexia has never been photographed with me, but she has been photographed with you in explicit and time-dated photographs. Oh, the look on your face, Jan. My dear, this part is simply business. I do care what you think and how you feel. It's almost distressing to know that I truly care for you so much, especially since part of your charm is that you have always had one foot out the door."

"I have never tried to leave."

"Do not delude yourself, dear boy. I have stopped you from even trying. And you're going to have a good life, but as Jan

Winters, not as Janvier Reed. I don't suppose it will help to tell you that you are going to make serious money now."

The client's bodyguard entered the room and stood still near the foyer. He nodded to the billionaire as the old man touched Jan on the shoulder.

"I'll see you briefly in a couple of weeks. A business lawyer will meet with you in your office today. Your office, Jan. Every trace of the Woman is gone, except her records and client lists. You will have access to every business detail and, of course, the finances. A new accountant will be waiting there for you this morning. Learn as much as you can, as fast as you can, but don't make foolish mistakes like taking on a child whore, not even to suit the whims of extremely rich men. Our Alexia could be a poster child for human trafficking, but it turned out for the best for both of you, don't you think? Neither of you is standing on the street, desperately trying to earn enough money to get your next fix. Never forget that you have me to thank for that."

The billionaire kissed him before he left.

26

Ms. Nancy stood next to a folding table with the coffee maker on it and asked Janvier if there was a reason he didn't want her to advertise the dog pee rooms. "You aren't holding off leasing them because of any lingering smell, are you? Because you can't smell anything. Go sniff them for yourself. The only thing in there is the lovely chemical odor of new carpet and new paint."

Although the idea in his head was distracting him, he did go check. He walked across the hall, unlocked the door and gave into the urge to take off his shoes and his one remaining sock. The new carpet was the same wheat color as his scarf, which was still in the chest at Señor Rijos' house. Janvier sat cross-legged, pushed the loose hair out of his eyes, and made a call. His phone told him that he'd blocked the number, and did he wish to continue making the call?

He touched 'yes', and the billionaire answered on the second ring.

"Jan?"

Janvier congratulated himself on how calm he was. He didn't

feel panicked at all. He had sat in a sunny spot on wheat colored carpet with his shoes off and called the billionaire.

"Janvier?"

"Call me Jan, please."

"Yes, I prefer that too. It's good to hear…" The billionaire's voice cracked. "I'm pleased you called me, Jan."

Janvier hadn't had much choice. The only way to get the old man out of Raleigh was to deal with him, but Janvier wasn't going to antagonize him. He wanted the new idea to take root.

Still feeling calm, he told the billionaire that he wanted to talk to him, to work out a deal where he would spend time with him. "In Raleigh. You come to me."

"I always have, haven't I? You refused to leave New York, so I came to you. Jan, you owe me. I laid the world at your feet, gave you everything. Why didn't you tell me when you started feeling like you wanted to hurt yourself?"

"Listen to me. If you want to yell at me, accuse me, I will sit and take it. You want to say supportive things to me, then I will sit and take that, too. You can tell me in detail how much you've given me and I will show you remorse, or whatever the hell you want, but we need to strike a deal first and part of that deal is that you leave this area alone, and you leave my friends alone. There will be no sex, but I think paying for my time is an arrangement that is familiar for us, and that will make you comfortable." For the first time, Janvier said the billionaire's first name. It almost made him gag. It made the billionaire speechless for a moment.

"Fine, Jan. How much do you want?"

"I have to work out the details, but I will let you know when and where."

They talked for a billable hour while Janvier worked out the plan. His heart raced, not because of the old man but because the plan might work. He felt scared and excited at the same time.

"And part of that plan will be the donations of some of your artifacts. I'm not asking you to part with anything that has meaning to you, but you own a lot simply to own them. You will find the correct home for every one of those trinkets. And you will do it in the spirit of someone who loves antiquity and wishes to share their collection with the world. There will be no bargaining on this one. No making deals. You will find the right place for each one, the legal ones and the illegal ones, and you will do this every single time I meet with you, in addition to the money."

The billionaire agreed to everything, even the exorbitant amounts of money, but said it had to be legitimate.

"It will be." By the end of the phone call, Janvier felt exhausted and was doing his chuckle thing. He let the old man tell him a funny story about his driver damaging the limo by avoiding a bird.

"A gull! We were in Casablanca and he almost gave me a heart attack. He caused five thousand dollars' worth of damage to the car for a gull! But I didn't have the heart to be mad. It was a nice-looking bird trying to catch a small snake that was crossing the road."

"What were you doing in Morocco?" Janvier didn't even feel nauseated anymore. For the last year, he'd been demonizing the man, who deserved it. He deserved every loathing impulse Janvier had. But he was also a lonely old man who was going to let Jan set the terms.

"Just traveling around. I've spent very little time in the states since you left New York. I went to Baltimore several times, but you wouldn't see me. I also have been to the Raleigh area twice."

"Don't sneak around me. I'll get the arrangement set up and we'll do this right. And no involving anyone who lives in this area. Speaking of which, did you sic Alexia on my family?"

"You're calling the Ravaterras your family? Or is that the Rijos father and son?"

Janvier almost hung up. "That's over the line. You have never spoken about your family, and we've left mine alone, too. Let's continue that."

The billionaire's voice had a slight whine to it. "There's nothing to talk about with my family. To me, they are strangers who work hard and make me money."

"That's beside the point. We continue the no-family rule. Now tell me about Alexia."

"That might be a little difficult since she obviously thought of you as her family. She took it hard when you left. Certainly, you and I were all she had. Our Alexia asked me if I wanted to continue the escort business and I said no, but if she wanted to quit, I'd buy her out, which is what I did. She has enough money to live anywhere, but she had nowhere to go. I think you understand that. Can I ask what she did to your…family?"

"She was beautiful at the wrong time to the wrong person."

The billionaire chuckled. "That's our girl. And you feel guilty about her."

"Very much." Janvier gave him a name of a Brazilian millionaire. "He always liked her and I think it was mutual. If he is still single, perhaps she should go see him. I expect Alexia would do well as a respectable, married woman."

"Yes, she would. Perhaps she could accompany me on one of the visits to Raleigh. Even though you're offering to sell me your time, I assume that we are all dressed during these visits?"

"Yes. No sex at all." The visits were going to send him running to his therapist afterwards anyway. In fact, he was sure his doctor was going to tell him that there was no way in hell he should do this. Janvier was going to do it anyway.

The old man sighed. "It's just as well. I have felt my age this last year. You still haven't told me how often you are going to allow me in the area?"

"I'll be in touch and give you the contact number. In the meantime, if you bring Alexia with you, give me a little warning."

"Unblock my number and I will."

The next call he should have made was to his therapist. Instead, he called Paige Ravaterra, but only after he sat for a few minutes while his racing heart slowed.

He looked up the Ravaterra's home phone number via the internet. The only other number he had was for Perry's cell phone. He wanted to speak to Paige, not Perry.

She answered on the third ring.

"Paige? This is Janvier Reed. I'm Nate's friend?" He was nervous. This had to work. He told her it was about her charity work, and that he had something she might be interested in. She said she was free that afternoon, so did he want her to stop by? Yes, he did.

As he hung up, Ms. Nancy stuck her head in again. "You have a bunch of calls that need to be returned."

Janvier didn't move from the floor. "Paige Ravaterra will be here in an hour. Could you show her in the minute she gets here?"

"Perry's wife? Pretty woman, lots of poise?"

"Yes."

"Well, okay. Do I show her into your office, which has furniture in it by the way, or do I show her into the bare office where you have no shoes on?"

He made no move to get up and dimly heard the "ding" of the elevator doors further down the hall. That didn't mean anything. There were other offices on that floor on the east side of the building, but Ms. Nancy looked down the hallway and then back at him.

"Shoes!"

It would take Paige at least forty-five minutes to make the trip, so it had to be business. He reached for his shoes as Ms. Nancy stood in the hallway and apologized to someone for the mess. "We're renovating. I'm the manager for Reed Properties. Can I help you?"

A familiar woman's voice floated from the hallway, saying she was a friend of his and thought she'd pop in if he wasn't busy. Ms. Nancy stood in the open doorway and looked down at him holding one sock in his hand. "He's not busy." She stepped aside.

"Amy!"

"Hi, Janvier! Are you busy? Because if you are, I can, you know, go away. I stopped by on impulse. I had an appointment with the optometrist in the building, Dr. Taylor? Do you know her? Donny told me that you bought this building. Hi."

"Hi." She looked great. "I have an appointment, but not for forty-five minutes. My office manager told me to use the time to put my shoes back on. Ms. Nancy Chopper, this is Doctor Amy Ravaterra, Perry's sister."

Ms. Nancy called, "How do you do?" as she headed back across the hall. "And you have calls to make."

Amy waved and dropped her voice a little. "It's okay if you're busy, Janvier. I wanted to say 'hi', but I do have to get back to work. I took a couple of hours off to get my eyes checked because the doctor doesn't do after-hour appointments. You know how they are. Doctors." She fluttered her hands.

Janvier nodded. "Some of them are really good-looking."

He shouldn't have said that. Amy blushed exactly the way Donny did. It was all nose and neck. Like her brother, she was awkwardly appealing. Arms and legs folding, she sat down on the carpet next to him.

"Oh, this carpet is new. Is that why you're barefooted? Trying it out?"

"Ah, let me tell you the saga of the dog pee offices." While they sat on the new carpet, he told her the story, omitting the fake euthanasia notice that he'd left on the consultant's door. He decided not to put the single sock back on and slipped his feet into his casual shoes.

"Why do you have only one sock?"

"Madeline's Barbie doll has a thing for dresses made from socks."

"Ah. Is that why your sock is colorful and completely mismatches your business casual attire?"

"Hey, a doll needs wardrobe choices." Cross-legged, they faced each other. "You know, this is the first time in my adult life that I can wear business casual and I still feel wrongly dressed. If it wasn't for the loud socks, I'd wear only suits to work. There's no thinking involved beyond the tie."

"You look fine." She put her hand on his knee, but it seemed innocent. His knee was the closest thing to her hand. "Janvier, I hope that you don't avoid Will because of what happened. He thinks a lot of what you are trying to do and so do I. We'd love to have dinner or have you over sometime. Maybe with Donny and Nate? I promise, we won't say anything about you meeting Will for the first time. I mean, it's pretty personal."

"I already told Nate that I'd met Will before. No details, of course." Janvier had never intended to see her again, much less with Will. "And thank you, Amy. I can't tell you how much it means to me to hear you say that."

"Well, I'm going to scoot. Please let's get something set up. This is such an insane month for everyone, so I'd love to have a just-for-fun evening." She awkwardly got up from the floor, and he smoothly took her arm to help her unfold.

Untangling Amy left them standing close together. For a long second, neither of them moved. She gave him a quick hug. It was over before he had time to realize it had started.

He walked her to the elevator, feeling like he should kiss her goodbye. He didn't. She stepped on and waved, and he returned the gesture.

As soon as he returned to his office, Ms. Nancy cornered him. "I've been trying to call the massage parlor all morning to tell them their monthly lease wasn't going to be renewed, but no one is answering. We probably are going to end up with them until February because we should give them adequate notice. Reed, do I need to go over our legal rights with evictions with you? Even with a month-to-month, you can't—"

He quietly stopped her. "They aren't going to be there next week."

She looked at him the way Señor Rijos used to if he talked back. Janvier modified his speech immediately. "I apologize, Ms. Nancy. You are the one with all the experience in this business, so it wouldn't be a bad idea to make a list of things I need to know, like eviction laws. I promise that I will learn them."

"Good thinking, Reed. I'm old. I need to know that when it's time for me to re-retire, you'll be able to walk without me holding your hand." She settled herself in her folding chair behind her folding table desk. "Go on now. Go into your office so I can show the next Ravaterra lady in. And return those calls."

He had furniture. There was a leather chair behind an old fashioned, heavy wooden desk. It looked like an antique and was in excellent shape. There was an upholstered chair on a swivel that could either face the desk or could face a matching simple chair and a small couch. He tried the couch and chairs.

They were too small for him, so he tried the new leather chair behind the desk. It fit.

He stuck his head out the door. "I like my furniture. Where's yours?"

Ms. Nancy had her computer open and looked at him over her glasses. "My desk is stylish, circa 1961. They call it mid-century modern, and I had to special order it. Your desk belonged to my uncle, so take care of it. And, by the way, giving you my uncle's desk is how I justified spending the money on my desk. Your phone messages are sorted by importance."

He made the calls.

An hour and ten minutes after he'd called her, Paige arrived. Her face was a polite mask as she entered the office. She wore a camelhair coat that matched her slacks perfectly.

"Thanks so much for coming over, Paige. I make a decent cup of coffee. Can I offer you a cup?"

A study in elegance, she accepted the coffee and relinquished her coat. "I must admit, I am curious. Your call was vague. Almost cryptic."

After closing his office door, he took a seat on the couch. It was slightly too low and slightly too short to be comfortable. "There's a new project I'd like to undertake. A charity to help sex workers. I'd like to call it The Alexia Project."

"Excuse me? The Alexia…?"

"To be honest with you, I'm nervous. This idea is not thought-out, but it is something I think I need to do on several levels. I badly want it to work and I think it's going to take an expertise I don't have. So, are you capable of running a start-up charity?"

"Yes, but ask me if I want to. Explain your Project. Do you have a mission statement?"

"No. Can you write one?"

She raised one, then both of her perfect eyebrows.

"Paige, this idea is only hours old, but I've put some things in motion already. I guess what I want is to fund things. I am not locked into doing a charity that funds existing organizations, but I am locked into helping sex workers. I'm asking if you can run it.

She struggled to hold her composure. "A charity? I have done extensive charity work before, Janvier. I simply…I've worked, just not for pay. But believe me, I am qualified. You want what exactly?"

"I want to start a fund. Some sex workers do what they do because they choose to, but an awful lot get into the business through predatory practices. I poked around online a little and it looks like there are several organizations that already exist. Most work with the poor and the trafficked. Unfortunately, from what I've seen, these places are underfunded at best. You'll be the one who raises the money needed and figures out if they're legit. I'll just work for you. I'm going to start you with two million, and set aside ten to twenty percent of the profits from my commercial businesses or whatever my tax attorney tells me to do. In addition, there's an obscenely rich man who will pay you for my time. He's going to end up being the real funding for this thing and yes, we are talking about a serious amount of money."

Her eyes followed his hand as he pushed his hair out of his eyes. Janvier surprised himself. He was nervous. "Paige, how much do you know about my past?"

For several seconds, she said nothing. Then she looked him in the eye.

"I know, Janvier. My husband told me a few things and his brother said something in passing, so I started looking for myself. To put it politely, you worked for an expensive escort service and I know that you went to several openings with your rich friend. I'm assuming you are talking about the same man? I thought that part of your life was over. Is it?"

"It's absolutely over, but he hasn't gone away. It was my intention never to speak to him again, but he's had his fingers all over the real estate in this area since I came home."

"I know."

"I've worked out another way for him to interact with me. He wants my time and I want the charity. But I need you. I need someone who will not look at him with stars in her eyes. Paige, are you interested?"

She held his eyes. "Fascinated, but tell me the details. Tell me enough to knock the stars out of my eyes."

"I was very, very lucky and I'm not being sarcastic. What happened to me doesn't happen often to young people in the trade and it was because of him. That's enough, isn't it?"

She shook her head with a slight, sharp movement. "No. Janvier, I can't even consider doing this without knowing more. I don't want any surprises. You're asking me to sign on with someone who doesn't even seem worried that he made his money by breaking the law. That's you, not your friend. Tell me why you were lucky and why your sugar daddy is willing to do this weird fundraising. That's what we are talking about, by the way. Not selling your time. Fundraising. Now talk to me."

She was right. Janvier looked down, not wanting to meet her eyes. It didn't work. He looked up and started talking.

"I was eighteen years old and the billionaire contracted with a madam for an inexperienced southern gentleman of no more than legal age. He liked me so much that he kept me. After a year or so, I wanted to get out of the business and come home, but he told me that if I left before he was ready for me to go…" He couldn't keep the anger out of his voice. "If I left, he'd publish photos that my family would be sure to see. My family. That was Nate and Nate's father. I was too young and too ashamed to understand that they would have wanted me home anyway. As I grew older, he entangled me further with an education and even a business to run. Alexia, too. He kept her with me. For seventeen years, that man made sure we understood how lucky we were while we prostituted ourselves and others. It's important you know that, Paige. I never forced anyone. I hired them, though. Sometimes that was probably the same thing, but I never checked."

She said nothing as he pulled himself together. After a moment, she touched his hand. It made more words come out of him.

"I hate him. Even worse, I've gone from thinking that I can't live with him over my shoulder to understanding that maybe I can. I want to control it, though. That is the reason I want to set up this charity."

He didn't see judgment in her face. She gave him a slight "go on" nod, so he took a breath and continued. "I wish I could say that I wanted to do this for the good it will do, but the truth is that I hope it helps me feel cleaner. And I haven't given a thought to saving anyone, although I have a huge amount of retribution to make. What I want is to control the billionaire's impact on my life and this will allow me to do so. I want you to run it because I trust you, and you probably have the background and education, and because it feels right."

Paige had a whole range of facial expressions that he hadn't seen on Thanksgiving.

"I'm qualified. Janvier, after buying these buildings, do you still have the kind of money to pay for a start-up? Will two million cut too close?"

"It will cut closer than I wish, but I financed enough to give myself wiggle room but not so much that I'm worried. I'm sure I can make a profit on the real estate and I don't intend to live like a millionaire, so I'll be fine financially."

"What about—is he—Jesus God! How can you stand to have anything to do with him?"

He shrugged. "Honestly, I don't know that I can. But if it doesn't work, is two million enough to cover first year cost?"

"Probably. Can I assume you will furnish the office space?"

"Is two rooms and a half bath okay for now?"

"Yes. Don't give me the money yet. We need a mission

statement and a tax-exempt code and…the woman, Alexia, what happened to her?"

"I hope she has a happily ever after in her future."

"So why are we naming a charity after her?"

"Because her family sold her into the business when she was a child."

"Shit." The elegant woman swore. It made him smile, but only for a moment. Paige looked angry, bewildered, and a lot of things that weren't elegant. "What do you call him?"

"I just think of him as 'the billionaire.' Thinking of him by name is too personal."

"And you are going to fundraise with that man?"

"Sort of. For a huge donation, I will sit and have lunch with him."

"Lunch?"

"Only that and nothing else."

"Janvier, sex would be a deal breaker for me. Are we clear? Good. No travel either, not for you. You don't go to Paris or to Kyoto to meet him for lunch. I'm not going to babysit you in another city. No overnights. Just lunch in Raleigh, right? How much money are we talking about?"

"Ask for half a million per lunch. He'll balk at that, but don't go much lower. He has nothing but money and he'll spend it."

She swore again.

"Paige, you haven't said yes. Are you going to take the job?"

For a moment, she said nothing. His heart sank. Then her face changed from angry to an expression completely different than any he'd seen so far.

She had dimples.

"Wow. I may be wrong," he said, "but that looks like a genuine smile. Does that mean yes?"

"God, Janvier. Yes, I am going to take the job. Rather, I am going to let you give me a charity, because you're right. If this thing gets going, it's mine."

She didn't look the same. Not at all. The hostess elegance was gone. She threw one hand up in the air. "Last night, I was depressed because being Perry's wife is all I am. Suddenly, I'm excited about the future. Which two rooms and a half-bath are mine?"

"The rooms across the hall. They've been refurbished and you can expand when you need to."

"Janvier, eventually I'm going to take over the whole floor, but don't worry. I'll let you keep these two rooms and your half bath. Besides the billionaire, are you comfortable with the idea of giving me a few well-connected names?"

"No, that's not going to happen. You need to understand that he is it. I'm not going to start pointing fingers at old clients."

"Well, half a million for a lunch equals a great 'it.' Don't you think that within a month, your old clients will know that you've become a charity? You're about to become the reclusive genius who is trying to clean up the sex industry. By the end of the next fiscal year, I predict the Alexia Project will be the favored place for the elite to take a tax deduction, especially if they get to whisper that they knew you when."

"God. Keep me reclusive, okay?"

"Sure. Besides, I intend to be the one in front of the camera. Oh. Do you want to focus on a specific group or anyone caught in the sex trade?"

"Anyone. And it's about us now, Paige, not me. What do you want?"

She spread her arms out. "This."

27

PERRY WAS PLEASED with how things had settled in with Julie over the last two months.

That night, she trotted out a beat-up electric wok and stir-fried chicken with all kinds of vegetables, raw cashews, and a ton of soy sauce. She called the combination "Approximate Cashew Chicken." It was way too salty and shouldn't have been good, but it was incredible. She did the dishes immediately afterward but made him help.

Julie was lighthearted. This was a novelty to Perry. He'd never spent time with someone who was naturally happy. She sincerely didn't worry about things like housework, but she wanted to please Perry so she kept the place picked up. She also knew he wanted her to pay off the lawyer, so she worked harder on it. Because of her commitment, he decided to reward her, and he went ahead and paid the legal bill for her.

The Approximate Cashew Chicken lingered a while after dinner, so they ate ice cream that had crumbled up peanut butter cups in it while watching a sappy movie about true love. Julie started giggling at the over-the-top dialogue and things just escalated. They ended up half naked on the couch, toying with sex while making fun of the movie. He went down on her, something he almost never did to anyone but his wife, but he had to get her to stop giggling.

They left the television on when they moved back to the bedroom. Maybe it was the long, drawn out foreplay or maybe it was the rather simple pleasure Julie took in sex, but for whatever reason, Perry exploded inside her. He couldn't remember the last time he'd ejaculated that hard. She curled up next to him, murmured something about going back into the living room to turn the television off, and Perry remembered nothing else until the TV projected a loud battle from the other room.

He woke, listening to the sounds of the televised war cries. Shit. It felt late.

Sitting up, he reached for his phone on the nightstand, but it wasn't there. It was in the living room with his pants. Perry got up and walked into the next room. The lights were on, the television had a close-up of someone gruesomely dead, and his phone was on the coffee table. It was almost four in the morning, and there was a text from Paige. "Big good news. Hurry home."

Shit. Shit. Shit.

Perry took a quick shower. He'd never once went home with another woman on him and he wasn't going to try that now. When he turned the water off, Julie brought him clean underwear.

"Honey, I'm so sorry. We both did the roll-over-and-go-to-sleep. Hurry up and dress, you need to get home."

He used his cruise control on the almost empty streets because his speed kept creeping up. A speeding ticket would eat up too much time.

Damn it, he hadn't brushed his teeth.

He pulled into his driveway an hour later and almost hit

Sarah Grace's car. He'd told her a dozen times to park tightly against the curb. He had to run onto the lawn to get around her. Glancing up, he saw a light on in his middle daughter's room. What was Beth doing still awake? Did it have anything to do with the big good news? Damn it, it was bad enough that he ignored Paige's message. He hated that maybe he'd missed something important for his quiet, easily-overlooked middle child.

Her bedroom door was open a crack, letting more light spill out. Perry knocked slightly as he pushed it open. She was sitting in bed with her computer open. He whispered, "Hey, Curls. What are you doing up?"

"Hi, Daddy. I was already awake so I decided to mess around online for a while. I looked up peat-bog mummies. It's so cool, though they were probably murdered or sacrificed, so that's bad."

"Honey, why don't you try to get a little more sleep? It's early."

"Not really, Daddy. It's five o'clock. I get up at six."

It struck him. His daughter hadn't even asked where he'd been. He needed her to believe that he was a good husband. It wasn't good for little girls to have fathers that were cheating husbands.

With a lump in his throat, he blew her a kiss. "Try to keep all that mucking around in peat bogs quiet. I'm going to grab some sleep."

"Okay, Dad. Good night or morning."

"Good night or morning to you too, Sweetheart."

He went into his bedroom and decided not to brush his teeth. It would wake Paige up, so he slipped out of his clothes and into bed wearing the boxers that smelled like Julie's laundry detergent.

Paige was awake. He could tell by how still she was, but he had nothing to say. An hour later, he got up and fixed his middle daughter some breakfast.

28

CAL LIKED ALMOST everything about Christmas. Even the music, which everybody complained about, made him feel good inside. The radio station he liked was playing nothing but Christmas music, alternating between Santa Claus type songs and Baby Jesus songs. He thought the first category was fun, and the serious songs made him feel all mushy inside.

He liked the way the shops were all festive and the way the streetlights had those sparkly wreaths hanging from them. Cal carried the bag with the name of the Christian Bookstore and started walking down the crowded parking lot to put it in his trunk before he finished his shopping. If he took his purchase into the toy store, he'd have to leave the package at the service center and he wasn't about to do that. He wasn't going to leave it on his front seat, either. Someone might see the purchase and break in. He didn't have time to reorder another present, and it was a good one.

A month earlier, he'd overheard Perry's middle daughter talking to her mother about the historical significance of the

Exodus. He was so impressed with that kid. Beth looked like Perry more than the other two girls. Not only that, she was bookish and sharp as a knife. She was all of eleven or twelve, and there she was, discussing the Bible.

As soon as he heard that conversation, he knew what to get the kid. He stood next to his open trunk and looked at the white book inside the bag. It had her name, Beth Ravaterra, printed in the same gold letters as the word "Bible." The edges of the thin pages were also bright gold. It had a ribbon attached to it in a deep blue color. Everything about the Bible was perfect. Slamming the trunk shut, Cal beamed with the knowledge that Perry's kid was going to love it. And today, he'd take care of the youngest one's gift, too. She was Perry's little ballerina. Megasmall Toys would have a bunch of ballet stuff and it was in the same mall as the Christian store.

As he walked all the way down the parking lot, Cal hummed a Christmas song. Even though he was getting older, he still had a nice tenor voice. Sometimes he thought about joining a church so he could sing in the choir, but he didn't want all the stuff that came with churches. He simply really, really liked Christmas, right down to the songs and the wrapping paper and the glittery lamp-pole wreathes.

He even liked what he spotted at the end of the strip mall. He'd never noticed it before, but the last store on the opposite end of the strip mall was a massage parlor. It wasn't a national chain. The fake snow sprayed on the windows pretty much obscured the view of the inside, and there weren't any big signs saying that they did pedicure or 'Ask us about our spa treatment.' The word "therapeutic" wasn't anywhere.

That looked interesting to Cal. He walked up closer to the last unit so he could read their signs. They had small, cheaply painted lettering that announced they specialized in "Relaxation, aroma therapy, and massage." There were two additional signs.

One said that said they had "LMT on premises," and one said "Help Needed." Cal went inside. The toy store wasn't going to close soon. He might as well give himself a Christmas present first.

Inside, the place was almost bare. A battered front desk had a chair behind it, but that was it for furniture. Painted particle board separated the areas from one another.

He chatted it up with the old señora at the front desk, trying to get her to commit to a price and maybe then steer her towards an enhanced price. He also wanted to find out who would be giving him the massage. After all, the señora had to be in her forties.

"So, do you do the relaxation massage yourself, or—"

The front door opened, and in walked Donny's friend from Thanksgiving dinner. Cal couldn't remember Frenchie's real name, but there was no mistaking his long hair. The guy recognized him, too, but he didn't call him by name. Instead, Frenchie spoke to the woman.

"Hi. I own these buildings. Your lease is over. Pack up your stuff and get out. If it doesn't take more than an hour, I'll give you back the rest of your rent for December."

The woman immediately lost her English. In rapid Spanish, she obviously told him she didn't understand. In equally rapid Spanish, Frenchie pointed at him.

Cal didn't speak Spanish, but he thought the guy said something like "detective de la policía" while he was looking at him. Maybe he even said it slow so Cal would understand. What did the poof think Cal was going to do—start flashing a fake badge?

The woman switched back to English. "Hey, I didn't do or say nothing that he could use. I'm licensed."

Cal puffed out his chest and took a step closer to Frenchie. "What the fuck are you doing and why are you involving me?"

The queer should have backed off a step, but he didn't. Instead, he leaned slightly towards Cal. Limp wristed boys might be okay with his brother's family, but Cal wasn't having that. He stepped back. The queer's mouth kind of twitched like he might smile. Cal took another step back.

Frenchie switched his attention back the woman. The guy swished his hair out of his eyes. "Want to produce that license for me?"

She immediately opened a drawer in the desk, but Frenchie asked, "An up-to-date legitimate license?" She looked daggers at him but didn't answer. Frenchie calmly asked her, "Did you fail to keep up the continuing education?"

Cal would have liked to push Frenchie out of the door, make him go away and leave the innocent little massage parlor alone, but he also didn't want to fucking get involved in whatever he was about to do. The guy looked unstable as hell, threatening that woman. Besides, the shit said he owned the building. Either way, Cal was going to get the hell out of there.

When he went to walk around him, Frenchie blocked him by stepping in front of the door and pulling the help wanted sign off the glass door. "Here. Let me help you pack." His hair fell into his face, and he gave it a toss back again. This time it didn't look like a gay thing. It looked angry. Over-the-top angry. What the fuck problem did Frenchie have with massage parlors?

But the guy got his anger under control. He stood in front of the door and, as calm as a melting ice-cube, asked if anyone else was in there. That unnerved Cal.

The woman looked unnerved, too. "Look, my staff doesn't come in until later."

Frenchie switched back to Spanish so Cal couldn't understand him, but he watched the woman crumple a little. She finally waved her hands in surrender and said, "Okay, okay. I don't want to make trouble for you, either. I'll go, but I want my rent back."

The woman looked daggers at Cal several times. He didn't know what in the hell to do, and he was a little pissed off that the señora hadn't told him that she didn't have any young ones available until later. Mostly, he wanted Frenchie to move the fuck away from the door.

She finally crossed her arms over her chest and said, "But it's going to take me more than an hour. I got to get a truck out here to get the beds out of the back."

Frenchie pulled out a business card and handed it to her. "Tomorrow, if you're gone, you can call this number and I will reimburse you for the rest of the month." He glanced at the make-shift walls. "Maybe you can even get some security deposit back, but I doubt it. Buenas tardes, señora." He held the door open for Cal, who scooted through.

As soon as the door closed behind them, Cal scolded the guy. "Look, impersonating a police officer is illegal. I'm not going to let some guy I barely know get me into trouble."

"Oh, I doubt if you were impersonating a police officer. I think you were trying to be a customer. Take it as a compliment. You look like a cop who needs to retire and there are worse things."

Frenchie started to head out to the parking lot, frowning. "Jeez, when I parked, there were two empty spaces on either side. Now look."

Cal had a thought as he walked away. "Hey. Hey!"

Frenchie was halfway in the middle of the traffic lane, but he turned around and looked at him. No cars were coming, but it would be funny if the guy got run over in front of the massage parlor. Would the señora unpack her Help Wanted sign and stay in business?

"You said you own this shopping mall, right? That's bullshit, right?"

Frenchie half-nodded, half-shrugged, and that made him flip his hair out of his eyes again.

"What do you get out of stomping all over that poor woman and making a fool out of me? What, did you come down here to do your Christmas shopping and get distracted? Decided to have a little fun with some helpless woman?"

Frenchie said, "Oh, I haven't done any Christmas shopping yet. I suppose I should do that." He gave a small shrug and turned without saying good-bye.

What a freak. "Hey, Frenchie!"

The man turned around in the middle of the road, making a car come to a complete stop.

"I'm going to tell my nephew about this. He needs to know that you're…" He twirled his finger at his forehead. "Fucking nuts."

The car tooted its horn. Cool as mint, Frenchie stood there and looked at Cal. "Sure. Say 'hi' to Perry for me. Or were you talking about Donny?"

Cal ignored him and walked towards his car, only to find his back tire was flat as a pancake. He could even see the big screw sticking out of one side. Cal hadn't changed a tire since he was a young man. He went around to the trunk and popped it open, wondering if there was a jack in with the spare. He moved the pretty white Bible bag and tugged at the carpet just as a car pulled up. Frenchie, the never-ending-annoyance, left his running car blocking Cal.

"Hey, you have a flat."

"No shit." Cal grabbed the bag with the Bible and slammed the trunk closed. He had a brilliant idea. Let the dumb shit change the tire for him. "Your car looks pretty new. You got a jack in there?"

"I have no idea." Damn, Frenchie didn't even pretend. "I have no idea how to change a tire. Do you?"

Cal, cool as anything, walked over to the passenger side door on Frenchie's car. "I left my jack in my garage. Drive me home and I'll get it. It's not far." Just to show the guy who was boss, he snapped his fingers and added, "Come on, come on, come on! Let's not take all day."

Stupid Frenchie drove like an old woman. What the hell was that guy's name anyway?

29

It was only a week before Christmas, and Janvier needed a present for Madeline. He hadn't been to the strip mall since Cal Ravaterra had the flat tire, and he was having a hard time putting the encounter out of his mind. He'd driven Cal home and was surprised that he lived in a nice, quiet neighborhood. Cal didn't get a jack from his garage. He didn't have a garage. He got out of the car and went into the house without a word.

The house was notable because it had a large magnolia tree in the tidy front yard. There was even a wrought-iron bench under the tree. It faced the house, not the street, but it looked good, almost genteel. It all seemed very un-Cal, but maybe Janvier just hadn't seen that side of the man.

The guy didn't come back out, so after about ten minutes, Janvier left. Donny's unpleasant uncle seemed easy to ignore, even if he was right that Janvier needed to do some Christmas shopping. He headed back to the strip mall.

He parked at the Megasmall Toy Store. Customers were exiting with piled-up grocery carts. He couldn't imagine buying that much stuff at a toy store, but a woman almost ran into him because she couldn't see around her cart.

Inside the store, it was madness on a commercial level. The aisles and the merchandise made a kaleidoscope of primary colors. Masses of people lined up at cash registers. Frantic Christmas music poured out of the ceiling, but the overwhelming noise was human in nature. A small child screamed in outrage right next to him. Monotone cashiers wished "Happy Holidays," and it all blended into chaos.

He turned around and got the hell out of there. Maybe his office manager could go buy Madeline a present or maybe there'd still be time to go online. With a week left, he could still get a toy or something.

An unknown number called his cell phone, but he ignored it while he hurried to his car. He jumped as he walked below a huge tinsel wreath with a candle in it and the damned thing blinked on. Shit, the piece of crap decorations did light up. Three cars waited for a parking space behind a woman who squeezed a small bike into her trunk as fast as she could. The parking lot had filled up in the few minutes he was in the store.

The car next to him had parked almost on the white line, so it took several K turns to get out of the spot. A fat minivan waited for his spot, but Janvier's car kept beeping a warning when he got too close to the next car, so it took him several tries to get out of the spot. Another beep made him jump again, even though he was out of the parking spot. It was his phone, telling him he had a voicemail message. Janvier scooted the car up enough to let the minivan park as he hit the phone's speaker.

A woman's voice hesitantly came from the phone. "Hi, Joni-vee-ay. This is Tessie Ravaterra? I'm Donny Ravaterra's sister? I cut your hair at my brother Perry Ravaterra's house."

Janvier wished he'd answered the phone. Tessie continued in a stronger, surer voice. "I work at Classic Pearl's Salon and I'm doing my customer files and I got your phone number from Donny. I hope that's okay. I wanted to put your information into my work computer in case you decide to come here as a client because you are supposed to get a trim before Christmas. It's reasonable and you would get the family discount, of course. I just wanted you to know that your phone number is now in the store's computer and I hope that's okay. Bye."

He hit redial, even though Janvier never talked on the phone while trying to drive. Tessie answered on the second ring.

"Hi, Tessie. It's Janvier. I'm sorry I missed your call."

A minivan discharged a skinny, irate looking woman. He waved his hand amicably and put his car in drive, carefully maneuvering it forward. Tessie said hi and hoped it was okay that she put his phone number in her computer.

"It's very okay. Listen, Tessie, I need a favor. I don't know anything about buying presents for little girls and I need to buy Madeline something for Christmas. Can you help me?" He meant to ask her for a suggestion on what Madeline would like, but her enthusiastic response seemed to indicate that Christmas shopping was something she enjoyed. He admitted that he hadn't bought anything for Nate, Donny or Señor Rijos.

Tessie sounded horrified. "You haven't shopped at all? Joni-vee-ay, it's almost Christmas!"

He swerved too close to a truck and scared himself while she gave him directions on how to get to her shop to pick her up. "Because I can go right now, if that's okay with you?"

It was. He hung up, drove, and was happy that he had a mission. Really, he was completely unqualified to shop for gifts. He used to make his mother presents in shop class. His junior year, he made bathroom shelves for both his mother and Señor Rijos. That year, he bought Nate a bag of grass.

Every Christmas in New York, he went into a small shop in Manhattan. There a man named Ahmed had his gifts for the billionaire and Alexia ready. The tiny, elderly Turkish man would show him some perfect piece of understated jewelry with a staggering price tag. Alexia never wore flashy, but he presented her with small earrings of rare diamonds, chokers of Australian pearls, and an antique gold ring with Arabic writing. It was very antique. The jeweler told him it was probably as old as Christmas. True or not, it made a nice present. Ahmed would also come up with incredible artifacts that he could present to the billionaire. Those, Janvier insisted, had to be authentic. If they weren't, the billionaire never mentioned it. Once, he'd picked out a gift by himself. He bought the peach colored sweater for Alexia because he saw it in a boutique window that was right next to the bookstore and the café. The sum of his shopping experience was going to Ahmed's, sweaters that looked like ice cream, homemade bathroom shelves, and some grass.

He didn't have any trouble finding Tessie's beauty shop and mercifully, the parking lot wasn't too crowded. The manager, an older woman wearing too much make-up, looked him up and down when he said he was there for Tessie.

"Hi and welcome, Hon. What's the name and do you have an appointment?"

Tessie appeared, ready to go. "This is Joni-vee-ay, I told you about him. He's in my family because he's like a brother to Nate, who is my brother-in-law. That means I can cut your hair, because I don't have a license so mostly I only get to shampoo hair, but I cut family's hair and that's you. This is my boss."

He loved that she said he was family. Extending his hand to the older woman, Janvier wondered if Perry or his father owned the hair salon just so Tessie could cut hair without a license. "Janvier Reed. How do you do?"

The heavy eyeliner woman said she did well, and how unfair it was that the Ravaterra family now had a Nate and a January.

"Lord, you are a pretty hunk of a man. Tessie, did you do his hair?" He bent over enough to let Tessie show off his hair.

It was only ten minutes into the evening and he was already having a wonderful time with Tessie. He carefully told her who he needed to buy for and she carefully expanded his list to include his therapist and his office manager. They wandered through a mobbed shopping mall while he told her that he had no idea about his therapist's personal tastes. "She's about the same age as your father. In fact, I think they're friends." They bought a blank Holiday card, and Tessie hand wrote a certificate for a haircut at her hair salon. Janvier was sure a haircut was inappropriate for one's therapist, but hell. The therapist would understand.

He listened carefully as she explained that he should give his office manager money even though Ms. Nancy just started working for him.

"Like the equivalent of a month's pay?" He'd already done that, but he didn't tell Tessie.

She nodded, pleased with him. At her suggestion, they also bought the office manager a crystal picture frame to put on her desk to hold her grandson's picture. "Just as a little something when you give her the money. It's nice to unwrap things."

They walked out of the store, and Janvier looked in the bag. "Tessie, you're good at this. Any ideas for Nate and Donny?"

"Oh, Donny's easy. He likes everything. Nate, maybe I need to think about."

"What about his father? Señor Rijos is older...Tessie?"

Apparently, the idea that he spent time with Nate's homophobic father offended her. He gently told her that Nate needed contact with his father even if it was through Janvier, and that Nate and his father disagreed strongly about the gay thing, but that didn't mean they didn't love each other. Tessie sighed and asked what Señor Rijos was like.

"If I had to use one word for him, I would say 'sophisticated'."

"Okay, then I know what to give him. Does he like lamps and is a hundred and thirty dollars too much to spend?"

They left the mall and drove to an antique shop that clung to life near the hippy haven of Carrboro. Driving and parking in the congested area was painful, but Janvier had his pride. He pretended that it didn't give him a heart attack to drive around the pretty town. The shop Tessie wanted was in an old saltbox house that looked like it needed to fall down, but there was too much stuff inside. Hell, it might have already collapsed. The shelves went up to the ceiling.

Tessie said she'd seen the "best thing there. Are you sure that Nate's dad is sophisticated? Because Nate's kind of not sophisticated. I mean, he's not crude or anything, but he's a jock."

"Don't let Nate fool you, sweetie. He has a side he never uses."

It was almost impossible to look at any one thing because there was so much inside that store. He held his breath as he followed Tessie through the claustrophobic aisles.

The lamp was still there, on the back wall. It stood, still wonderful in Tessie's eyes---a hookah that had been converted into a lamp. "Isn't it the best thing? I think it's perfect for someone sophisticated."

Oh Lord. The hookah was brass and green glass with inlays of a shiny, black stone. "Tessie, I'd love to buy this thing for you, since you've been such a help to me with this shopping."

She wouldn't hear of it. The lamp was for Nate's father or nobody. Tessie had the most wonderful, crooked smile. Janvier had no choice but admit that she was right. "The lamp is perfect. Yes, it is."

Carrying it to the register, he spotted a football jersey hanging on the back wall. It was a Redskin's jersey with the name "Theismann" on the back and a faded signature on the number seven. "There's Nate's Christmas present."

He asked the proprietor to get the jersey. It took the cigarette smelling woman a minute to realize that he wasn't trying to dicker on the price. He just wanted the jersey and was willing to pay the whole fifty-seven dollars.

When they went up front to make their purchases, Tessie spotted an old Playboy magazine in the glass case. "Look, it's the one where Samantha Bryant took off her top."

Janvier vaguely remembered a leggy actress by that name, but Tessie's excitement surprised him.

"Donny loved Samantha Bryant and he used to get in trouble for swiping Dad's Playboys. He got in trouble for swiping this one because Dad never found it!"

They bought the Playboy for Donny's present.

That just left Madeline. "The most fun saved for last," Tessie announced before giving him instructions back to the Megasmall Toy Store. It was fully dark by then. At least the lamp-post tinsel decorations weren't blinking anymore. Most of them weren't, anyway.

Janvier took a deep breath and followed Tessie into Toy Hell. She didn't even flinch on her way in. He did. The same sensory overload hit him, but he toughed it out. In fact, he felt so improved that he noticed the electronic section on the way to the dolls. He stopped cold. "I'm going to buy her a computer."

Tessie was patient with him. She explained that Madeline already had an age appropriate computer. "She's Donny's little girl and he likes computers and stuff."

They continued to the doll section. Tessie explained to him that most of the fashionable doll things were still too old for Madeline. "See, every package has the right ages on it. You're not allowed to buy for under the age they say."

"She's four, right? Hey, all the packages say eight-and-up."

There were plenty of things that were for three-and-over, but none of them looked like a showstopper. Tessie floated through the plastic smelling aisle with a wistful look on her face. "Joni-vee-ay, do you want to have lots of children?"

He moved out of the way of three small girls and two tired looking mothers. "I don't know, Tessie. I haven't given it much thought. How about you?"

"Yeah, I want lots of kids. I go on dates and maybe sometime I'll get married. Is this a date with you? Oh look, they have Disney princess dresses. Let's get Madeline one of these. She loves playing dress-up."

A date? Oh God.

The dress-up gowns were poufy and had sparkles. He grabbed five or six of them off the rack. Janvier didn't want to hurt Tessie's feelings. He'd probably marry her rather than hurt her feelings. No. There would be no relationship with Tessie. It was one thing for Donny to tolerate him because he was a friend of Nate's, but he was sure that the entire Ravaterra clan would stop him well before he got anywhere near Tessie in a romantic way.

He clutched the princess gowns to his chest. "I mean, I think you are the prettiest, most wonderful woman, but I'm not ready to date right now. Is that okay?"

"Sure. I told Amy I was bringing you over for dinner, but I didn't say it was a date."

Oh God, no. Janvier tried to keep up with what she was saying. The canned music was so damned loud. "What?"

Tessie had a slightly worried look on her face. "I didn't think it was a date, even though you are handsome and all. I have a date tomorrow night with a guy named Pete. I went out with him last week, too. We like each other. Thanks for saying I'm pretty. I'm not."

"You look very much like Donny and almost exactly like Amy. They're beautiful, aren't they?" She beamed at him. Her smile wasn't as lopsided as Amy's or Donny's, but it held the same charm.

"So what is this about dinner with Amy?"

"When we finish shopping. I'm supposed to go to Amy's house for dinner and I called her and she said bring you, too. Oh, Joni-vee-ay. I bet she thinks this is a date."

No. No-no-no. It had been such a short time since Thanksgiving. He'd seen Amy the one time she came over to his office, but he hadn't seen Will. What had happened to his decision to stay away from the extended family? He stood in the toy store, clutching tiny, sparkling dresses, and started to sweat. "Tessie, I don't think I can go."

She nodded. "It's okay. They are expecting you. Will is a good cook. I think Madeline would like that dress the best. It's her favorite princess. She likes that one, too. Oh, they are so expensive. I'd say get them both, but that's too much money."

Janvier grabbed the two she pointed out and dumped the rest on the shelf.

"Tessie, sweetheart, please…" He watched her replace the dresses on the rack and quietly felt panic rise in him. He didn't want to see Amy and Will. He badly wanted to see Amy and Will.

Tessie checked the size on the two gowns he held. "Come on, let's go pay for these. We need to hurry up and go to Amy's house. Are you sure you want both dresses? That's expensive."

At the registers, Tessie told him to pick out some wrapping paper and added tape and a bag of bows because she didn't think he was a tie-a-bow type. Then she made him put back the jar of bubbles because it was wintertime, and she made him put back the Silly-Putty because Donny would kill him, and she made him put back the Christmas earrings because Madeline's ears weren't pierced.

Tessie's ears were pierced, so he bought them for her. She smiled as she added the little gold bells to the dresses and the paper. The two princess dresses were too expensive to have shed sparkles all over the front of his clothing, but they had anyway.

Outside the store, he tried dusting the sparkles off his jacket. Some came off. Some stuck to his hands, clothes, and everything else. "Is Will going to be over at Amy's house?"

"Sure. He lives there. I have glitter on me, too."

For the third time that day, he squeezed his car out of the same packed parking lot. He did it while remembering how Will looked laying on that bed, watching him.

Amy and Will lived in a townhouse less than a mile from Nate's old duplex. Amy's townhouse units were older, built in the eighties and tucked back into the woods. Tessie opened the door and walked in. "Hi. We're here!"

He followed her in, closed the door behind him, and hesitated in the foyer. He badly wanted to leave, but instead he followed Tessie. Will came out of the kitchen and joined Amy in the main room where she was putting ornaments on a small tree.

They looked happy to see him. Amy pointed to the front of his jacket. "Janvier, hi. I hear the two of you have been shopping. Is that where you got the glittery clothes?"

"Tessie and I have spent the evening together. She babysat me through the extremely confusing process of Christmas shopping."

Drying his hands, Will hugged Tessie. "Oh, God. I shouldn't admit this, but I love Christmas shopping. We bought our presents before Thanksgiving."

"Before Tessie rescued me, I went into a Megasmall Toy without a life line. I didn't get far in before I had to fall to the ground and feel my way back out." Will was near him. Smiling. Janvier felt sweat dampen his shirt.

Tessie blurted out "Joni-vee-ay and I aren't on a date."

Janvier tried to sound calm, but he thought it sounded like he stammered when he said, "Tessie was sweet enough to help me shop and gentle enough to let me know that it was platonic."

Amy ignored the whole "aren't on a date" conversation. She showed Tessie a tree ornament that apparently had been M.I.A. the last several Christmases. The semi-decorated tree distracted them. Apparently, Amy had waited for Tessie before placing several special ornaments on the tree.

Will motioned for Janvier to follow him back to the kitchen. "Do you think you can chop veggies without getting glitter on them? We're doing tacos tonight. I made a promise to help decorate the tree and I figure if I drag dinner out enough, the twins will have it finished."

As soon as they were in the kitchen, Will told him to wash his hands and asked him if there was some confusion on Tessie's part about whether it was a date.

"No, I don't think so. It surprised me when she came up with that. I admit, I've had a fantastic afternoon, and I do not want to hurt her feelings, but…"

Will handed him a half-diced up onion on a cutting board. "Janvier, do me a favor?" His voice was level, even gentle. "Just based on what happened between us three years ago, could you not date Tessie?" He met Janvier's eyes. "Even if it means hurting her feelings, I must admit, all afternoon, I kept wondering about it and I didn't like it."

"Don't give it a thought, Will. I told you. It's not a date." He started to chop the onion.

"Good, because I was a little jealous."

The onion made Janvier's eyes sting, and he rubbed one without thinking about it.

"Oh, God, Janvier. Don't touch your eyes. Here. Lean over the sink." Will put one hand on the back of his head and gently rinsed his eyes with water.

Will had to know that he was seriously messing with Janvier. Did he?

He handed Janvier a paper towel. "Haven't you chopped up onion before?"

Janvier's nose was running, his face was dripping, and he felt irrationally like laughing. "Not in a long, long time."

"Oh, come on. You grew up with Nate and his father is a chef, to say the least."

"He didn't let us cook." Lord, how could he feel so flirty and wipe his nose on a paper towel at the same time?

"I'd say that was a failure on his part, but maybe he understood that some people are dangerous in the kitchen. There, your eyes are going to look like you've been crying, but you'll live. I'll finish cutting the onion. Can you put that sheet with the taco shells in the oven without hurting yourself?"

Janvier threw away the paper towel and gave his hands a wash. He almost tipped the shells off the cooking sheet before he got them into the oven. The meat and the sauce smelled fantastic. "So, before I tried to blind myself, you said you were jealous?"

Will carefully added the diced onion to the rest of the vegetables. "Yeah. I think Amy was a little confused, too. She called Donny and asked if you were likely to ask Tessie out. This salsa is going to be mild. That's okay with you, isn't it?"

Janvier blinked at him. "What did Donny say?"

Will smiled. Deep lines radiated from his blue-blue eyes. "I didn't ask."

Janvier's penis stirred. He remembered Will, lying in the bed, watching him. Janvier blurted out, "After Thanksgiving, I decided that I'd just avoid you and Amy. She stopped by my office. She had an eye appointment in my building."

"I know. You worry about everything, don't you?" It wasn't a question. "The Ravaterras are close, Janvier. I don't think you can avoid us. Although, in the last few weeks, I wish I hadn't told Amy about our adventure in New York."

Somewhere in the recesses of the townhouse, a toilet flushed. Grimly, Janvier nodded. "She didn't seem upset at Thanksgiving, but she's upset now, right?"

Will looked surprised. "No. Why?"

"You said you wish you hadn't told her."

"Yeah. Then I wouldn't have to wonder why she's so intrigued by it all. By you."

Janvier had nothing. There were absolutely no words in his head. Intrigued? "I...um..."

Will agreed. "'I, um' is pretty much what I think, too, but Amy is far more complicated than I am."

They managed to get the food to the dining room without incident, even though Janvier's left eye still stung a little. The twins drifted into the room, and immediately Amy asked Janvier what was wrong with his eyes.

"I rubbed onion juice into one of them."

She took Janvier over to the light and stood close to him, one hand on his arm, and told him to lean down and look up. He did what she said, feeling the heat from her hand on his arm, feeling her body so close to him.

"Look to the side. Now back to the other side." Her hair smelled clean. He shifted his eyes to hers. God, she was so close to him.

"My diagnosis is that you're more of a dishwasher than a cook."

They ate tacos, passing the sour cream and the guacamole around the dining room table. It was salty-good, and Janvier had to make himself eat slowly. There was peach ice cream for dessert. He had no idea if Will remembered the peach ice cream in New York or not.

After dinner, Tessie decided to gift-wrap everything they bought. "If Joni-vee-ay doesn't know how to buy presents, then he probably doesn't know how to wrap them, either."

Without a care in the world, Tessie dug into Amy's supply of wrapping paper and added the rolls that he'd purchased. Snips of red and green paper littered the living room by the time they were finished. Will ended up with one of Tessie's Christmas bell earrings dangling from one ear to prove that he'd once pierced his ears and they hadn't closed. Amy thought the jersey was great, the Playboy was better, but there were strange looks when it came to the hookah lamp until Tessie held it up and asked them if they didn't think it was the most perfect thing for a sophisticated man.

Christmas lights reflecting off his earring, Will said the lamp was "wonderful."

The twins looked through the Playboy before they wrapped it. They did not offer either of the men a peek. After the wrapping, Janvier left Tessie at Amy's house. Will said he'd run her home, but he expected she'd sleep in the guest room that night.

"It's okay. It happens often enough. Amy has pajamas that will fit her. Janvier, I'm glad she was with you today. Thanks for giving her a good time." He carried the massively wrapped hookah lamp out to the car for him.

It took both of them to arrange the lamp and the other presents in the trunk in such a way that didn't endanger wrapping paper, especially around the brass monstrosity. While they were bending over, their shoulders brushed up against each other.

Will did not pull away.

They stood, too close. Janvier reached up and touched the bell hanging off Will's ear. He let his fingertip trace along Will's jaw line.

Will waited for several seconds before he stepped back. "Wow. Janvier, you are still…" He put his fingers on his jaw line. "I can still feel your fingers. And here I was thinking about the way you look at Amy."

"For what it's worth, I would have touched her the same way."

Will clapped him on the shoulder, which was a completely non-intimate gesture. "You are an interesting man, Janvier Reed. I'll see you at Christmas dinner. By the way, it is tradition for everyone to bring Dr. Ravaterra a present."

As Will walked away, he trailed a finger across Janvier's chest. Janvier couldn't speak for a moment. Before Will reached the front door, Janvier called out, "Which Dr. Ravaterra? There are three of them."

Under the door light, Will looked back at him. "And none of them want a hookah. Goodnight, Janvier."

30

WALKING ACROSS THE PARKING LOT, Perry glanced at the stone steps that led to his brother's condo. Donny had made a nice job out of some subtle evergreen decorations on their door. Perry had been the main architect on the renovations to the old fieldstone warehouse, and he still felt proud of the work. If Donny hadn't bought the unit at the top of the stone stairs, Perry would have bought it himself. Instead, he bought one of the small condos, and Julie was the fourth girlfriend he'd kept there.

He walked slowly to his condo, almost wishing he could sit down and talk to his brother about the arrangement Paige had just made with Janvier Reed. His brother wouldn't see any problem with it, and Perry knew that. He walked up to the second floor and noticed that Julie had placed a welcome mat with a huge Santa face on it in front of the condo's door.

Usually his wife would be busy making Christmas centerpieces for some charitable dinner and combing over the family's menu with the caterers. This time, however, Paige had simply told them to fix the same thing as they had for

Thanksgiving. He couldn't even talk to her because it took nothing for her to go off on some tangent about "sex workers." Since she didn't do any field work for the charity, Perry felt like he couldn't object.

God, he couldn't believe Janvier Reed had thrown Paige into his former cesspool. Maybe if Paige knew how he felt, they could switch it to a medical charity instead. Janvier would still be her "partner," but it would be cleaner. That would be so damned much better.

Maybe his wife's preoccupation with Janvier's sex charity was why he wanted his girlfriend out of the way during Christmas. He wiped his feet on Santa's face and opened the condo's door.

A few minutes later, Julie was squealing with delight at what he gave her for Christmas.

"God, Perry, you are such a sweetheart!" Julie jumped up and hugged him hard around the neck, excited to have a plane trip back to the Midwest. It was ridiculous how much money he'd spent on Julie. She was worth it, except when she squealed. He wished she wouldn't do that. He also wished for a Christmas where he wasn't trying to balance home with a girlfriend.

Holding the plane tickets, Julie twirled in a circle like a little girl. He didn't like it when she did that, either.

"You are the best, Perry. I've told my family about you, except for the married part. I said you were divorced. Don't worry. I changed your last name to Terrarava. My dad asked what ethnicity it was and I didn't want to say 'Italian,' so I said 'Hungarian.' I have no idea why."

Julie looked coquettishly up at him. "You know, I was kind of hoping you were going to get me one of those little dogs for Christmas, you know, like the Chihuahua at the pound? But a plane ticket is even better."

"No, no pets, remember? We talked about that."

"I know. Another trip home is better anyway!"

It was just for the holidays, only five days. He wasn't tired of Julie. He didn't want it to be over. She was almost the perfect girlfriend, and this was almost the perfect setting. For once, his uncle wasn't involved. The arrangement was so much better without having to handle Cal as well. Perry wasn't tired of this game. He was only distracted.

"Oh, Perry, here I am acting like a kid seeing Santa Claus and you look all pensive. What's wrong?"

"Oh, it's nothing. I'm glad you're happy."

"Yes, I am!" She tipped her face up, expecting a kiss.

It surprised Perry when, instead of kissing her, he said, "Julie, this isn't going to work out. You're great, but I don't want to do this anymore."

31

CAL CALLED several times to find out if he could come over and watch the game at his nephew's house. Perry hadn't answered, which meant he was at a business meeting or with a girlfriend. It had to be business because his nephew hadn't had a girlfriend in a long time. It was a shame. That gift shop girl, Honey-Butt, Julie-Fucking-Cooper, had been perfect. Cal had checked out her apartment and everything, but Perry had turned it down.

Well, his nephew was going to miss out on an evening watching the game with his good ol' Uncle Cal.

At least he didn't have to make that drive into Raleigh. It was getting dark so damned early—that was the one thing that he didn't like about that time of year. That, and the cold, miserable drizzle that passed for winter weather in North Carolina. Cal didn't want to admit it, but driving at night was getting tough and when you added rain into that, the resulting sum was blurry lights making halos all over the windshield. He was going to be too old to drive at night someday, and then Perry would be sorry he hadn't spent more evenings with Cal, watching some games and eating Paige's little snacks.

Gift wrapping was a good idea. He would enjoy the evening wrapping presents, even if his nephew was ignoring him. No, Perry wasn't ignoring him. He was just busy, and not with a girlfriend, either. Perry didn't lie to him. His nephew was an honest person, especially to him. Perry didn't talk about his girlfriends to anyone but Cal, but he also didn't lie about them. They had a special bond, and nothing would ever change that.

Cal pulled out his gift wrap collection. It was a large, well organized cardboard box, fully stocked with ribbons and tape. Weirdly, he'd learned gift wrapping in prison one year. The church ladies had brought in little Bibles for the prisoners, and some of the prisoners got to wrap them. Cal thought the whole thing was stupid at first, but by the time they showed him how to fold the paper's edges and how to tie the ribbon, he was sold on the neatness and efficiency of the whole thing.

After getting his wrapping paper situated, he pulled out the presents. Little Beth's Bible was white whereas the prisoners' Bibles had been black, but they both had the same gold letters and soft, thin pages. He'd wrap that first.

This year, Cal bought shiny red wrapping paper. It was more expensive than the printed kind, but it was pretty. He bought white ribbon, too. Not the curling type—that was too easy. Very few people understood that the package was part of the gift. Spending a little time on the wrapping counted. Ensconced in his living room, Cal forgot about watching the game. Instead, he dug his favorite video out of the coffee table's little drawer. He'd had the home movies recorded to a disk, and doing something as special as wrapping presents required something good happening in the background.

Cal had just finished wrapping the white Bible when the video reached the part with Perry's mother at the lake. He watched, slack jawed, as Selma waved to the camera. When that part was over, he went back to work on the packages. The next part was just a chunk of his brother's med school graduation. He didn't need to see that shit again.

The last package was for Perry's oldest girl, Sarah Grace. She'd been born while he was in jail, and here she was, almost all grown up. After making an elegant bow, he added a sprig of plastic holly. It looked great. He had bought her a sampler set of perfumes from Wal-Mart. There were three rows of tiny bottles, six to a row, with names like 'Misty Stars' and 'Butterfly Kisses.' The teenager was going to love it. Cal had done well with all the Christmas gifts that year.

He restarted the video at the beginning while he put away the wrapping paper. He piled the presents in the corner of the living room and admired the way they looked like a holiday decoration all by themselves.

On the television, the video went to black and white. Teenaged Selma, Perry's mother, waved at him to stop filming her. She was sweetly embarrassed.

Old, fat Cal sat in his chair and chuckled back at her. He and Selma had had the best time at the lake. They were there all the time. He'd fallen in love with her the first time he saw her in school, but it was that warm spring that made it into something real. That lake was special…at least until everything went to hell the last time they'd been there right before their high school graduation. Thinking about that day, he skimmed over the real details but let the pain of loss wash over him. It should have been so different. His whole life should have been different.

———

Selma's big fear was the Vietnam draft. She had only a vague idea of how the draft worked, but she didn't want it to get him before he could go to college. His brother, Adam, was pre-med, a straight A student, and wasn't going to Vietnam. Selma figured Cal was going to be pre-med, too.

She didn't know that his academic and juvie records would keep him out of good colleges. His parents had smoothed over the little problems he'd had over the years, but even they couldn't fake good grades. Selma didn't know all that. She thought Cal had already chosen to go to Duke. She kept talking about being Dr. and Mrs. Ravaterra. They'd get married after he had his undergraduate degree but before med school. She had it all planned.

He was going to marry her, but not in five more years. He had a surprise for Selma. Next door to his parents was an old lady. Ms. Linda was probably as rich as Cal's parents but wouldn't hire help. Cal and Adam had to do chores for her. In fact, doing chores for the old biddy was what had made it possible for Cal to propose.

Ms. Linda had a big ring that was, in fact, a large diamond made out of a bunch of smaller ones. The diamond ring dangled from her scrawny finger, but it never slipped over her gnarled knuckle. The teenaged Cal couldn't imagine someone horny enough for that old bag of bones to buy her a ring like that.

His father said that before he could take the car to the lake with Selma, he had to go next door and help the old woman get some stuff out of her attic. Cal didn't bother to argue with his father. It was a waste of time, so he hauled himself over to her place.

Cal knocked on the backdoor while opening it, as usual. "Ms. Linda? Ma'am?"

She was on the kitchen floor, on her back, with her dress bunched up to her panties. She'd wet herself. Her thighs, white, loose bags of flesh, trembled in an ugly way. Her hands clawed feebly at her chest. She saw him, waved one of those blue-tipped claws at him. The diamond ring looked like it was about to fall off as she flapped that hand.

Cal didn't hesitate. Standing over her, he pulled the ring off her finger. It wasn't that hard to get it over the knuckle.

With a thin sound, she cried out before she choked hard and started vomiting. He straddled her, stepping on her dress so she couldn't roll over while he slipped the ring into his pocket.

Her tongue was pushing the vomit out of her mouth. Her nostrils flared as her eyes bugged out. The skin around her mouth was blue tinged. Cal bent and slipped his fingers into her nostrils. He'd heard that it didn't leave bruises if you did it that way. He was supposed to stick something in her mouth too, but she had puke in there. It'd do the job just as good.

She batted at his hand, but finally her eyeballs rolled back in her head. Her eyelids were still open in little slits, and he could see her blood-shot whites. It was disgusting. Unconscious, her chest heaved and she sucked in the vomit. He was almost afraid she'd blow like old faithful, but she didn't. Her chest hitched once, twice, and was still. He stayed still, keeping her nose plugged while he counted to fifty slowly.

Cal straightened up. He walked over to the sink and washed his fingertips. They felt nasty, like they had snot on them. He used the scrub brush next to the sink to clean his fingernails and then got an idea. The diamond ring came out of his pocket. It was a little cruddy. He lathered up the scrub brush and gave the ring a good cleaning. Locking the old woman's door behind him, he went home where his dad asked how Ms. Linda was. It occurred to him to say she wasn't feeling good, but his father was a cardiologist and a major square. He'd probably run right over there and check on her. Cal already had the car keys in his hand, the ring in his pocket, and a plan forming in his head, so he simply said, "She's fine."

He surprised Selma all right. At the lake, he suggested that maybe Vietnam wasn't a bad idea. A young enlisted man could earn enough to support a wife and even a family. He would take care of her. Besides, his mother had all the real money. She wouldn't be able to resist a grandchild, so they should start one right away. They'd live just fine.

WATCHING the video of Selma setting up a picnic on a blanket, Cal blanked over what had happened that day. He didn't remember when Selma said "Hell no." She was going to marry a doctor. If he wasn't going to college, he could take her home. She didn't want that old-fashioned ring, where did he get it?

Cal didn't think about how angry he became with her. He didn't remember feeling Selma's finger joint dislocate as he shoved the ring on her finger or how she ran away from him. Sitting in his leather lounge chair, he didn't think about how the prosecutor told his parents Ms. Linda had scratches and bruises inside her nose, but he couldn't prove that the eighteen-year-old helped her to die. However, he sure as hell could prove that Cal left her there, dead or alive, after stealing the ring.

His parents didn't pay for much of a legal defense. The lawyer kept talking about taking a plea or some such shit because of Cal's juvie record. They didn't even go to trial. By the time he got out, the draft was over and America's involvement in Vietnam was winding down.

While he was in jail, Selma had seduced his brother and had a baby. Adam was supposed to be the better brother, but he'd knocked her up and refused to marry her. Cal was both relieved that Selma hadn't married his brother and furious that his brother would do that to her. He hated Adam, but his brother took care of him, financially and with the legal system. He had no choice but to live as if it was all okay.

The video playing on the television showed baby Perry

figuring out how to walk on chubby legs. Selma stood awkwardly in the background. Cal's eyes lingered on her. She had gotten her figure back fast after Perry was born. In those days, her hair was a platinum blond cloud. She didn't buy into the whole hippy thing with the long, straight hair or the braless look. She preferred the blond bombshell look. Marilyn Monroe had nothing on Selma.

Cal smiled vacantly at the television as Perry chased a butterfly and couldn't make his little legs go fast enough. The blond, curly-haired toddler sat down hard and his chin quivered, but he didn't cry. Cal's little man wasn't a crybaby.

In his mind, Selma had said yes to the ring and the plan and, in her happiness, she laid down with Cal. The baby on the screen was his and Selma's. Little Perry was his. Sitting in his chair with his unfocused eyes staring at the pile of presents, he saw the life he should have had. By now, he would have been retired from the Army. Selma and he would have finished wrapping the presents for their granddaughters. She was the one who knew to put the sprig of plastic holly on the ribbons, not him. He was all thumbs when it came to that kind of thing. She'd laugh at his clumsy attempts and put pieces of tape on the end of his nose. She was older, but still lovely with the lights of the tree reflecting off her platinum hair. Even though their Perry was grown up, Selma had insisted that they had an artfully decorated tree because the grandchildren were over there all the time. As soon as the wrapping was finished, his wife would announce that she needed to get started on the pies so would he mind cleaning up the wrapping paper?

He'd remind her that he liked pecan pie, but the simple kind, and she'd laugh and give his nose a little kiss after she plucked off the piece of tape. "I love you, Major Ravaterra, but pecan pie is the only simple thing about you!"

"I love you too, Mrs. Ravaterra. I love you. I love you."

32

AT FOUR-THIRTY in the afternoon on Christmas Eve, Donny worried because Nate was late getting home and Janvier showed up early. Although he needed a trim, Janvier was Mass ready with a good suit and his hair neat.

"I'm sorry he's late, Janvier. I think you're going to be late for Mass. What's in the bag?"

"They have another Mass a little later. I had breakfast with Señor Rijos this morning. He sent presents."

Madeline piped up in her over-excited voice. "I'm going to see Baby Jesus tonight with my granddaddy! I have a green dress with a red sash on it."

"Way cool, Madeline!"

Donny watched him put the stuff on the kitchen table next to Madeline, who was having an early dinner. She'd been going full-tilt all day. She had started the morning with a visit to scary Santa Claus and was going to end it by going to church with granddaddy. She should be home and asleep by eight.

His little girl ignored her dinner while she investigated the contents of the bag.

"Careful of this, Madeline." Janvier pulled a menu out of the bag. It was one of Angelica's.

"Why is he sending a menu to Nate?"

Janvier held it out to him. Apparently, one of the area's college coaches had dinner at Angelica's.

"Nice autograph," Donny whistled.

"Very. I'm jealous."

"Nate's going to love this. Oh, Madeline, be careful."

She pulled a silver-plated hairbrush out of the bag. She squealed, "Is this for me?"

"I don't know, kiddo. It was Nate's mother's. Abuelo said it needed to live here now."

She took two hands to try to brush her bangs, getting some of her neatly braided hair with it. Donny shook his head.

"Honey, I'm sorry. I think maybe we'll brush your hair with it when you get ready for church, but we don't brush our hair at the table. Do we, Janvier? And be careful with the brush, Madeline. You don't want to break it."

Janvier ate half the child's chicken pieces. "Okay. I think there's a comb in there, too. Do hairbrushes break?"

As Madeline dug for the tarnished comb, Donny dryly asked, "Do you want your own plate?"

"No. I'll share hers."

Before Janvier had come back into their lives, Nate and Donny discussed having a second child. Although Nate was hesitant, he wasn't completely opposed to the idea. They looked up some adoption options and they even went to the fertility clinic and got some information on surrogates and freezing sperm. At the time, Donny had no idea that their second child was going to be male, six feet tall, and named Janvier.

"This comb isn't as shiny as the brush. Uncle, can you brush my hair?"

"Sure. Whoop! There, I did it and braided it right back up. Try eating your dinner and maybe we'll talk."

"I can't! You already ate all my chicken nuggets."

"Those were nuggets? Well, I didn't eat the green beans."

With an I-dare-you-to-tell-her-they-aren't-nuggets look on his face, Donny dumped the rest of the cubes of free range chicken onto Madeline's plate. She picked one up and fed it to Janvier. "These aren't like the nuggets at my school."

Janvier picked up a green bean with his fingers and told Madeline to make like a baby bird. She yelled, "Cheep! Cheep!" He put the bean in her mouth and ate one of her pieces of cheese.

"You want to give your hands a little wash, Janvier? I have no idea where you've been. Madeline, put the brush down during dinner. It's rude to have brushes and combs on the table."

Janvier got up and went to the sink, washed his hands, and held them out for Donny's inspection. "Señor Rijos sent a present for you, too, Donny. It's not in the bag, though. He gave it to me after I gave him the hookah lamp."

"How did that go over?"

"He looked at me like I was crazy until I told him the story of the shopping expedition. I gotta tell you, he laughed himself silly at the thought of me in an M-e-g-a t-o-y store, and he's absolutely charmed by the whole thing with Tessie. I think he's going to treasure that hookah lamp. Then he gave me this stuff."

He took a worn-thin wedding band out of his pocket and handed it to him. Inside, there were initials that looked like B.R. "He said for me to give it to you, that you could get it sized. Donny, he's coming around."

His father-in-law had already caused so much pain. Donny wasn't sure if he wanted him to come around, or what to do with the woman's ring, but he was sure that Nate would forgive his father everything, so he'd go along.

Nate and he already had their rings. Nate couldn't wear his to work because it was too easy to catch it on a piece of equipment. Sometimes he forgot to put his ring back on. Maybe if they had his father's ring sized for him, he would be better about remembering.

Nate burst through the door, and Donny shoved the ring in his pocket.

"Sorry I'm late, but we were running a special on heart attacks today. Good, Janvier, you're already here. Hi, Honey."

He gave quick kisses to Donny and Madeline. He got as far as the brush, which he picked up with a question in his eyes.

Janvier briefly told him that he'd had breakfast with his dad. "I'll tell you about it on the way to church, unless you want to go to a later Mass."

Nate said, "Oh, hell no. Let's get this over with. What is that, Dad's menu? Who signed it? Oh wow, Oh Daddy-mine! This is going to be framed and hung in the living room."

Donny rolled his eyes. No, it wasn't. "Go get changed, Nate. If you go to Mass dressed like that, you'll have parishioners lined up asking you to take their pulses."

Nate took the menu to the bathroom with him.

"Janvier, don't mention the r-i-n-g, okay? Let me deal with it."

Janvier ate the last green bean. "Sure. So how is Perry? How's he taking to being married to a working woman?"

"He's thrilled to death that she's now working with p-r-o-s-t-i-t-u-t-e-s. And that's sarcasm, in case you missed it."

"Actually, she's working with people who work with them."

"I'm sure she's euphoric to have her own charity, but you're going to watch out for her, right? Like she was one of your own."

"Donny, Paige does not need watching. She knows her stuff,

and I think she considers me one of her own. I'm a duckling to her great, big swan."

Donny sighed. For a duckling, Janvier caused a big wake everywhere he went.

33

AT EIGHT-THIRTY P.M., Nate was back from Mass, but Madeline wasn't back from church with her Granddaddy. Donny picked up her beat-up Barbie doll from the dining room chair. Nate made sandwiches while Donny contemplated the Barbie. The doll wore a brand new red cut-off-sock dress. Like all the rest of Barbie's dresses, the sock was way too big. This one bagged away from her plastic boobs.

Donny hadn't even noticed Janvier taking off his shoe before they went to Mass.

He wished his dad would hurry up and get her home. Madeline was going to be tired and wound up. He was glad Janvier hadn't come back from Mass with Nate. He'd wind her up even more.

His dad called from the parking lot and said Madeline was asleep and he wasn't going to carry her up the stairs. Nate, still in his church suit, ran down to get her. Donny went back into the kitchen while Nate put her to bed. On a whim, he opened a bottle of wine and sliced up a tomato for Nate's ham club. By the time Nate came back in, Donny sipped at his wine and held up the wedding ring.

"This was one of the presents your father sent. Janvier said it was my gift."

Nate took the ring. It was a minute before he said anything. "Janvier didn't tell me about this."

"I asked him not to. It is your mother's, isn't it?"

"No, my grandmother's. The initials are for Bella Rijos. I never thought of this, but I'm betting that my mother was buried wearing hers. Why did he give you this ring? Did he say what you were supposed to do with it?"

"No. Honey, do you think this means he's coming around? I think Janvier thinks it does."

Nate didn't say a thing. Donny put the glass down and slipped his arm around him.

Still looking at the ring, Nate asked, "Donny, what makes it okay for Dad to see Janvier and not me? Why the hell does my father ask him about Madeline and send presents through him? Why doesn't he just come over and be a grandfather? How the hell hard is it to take a Bible study that explains the whole God and gays thing? God damn it, Donny!"

"Your father is a rotten, mean old man who loves you very much. He loves you and you love him and I'm so sorry that it's so fucking stupid."

Nate took a chain off his neck. His wedding band was still on there from work. He wore it on the chain to Mass, but maybe that was an accident. Maybe not. He might have run into some old friends of his father's. Nate unhooked the chain, slid his ring off, and put it back on his finger. He slid his grandmother's ring on the chain and put it around Donny's neck.

"Don't say anything to Janvier, Donny. I know, it's not reasonable but damn it, he's my father, not his. Dad washed his hands of me because I'm gay, but he let Janvier come back from spending years fucking everyone in the world and I hate that I just said that!" He put his arms around Donny. "I mean, thank God Janvier's home. Thank God we have him back. But damn it, why does my dad...why?"

Donny let Nate vent. He didn't point out the dinners were the only way Señor Rijos had of keeping in touch with Nate. He didn't point out that Señor Rijos also was hanging on to Janvier with both hands, just like Nate was. He slid Nate's sandwich to him and let him talk. Nate was winding down when he said that he felt like a shit for being so damned jealous.

"Yeah. I know how that feels."

Nate bit into the sandwich. "Oh, you think?"

"Absolutely. Nate, I feel jealous over every pretty woman who looks at you."

"Yeah, I know that, but I don't understand it. I mean, why women?"

"I don't know. It's efficient, I suppose. I get to be jealous and insecure about your sexuality all at once. Give me a bite of that sandwich and take a sip of this wine."

"You have your own sandwich and I don't like red wine."

"Bull. You grew up in that restaurant. You just like beer better."

By eleven o'clock, the wine bottle was empty and they were curled up on the couch, spent, and wrapped in a quilt that Nate had found at a yard sale. Several of the squares had stuffing poking out, but it washed up well and it was big enough for two naked men to cover themselves in case a little girl woke up.

Donny dozed a little, but Nate mumbled that it was time for Santa to show up.

"Yeah. We need to get up and get her presents out."

Neither of them moved.

"Hey, I want to give you your present." Nate fished for his pants on the floor and dug a piece of paper out of his pocket.

"Merry Christmas. I hope you know how much I love you, because damn, Donny."

He knew what it was as soon as he saw the letterhead for a fertility clinic. Wrapped up in Nate and a quilt, Donny grinned hard enough to close one eye. "Oh, Honey. You froze sperm for me?"

"Merry Christmas. I don't want to talk about it."

"Was it hard? I mean, was it difficult to do in the little room?"

"No, they had good porn. I do not want to talk about it. What did you get me?"

"Only that bicycle you wanted. It's not nearly as good as frozen sperm for a surrogate."

"Did you get a bike for Janvier, too?"

"Yeah, but his isn't black. They only had one black one left, so Janvier has a silver one."

"Oh, not as cool, but good. I love you, Donny."

He waved the piece of paper. "Yeah, I know! I love you too, Nate."

34

CAL'S HANDS smelled Christmassy from the soap. It was a nice touch.

Perry's wife was in the hall when he came out of the toilet. She had one of those little computers in her hand and was looking something up. Cal found out over dinner that Frenchie had hooked her up with some cushy job. He better not hit on her. Cal would not tolerate that.

Paige had her back to him and apparently hadn't noticed him standing in the hall behind her, close enough to touch her. She had her hair in some sort of classy up-do, and he noticed that, from the back, she had a nice neck. Paige was in her middle forties, but she still had that divot at the top of her neck where it met the skull. A few strands of hair were loose right around that divot. It was nice.

Why Perry would let his wife work for that guy was beyond him. Cal was going to check it out. She was still attractive, but not like when she was young. Now she'd be vulnerable to any attention from a guy as smooth as Frenchie.

Paige turned around and jumped, giving a little squeak. "Damn it, Cal! Why are you sneaking up on me?"

She swore at him! Women like Paige didn't get all jumpy for no reason. Cal felt a flutter of relief. He had something important to do. He was going to follow the guy with the unpronounceable name.

"I'm just coming out of the bathroom, Paige." He held up his hands in fake innocence. "I guess you didn't see me."

She immediately went back to being the regular Paige. She took his arm and led him back towards the family room. "Oh, I'm sorry I snapped at you. You're right, Uncle Cal. I am a little preoccupied. The Alexia Project is such a huge undertaking. I'm having a difficult time focusing on anything else."

Perry's oldest daughter came down the hall towards them and overheard what her mother said. "Yeah. Mr. Reed's all rehabilitated, so now Mom and he are going to clean up the streets and save all the hookers."

Before Cal could absorb what the girl just said, Paige cut her off. "Sarah Grace! I am not going to tolerate that sort of talk, do you understand? Mr. Reed is deserving of respect and so is The Alexia Project. Trash talk diminishes everything, especially the person speaking!"

Sarah Grace apologized but added that, "Anyone who would give Granddaddy a kitten for a Christmas present is okay with me. I think Mr. Reed's cool, Mom, especially since he turned his life around and is with you on the charity. I think what you two are doing is great."

Rehabilitated Hookers? What the hell was she talking about? And how was it that Perry's kid knew about this shit and he didn't? It was obvious that Paige was going to take them both to the family room, so Cal got in one question. "Does everyone know about Reed?"

Paige stopped, frowning, at the entrance to the family room.

The line between her eyebrows looked hard. "The younger girls do not, Cal. Please keep that in mind. Some common knowledge is only for grownups, and we will all respect Mr. Reed's privacy."

No. He wouldn't, but Paige didn't need to know that.

Back in the family room, everyone was moving around. The girls were still playing with the kitten. It was just a gray tabby, some no-big-deal kitten, but from the moment Frenchie arrived that morning and handed it to his brother, the kids all forgot everything else. They barely noticed his presents. All those ungrateful brats wanted was to get their hands on that animal.

In the family room, Frenchie stood with the smart twin and the toothpick. The guy leaned toward Amy a little, laughing at something she said like it was the funniest thing in the world.

He couldn't believe it. That fucker was flirting with her right there in front of everybody! Then Frenchie looked up and met Cal's gaze. For that split second, there was nothing amused in the guy's expression.

Cal looked at the floor.

35

PERRY STARTED out that Christmas morning irritated with Cal, and it hadn't gotten better. When his uncle first arrived, he had looked right past Paige and announced that he was starving and got a piece of pie before dinner. He was grumpier than usual at dinner, and now with everyone having a good time, his uncle marched up to him while Perry was on the rug with the kids, trying to get his old golden retriever to make nice with the kitten. His poor old dog was caught somewhere between predator and being terrified of the kitten's tiny needle claws.

"Perry, we need to talk. Right now. Office."

Oh, bullshit. His uncle was not going to pull that kind of attitude on Christmas day in front of the children. "I can't, Cal. I'm holding onto the dog."

The aging golden retriever lay on the floor next to him, and Madeline sat across from him holding the kitten. Perry's two younger daughters tried coaxing the dog while Tessie sat on a footstool and worried.

His sister stopped chewing her thumbnail long enough to fret at Cal. "He can't let the dog go, Uncle Cal, don't you see that? Don't let the dog go, okay, Perry? Okay?"

"No problem, Tessie. I've got him." He had his hand on the golden retriever's collar. The sweet dog rolled his eyes up at Perry, begging him to make sense of a universe gone awry.

All the girls looked up at Cal waiting to see what was going to happen next.

His uncle crossed his arms across his chest. "We have a situation."

"Uncle Cal, give me a minute to put the dog outside, and I'll meet you in the office." He then ignored his uncle and paid attention to the kitten. The little gray tabby wanted off Madeline's lap. "It's okay, Honey. Let her go." He kept his hand on his dog's collar.

Madeline did. The kitten scrambled off her lap and walked right up to the dog, touching noses. Every inch of the dog trembled.

The kitten sat down and cleaned itself, inches from the dog. Little girl laughter erupted, startling the kitten. She immediately took shelter under the dog's chin.

His old golden looked up at him with tortured, brown eyes. "Okay! I think that's enough for our old buddy. Girls, why don't you take the kitten to the litter box and see if she'll do something? I think the dog is ready to take a backyard break, too." Dropping his voice to a conspirator level, he whispered. "I do think the kitten scared the pee-pee out of him"

He took his dog out onto the deck and spent several minutes petting him and telling him that he was "The man! The fierce, kitten-tolerating Man!"

Perry had to admit, he liked the whole kitten thing. Janvier had driven his own car over to the house, come in with the kitten, and made a bee-line for Perry's dad. He had announced that

"Will said it is customary to bring you a present, so here." He handed Perry's speechless father a kitten.

Perry's golden retriever had been a Christmas present also, fourteen years earlier. He gave the old dog one more ear rub. "You did good, buddy boy. Christmas day is almost over. I should go in and see what's bugging Cal now. Want to trade places? Huh?"

The dog's eyes promised unending love. Perry accepted a wet kiss and gave the dog a dry kiss on the top of his almost white head.

He went back in, gave Will a pat on the shoulder, and gave Tessie a quick hug as he made his way to the hallway. Cal was in his front office, off the alcove. Perry shut the door behind him. Whatever it was that was bugging his uncle probably wouldn't be for anyone else's ears. The one architectural detail he wished he'd changed about that house was the front office. He'd placed the window in a way that didn't mess up the organic look from the outside, but from the inside it was always shadowy.

Cal stood in front of the badly placed window, his hands on his hips and his feet spread slightly apart. "What's Frenchie's story?"

"He's a friend of Nate's. Grew up with him, apparently like a brother."

"Don't bullshit me, Perry. What's the deal? Why did Sarah Grace say something about hookers and call him 'reformed' and what the fuck has he gotten your wife into?"

Perry felt the hair rise on the back of his neck. He didn't like Cal talking about his wife and daughter in that tone of voice. "I wasn't aware that Sarah Grace knew about him, but I suppose it makes sense that Paige told her, in light of the charity."

Obviously, Paige wasn't going to back down off the Alexia Project. Cal was right about one thing. Janvier Reed had climbed off his billionaire sugar daddy and dropped all his prostitution baggage right into the middle of the Ravaterra family.

Perry also wondered whether Janvier's past was going to legally catch up with him. Hopefully, he'd keep his mouth shut about his wealthy clients, and his wealthy clients would keep him from any legal trouble.

Cal's lower lip stuck out far enough to show the smooth, inner skin.

Perry made himself look and sound sincere. "Sorry, Cal. I didn't realize you didn't know. Janvier Reed was a high-priced escort in New York. He got out of the business. He's funded the charity that Paige is starting to help sex workers get off the job."

"Shit, Perry. Why'd you let your wife get mixed up in something like that? Why is that douche here in the first place? Did you know about all this when he came over on Thanksgiving? What the fuck…"

An idea popped open inside of Perry like a massive boil erupting. If Cal pushed this, it wouldn't be Perry who would smack him down, it would be Paige. If Perry made his wife choose between running her own charity and her husband with his crabby uncle, his wife would choose the charity. In his moment of clarity, Perry knew that if he let Cal do something to Janvier, his wife would scrape him off like old leftovers.

And he wouldn't blame her.

Of course, it was ridiculous to think that his wife would leave him because she had a job. She could have had a job anytime she wanted, and she had a trust fund that made his family money look timid. She didn't need a job to empower her. The idea was absurd, but it wasn't going to go away. His wife was going to leave him and not because of the charity, but because she didn't have the time or passion to put up with him anymore. And she certainly would not put up with Cal getting in the way.

His uncle looked him in the eye. "Look, Perry. You gotta

make your wife realize that this is over the line. She can't go dragging you and your family into the gutter like this."

"Paige has trained her whole life for this and I'm not about to tell her how to do her job. She wouldn't tolerate it if I tried. She won't tolerate it from you, either. Do you understand?"

"You're being dense, Perry. Has it occurred to you that maybe there's a little something else going on? I'm just saying, lots of women her age get bored and start looking around and there's this exotic guy who offers them a job. I've seen it more times than I can say. Women Paige's age get needy and want someone to coddle them, to make them feel pretty and young again. Tell you what. I'll follow them and maybe—"

"Cal, listen to me. Listen!" Perry took a deep breath and wondered why he was Cal's babysitter. Why didn't his uncle talk to his dad about shit like this? "

"She's not sleeping around and even if she was, who the fuck am I to say she can't? Think about that for a minute!"

It echoed through his head again. Paige was going to leave him. She was going to leave him because he was a shitty husband. She was going to leave him because Perry was just an annoyance to her now. The first time she looked in her rearview mirror and saw his pathetic uncle following her, she'd leave him.

"But Perry, I can find out. I'll help you."

"No, Cal. Leave them alone."

"You're being a fool."

Perry didn't yell. In fact, he spoke quietly, forcefully. "Maybe you better leave, Cal, because if you make me choose between my wife and you, you will lose every time. Leave her alone."

Cal rocked back as if he'd been hit.

Perry tried to lighten his tone. "I'm sorry. It's just that Paige is completely qualified to do what she's doing. She's not on the streets, she's at the bank. She's not sleeping around. She's going to become the head of a major fund-raising enterprise, and I'm proud of her. I don't want you checking her out because that would send a different message, wouldn't it?"

His uncle puffed his chest out again. "Well, why didn't you say that in the first place, Perry? I thought you were keeping some shit from me."

God damn it, his closest confidant was this sad old man. He gave Cal a pat on the shoulder. "Keep something from you? Shit, Cal. You're my good old uncle, aren't you?"

36

Janvier did not trust Cal Ravaterra. He didn't like the small sneer he had on his face when he looked at anyone except Perry. He didn't like the way Cal bumped up against the elder Dr. Ravaterra's trophy wife, smirking when she was obviously uncomfortable. He did not like Donny's uncle, and he was sure the feeling was mutual. Still, he didn't think the man smashed into his car on purpose.

Cal, backing up too fast, slammed into Janvier's parked sedan. Sarah Grace was taking the kitten out to her granddad's car and saw the accident. Shivering outside with most of the family, she whispered, "He was going too fast, Mr. Reed. Way too fast." She was still holding the kitten. It mewed pathetically.

"I'm sure he was, Sarah Grace, but I think I'll keep it simple for the sake of Christmas. It isn't much of an accident, after all. It's a little cold out here. Maybe you better go ahead and put the kitten in your granddad's car. I already put the cat carrier in there."

The accident only messed up Cal's bumper, but it smashed in

one of Janvier's fenders, which rendered his car unusable. Cal sputtered that Janvier shouldn't have parked in the middle of the driveway. "He's two feet from the curb!"

Janvier agreed because it was easier and who knows, maybe it was his fault. However, it was Christmas and the damage wasn't bad, so he didn't advise calling police and tow trucks. "Let's leave the cars and deal with it tomorrow, Cal. What do you say?"

Cal said something about Janvier's insurance paying for the damage and "none of this no-fault shit, either."

Out of earshot, Perry told Janvier not to worry about it. He took care of Cal's insurance and he'd put in the claim the next day. "Just leave it. Do you want me to call Donny and Nate back? They can't have gotten too far."

The elder Dr. Ravaterra declared Cal's car drivable but damaged. "You broke one of your brake lights, so be careful driving home."

"Take parking lessons, why don't you?" Cal snarled at Janvier before getting in his car.

Amy spoke up. "Don't call Donny to come back. We go right by Janvier's place. We'll take him home."

It seemed like a good idea until Janvier saw Will's convertible. The two-door car had the top up, but he could tell that the area behind the front seats was more of a suggestion than a real backseat.

Amy tattled on Will. "He never lets anyone else drive, so the backseat is you or me."

Janvier interrupted her before she could offer. "I'll be happy to fold myself into a small package and ride in the back."

Amy told Janvier that his argument was chivalrous but unnecessary. "I'm about eight inches shorter than you and have about forty percent less mass."

He held the front seat up so she could climb into the back.

He had to admit, she folded up nicely. "Is it safe for you back there? Are there seat belts?"

"Yep. And this car has so many airbags that if we get into an accident, it turns into bubble wrap."

About three hours earlier, he'd found a word to describe how he felt. 'Giddy.' All Christmas Day he was enjoying himself so much that he felt giddy. He had to control himself because he wanted to smile like a lunatic most of the day. It was different from Thanksgiving. This time, he sought out Will and Amy. The gifts went over big, even the kitten, and when Tessie asked how Nate's dad liked the lamp, he told her the truth. Señor Rijos loved it. Tessie beamed to know that the lamp had found the right home.

The pediatrician held up the ten-week-old kitten. "Tessie, did you help Janvier pick out my gift, too?"

"No, Dad. The kitten was a surprise. What are you going to name her?"

Adam Ravaterra looked at Janvier. "December."

There was touching all day. Nate hugged him. Tessie hugged him. Madeline climbed into his lap once. All the women, especially Amy, touched him while they talked to him. Paige had a hard time not discussing The Alexia Project. She touched his arm a couple of times, almost vibrating with the effort of not giving him the latest news.

He felt relaxed around Will, but perhaps not at all relaxed. When he was in New York, he thought he was attracted to Will because of his accent and his own homesickness. But now? Now, Will brushed against him and a jolt shot through Janvier that was almost narcotic.

Amy leaned against him once. He could have lived the rest of his life in that moment.

The giddy feeling was still strong as he slid into the passenger seat of Will's convertible. The front seat let him stretch his legs out. "Amy, I can move this seat up."

"No, I'm good."

He moved it up a little anyway. As they drove away, Will shifted gears. The ambient light from the dashboard was enough to see his hand on the gearshift and to see his thighs change position as he worked the clutch.

"Amy's wrong, you know. I do let other people drive this car, but the one time I let her try, she drove timidly. This is a nice car. It does not deserve timidity."

Amy smacked the back of the driver's seat. Will ran his fingertips over the steering wheel. "So, Janvier, do you want to drive?"

"Nate spent this afternoon telling stories about my lack of driving skill, and Cal had a few things to say about my ability to park. If you wanted me to drive, you would have made that offer before we were on the road."

From the dim recesses of the backseat, Amy spoke up. "Oh, he might. He's been flirting with you all afternoon. He might let you boldly drive his car."

In the dark, Janvier shook his head. "I'm afraid Nate wasn't lying. I'm an old woman driving in the slow lane. I'm also gearshift illiterate. I have no idea how to make all four limbs do different things at the same time."

Will reached for the gearshift. "Janvier, that's just wrong. Shifting gears is built into the Y chromosome. Put your hand over mine."

They were coming to the light on the main road. Janvier covered Will's hand with his own and felt Will's fingers tighten on the knob. He felt the smooth-strong movement as he shifted.

"Aw, no." He took his hand off Will's and let it fall limply into his lap. "The two of you are killing me with all the flirting, you know."

The light turned green, and Will's thighs and hands worked in the low light. Amy reached between the seats and touched Janvier's arm. Her voice was sincere when she asked him if they were making him uncomfortable.

"Yes, of course it makes me uncomfortable. You're tormenting me and I love it."

Will shifted again. "Since the first time Amy laid eyes on you, Janvier, she's asked me to describe minute by minute, blow by literal blow, what the two of us did together. She's had me pinned, naked and talking, and never once asked me if I was uncomfortable."

Amy made an actual gasp noise. "Oh God, Will! Don't tell him that."

"Blow by literal blow, Janvier."

Janvier reached back and found one of Amy's ankles. She had on blue jeans and thick socks. "Amy, if he told you I blew him, he didn't tell you the truth." His thumb pushed her sock down enough that he found skin.

Will laughed out loud, and Amy mumbled something about being a doctor and "knowing it is truly possible to die from embarrassment." She didn't pull her leg away.

From the backseat, she almost whispered, "Lord, Janvier. I mean, he did tell me about it before I met you, and…you know. I asked for details."

"Before she met you, she wanted to know about your HIV status and whether we used a condom. After she met you, she wanted to know whether you felt heavy when you were on top of me."

"Seriously, Will! Shut up! I apologize, Janvier. He's being horrible."

"He's pretty good at being horrible."

There was light traffic, but Will had to accelerate to merge onto the interstate. The car responded to the driver and flew across the lanes. "What are you holding onto, Janvier?"

"Your girlfriend's leg."

His hand was under the cuff of her sock, fully on her skin. She reached over and stroked his wrist. "You know, Janvier, I'd never done anything too dangerous until I met Will and even then, he's good on paper. I mean, no one would take him for the hire two-prostitutes and then sleep with the pimp type."

He let go of her ankle. Amy calling him a pimp cut right into him. Immediately, he remembered Will saying "I let a pimp fuck me…"

"Amy!" Will barked. "He's never liked being called a pimp and he certainly isn't one anymore."

"I'm sorry." There was a click as she undid her seat belt. She slid forward, reaching for his arm as she apologized.

Will slowed the car down, and Janvier snapped, "Put your seatbelt back on, Amy." He turned in his seat and softened his voice. "Please. It scares the hell out of me, put it back on."

"Okay, okay." She put it back on. "Janvier, I'm really sorry."

"No, don't be. Look, Amy, I was a pimp. Being overly sensitive about the word doesn't change a thing. I just don't want you to think of me that way."

"I don't, and I'm so sorry, Janvier."

They made conversation for the rest of the drive, but it didn't reach the giddy level again. Janvier's erection was gone, and his limp penis reminded him that some things never changed.

They pulled up in front of his duplex. Janvier climbed out of the car, and then lifted the seat so Amy could get out of the backseat.

"My foot's asleep," she said quietly.

He held her hand, helping her as she untangled herself. She did a hop and came out of the backseat.

There was a hesitation, and then her arms slid around him. Amy hugged him in a way that could be innocent, but her hands reached inside his unzipped coat and pressed against his back. He wished she wasn't wearing a coat. He wished he could feel her as well.

Janvier kissed her temple, her forehead. She lifted her face, and he kissed her cheeks, and then her lips. Her kiss was soft and warm.

It was almost painful to let her go, but that's what he did. He took her hands from his sides and held them together. Let his lips linger on hers a moment more. Made it stop.

"Goodnight. Merry Christmas. Amy, I think maybe… I don't know. Goodnight."

He reached the walk to his duplex before she said, "Janvier, wait!"

Standing under the glow from the open car door, she was beautiful. When Will also got out of the car, Janvier's heart leapt. Maybe this was going to become something more. Maybe not. Will had left the car running. The exhaust made white billows in the near-freezing air.

Amy stayed where she was, but Will came up a little further. "Janvier, I'm worried. Amy and I…we have a crush on you, but I don't want to mess with your head. We can still back up and go back to friendly. If this is too much, say so."

"So."

Will nodded. The expression on his face was resignation. "Yeah. I guess it is too—"

Janvier kissed Will. Hard.

A moment later, Will whispered, "So."

They left. They got in the car and left him with his jumbled up, giddy thoughts and his erection and his horrible feeling that this could not happen because it was a sure way of screwing up his life, which was just starting to work out.

Janvier stood on the sidewalk and watched them do a U-turn.

Will drove the convertible back by his house again and put the window down. "New Year's Eve at our house. A bunch of people are coming and we'll try out our just-friends, no flirting or making anyone feel uncomfortable thing. I'll even pretend like I don't know that January first is your birthday."

Janvier waved as the convertible sped away again.

He should feel like shit, but he didn't. He knew he should be so upset that he would head to his bathroom with something sharp. Still, he hadn't replaced the razor blade. The most lethal things in his house were a new refill of anti-depressants and a dull steak knife.

He felt pretty damn good. He didn't even have the urge to put the pewter-bud vase in his mouth.

Damn. Giddy.

37

THREE DAYS AFTER CHRISTMAS, Janvier turned his car over to the hotel's parking valet. The parking lot was full of cars that glittered with gray light as the rain tried to freeze on hoods and windshields. Normally, he wouldn't have considered driving in such bad conditions, but the signs that said "Bridge freezes before road" gave him something to concentrate on so he didn't have to think about the billionaire. Janvier had a last-minute appointment with the man he hadn't seen in over a year. When he handed the parking valet his keys, he felt trapped, but he went on.

The high he'd felt on Christmas day had worn off as soon as Paige called him and let him know the billionaire was in town.

"He wanted to meet with you. I told him 'no.' He had to wait until after the official launch of the charity. I mean, I can legally go ahead and put the money into a holding pattern, but I don't want that man to ever take the upper hand with me. He agreed he needed to follow my rules but that he needed to see for himself that you were okay. He said he flew down here as an impromptu Christmas present to himself, and Janvier, he offered a million dollars just for an hour of your time. I told him I would check with you, but now I feel bad about it. I should have just refused."

Janvier lied and told her it was fine. He thought he would have another couple of months to get ready, to tell his therapist about the set-up, and to push himself just to sit down with the old man.

He didn't. He had no time left at all.

Now at the hotel, he found he couldn't go another step. Janvier stood near the hotel's glass doors and flexed his gloved hands. Clutching the steering wheel had left his fingers stiff. He tried to be subtle as he stretched them out, but they closed into fists. He didn't want it to be too obvious that his hands shook and frankly, the fists felt right.

He reminded himself that when he first came up with the idea of the charity, he'd called the billionaire. That conversation had not been difficult for him. Janvier ran over the rules in his head. The fact that there were rules helped enormously. The rate that Paige and the billionaire settled upon was two hundred and fifty thousand per meeting, which would happen no more than twenty-four times a year, and each meeting would last between one hour and two. All contact would be cleared with Paige first, and that included billable phone calls. The meetings were to be at a hotel in Raleigh, but not in any room where there was a bed. There would be no physical contact, sexual or otherwise, and no removal of any clothing. The rules were in concrete, period.

At any time and for any reason, Janvier could cancel. That went for phone calls, meetings, or the whole arrangement. If he told the billionaire to leave him alone, in theory the billionaire would. The old man agreed to all of it before he immediately broke the rules by wanting an early meeting.

Janvier should walk away just to keep the old man from exercising any control.

Standing at the hotel's entrance, Janvier told himself that he could do this. It would probably only take a year or so, and the old man would get tired of making trips to Raleigh just to have tea with him. After that, the word would be out about the charity, and he could stop.

Just one year.

His therapist wasn't the only one he hadn't told about the meetings. They all knew about the charity and that Janvier was going to help, but he'd not told Nate about meeting with the billionaire. Shame washed over him. He should have told them. Why did he think this would make him feel cleaner?

He looked up to see a familiar face stepping through the hotel's door. Wearing a plain, gray suit, a Japanese man walked over to where Janvier stupidly just stood. When they were a few feet apart, they both bowed.

Janvier pulled himself together. It was one thing to fall apart in his head, but he would not embarrass himself in front of someone he respected. He had to admit, there was a pleasant familiarity to greeting the bodyguard.

They walked through the lobby and entered a discreetly placed elevator. The gray-suited man slid a keycard into a slot. Once the doors shut, the bodyguard quietly said, "It is good to find you well. We were all concerned."

Janvier thanked him and asked quickly, "It's good to see you again. How is your wife doing?"

"She's great. Cancer-free for two years now. We have a new grandchild, a girl."

Impulsively, he gave the man a shoulder-bump, and the bodyguard smiled hugely at him. By the time the elevator doors opened, both men had resumed their formal stances. He silently followed the bodyguard off the elevator.

Inside the suite's living area, the casually dressed billionaire held his Alexia-made, blue coffee mug. Janvier stood tall and simply nodded his head at the billionaire despite the sweat that broke out on his neck and between his shoulders.

With the slightest tremble in his voice, the billionaire said, "Good afternoon, Jan."

Janvier returned the greeting. "Good afternoon. I hope your holiday was pleasant." The maid took his coat and gloves. Janvier handed them over without comment. The older servant prided herself on being invisible. Thanking her would be offensive, but she did take a fleeting moment when she met Janvier's eye. There was a hint of a smile exchanged before she slipped from the room.

The billionaire had a slight flush to his skin. He didn't meet Janvier's eye.

"Please, Jan, sit. The coffee must taste wonderful after being out in this weather. It isn't the sort of temperature associated with the South, is it?"

Janvier sat where indicated and took a porcelain cup of coffee. "You're right. The coffee is wonderful."

The billionaire twitched a half smile and clutched at the handmade coffee mug. "I'm glad to see you." He finally raised his eyes and skimmed over Janvier. "Even with the shaggy hair and the whole unkempt look, it's so good to see you. The Ravaterras, do they like you looking that way?"

Janvier took his time with his coffee. It warmed him. He sipped, then looked the billionaire right back in the eye. "I believe part of the deal is that you pretend you don't know about the Ravaterras. That makes what I'm doing here somewhat easier."

The old man rubbed his thumb over the place on his coffee mug where Alexia had kissed the wet clay.

"Ah yes. Only Paige Ravaterra counts. The rest, I keep my fingers off."

"You keep your fingers off Paige as well. I know that you know all about me. You know what I drive, where I live, what property I own, and what happened to my socks."

The billionaire looked slightly confused. "Socks?"

It was irrational, but it helped that the billionaire didn't know that a worn-out Barbie doll wore his socks.

The billionaire was only an old man. That's all. He'd had some of the extra skin on his neck removed. That surprised Jan because the old man wasn't particularly vain, and he was somewhat nervous about anesthesia.

Jan saw movement near the bedroom and stood. "Alexia?"

He didn't smile when he saw her, but he almost wanted to. Instead, he thought of the impact she'd had on Donny. Of course, she looked fantastic.

Impulsively hugging her, he told her how sorry he was that he'd left like that. "I was only thinking of myself. I was so far gone that I couldn't get out of my own head. Alexia, I'm sorry. Please forgive me."

It was almost as if he'd missed her.

She pushed slightly away and looked up at him with her tear-filled eyes sparkling.

"If I'd known that you were so desperate to leave, maybe I could have forgiven you for running away. But you said nothing to us. No, I don't forgive you."

She pushed herself further from him but kept her hand on his chest. "And Jan, I don't appreciate you telling him who should marry me. If I wanted to marry the Brazilian, I would have. All I want from you is to tell you that you are one ugly, arrogant, mean, horrid, conceited fool who didn't realize that he lived in paradise and didn't appreciate all that we did for you. For you!"

She hit him, hard, on the chest but then kept her hand there. Janvier knew she could feel the dampness from his sweat, but she didn't mention it. She only said a couple of well-rehearsed, elegant phrases designed to insult.

Janvier knew she wouldn't hit him again. She probably wasn't even angry. That would be too personal for her. She was playing a role that she was supposed to play…maybe. He could never tell if she had any emotions at all.

"You look beautiful, Alexia. You caused a real mess with my friends, you know."

"I don't care."

Now that was true. It wouldn't do any good to order her never to do that again. She probably wouldn't, unless she felt like it. At least Donny knew who she was now. Donny would probably invite her in, give her tea, and hold her hand while she dabbed at the tears leaking out of her glittering, amazing eyes.

Her left hand was on his chest. In a surprisingly real gesture, he covered it with his hand, and she lifted her ring finger enough for him to feel the ring. She wore the thick ring Janvier had given the billionaire, the antique band of beaten gold that dated back to the time of Jesus, but she wore it on her left ring finger. Janvier took her left hand and looked at her questioningly. She pointed to the billionaire with her right.

The old man shrugged. "My wife passed away while you were in the hospital."

Janvier knew that it had been years since the billionaire even spoke with his wife. Her death probably meant nothing to him, but Janvier said, "My condolences to your children." Still holding Alexia's left hand, he asked, "When did this happen?"

She answered him coldly. "When you suggested that I marry the Brazilian."

The billionaire motioned for them to sit down. "That's not true. We were already married by then. I could not stand to lose both of you, and Alexia knew that. She decided she was going to marry one of us, and she threatened to move to Raleigh."

Alexia melted her body against him in a parody of a hug. God, Alexia thought he would have married her. He put his arm around her waist in a gesture that was still familiar.

Over the top of Alexia's head, Janvier looked down at the seated billionaire. "You got an iron-clad pre-nup, didn't you?"

"Of course. Haven't I made sure that both of you are independently wealthy? And both of you will have been taken care of in my will. Sit down, sit down. Jan, are you going to refuse what I have bequeathed to you?"

Holding Alexia's hand, he sat across from the billionaire. She was close enough to be intimate, but the way the billionaire took credit for Janvier's money snapped him back to the reality of the meeting. "I absolutely will refuse to inherit. You have no reason to leave me any money. Instead, give it to the Alexia Project."

The butler placed a tray on the table with small sandwiches and the almond cookies that Alexia liked. "I see you still get those little cookies."

She abruptly put her hand up. "Stop talking to me. I didn't ask you to be here. It's so obvious that you don't want anything to do with either one of us, but he wants you here and I wasn't about to be left out. I'm here, but talk to him. Just do that verbal sparring thing to see which of you gets to control whatever stupid, stupid conversation you're going to have. God, I am so angry with you!"

"Yeah, well, Alexia, I'm kind of mad at you for doing that thing to Donny Ravaterra. Why'd you do that?"

"Do what? Pop in? Say 'hello?' He's a strange looking man."

"He's one of the sweetest people you've ever met. Please respect that."

She lifted an eyebrow and pointed to the billionaire. "If I shower your Ravaterras with respect, will you remember how to respect him? Will you respect the fact that this man loves you and wants to spend time with you?"

Love. The billionaire did love him, but Janvier had never had any choice in the matter. There was a lot of anger in him, but he didn't show it. He answered honestly. "I don't know. I'll try."

She pulled off the antique ring. "Here, you wear it. You wear it because you are going to promise us that you will sit here, just like we arranged, for about ninety minutes. You aren't going to worry about your precious mental state or relive all your past traumas. For now, you are going to make nice talk with someone who loves you."

"I'll try."

She pushed the ring into his hand. "Put it on, Jan."

"But it's your wedding...."

The billionaire's voice was level but did not sound calm. "Please, Jan. If she wants to claim you with a ring, let her."

It was all about power. Apparently, Alexia needed some as well. He put the ring on his little finger. It went halfway down and stuck between the joints.

Alexia pressed her hand against his chest. "Have it sized."

"I might be one cold-hearted, self-centered idiot, but I'm not going to have a two-thousand-year-old ring sized. And since we are also talking about finding homes for all your artifacts, let's start with this one. Alexia, I think your finger is the perfect place for his ring." He pulled the ring off and handed it back to her. She looked away, so he put it on the table before he reached over and took the blue mug from the billionaire. "I'll take this instead. I think it's worth more."

The billionaire took Janvier's china cup. The butler appeared and refilled the aromatic coffee into the thin porcelain as if this was what happened all the time. Again, just for a second, the servant met his eye.

He sipped from the blue mug. The coffee was cooling off.

Alexia picked up her ring. "And you don't push me around,

271

Jan. I don't appreciate the way you named your charity. How presumptuous." She curled her perfect lip.

"You were a just a child, Alexia."

She waved a dismissing hand. The billionaire agreed with Jan. "You were too young, but that was in the past. Let's talk of lighter subjects and save the deep analysis of our lives for some other meeting." Jan let the billionaire set the tone and subject. They talked about the New York penthouse and the unresolved dilemma of the aging swimming pool.

"It's an old building. Do we redo supports? Replace the pool with a lighter weight steel one?"

Janvier didn't hesitate. "Get rid of it."

He could do this. He knew how to do this. Janvier laughed at all the right places, looked concerned when called for, and gave the billionaire all the attention the old man needed. It felt easy, the way rewatching an old movie felt easy.

Ninety minutes after he'd sat down, Janvier left with the blue mug. Waiting under the sheltered valet drive, he was sure his next therapy session was going to be a tough one because he was going to have to admit so many things, including how simple it was just to slip into the old routine. Buttoning up his coat, Janvier knew that in therapy, he would have to admit that after meeting with the billionaire, he didn't feel suicidal. He wasn't even in a bad mood, even if his hands insisted on shaking.

The valet brought his car around, and he put the mug in the glove compartment, cradled between the owner's manual and his gloves. As he drove home, he hardly noticed that the temperature had climbed enough to turn the freezing rain into a dull drizzle.

Nate called on the way home, and Janvier managed to stay in his lane as he touched the phone button. Still he clutched the wheel hard when he said, "Hello, Nate?"

"Hey, Buddy, do me a favor. Donny came down sick last night after we came home. He has the stomach bug. Sorry about exposing you yesterday, but I can't get off work. Madeline is already at her preschool, and I know that Donny is going to be fine, but I'd feel better if you could stop by. Could you maybe stay with him a while? You've already been exposed."

"Okay."

"Cool. I gotta run. You have the key, right?"

He wanted to double check his keychain, but that would mean taking his eyes off the road while talking on the phone. "Yeah, I do. Go on. I'll be there soon."

It would be okay, although he did wish cars wouldn't pass on both sides at the same time.

38

DONNY SAT ON THE TOILET, boxers around his ankles, and held a small bathroom trashcan in his lap. Another wave of cramping hit him, making him think that dying was not a bad idea. In a miserable voice, he whispered, "Donato Ravaterra, PhD., shit himself to death at the age of thirty-three. It was a shame. He was nice."

He threw up a little more into the trashcan and shivered as sweat cooled on his skin. So much for the ginger ale he'd tried to drink. The trashcan had a nice clean plastic liner in it. A larger, black trash bag was on the floor next to the sink. It already held four or five used small trashcan bags, tied and discarded properly.

"The late Donato Ravaterra was fastidious, even when dying. That's how nice he was."

He put the trashcan down, cleaned himself, flushed, and repeated the procedure. He washed his hands, wiped the toilet down, and re-washed his hands. When Nate had left that morning, he said he was going to get back to check on him at lunch, or he'd send Janvier to look in on him. Donny didn't want either of them to see anything more than tidied up trash bags. He washed his hands one more time and wondered if he'd survive a shower.

It seemed like far too much work. He leaned against the vanity and looked at his miserable self in the mirror.

"Etcetera, etcetera. The late, gay Doctor Donato leaves behind his very handsome husband, whom he bequeaths to the women of the world because our dear, late Ravaterra has it stuck in his head that Nate is secretly straight and panting after every woman who comes to our door wearing a peach colored sweater."

God, don't think of peaches.

Had Madeline felt this bad when she had the stomach thing? She threw up three or four times, but the diarrhea wasn't too bad. At the time, he was so worried about peach sweater woman showing up at the door that he'd zoned out on Madeline. Ah, daddy guilt to go with his nausea. Peach colored nausea.

Crap!

Donny threw up into the toilet and then managed to turn around and sit down in time. He put his head in his hands. Through the throw-up odor, he could smell soap on his hands. He breathed through his mouth as he continued his eulogy.

"While the Ravaterras probably have a direct paternal line right back to Italy, the male name-bearers have long had affection for blond, protestant women. Therefore, they are diluted Italian. Name only, really. And no one truly understands what possessed the Elder Doctor Ravaterra to give his son Donato such an ethnic name."

Not just his dad. They. His mother was still alive then. He'd asked his dad once about his name. His dad said that his mother liked it and that he was mush in her hands.

His headstone, bearing the name Donato Ravaterra, would make it seem as if a large, burly man was buried in the plot. The name sounded like someone with dark flashing eyes, like Nate, only Italian. Someone buried under a Donato Ravaterra headstone shouldn't be a skinny, pale corpse who'd shit himself to death.

Donny re-cleaned the toilet, re-cleaned his hands, re-cleaned everything. After re-rinsing his mouth, he went back into the bedroom, and collapsed face down on the bed. He heard the front door open, but so what? It was either a friend or foe. Maybe the foe would be kind enough to murder him in his stupor.

He'd probably be cremated. There would be no grave; therefore, he would have no virile looking headstone. That would be better anyway. He couldn't live up to being a big, burly corpse under an Italian-named headstone.

Whoever was in the living room, it sounded like they were milling around. Donny propped himself up on one shaky elbow and listened. "Hello?" His voice sounded as high as an adolescent's and as feeble as an old man's.

Who was that? It wasn't Nate checking on him. The front door sounded like it opened and closed again. Donny got up onto trembling legs and walked into the living room. Everything was in place. Besides him, the condo was empty. Shivering, he went over to the front door. It wasn't locked, and that was a little strange. He went to the front window, which afforded some view of the parking lot.

His uncle was walking away from the steps. Or some guy who looked like his uncle. Had he been inside? No. Donny probably just heard someone knocking on the door. The man moved out of sight, and Donny thought maybe he'd hallucinated the whole thing. Still, he locked the door.

An hour later, Donny woke up when Janvier tiptoed into the bedroom. He carried a small grocery bag and sat on Nate's side of the bed. It didn't jiggle the mattress too much.

"'Lo, Janvier." Please go away. "Did Nate call you?"

Donny needed to go back to sleep. In fact, he was having a hard time keeping his eyes open.

"Yeah. God, Donny. This is heartbreaking. You're so sick."

"Sleep is good for sick people."

Janvier stroked his hair. "I'm sorry to wake you up. Let me go through Nate's list so I can call him back."

Donny cracked one eye open enough to see Janvier take a brand new digital thermometer out of the bag and a bottle of Gatorade. He also reached over and lightly pinched Donny's arm.

"Tell Nate that I'm only slightly dehydrated and thanks for the Gatorade. That's my favorite color." Wrong flavor. Right color.

"I'm supposed to watch you drink some. Temperature first though."

Janvier held the thermometer out like a miniature sword. At least it was not a baby thermometer.

"Janvier, you need to put a probe cover on it."

His clueless buddy inspected the box. "Oh, like a condom for the thermometer." A second later, ten free probe covers flew all over the bed.

"Janvier, give me that thing. You know you're being exposed to some nasty germs, don't you?"

Donny stuck the thermometer in his mouth and dozed off in the thirty seconds it took to make the thing beep three times. It read one hundred one, point two degrees. Good. He was getting better. He took four sips of the electrolyte drink and explained to Janvier why it wasn't a good idea to gulp down more. The words wore him out. One more sip and he had to go back to sleep.

"Oh, yeah. Uncle Cal snuck in here, I think." Janvier could help him find out if his uncle had a key to the condo, Donny thought, as he slipped back into sleep.

At some point, he opened his eyes again. He was dreaming

that he was dying all alone, but Janvier sat on Nate's side of the bed, reading a book. It was okay, then. He wasn't alone and besides, if Cal came creeping back, then Janvier would take care of that, too. It was okay. Janvier was a good man. Cal wasn't.

"Good, you're awake. How are you feeling?" Janvier made him take little sips again. "Come on, Donny. Nate said whenever you were awake that you had to drink a little more."

Donny wished he would go away so he could die alone.

39

CAL PARKED at the end of the duplexes. It was New Year's Eve and dark. Cal didn't worry too much that Frenchie would recognize the plain car, even if he had been looking for it.

He didn't get Frenchie. The guy had money, serious money, so why was he living in some shitty duplex? He had a bike chained up to the minuscule porch, but nothing else. His car was okay, but not a big deal. Obviously, the guy was lying about who he was and what he was doing. Wait until Paige found out about that detail. Her charity money-boy was poor enough to live in a dump that probably didn't even cost a hundred thousand.

Cal had followed him and tried to do some sleuthing during the week between the holidays, but he hadn't found much. He even had a close call when he checked out the Toothpick's place a few days after Christmas.

He'd let himself in because Perry said Frenchie was over there a lot, but Cal thought no one was home. It had sure scared the shit out of him when someone had called from the other room. Someone was home, but they must have been asleep or

279

something because they didn't come after him. He moved fast and got out of there. He didn't even bother to go check out the small condo. He just got the hell out.

He didn't figure a party boy like Frenchie was going to stay home on New Year's Eve, so he was prepared to find out who he partied with when no one was looking. The asshole came out, strapping on a bike helmet. The bike had a light on it and the guy wore a reflective helmet, but shit, it was New Year's Eve. Drunks were going to be all over the place.

Frenchie rode the bike right into the woods onto some path. In the fucking dark! Cal could make out the headlight, so after a heart-fluttering moment he figured that Frenchie was headed for the highway.

Cal drove to the intersection as fast as he could, and he made it in time to see the reflective bike disappear down the road on the other side of the highway. It was hard as hell to follow the bike, and Cal ended up losing him in a neighborhood. He had to drive back and forth a couple of times before he finally spotted the bike in a row of high-end townhouses. It was chained to a For Sale sign in front of one of the units, but the townhouse next to that one looked like there was a party going on.

That was stupid to chain the bike to a shoved-into-ground sign.

Cal found a parking spot where he could see the party. It wasn't as concealed as he liked, but it gave him a view of who was coming and going.

Dummy-Tessie walked up to the townhouse with Toothpick's Mexican boyfriend, but there was no sign of the Toothpick himself. The front door opened, and the smart twin welcomed them in. Shit. The fancy-pants townhouse probably belonged to her. Perry was not going to be interested in Frenchie's partying with the toothpick and the twins. Cal was going to have nothing to report.

He knew it wasn't going to be easy to get something on Frenchie. Surveillance took patience and practice. Eventually he'd figure something out, but in the meantime, he'd have to make do with a stupid New Year's Eve party.

He had lots of snacks in the car, a pee jar, and he could use the time to figure out how to take pictures with his new phone.

The party went on, and Cal daydreamed. He thought about how two of the three younger Ravaterra children were in that townhouse and how cool it would be if the place exploded or something. It was a shame it hadn't occurred to him to take care of those extra kids when they were all babies, but if all those kids had ended up at the bottom of the stairs, they probably would have spent more time investigating the bitch's death.

At least Perry looked like a combination of Selma and Ravaterra. Those last three kids were all skinny as lampposts with crooked faces. There was no Ravaterra in their looks. All three of them were physical copies of that raging bitch that was his brother's first wife.

The party went on, but Cal waited and thought about that old farmhouse that his brother had fixed up when he married that bitch. It was a big, old place with twelve-foot ceilings and three chimneys. He wondered who owned that house now, or if someone bought the place for the land and leveled the house. Maybe not. It was a nice place if you liked antiques. The fact that a woman died falling down the steep steps would probably give it more value as a haunted house.

———

THIRTY-SOME YEARS EARLIER, Cal went to that very house. It was an old, antebellum farmhouse that his brother and the bitch were redoing, one room at a time. New houses sprouted up around it, but the old house sat on ten acres of wooded property.

It was his brother's house. Cal should have been able to put his hand on the door and just walk in, but he was never that comfortable with her so he knocked. The bitch answered the door.

She opened the door quickly, tucking her hair behind her ears nervously. That was the one thing Cal had liked about her. He'd made her nervous as hell.

"Cal, what are you doing here?" Her tone was light, but she didn't look terribly happy. "Adam's at work and Perry's in school."

"I know. I wanted to stop by when Perry wasn't here, to see if I could get you to change your mind about letting him go to the game."

She frowned slightly. "Come in, but be quiet. I have all three babies asleep at the same time."

He followed her back to the kitchen. She'd just had twins when she got pregnant again. She'd had three babies in two years. Following her, he noticed that she was back to being skinny like always, but now her waist was gone. She wore stretchy pants and her body went straight up and down. From the back, her t-shirt clung to some loose skin over the waistband. Her butt was gone, but she'd never had one anyway. Cal could not imagine what his brother saw in her.

She was polite but didn't budge about Perry's punishment. The fifth-grade teacher caught him copying off some other kid's test paper. Skinny bitch mom said she was sorry because she knew it was going to be the first time that Cal and Perry would have gotten to go somewhere by themselves. Adam was too busy at work and now with the twins and the new baby boy, they finally said Cal could take Perry to a game. But then she grounded him, just for doing what all kids do.

She didn't think all kids copied homework. "This isn't

something I can gloss over. Perry is going to have to take his punishment."

The bitch was acting as if she was Perry's real mother. She wasn't. Selma was. Selma should not have ever married that Swedish doctor and moved to Europe. She should never have let the bitch take charge of Perry's life.

A squeak sounded from the baby monitor.

"Oh, one of the twins is waking up. Stay put, Cal. I'll be right back."

He listened to her footsteps on the old wooden staircase.

Cal went up the stairs quietly. From the bedroom to the right of the stairs, he could hear her talking softly to a toddler. Directly across from the stairs was a half-opened door. Cal slid into the room and shut the door exactly as it had been before.

He was in the master bedroom. Near the bed was a bassinet. Cal didn't even glance at the lump in the bassinet.

He watched through the crack in the door and stepped back out of sight when the bitch came out of the other bedroom, the toddler on her hip.

There was a moment at the top of the stairs. The woman had her back to him, but the toddler saw him, her round eyes widening as he silently opened the door. The bitch turned, surprise on her face as she looked over her shoulder.

It took nothing to push her. She twisted, maybe trying to protect the little girl, and she hit so fucking hard, Cal heard the sound as the back of her head hit the wooden step. She let go of the baby then, and they both fell. From the top of the stairs, it was like watching a human avalanche. It was so loud, too. He never thought such a thing could be so loud. One of the babies started crying, but it wasn't the one at the foot of the stairs. That one didn't move.

It was an accident. He was angry, that's all. He hadn't meant to kill her or brain damage the little girl. He was just angry. He had started to go down the stairs, but he remembered there were stairs in the back of the house also and that way he wouldn't have to step over them. Using his shirt tail to wipe the door handle on the master bedroom, Cal got the hell out of there. No one ever even knew he'd been there.

————

By now, Cal was good at not getting caught. He hadn't been caught all those years ago, and he wouldn't be caught following Frenchie around. Light spilled out of every window in the smart twin's townhouse. There seemed to be a fair number of people at the party, probably drinking, laughing too loud at nothing, and doing a little groping. He wondered about Frenchie. Did he swing both ways? Given his past, he probably grabbed everything that moved. Well, Cal could and would record every disgusting thing about the guy. That was the trick. All he had to do was be patient.

40

JANUARY 1, 2014

JANVIER FELT the blood rushing up his neck. Amy had one of his hands, Tessie the other. He could hardly breathe. Two minutes after everyone yelled "Happy New Year," all thirty or so of the partiers started singing "Happy Birthday." They lined up under the banner that proclaimed: "Happy New Year Everybody and Happy Birthday Janvier." Even still-sick Donny was skyping on the computer screen, singing with everyone else.

The song ended with applause and hugging. Red faced, Janvier said, "Thank you." He had no other words. "I mean it. Thank you."

It didn't end there. Gifts came out. His office manager gave him a catalogue of upscale office furniture with appropriate pages marked. He laughed and said he'd simply forgotten that what he wanted for his birthday were bigger chairs.

Paige and Perry gave him an ancient bowl, the picture of the

Phoenix rising out of the ashes still visible on the glaze. He couldn't imagine what Paige paid for the thing. It belonged in a museum.

Tessie held a squirming, blanket wrapped package. It was yowling, so she went next. She handed Janvier an envelope while bouncing the blanket as if she was trying to comfort a baby.

"Here, Joni-vee-ay. It's a gift certificate for a haircut. That's from me. This is from my dad." She pulled the blanket back to produce a pissed-off, longhaired kitten.

"Dad said to say happy birthday and that he hoped you weren't allergic because…" Tessie paused, trying to remember exactly what her father said. "You gave him a tabby cat but this sucker is a Persian cat and is going to shed for decades. He said 'sucker.' I didn't."

She handed him the kitten, which immediately attached itself to his chest via needle claws. He had to think fast. "Oh, Tessie. Oh, this is great, but Honey, I like paying you for haircuts. Ow. I love tipping you and paying for my haircuts, so instead of this gift certificate, can I ask you for a different present?"

Good God, the kitten was needle Velcro. Every time he unstuck one paw, four or five others attached painfully somewhere else.

Tessie looked at him with innocent, round eyes. "What do you want?"

Janvier pulled the kitten gently away from his injured body and handed it back to Tessie. "I want you to take care of my birthday kitten for me, forever. Name it January."

Tessie's face lit up. She cuddled the kitten to her. "I'd love to Joni-vee-ay, but we already have a kitten at our house. Remember, you gave Dad one for Christmas."

"Yes, Sweetheart. I did."

Tessie got the joke. "Oh, and if I keep this one, we'll have two and that's funny because Dad thought he was getting even with you!"

Janvier kissed her on the forehead, and the kitten meowed at him.

Nate needed to be at the rescue squad, so he left with birthday wishes and a hug.

"I love you, man."

"Back at you, Nate."

For the next couple of hours, Janvier helped Will serve mushroom caps stuffed with crabmeat and beers out of several coolers. There was a time when he would have felt out of place after Nate left. Now he felt right at home.

Amy pushed him into the kitchen. "Help me with something. So, are you having a good party?" She looked up at him.

"Hi. Do you know how beautiful you are?"

"You've been drinking."

"A little bit, yes. Amy, do you know how beautiful you are?"

"I know you think so. Janvier, do you know how beautiful you are?"

He had been drinking. He also felt extremely happy. "Amy, will you and Will marry me?"

She touched his waist. "That does sound good, doesn't it?"

One of her neighbors came up, looking to say goodnight. About a third of the partiers were already gone. The neighbor, a large, loud man with his large, loud wife, clapped him on the back.

"Happy Birthday, Jon. I hope you don't mind me shortening your name. That's a mouthful, what you got. Besides, you seem like a Jon sort of guy. Hey, were you the first baby of the new year back in the hospital where you were born?"

"No. Missed it by several hours."

Why did Amy say that the idea of the three of them together sounded wonderful?

Tessie left with Perry and Paige, taking the kitten. "I was going to stay tonight and help Amy clean up, but she said you were going to sleep in the guest room because you're drunk. Are you drunk?"

Janvier knew. This was going to happen.

"Yep." Anyway, he'd had way too much to drink to get back on that bike. "Make sure you wake up your dad and show him the kitten, okay?"

Tessie giggled. "Happy Birthday and thanks for letting me take care of your kitten!"

Will walked Tessie out to the car. Amy herded the last of the partiers towards their purses and coats.

"Happy Birthday. Happy New Year. Happy, happy."

It was a little after three, and the townhouse was a wreck. Janvier stood alone in the living room, listening as Amy and Will sent away the last of the guests.

He wasn't even sure what they had in mind. Whatever it was, he told himself to imagine explaining it to Donny.

What did they want? Expect? What if they wanted nothing from him? What if they were going to suggest that he stay in the guest room? God, that would break his heart.

They came back in the room, holding hands.

Janvier told himself to walk out the door. Go.

Amy tried to say something but ended up fluttering her free hand.

Will reached for him and pulled Amy along. His free arm went around Janvier, and Will kissed him.

The kiss went from soft to hard. Janvier could feel Amy's body to the side. She slid her arms around too, but Will's mouth was on his and Janvier took the kiss, took it as deeply as he could.

He let go of Will. He used both arms to hold Amy while his mouth found hers. The kiss was warm, full. He felt like he needed her every bit as much as he wanted Will.

Will guided them up the stairs to the bedroom.

Janvier orchestrated the removal of clothes. He'd done this too many times professionally not to know what to do, what to touch, what to kiss. He was terrified that they'd see how often he'd done this. He was terrified that his erection would go away. He was just plain terrified.

But he knew what to do and he kept doing it. It was a lazy pace, and when one of them stumbled, he knew what to do. He stalled getting into bed, intending to draw out the nude-and-standing part until…but Amy took his hand and she led him to the bed, and he forgot that it was supposed to be lazy.

He had a moment where he felt awkward, fumbling, and he silently grabbed for control. After all, it was the same setup—two men and one woman. But Will wasn't the billionaire and Amy wasn't Alexia. It was the same, he knew what to do, but… it was so different. They didn't focus on one person. They weren't doing… they weren't. They weren't.

They loved him. He melted into Will. Amy melted into him. He panicked because he wasn't doing what he was supposed to do, but even the panic felt like letting go.

Janvier struggled to pay attention to what they were feeling. He felt Amy working towards an orgasm, and it was the most wonderful thing to give her, to feel her need him, to want him. Together with Will they loved her, needed her.

He fought control. He had to make Will… had to wait… control… He felt Will's release and that should have been that, but it wasn't.

Amy and Will took control. They took it. He panicked, but now he was drowning in them. Now he was making love. Now, out of control, he let go while Will loved him and Amy held him and whispered that it was okay, it was okay.

41

PERRY LOVED COOKING with his daughters, even though they bickered. When Cal showed up, Perry's girls were making cornbread to take to a New Year's Day party. Little Elaine got to measure the water but was upset because Sarah Grace wouldn't let her break the egg.

"You'll get shell pieces in the mix!"

Perry was amused but had a little bit of a headache.

Beth preheated the oven like she'd been doing it all her young life and informed her sisters not to get the mix too smooth. "It needs to be lumpy."

Sarah Grace broke the egg and pieces of the shell went into the mix. Elaine declared that using her fingers to pick pieces out was "Disgusting!" The girls stopped bickering and silently picked eggshells out of the mix as soon as Cal stomped into the kitchen.

Ten minutes after Perry shooed his uncle into his office, he ordered his uncle to go home. It wasn't a request. In a low voice, Perry told him to "get back to your own house and I'll deal with you later." Eggshells in cornbread weren't disgusting, but his uncle was. A few minutes after Cal left, Perrry drove off, not saying bye to his daughters or his wife and barely noticing the look on his uncle's face.

Perry parked in front of his sister's house angrier than he'd ever been before. Cal had told him all about what he'd seen through the window. How could that man-whore do this? Make a sex tape with his sister and Will? How the hell did he even talk her into something like this?

It flicked through his mind that Cal might have made it all up. He had no doubt that Reed was capable of dropping his pants in front of a camera, but his sister and Will weren't.

Shit!

He needed to find out what the hell the story was, but he couldn't be calm. Not this time. If it was all bullshit, then he'd make his apologies later, but he'd had it with Janvier Reed. Overall, completely, had it with him.

It was one o'clock in the afternoon, and the son-of-a-bitch was coming out of Amy's townhouse with a bicycle helmet. There was a bike chained to the For-Sale sign on the unit next door. Perry assumed it was Janvier's bike.

He looked a little rumpled. God damn it, he'd spent the night.

Cal might have been right when he said he looked through the back window after the party broke up and saw the three of them kissing and groping each other with a camera set up. His uncle went into some detail about what clothing was coming off, but Perry stopped him. He didn't want to hear it even if Cal wanted to say it.

And now, the birthday boy was blinking in the sunlight. "Hey, Perry." Instead of putting his bike helmet on, he dropped it next to the bike.

Perry crammed his fists into his jacket. He kept his voice even when he spoke, but it was not a suggestion when he said, "Happy Birthday, Reed. How about going back inside?"

Standing in the still-messy living room, he told them Cal's story. "He said he stood right out there, on the back deck. Now how about someone explain it all away for me?"

Janvier and Will looked surprised, but it was Amy who pulled the best defense-is-a-good-offense trick.

"What the fuck do you think you're doing siccing your pet bulldog on me, Perry? What I do in my home is no one's business except these two men, and hell no, I am not putting up with Cal peeking through my windows!"

Of course. Of fucking course. His sister had herself a three-way, and Janvier Reed probably knew exactly how to run one of those.

"At least tell me there wasn't a camera."

Janvier had the nerve to look irritated. "No, of course not. I'm not sure what Cal thought he was doing, but—"

"But you're not denying the three of you—God, that's disgusting. Reed, if I do nothing else, I'm going to give my family an enema and wash you out, do you understand?"

Amy almost turned purple with rage. "No, Perry, you're going to mind your own God-damned business, do you understand? Who said you had a right to have an opinion about anything?"

This wasn't going the way he wanted it to go. Janvier Reed didn't look scared or caught. He had that look on his face, like he could see inside Perry's mind.

Janvier also knew how to speak evenly. "Perry, did you send Cal here?"

On the defensive, Perry found himself shaking his head. "Look, Reed, you plopped yourself down into *my* family..."

Will and Amy both opened their mouths, but Janvier held up his hand.

"Because I think Cal has a dangerous streak in him. You can aim him at me all you want, but not at your sister, Perry. Not at Amy or Will."

Perry forgot how to compose himself. "I didn't—what the hell are you talking about, I didn't aim him—he's her uncle, too!"

Will finally got a word in. "If he took photos last night of anything that would be embarrassing, I will have him arrested. You know that, don't you?"

Amy agreed. "Perry, I'm choosing to believe that you didn't know what Cal was doing, but our idiot uncle won't listen to me. He will listen to you. You're going to have to tell him that he crossed a big line here. If you don't, I will, and I'll do it in a way that makes sure he hears me. Got it?"

God knows what Cal would do if Amy started yelling at him. And she was right. He was the only one Cal would listen to. Janvier Reed, the emotional leech, the professional fucker who had just taken advantage of his little sister, took Perry's arm.

"Come on, I'll walk you out."

He couldn't believe how badly this was going. He yanked his arm away from Reed's touch and almost balled up his fist. Perry wanted to hit him. He hadn't been in a fight since he was a small child, but he wanted to hurt the guy.

And Janvier knew it. They met each other's eyes in a way that should have been aggressive, but the pimp looked at Perry with something like understanding.

Before they walked out, Will said, "Hey, when Amy ends up marrying Janvier instead of me, don't you think he should take her last name, Perry? I mean, Janvier Ravaterra. That's exotic but it works, don't you think?"

Marry? It wasn't the first night Janvier and Amy were together? What the hell was going on? It didn't matter because Perry would never accept Janvier as part of the Ravaterra family.

Never. He turned and walked out of the house with Reed right behind him and Will's laugh stinging his ears.

There was no way he was letting Janvier further into his family. Perry knew just how to do that. Once outside, Janvier called for him to stop, but Perry kept walking towards his car.

"Perry, wait. I need to know that you heard me about Cal."

He turned and looked him in the eye. Janvier still had that soft-eyed thing working, and Perry had never wanted to hurt someone so much in his life.

"Stay the fuck away from my sister and my family, Janvier. Get out of our lives. Get out!"

"That's up to your sister and to Donny, Perry. Not you and not even me. But I need to know that Cal's not going to be a problem for Amy and Will. He's out of control. I need to know that you won't—"

"Cal is her uncle, too. You don't have to worry about him, but you do have to worry about me. Do you get that? Reed, tell me you understand."

His long hair falling in his eyes, the whore nodded. "But understand me, Perry. Cal will do anything to please you. If he hurts Amy or Will or does something to hurt anyone in the Ravaterra family, I will stop him."

"I am the Ravaterra family."

Janvier only nodded slightly at that.

Perry got in his car and drove away. He didn't go to his uncle's. He needed to be a lot calmer first. If he went to see Cal now, he'd do something that would make it worse.

Something had to give. Janvier said he didn't trust Cal. Perry didn't trust him either, but he knew how to control him. He needed to focus on getting Janvier out of his family first, and then he'd deal with Cal.

Getting him out of his family would mean getting him away

from Paige. She wouldn't do it. His wife would not let Janvier Reed go.

Perry went home and without saying a word to his family, he went into his office. Within a few minutes, he found the phone number filed away after the dinner.

"I need to talk to him as soon as possible," he said to the person on the other end. "Tell him it's about Janvier Reed."

"He will see you in the morning. A car will pick you up at JFK at ten." The voice went on to tell him where he should be waiting and hung up.

That call finished, Perry took a minute to stare out his shady, badly placed window before he booked a flight for the morning that would get him to New York in time for the meeting. Perry was determined to get rid of Janvier, but it was going to have a deep impact on his family, and that included his wife. He needed to do it cleanly and worry about the fall-out afterwards.

God damn Janvier! He was like a brother-in-law to Donny, an extra boyfriend to Amy, and a business partner to his wife. How had he done so much in just a few months?

If he got rid of Janvier by himself, his family would be furious with him. His wife would leave him. Hopefully, Perry could throw him back in his own dirty little pool and walk away from him cleanly. With a little help from the billionaire, maybe he could do just that.

He needed to spend the rest of the day figuring out a plan, something to approach the billionaire with that would make a difference.

His wife tapped on his office door and instead of inviting Paige in, Perry went out to the foyer.

"I'm sorry, Honey. I'm a little distracted. Something's come up with work…"

There were boxes stacked up next to the altar and on top of

the old pew. He hadn't seen them when he stormed into the house.

He looked around the foyer again. The pew was stacked with moving boxes. Moving boxes! Perry went from angry to desperate in the space of time it took Paige to add her gardening gloves to one of the boxes.

"Paige, no. Please, no. Honey, listen to me. Oh, God, no."

She closed the box. "I made this decision around Thanksgiving when I found out you had yet another girlfriend. It was Cal that made me decide. He doesn't know about the girlfriend, does he? That's different. But I decided you'd finally found someone you liked too much to sic Cal on them."

It was the second time a loved one accused him of having "sicced" Cal on someone.

"I don't care anything about her. It's over anyway."

"Wow, that's a shame. You should care something about the women that you keep stashing in the small condo, Perry. Has having a mistress become so routine for you? How sad, for both of us."

"Paige, please, don't. Don't. Stop. I have given up my girlfriend. She's still in the condo, but only because she hasn't found another place yet. I told her it was over because I was just going through the motions and you're right. It was ridiculous. I love you. I don't want anyone else besides you."

God, he had known this was coming, but he had no idea how much it would hurt and how surreal it would feel. He sat down on the edge of the antique pew next to a box labeled "Beth's room."

"The girls…."

"They left for the Beans and Greens party." Paige didn't sit. "This isn't about the affair, Perry. In fact, it isn't even about you. I don't want this life anymore."

"Is it because of the charity? I'll give you all my money! I don't even trust Janvier, but I've been as supportive as I can be."

"Umm, well I do trust him and I told you, I made this decision before the charity. One has nothing to do with the other."

Perry stood and pulled out the only concrete anti-Janvier thing he had.

"You don't understand, Paige, about him. Janvier. He's sleeping with Amy and Will. Both of them. At the same time."

Paige looked amused. "That's none of my business but it doesn't surprise me. The 'same time' part does, but there's been chemistry from day one. I just figured she'd leave Will for him. Look, Perry, I don't want to talk about Amy or Janvier."

"Please don't leave me, Paige."

She ran her hand along his jaw. "Perry, we've had a terrible marriage. There's love, but neither of us respect each other. I made an offer on a house in Durham a couple of weeks ago, but I've arranged to do a rent-first thing until the closing. We can talk to the girls tonight, and the movers are coming in the morning. It's all set up."

He shook his head, begging her. "I do respect you, Paige. You've always been too good for me."

"Maybe we need to redefine the word 'respect.' Sweetheart, tomorrow, it would be best if you weren't here. The new house is in a lovely neighborhood, near the golf course. It's a little closer to the girls' schools and we'll share custody, of course. I think the girls knew this was coming, but we can talk to them together as soon as they come home."

"Paige, God, please don't do this. I love you. I love you so God-damned much."

She turned to him, tears in her eyes, and flashing her dimples. "You know what my daydream is, Perry? That we'd break up and you couldn't live without me, so you'd start trying to impress me.

You'd pay attention to me. You'd treat me like a real lover, one that matters. Me, Perry. Just me."

"Yes, I will. I promise."

"Then understand that I'm going to stop being your wife. I don't like that role at all."

42

WITHOUT DETAILS, Janvier told Donny and Nate as evenly and honestly as he could. It wasn't as bad as he thought it would be. Still, it was hard to tell Donny that he'd spent the night with his sister and her fiancée and that their nasty old uncle had spied on them and reported an exaggerated story.

"This was probably a one-time thing. God knows I want something more, but I think maybe it was just last night. Amy, Will, and I haven't discussed much. Except for Cal, I wouldn't be talking about this to anyone, not yet. But Amy told me to talk to you before Perry does."

Neither Donny nor Nate spoke. The silence stretched to three seconds.

"Please, guys. Say something."

They were in Nate's living room with Madeline ensconced again in her dads' bedroom with a Disney movie blaring so she wouldn't hear the conversation. She was starting to love it when they had "discussions."

Nate, still wearing his uniform, wasn't saying much, but he looked upset.

Donny, wearing jeans that looked about an inch short, looked like he was about to be sick again. "This is so perfectly you, Janvier. And now I know what kind of husband Will would make and I assume Amy is at home crying?"

"She's at the hospital. She was on call."

Donny held up his hand in a shut-up gesture. "You are such a wrecking-ball, Janvier. Look, do me a favor and stay away from my sister. How hard could that be? Stay away from her and maybe she can fix her relationship with Will, okay?"

Nate agreed but for different reasons. "Yeah, sure. Amy needs to stay away from Janvier too. Jesus! Janvier got out of a mental hospital about four months ago, and Amy decides it's time to use him for a three-way? Forget it!"

Oh, God. Janvier hadn't seen that coming. "No, no! Nate, it wasn't like that."

His old friend wasn't having it. "No, I'm sure for you it wasn't. What about for them, huh? Donny, you're taking razors out of his house and your sister decides he's well enough to mess with him emotionally? So now what? We put him back on our couch so we can keep an eye on him? Check his pockets for sharp objects?"

Damn it, now Nate and Donny were going to start fighting. He really was a wrecking ball.

"Stop it, Nate. It wasn't like that and frankly, the last thing I want to do is start putting what happened in therapeutic terms. Donny, I care for Amy. I care for her." He almost said "Amy and Will," but that wouldn't help a thing.

But it would be true, and that was important when dealing with Donny.

"I'm trying to be honest here. I wish I could say that I will leave Amy and Will alone, but I'm half in love and I don't think

I'm in control of this. I suspect Amy is. And Nate, I don't know if it will go any further. If it doesn't, I'm going to hurt like hell. Will it help if I promise you that I will pick up the phone if I get in trouble? I will."

Nate's dark eyes looked at him. "If you even have the slightest urge to hurt yourself, you call. You call me first."

Donny was still upset. Janvier didn't know how to get around that, but he tried to lighten it up a little.

"There is one more thing I want from you, Donny. Can I have your permission to deal with your uncle? Because I don't trust him around Amy or Will."

"Did Perry send him?" Donny asked.

"No, I don't think so, although Cal obviously thought it was okay to spy on Amy. I keep telling myself to let Perry handle Cal, but I need to have some control here. I need Cal to understand a few things, but first I want you to say that it's okay."

Donny shrugged. "Sure. Perry's not going to handle it. He's going to tell Cal he was a bad old man and that will be that. My dad is going to yell—shit! I don't care about my uncle. Stop distracting me, Janvier. I don't care if you deal with Cal. I have to deal with you. I have to figure out a way to tell you that a threesome with my sister is *not* okay, and whatever Will is to you is *not* okay, and all of this is *not* okay."

Nate put his arm around Janvier's shoulder, hugged him, and said, "But it'll *be* okay."

Donny only had time to look at him incredulously before Madeline yelled from the other room that she went poop in their bathroom and needed her daddy. She was obviously on the other side of the door, not still in the bathroom.

Donny looked at the bedroom door and back at Janvier. Almost gently, Donny said "I figure you are going to do something about Cal, but make sure you don't take it too far.

Nate would be a bitch to live with if you go on trial. And stay away from my sister."

Nate said, "Make sure you tell me exactly when you go too far with Cal, so I can alibi you. There won't be a trial."

Janvier looked Donny in the eye. "As far as Amy goes, I'll stay away from her if that's what she wants. But if she wants me there, then I will be with her."

Madeline yelled from the bedroom. "Daddy, I need you to help me. Now!"

Donny put his hand over his face. He was crying. No. He was laughing. Donny wiped his eyes.

"God, I have a fucked-up family. I thought Amy was the normal one. Turns out it's me. I'm going to go clean up whatever needs cleaning and then watch cartoons with Madeline. I suggest you two go to the gym and lift weights until one of you pops. Janvier, leave my sister alone."

"Donny?"

He stopped at the bedroom doorway.

"I'm probably not going to do that."

Donny kind of nodded. "I know." He closed the bedroom door behind him.

Janvier and Nate looked at each other. He honestly had no idea what to do next.

Nate crossed his arms and tried to frown. "So, do you want to talk about it?"

"No. Do you?"

"Not really. Both of them, huh?"

"Yeah."

"Okay. You want to get out of here?"

Janvier nodded. Oh God yes. He wanted to go to the gym and just workout. He wanted to not feel anything or think about anything. He wanted to use up the rest of the day so it would get to tomorrow and wouldn't be so bad. "You gotta change out of your uniform?"

Nate pulled off his uniform top and put his coat on over his undershirt. "I'm not going to go change. I'm not going in that bedroom for anything. He's pissed off."

"Yeah. Sorry."

Nate inched towards the door. "Donny telling us to go to the gym is sort of like getting out of a math test and being told to go to football practice, isn't it?"

They bolted. As they ran down the stairs, Janvier said, "Listen there's something else you should know about. The charity and all, I've arranged…"

He told Nate about the billionaire and the arrangement on the way to the gym. And he made the same promise that he'd made to his therapist and to Paige. If he couldn't handle it, he'd quit, no matter what.

At least Nate believed that was true. Maybe.

43

PERRY TRIED to sleep in the guest room. The talk with the girls was every bit as painful as he'd thought it would be. He had expected tears and accusations. He hadn't expected calm. The girls had questions about how their day-to-day lives were going to change but seemed to take for granted that both their parents still loved them and would be in their lives. When they found out that they wouldn't have to change schools and that their friends could still come to the new house, the relief was obvious. Only sensitive Beth, his middle child and his deep thinker of thoughts, asked whether they were getting a divorce. To his great relief, Paige answered, "No. We haven't even talked about that. We're going to live separately and see how that goes."

The next morning, he got up before dawn and drove to the airport. Paige was up, and it was awkward and obvious that she wanted him out of the house before the moving van came. She walked him to the door. "Have a good trip, Perry."

Paige kissed him. It was a simple pressing of the lips together, but it was a kiss.

On the flight to New York, Perry thought of all the shit that was happening because of Janvier. He was doing what his dad called "poking the bruise to see if it still hurts."

Only one day had passed since the pimp's three-way with Amy and Will. It still disgusted him, but he was surprised he hadn't seen it coming. She'd drooled over that man since Thanksgiving. Perry had just missed the part where Amy wanted both Will and Janvier.

Below the window, clouds began obscuring the landscape, and Perry admitted to himself that Amy wasn't terribly worried about what he thought. She was furious with him because she believed he'd sicced Cal on her.

He hadn't. In fact, it never occurred to him that Cal might trip Amy up as casually as he would a stranger. Perry had had a brief, angry phone call with his uncle the night before.

His uncle sputtered into the phone. "I fucking just wanted you to know what was going on with Frenchie and your sister. Since when do you care about who I spy on? So what if she feels violated? I bet Frenchie violated the hell out of her and she loved it!"

Uncle Cal was a nasty old man who spoke about Amy like she was nothing more than some slut, and that infuriated Perry. And, he had to admit, it scared him.

He'd ended up telling Cal to do nothing, nothing at all. "I have a lot on my hands the next couple of days and I'll deal with you when I get back. Do nothing, Cal. Do some landscaping around that bench in your front yard. That's it. Nothing else. Do you understand?"

He'd implied that he'd be gone for several days, but the trip to New York was a one-day deal. He'd be home by late afternoon or early evening. Rather than go to his quiet, empty house, he'd go to Cal's and deflect all his anger on his unredeemable uncle. Shit. In the meantime, he needed to stop thinking about Amy and Cal and just concentrate on Janvier.

It didn't help that on the way to the airport Donny called and told him that Julie had come over to the condo.

"We came home and she was sitting on the steps to our condo. She wanted you to know that she really loves you. I assured her that I'd pass the message on, but Perry, I had Madeline with me and I didn't like having to explain this to her."

"I'm sorry Julie bothered you and I'll take care of it." He'd get rid of Julie by throwing money at her, but he needed to take care of the billionaire first. He wasn't even sure what he was going to say to the old man.

Between the landing and the chauffeured car, Perry tried to get some of his thoughts in order. He couldn't just walk into the billionaire's home and start spouting that he was pissed off at Janvier and he wanted the old man to do something about it.

It was just above freezing in New York, which was good. The drizzle seemed to slow down, which was also good. Normally, Perry found New York both exciting and claustrophobic.

A middle-aged Japanese man opened the door for him. There was no doubt in Perry's mind that he was a bodyguard. He remembered him from Angelica's. In the restaurant, the man had sat at a small table directly behind the billionaire but eaten nothing.

The bodyguard gave a short bow and motioned him inside.

The billionaire's penthouse was in an old princess of a building. There were architectural details that should have caught Perry's eye, but all he could think of was the moving van that was in his driveway right at that moment and how his whole life was being loaded into boxes marked with his daughters' names. Elaine's toys. Sarah Grace's bedroom. Beth's room-fragile, handle with care. The children packed the stuff they wanted during the week, and left everything else. After all, they still lived at Dad's house, too.

When the elevator stopped on the top floor, the bodyguard used a keycard to open the doors and tapped in a passcode. They stepped into a private entry that looked like a museum. The bodyguard stood next to floor-to-ceiling glass frames that covered the wall and contained pieces of broken pottery and primitive clay statues. There were several carved pieces of jade and ivory as well. Small signs in Japanese identified each piece. Perry didn't need an interpreter to understand that he was looking at some seriously old relics.

The assistant stood to one side, letting Perry take in the artifacts. "I would be happy to translate, Mr. Ravaterra."

"This one, if you wouldn't mind." Perry pointed to a small, worn statue of a man. The primitive sculpture probably once had distinct features. Now its mouth was open in a scream, and its eyes looked gouged out.

"It is from the later part of the period that is roughly translated as 'Cord Marked.' This is a statue of a man, of course. It is about two thousand years old." The assistant pointed to a plain pot. "This is the oldest piece here. It is from ten thousand years B.C. and the markings around the edge were made from pressing a cord into the wet clay."

Perry looked back at the screaming statue with the gouged-out eyes. The figurine shouldn't be in a foyer. All the items should be in a museum where groups of children would look with disinterest until one of them, like his daughter Beth, would look at it and try to contemplate the weight of thousands of years.

"Would you like to go in now, Mr. Ravaterra?"

"Why does he keep these things in the foyer?"

Although he didn't answer the question, the man had the slightest flicker of expression. "This way please, Mr. Ravaterra."

He followed the bodyguard into the neutrally decorated living room that lacked charm or personality. The sterile cleanliness, the slate floors, and black marble coffee table gave a clean, hard look to the room. Even the cream upholstery looked impenetrable. Three pieces of ancient-looking black slabs hung on the wall, depicting hunting scenes. If they were art, they failed to bring any softness to the space. If they were artifacts, the beveled cut-lines around the edges were obscene.

Perry was relieved of his coat and informed that the billionaire would be with him shortly. As he walked over to the double glass doors to look at the rooftop patio, a female servant in a black silk tunic and matching pants placed a tea tray on the table.

A rooftop pool occupied much of the patio. He couldn't imagine how much they had to mutilate the substructure of the old building to add the pool to the rooftop. Despite the cold, Perry opened the door and walked out. Even though the forecast didn't call for more snow, the gray-bellied sky felt like it was only a few feet above his head.

Lamps turned on around the patio, doing nothing to improve the morning light. He walked to the edge of the empty pool, near a metal ladder. The deepest end was only about seven feet deep and the whole thing was slightly more than thirty feet long, but it was showing its age. Several cracks marred the tile in the pool. They needed to repair or remove it, and Perry hoped it was the latter. The thing was an eyesore on the old building.

The billionaire stood inside, watching him. For a moment, Perry returned his stare. He could see his own reflection superimposed on the glass. With reluctance, he went back inside and formally greeted the man.

The billionaire nodded towards the tea set. "Please join me. Or, if you wish, I will have the staff prepare a brunch for you."

The pool loomed behind him. In his head, Perry saw the structural supports as blue prints. It took serious reconstruction to hold water high on top of an old building. "No thank you. Just coffee would be fine."

Perry felt his hands shaking and ordered them to stop. "First, let me thank you for agreeing to see me on such short notice."

The old man waved his hand as if it was nothing. "I wouldn't have if you said you needed to discuss work. Saying you needed to discuss my Jan gets you through immediately. So please tell me you didn't use him as a ruse to show me some business deal."

Perry bristled at the idea he'd use Janvier to further his own career. He did not want to think about the fact that he also bristled at the way the billionaire called Janvier "his Jan." He met the man's eye. "I haven't used him as a business ruse. However, you've been in Raleigh, and by now you've purchased the land adjacent to his buildings. You invited me to dinner to discuss your plans for the lots. It's a sideways approach to Janvier. I believe you want him back in your life and I'm guessing that isn't okay with him."

"We've reached an agreement."

"Excuse me?" Was Janvier with his sister while fucking that old man? "What agreement?"

The billionaire looked amused. "As much as I want to know why you are feeling so defensive, Ravaterra, I have a feeling Jan wouldn't appreciate me toying with you. I've reached a simple agreement that will allow me to chat with him occasionally. Only chat. Your wife was very clear about the parameters of the agreement. It fills my needs and it gives your wife's charity a financial boost that I don't believe she could find anywhere else." The old man could have left it at that, but he didn't. "I believe that makes Jan indispensable to her."

"Excuse me." Perry got up and walked back over to the glass doors overlooking the patio. Paige knew about the weird arrangement. She really had cut Perry out of her life.

Behind him, the billionaire told him that he had, indeed, purchased the land.

"But I've tabled the idea of building. I'll give the land to him, or to the little charity he set up with your wife. So tell me, Ravaterra, what do you want from me?"

Staring at the ruined patio, Perry asked something that felt important, but he didn't know why. "Did he make this arrangement? Or did you?"

"We made it through your wife. She is an admirable woman, firm in her negotiations, and firm about what is acceptable behavior on my part. It's been a long time since a woman took an upper hand with me. I rather enjoyed it. Oh, don't look like that, Ravaterra. Your wife is extremely professional, and I believe if I so much as patted Jan on the knee, she'd dissolve the agreement."

The billionaire's reflection was not smiling anymore, but he still looked amused. "If I wasn't mostly retired, I'd think about hiring her myself. But of course, she's following a dream, isn't she? Since I am retired, I have little to do but spend my money, and this is far more fun than politics or buying my young wife some trinkets. Did you know that Jan bought the ring that we used for a wedding band? He gave it to me as a Christmas present in this room, seven years ago."

Perry turned towards the billionaire but backed up almost to the patio glass. "I'm glad to hear that Paige has worked something out with you, but I want Janvier out of my family's life. I think you can help me with that."

"Your family? Yes, I imagine it was difficult when he first showed up. You must have worried about having him around. You have a daughter who is only eighteen, don't you?"

Perry tried to keep his voice level, but there was a definite tremble. "I don't want you to mention one of my daughters again."

The old man nodded. "I have no interest in your family. What has my Jan done to bring you all the way to New York?"

"Nothing. I just want him gone."

"And how would I do that, Mr. Ravaterra? Kidnap Jan? Keep him prisoner in this building? I don't think he'd last long under those conditions." Surprisingly, the billionaire's voice also had a slight tremor. "He has a troubling instinct that I believe he inherited from his mother."

Perry said the only thing he'd thought up on the ride over. "You are a profoundly wealthy man. You could set things up so he is committed...an involuntary commitment. A danger to himself. I have no doubt that you could get him back here and out of North Carolina."

"Perhaps you think I want Jan to hate me, more than he already does. I promise you, I do not. However, I don't care how he feels about you. So tell me, what is driving this emergency meeting? What compelled you to get on a plane and make a day trip to New York? Come on, Ravaterra. What has my Jan done now?"

Perry took one more step back. His jacket brushed against the glass doors. "Your Jan is wading in some serious trouble. He's decided that he's going to have a romantic entanglement that involves someone in my family. This is going to implode, to say the least. He's going to keep messing up until his precious Nate doesn't want anything to do with him. I promise when Nate's father finds out that Janvier's been screwing another man, he'll scrape him off as well. What do you suppose 'your Jan' will do then? How fast will his 'troubling instinct' resurface?"

The older man gave a heavy, heart-felt sigh. He spoke up so Perry could hear him from across the room. "I admit I don't like the idea that he's formed a romantic entanglement, but that is simple jealousy on my part." He seemed to stare past Perry at the patio. "It's funny how Jan gets into families, isn't it? I believe the

Rijos family still considers him as one of their own, despite the way he ran away from them. I certainly do, despite the way he ran away from me. Maybe you'll get lucky. Maybe he'll run away from you, too."

Perry felt the cold of the patio glass brush against his back. "I doubt he considers himself part of your family."

The old man looked both fierce and fragile. "He's mine. He will always be mine. If you don't believe me, ask your wife. Or ask mine. I think this meeting is over, Ravaterra. And, by the way, if Jan hurts himself in any way because of you or any member of your family, you will discover just how much he means to me. It is in both our interests if the Ravaterras simply accept him into the family."

That old man had no concept of family. Perry was sure of that. He walked stiffly from the room but had to stand in the foyer and wait for the God-damned elevator. Enclosed in the glass wall, the little statue of a man looked back at him. Even with the artifact's antiquity, he could see the marks where the ropes had been pressed into the clay. Perry had an urge to smash the glass to set the ancient statue free.

The elevator doors opened and the bodyguard simply said, "It's time to go."

44

CAL SAT IN HIS CAR, glowering. He'd followed Frenchie to the condos about an hour earlier and watched as the guy ran up the stone steps and tried the door handle of the Toothpick's place. The fucker let himself in.

The evening before, Perry had chewed Cal out. It wasn't his fault that following Frenchie led to Amy and her swings-both-ways boyfriend. Through the phone, his nephew had yelled at him. Cal still felt stung over the dressing down, but his nephew wasn't mad at him. He was just pissed off about the three-way and took it out on his good ol' uncle.

Anyway, he was doing Perry a huge favor by spying on the guy. The other night, he couldn't believe it when he looked through the windows and saw the twin and her husband kissing on Frenchie. No clothes came off then, but it was obvious what was about to happen when they went upstairs. Cal embellished a little when he told Perry, adding a video camera and removing clothing, but that was just to get Perry to where he needed to be.

And what had Perry done? Bit his fucking head off for spying on his innocent little sister!

Cal was determined to stay on Frenchie until he had something else to report. He parked in his usual spot, which was all the way down in the parking lot and halfway behind a dumpster. He could see not only the front of the stone-step building where the toothpick lived, but also Perry's little smaller condo that overlooked the parking lot. Perry shouldn't have rented the unit to that old professor; he should have kept it for the next whore. But no. Perry was going soft. There was a light on in the window of the small condo. The professor-tenant was home. Whoop-da-do.

45

DRIVING FROM THE AIRPORT, Perry didn't want to go home, not yet. The movers might still be there, and he didn't want to actually see Paige leave him. He was exhausted and a little ashamed of himself for going to New York. Why did he think the billionaire would help him?

He didn't want to go to Cal's either. Frankly, Perry was just too tired to deal with him. He'd deal with Julie first, then maybe he'd be up to taking on Cal.

Perry stood in the small condo's messy living room and kept it short and sweet. "My brother tells me you've been lurking in front of his place. I told you not to contact him and that includes sitting on the steps to his home."

She simpered, still trying seduction. God, she disgusted him. The apartment stank of garbage, probably unemptied since before she went on her trip to her parents. She was ridiculous, plucking at his shirt and brushing her breasts against his arm.

Gently, he pushed her away from him. "Julie, it's over. I will give you to the end of the month, and I still intend to help you with that first and last month on a new place, but you have to get out."

She would have kept him there for an hour, alternating between anger and pouting, but he wasn't up to it. He couldn't be nice, not tonight. He was tired and all he wanted to do was see Paige.

"Get your shit together, Julie. We were done before you went to my brother's, but now I'm seriously pissed off. Do you understand?"

She rubbed against him. "Perry, I don't want your money. I want you."

He stepped away from her. "You've been a pretty good whore and you've certainly earned all the money you didn't want. Good-bye, Julie." He almost added, "clean this place up," but hiring a housekeeping service would be less trouble. She looked shocked and he felt a little shocked himself, but he left the apartment without looking back.

Perry got in his car and drove to Paige's address in Durham. Her new house was nice with pale bricks and arched windows. The multi-level roof was visually appealing, even if he could see a corner that would eventually become a drainage problem. He'd hire someone to fix it before it became a problem. The garage door was open. He could see empty boxes piled up, including several that looked like they had contained new china or lamps.

His breath caught. Of course, she'd bought new furniture. She wouldn't leave him with an empty house. His old house still had all the old furniture and dishes.

With a massive exhale, Perry let it sink in. Paige had left him. She bought this house and bought new things to put in her house.

His youngest daughter came running out of the house yelling, "Daddy!"

He got out of the car, discreetly wiping his eyes. "Hey, sugar-girl. You shouldn't be outside in your ballet slippers. How do you like your new room?"

"Daddy, I'm so sad about this. Do you and Mommy have to be divorced?"

"Mommy and I have lots to talk about, but I think it's all going to be okay." He followed her into the house. Under the moving-day mess, the house was nice.

His eight-year-old looked at him with a rather adult expression on her face. "Are you and Mommy getting a divorce or not? Because my friend says that's what a separation is."

"Nope. They're different. This is only a separation, not a divorce. So, do you like your new room?"

"Yeah, kind of, but it's weird. I'm glad my real bed is still at your house."

Your house. God. "Where's Mom?"

"In the back yard. She had to hose dog poop off the deck. Mom said he had nervous diarrhea."

"Oh, maybe I'd better go help."

Paige didn't look unhappy to see him. Messy in jeans and an old sweatshirt, she looked like she was okay that he was there. She was cleaning the deck where the old dog hadn't made it to the yard. Her expression was less than pleased.

Perry offered to help, but she said she was almost finished. He resisted the urge to tell her to disconnect the hose after she'd finished. It was likely to get below freezing that night. He'd check the hose before he left, and he was sure she was going to make him leave at some point.

The dog was overjoyed to see him. Perry gave ear, throat, and belly rubs before Paige, while disconnecting the hose, told Sarah Grace to give him a tour. The house was about ten years old and in a neighborhood with several quiet cul-de-sacs. Paige's house had a variation of a layout that was standard for expensive houses. His father's had almost the same design, which involved large rooms with plenty of light. He didn't disapprove.

Sarah Grace kept clinging to his arm as she led him around the house. The tour ended upstairs with his daughter showing him the bedrooms.

"This one is Mom's. I don't know if I should show you, so just take a quick peek." She opened and closed the door on a room that looked like a bedroom-in-progress.

Perry winked at his daughter. "Nice. I think you hit the end of my nose with the door."

Paige yelled upstairs, asking if he had cash for a tip because she'd ordered pizza and forgot to put the tip on her card.

He'd never heard Paige yell from one end of a house to another. He sat down on the top step, tears in his eyes and a lump in his throat, and handed Sarah Grace his wallet. "Go give this to your mother."

Sarah Grace threw his wallet down the stairs to the empty foyer. "Here!" His daughter sat down next to him and put her arms around him. "Poor Daddy. God, I feel so bad for you."

"Don't, baby. I deserve this. And your mother is trying hard not to make it horrible for me, so how about you go get my wallet, go hand her the money, and be nice to her because this is all my fault."

"Daddy, do you have a girlfriend or something? Or does Mom? I mean, like Mr. Reed or something?"

"No. No, your mother is not the type to have affairs. I was. I don't have a girlfriend anymore, but to be honest, I've had several. This is all completely and totally my fault. I'm hoping that your mother will start dating me and that maybe we can work our way back to each other because I'm still deeply in love with her. Please, go get my wallet and be nice to your mother, Sarah Grace."

She hugged his arm. "Men *suck!*"

The doorbell rang.

Sarah Grace ran down the stairs and picked up the wallet before her mother got to the door. Paige let her tip the pizza man while she looked up the stairs. His wife gave him the sweetest of smiles.

"I got you some of Nate's stinky beer. I know you like it. Come on downstairs, Perry."

He did.

46

CAL NEEDED glasses to read anything up close, but there was nothing wrong with his distance vision. Earlier, he'd watched his nephew leave the building where the small condo was. He also watched Honey Butt staring out the living room window, wiping her eyes.

Perry had lied to him. For the next hour, he sat in the car and thought about it. Perry lied about banging Honey Butt. He lied about the old professor renting the condo. Perry had probably lied to him about other things, but nothing, nothing was as bad as this.

The streetlights flickered on in the parking lot. Cal didn't know what time it was, but the days were short on January second. Only a few cars still came and went out of the parking lot. Lights were on in most of the units, including the stone-step condo across the way. He'd watched Donny and his little family come home and go into the big condo, one building over. The lights were already on there because Frenchie was still inside. Frenchie didn't matter anymore. Nothing mattered anymore.

Perry had lied to him.

Cal barely realized he'd reached a decision when he finally got out of the car. No one saw him go up the stairs. Television noise came from a few apartments, but it was mostly quiet. How long had that little whore been in that unit? Why didn't Perry tell him? When Cal was checking Julie out, had she seen him? Maybe she was scared of him and didn't want Perry to tell him.

If Honey Butt had talked Perry into lying to him, then she was right to be afraid.

Or maybe the whole thing was recent. Maybe Perry hadn't had time to tell him and then the threesome thing happened and maybe he just hadn't told him yet.

Maybe anything. Maybe Perry fucking lied to his good ol' uncle.

On the second floor, one condo shared a wall with Perry's unit and that one had loud music playing. Last time he looked, a couple of rich-kid students lived there. The two units across the hall might as well have been down the street. The hallway was at least ten feet across, and the units didn't share any interior walls.

Smoothing his hair down, he listened at the door for a moment. He heard nothing.

Cal dug the key out of his pocket and opened the door quietly, but it caught on the security chain. He stood there, holding the door open as far as it would go but standing out of sight.

"Hello?" Honey Butt's tiny little voice reached him through the open crack.

The chain broke free as soon as he hit the door with his shoulder. It knocked into her, and she stumbled back, holding her face and trying to scream, but she only produced this little, thin "eee" sound.

He was on her.

He grabbed her, one hand on the back of her head and one

over her mouth as he used his foot to close the door. It only took a few seconds to get her on the couch and climb on her.

Pressing down, he watched her struggle. He thought that maybe he wasn't going to kill her because she could tell him if there was some reason Perry had lied, but he needed to make her understand that he was in charge.

Cal straddled her, his hand over her mouth, and noticed how the door must have hit the side of her nose. It didn't feel broken, but one of her eyes had a line across it and was swelling up.

"Be still."

She kept thrashing.

"I said, be still." He removed his hand from her mouth so she could breathe. The little whore was going to answer his questions, and he had a lot of them.

"I fucking told you to be still. Are you hearing me, Girlie?" He put his hands on her neck, nice and easy, but squeezed enough for her to get the message.

Her mouth open, she gulped air and didn't answer him, but she was still. Very still.

He was rock hard. It didn't even bother him that she had snot under her nose.

"Now very quietly, answer me. How long have you been with Perry?" He gave her neck another small squeeze while he shifted a little more weight on her. "Pay attention, Honey Butt. What do you do for him? Suck him? Fuck him?"

"I…yes…both. Please…"

"And how long has it been going on?"

"I don't know, like a couple of months, maybe a little more? That's all. Please, he told me to leave. I didn't do anything. I didn't mean to go to his brother's place. Please…"

So not only had Perry lied to him, everyone else knew about Honey Butt, too. Toothpick must have been laughing at Cal. They all knew.

The important thing was to send a message to Perry. He let go of her neck. The first blow landed on the side of her temple. The second one made her eyes roll back. She went limp under him.

She wasn't dead, not yet anyway. He grabbed a dirty wad of paper towels off the coffee table. They had some tomato food crap on it, but he shoved the towels in her mouth. Before he even got off her, she started to come around. She'd only been out a few seconds, so he hadn't hurt her that badly. She tried to gag out the paper towels. He didn't let her.

But he didn't have any choice at this point, did he? Shit, if she lived, all beaten up, Perry would get the message big time. Besides, the girl would probably have him arrested and with his record, he'd do time.

Cal wasn't doing time for anyone, especially not some whore. No, Perry would get the message if the girl went missing. He'd see the apartment, the little splatter of blood on the couch, but there was no way Perry would call the cops. Honey Butt would just disappear and his nephew would understand that he couldn't mess with Cal. Ever.

The dazed girl struggled to push him off her. God, he was so pissed off that he just started beating her. She screamed into the mess in her mouth, almost loudly enough to be a problem. He hit her in the collarbone hard enough that he heard it crack.

"Be fucking still, you disgusting little whore!"

She was nothing, a tiny thing, lying still now. She stared up at him with the one eye that wasn't swollen shut.

He had to think, damn it!

Perry had just been there.

If he killed her in the apartment, especially if Perry's stuff was inside her, they would think his nephew did it. Cal wouldn't frame Perry, even if Perry had betrayed him. Cal wouldn't do that. He also couldn't carry her out of there by himself. She was little, but he wasn't sure he was up to carrying a dead body. Cal had to get the whore out of the apartment first and kill her where he intended to hide her body.

"Get up. Come on, get up."

She was awake. He yanked her to her feet. Blood was all over her face and some of it dripped on the carpet. That was no good. He only wanted a little blood, just for Perry's sake. Too much, and Perry would think he'd hurt the girl instead of just giving her a little punishment.

Cal knew a place in the woods, out by where Frenchie lived. He could leave her there. This time of year, she wouldn't even stink too much. It would be months before it was warm enough to make that smell. By then the foxes and shit would have been at her. It'd be hard to prove anything. And, if someone found her body, he could call the cops and leave an anonymous message that Mr. Janvier Reed was seen riding his bike through those woods at night.

She plucked at the paper towel mess in her mouth. Cal swatted her hand away.

He got her into her coat and told her not to zip it up. If she was trying to hold her coat closed, she'd be less likely do anything stupid once they got into the parking lot. For extra measure, he tore her blouse open. She wasn't wearing a bra.

"You hold that coat closed, got it?"

There was a green scarf in the closet, one of those that looked like a long piece of regular fabric. He had an idea and snatched it out of the closet.

Honey Butt's face was a mess. One eye was swollen shut, already purple where the door had hit her. The other one had blood on the eyelid crusting in her lashes. The little bitch had the nerve to look at him and, through her gag, mumble a clear "Why?"

Earlier, she'd said that Perry told her to leave.

"You went to his brother's place, didn't you?"

She nodded.

"Perry told me to come over and teach you a lesson. He even told me I could fuck you to remind you that you're just a whore, but I don't do seconds."

She started to cry. Honey Butt looked so helpless that he felt his groin tighten up again.

"Okay, the worst is over now. We just need to go see Perry. He needs to know that you've learned your lesson, that's all. You can spit those towels out in a minute, that's a good girl. But you damned well better keep quiet, you understand? I have to make sure you don't pull something on the way to the car, you know?"

She looked up at him with her one open eye, the red wad of paper hanging out of her mouth and her coat gaping open. It was obvious that she was having a hard time breathing through her nose. With his fingertips, he pulled the paper towels out and then immediately wrapped the scarf around her mouth and nose, obscuring most of her face and effectively gagging her. One of the scarf ends came back around her neck. He made a loose knot at her neck and pulled the hood of her coat up over her head. It was hard to see any of her face.

"Now we're going to walk, real nice, out of here. You're going to walk with one hand holding your coat closed and one hand looped through my arm, like this. You pull anything, and I'm going to jerk the end of this pretty green scarf. The way that knot is fixed, it should break your neck. Be bad, and you're dead. Got it?"

One glittering eye peeked out from beneath the hood.

Honey Butt linked her arm through his and held her coat closed. She behaved in the empty hallway while he locked the door. He realized she was only wearing socks as they went down the stairs. If someone saw that, they'd notice, but there was no one around. The only thing he heard was muffled television noise.

However, as soon as they stepped out of the entrance she tore loose, the scarf tearing out of his hand. The whore did a slightly muffled scream and ran towards the other parking lot. Cal's fingertips brushed against her flapping coat, but she ran fast. In the parking lot lights, he could see her hunker down and plow through the landscaping, heading straight for the other building.

He couldn't catch her.

Damn it, he ran for his car, already thinking that he hadn't told her who he was. He jammed his key into the ignition. All Perry would have to do is deny he knew anything about it. That was true, and maybe Perry was somewhere where he could be alibied.

He drove off, looking back in time to see her scrambling up the stone steps to the big condo where Toothpick lived.

JANVIER THOUGHT Donny was still in the kitchen. He jumped and almost dropped the scissors when Donny snapped, "Janvier, stop it! You're going to give her a foot fetish."

Madeline, wearing footy pajamas and with her hair still a little wet from a washing, tried to convince her daddy that Barbie absolutely needed a blue dress with little clouds on it.

"Uncle bought special socks just for me and Barbie!"

Donny was less than amused. "Just for Barbie and me, not me and Barbie. And Honey, Uncle Janvier isn't allowed to play with sharp implements." He held out his hand. "Scissors." Janvier heard Nate laugh from the direction of the kitchen as he put the blunt safety scissors into Donny's hand—handle first, of course.

The cloud socks would come back again. He put the halfway cut sock into his pocket and winked at the little girl. "It's bedtime anyway. Sweet dreams, Madeline."

His stomach rolled a little bit as Madeline ran to get a kiss from Nate. God, he hoped he hadn't caught the stomach bug. Donny waggled the safety scissors at him.

"I think I'll go home now Donny, before you get inventive with those safety scissors."

"Inventive? I was thinking of giving you a haircut."

Madeline came back and took Donny's hand. Her footy pajamas made wispy noises on the wooden floor.

Before they disappeared into Madeline's room, she blew Janvier a kiss, and her daddy discreetly waved goodbye, perhaps just using one finger. Janvier thought Donny wasn't finished being mad at him about his sister and Will, but he would be eventually. He was a forgiving soul.

He went into the kitchen to say goodnight to Nate, who was finishing up the dishes.

"I'm going to hit the road, Nate."

"Can Donny hear us?"

"No. He's putting her to bed."

"Have you heard from your partners in family drama?"

"Yeah. Amy called last night, and talking to her was so good, it hurt. That's kind of why I want to go home. I'm hoping she'll call again. I don't want to talk to her around Donny."

"You can't call her yourself?"

"Probably, but my instinct is to let her decide when. She did ask me out, though. This coming weekend. She and Will want to have dinner with me."

Nate rinsed the soap suds out of the sink and off his hands. "Sounds complicated. Have you talked to Will?"

"Yeah. Today. It was good. Really good."

"You're a mess, my friend. Do not let those two get you all mixed up, okay? That's all I'm going to say on the matter. Just don't let your head get messed up."

"Speaking of which, I also talked to your dad. I didn't want to say anything in front of Madeline, but your Dad's trip to Mexico went well and he wants me to join him for dinner on

Wednesday. He said that if you and Donny would like to come as well, it would be okay with him."

Nate didn't answer. He simply dried his hands. After a long moment, he said "Maybe. I'll talk to Donny."

"Okay. Goodnight, Nate. Gym tomorrow evening, right?"

"Right."

Nate went back to finishing the dishes, and Janvier put on his coat. He opened the front door and a bleeding child-sized person fell into his arms. He yelled, "Nate! God, Nate!"

She wasn't a child. Her coat fell open and showed a woman's body. She clawed at the scarf around her neck.

Janvier got her inside the door as he bellowed, "NATE!"

Swollen lips slurred the woman's words. Her face was swollen and purple. Even her neck….

Nate was there, speaking in calm, soothing tones. He had his phone and was starting to examine her. He spoke into the phone using the same calm tones and spoke to someone over Janvier's shoulder. "Get my kit. Janvier, get Madeline out of here."

Oh God. Both Donny and Madeline were back in the room, but Donny was trying to shove her behind him. Janvier ran over to the hall and picked her up. He took the little girl back to her bedroom, ignoring the questions that spilled out of her. She wiggled, trying to get away from him.

"I want to go see what happened to that person. Where's my Daddy? Is Nate helping her?"

"Some lady is hurt, Madeline. We should let Nate take care of her, okay? We should stay back here so we don't get in the way. Okay?"

Her eyes huge, she nodded.

He sat on her bed, holding her like she was a baby. "Uh, read a story. Maybe we can read a story."

Donny opened the door and stuck his head in. "Oh, good, Madeline. Can you be a big girl and stay on the bed for a minute while I talk to Janvier out here in the hallway? Okay, sweetheart. That's my big girl."

He pulled Janvier down the hallway until they were in front of the window overlooking the lake.

"That's Perry's girlfriend. Her name's Julie Cooper. She said that an older man showed up saying Perry sent him to beat her because she sat on my front steps."

"Cal."

Donny continued, in a calmly-panicked way. "From the description, I'd say it was Cal, but there is no way Perry told him to do this. No way!"

"No, I'm sure he didn't. How bad is she?"

"I don't know. She isn't going to die, but she's badly hurt. She keeps saying Cal is going to kill her. The police will be here in a minute, but before they get here, Janvier, can you go find Perry? Paige moved to Durham today. He might be over there."

Janvier felt in control as he looked into Donny's eyes. "I'm going to fight like hell for this family, with or without your permission. Do you understand that?"

Donny held his gaze. "Yes. The Ravaterras are your family, too. Help Perry. Help us."

Janvier skirted Nate and the beaten woman and ran down the stone steps. He was already in his car when he heard the first sirens coming. For once, he backed out smoothly and put the car in drive, turning out of the parking lot just before a police car turned in.

He'd taken Cal home after the flat tire incident, and he knew the man lived near the strip mall. He managed to tell the GPS where to go without stopping the car.

Janvier wasn't sure Cal would go home, but where else would he go? Dr. Ravaterra maybe, but probably not. His brother would want an explanation, and he didn't think Cal would want to give him one. If Cal wasn't at home, Janvier would try Perry's house in Raleigh. If Cal was at his house, what the hell was Janvier going to do? Convince the old ass to turn himself in? Give him money to disappear? Did he trust Cal to stay gone? Hell, no. Sweating, and barely doing the speed limit, Janvier drove as fast as he could.

He hadn't been sure of the house number, but he got it right. Janvier could see Cal's car and the dark shape of the magnolia tree in the front yard. He pulled in to the narrow driveway in a way that blocked Cal's parked car.

Lights were on inside the house. Janvier didn't knock or ring the bell. He walked straight into a small living room. Cal was coming down the hallway with a suitcase.

Almost casually, Janvier said, "There's nowhere to go, and no one who wants you."

Cal startled when he saw Janvier but recovered quickly. "Get the fuck out of my house, Frenchie. You got no business with me."

"Oh, I doubt it is your house, Cal. Who owns it? Your brother or Perry? Where are you planning to run?"

Cal flung the suitcase hard enough to bang it against the narrow hallway wall. "You get out." Spittle flew from his mouth. "You get out."

Janvier held up his hands, palms out. "Calm down, Cal. You've messed up, but we can figure out something that won't hurt the family too much. We need to protect the rest of the Ravaterras."

"Hurt the family? You have no place in the Ravaterra family. Anyway, what the hell are you talking about? I went to talk to Perry's whore and things got carried away." He touched a small scratch on his face. "It doesn't have a fucking thing to do with my family."

Janvier's mouth was uncomfortably dry, and his stomach felt sour. "Please, Cal. Did you do it to hurt Perry? Because it will.

Hey, would you mind if I helped myself to a glass of water? I'm thirsty as hell."

Cal's face was an angry shade of red. "Yeah, I fucking mind. What are you talking about, hurting Perry? He's like my own. I'd never do anything to hurt him."

"Like your own? No way. Not after what you did to his girlfriend." Janvier walked into the tidy kitchen, extremely thirsty. It was almost painful.

A tight, small noise escaped from Cal's throat. He followed Janvier into the kitchen. "I'd never hurt him. He's like my own kid. He should have been my kid. Did you know I was engaged to his mother? Yeah. Perry could have been mine. He really could."

"Well, that explains your special bond. Are your glasses up here?"

"You don't know about Perry. All his life, I've taken care of him. You don't know."

The glasses were in the cabinet next to the sink and he wasn't finished yelling about Perry. spun on some daydream about how he was going to marry Perry's mother and how he was going to enlist for Vietnam. "Selma loved me. Don't you ever forget that. She was mine. Mine!"

Janvier filled the glass with cold tap water and drained it while Cal went on about Perry's mother.

"She was with me. Me, not Adam. We were on a blanket by a lake and I'd asked her to marry me. That's when Perry was conceived."

Janvier hated it, but a plan took shape in his mind. He needed to keep Cal talking for it to work. "I think you're off by a few years and by a fair amount of truth, Cal, but all that isn't any of my business. Man, I needed water. I'm sorry. I didn't even ask if you wanted some."

The water sloshed uncomfortably in his stomach. Janvier briefly wondered if he'd caught the stomach bug or if he was nauseated because of what he was going to do to Cal. He didn't let himself show the queasiness. Instead, he leaned against the counter and stared at Cal. God, he hoped he had time before the police came. Or maybe he hoped he didn't.

Cal blustered, but he was still talking. "You need to hear this, Frenchie. You need to know. I'm about to disappear and you need to tell Perry." Cal's face crumpled. For a second, the tough old man looked close to tears. "You tell him for me, okay?"

"Okay."

"I took care of Perry all these years, even when he was a kid. I've taken good care of him, whether it was with family or some of his whores. When he was a boy, that lopsided, skinny-assed bitch stepmother tried to mess up his life, so I took care of her. I stopped her, and I did it for Perry. Same as now. Perry's whore was making trouble. He should be grateful I let her walk away. You tell Perry that. You tell him."

Janvier's stomach turned. "'Lopsided step-mother? Oh God, no."

A dog barked several doors down. Cal squared his shoulders. "Never mind. You just tell him. Tell him that he was important to me, okay? You tell him."

Janvier moved over to the kitchen entryway and leaned against the doorjamb. Softly, Janvier said, "Cal, you said that you took care of a skinny assed bitch, a stepmother. Donny's mother was the only real stepmother Perry ever had. Tell me what you did to take care of her." He felt like vomiting the water back up, but this time it wasn't because what he wanted Cal to do. "Tell me about the skinny step-mother. Did she have a lop-sided smile?"

Cal tried to shoved him out of the way. Janvier simply rocked back a little.

"Nice try, old man. I'm not exactly a tiny little woman." He didn't move out of the doorway.

"Fuck you, Frenchie. Get the hell out of my house or get the hell out of my way. I gotta leave. Janvier stepped back enough to let Cal storm out of the kitchen.

He had seen the mother's picture often enough at Donny's house, and Amy had a matching one on her wall. The photo showed a skinny woman with a lopsided smile and Cal had just confessed to killing her. Rage spread through him, and Janvier became intent on making this man go away. With a controlled, conversational voice, he asked, "Did you push her down those stairs, Cal?"

Cal flipped his middle finger up and hauled the suitcase out of the hallway.

Janvier needed to be completely calm. It was the only way this would work. He needed pimp levels of control. "Cal, you have nowhere to go. No money. No way to hide. Put that down and go get your gun."

Cal grabbed his coat from the back of a chair. "I'm an ex-con, asshole. What makes you think I have a gun?"

Janvier shrugged. "You probably keep it in your nightstand, or are you one of those idiots who puts it under a pillow?" He turned his back to the old man and refilled the glass with water. When he went back to the living room, Cal stood next to the opened suitcase, Glock 45 in his hand. He pointed it right at Janvier's belly.

Janvier barely glanced at the gun "You're one fucking stupid human being."

Cal held the Glock on him. "Yeah, well, this whole night has been fucking-stupid. Any reason why I shouldn't shoot you now? Maybe help myself to your credit cards?"

"Because I'm the only one who can give you back Perry. That's what you want, isn't it? You want Perry to forgive you, to love you again?"

"He lied to me."

Janvier took a seat on the couch and put his feet on the coffee table. He motioned for the older man to join him, but Cal stood where he was, still pointing the gun at him.

"I expect Perry's lying hurt you, but that doesn't change much. Cal, you're done. You killed yourself tonight, but you know that already, don't you?"

The furniture was old but sturdy. Janvier liked the house. He even felt guilty when he put the glass down on the coffee table without a coaster.

"Perry's going to want you dead. You beat the crap out of her. I don't shock easily, but that woman shocked the shit out of me. Cal, Perry is going to hate you for this, and that's going to damage the hell out of him. Without me, Perry's going to let you rot in jail."

Perry's uncle was breathing hard. Janvier had a moment of sympathy for the old man, but then he remembered the photo of the woman with the lop-sided smile and the badly beaten young woman on the floor of Donny's apartment. The sympathy disappeared.

Cal snapped, "You don't know shit about Perry." He started for the door.

"Yes, I do. He's a decent man in several ways. The whole family is going to suffer. You'll go on trial, they'll dig up every nasty thing you've ever done for Perry and put it out for everyone to see. The whole family will go through hell, not just Perry."

Cal stopped and turned toward Janvier, the gun low but still pointed at him. "Perry would never hurt me."

"Bullshit. Down deep, Perry's a good man. As soon as he sees those bruises on his girlfriend's face, he'll want to tear your heart out. Stop pointing that thing at me and sit down. Sit down, Cal."

Cal didn't react.

"I wonder why the cops aren't here yet. It doesn't matter. They'll be here soon. Sure, go ahead and leave. I'm parked behind you. Do you want my keys, or do you want to use the minute or two we have left to sit the fuck down and listen to me?"

Cal crossed the room without taking his eyes off Janvier. The leather recliner made a wheezing sigh as Cal sat down. The old man still had his finger on the trigger, but the gun's muzzle drooped. "Okay, I'm listening. I'm being still, and I'm listening. Is that okay with you, Frenchie?"

Janvier shrugged. "My opinion doesn't count. Perry's does because his is the only opinion you've ever cared about, isn't it?"

Cal twitched but didn't answer.

"If you walk out of here, I will make sure that Perry knows about the stepmother you pushed down the stairs."

When Cal's gun came back up, Janvier held out his phone.

"Already texted it to myself. Kill me and they'll find it. Blow your brains out, end it, and I'll tell him that Julie Cooper started slapping you, that things went bad, and that you couldn't face him. I'll make sure he knows you died thinking about him. Listen to me, asshole. Killing yourself is the only thing that will make Perry feel guilty instead of despising you."

Cal was sweating. "I don't need you to tell me this shit."

"You need me to talk you into putting that gun against your head, and you need me to talk to Perry afterwards. That's what you need me to do. Think about it, Cal. If you don't, you're going back to jail for the rest of your life. You beat that woman. You meant to kill her, didn't you? Cal, it's over. Die and he's going to give your eulogy with tears in his eyes. Live, and he's going to hate you every day thereafter. It's up to you."

Cal sat with his hands in his lap. The gun dangled against his thigh.

Janvier took another swallow of water. It was cold and good, even if it had a slight metallic under-taste. "Stay with me, Cal. No zoning out. The police will be here soon. I only saw her for a few seconds, but it was bad. Cal, I'm the only one who can help you now."

"You need to leave me alone." The gun came up. Cal's eyes were slits in his puffy face. "Get the fuck out of here, because maybe you're right. Maybe I need to eat this gun, but damn if I won't take you out, too."

Calm. Pimp levels of control.

"Kill yourself and leave me alive and I promise you this: I'll tell Perry how much he meant to you. I'll keep telling him until he hears me. I'll make sure that he knows you died because you love him."

He'd tell Perry nothing.

"If you live, then the news at eleven will talk about the whole family, and I can tell you right now, they won't recover from this." That was true. It would fuel every dirty-laundry news show in the area, but protecting the family's name wasn't doing it for Cal. Janvier switched back to Perry's forgiveness.

"Imagine how Perry is going to feel when his little girls find out from the news about his affairs. Imagine them listening to that whore say that Perry put you up to this. Die and there's nothing but a mention on tonight's news. A brief mention of your name. No pointing fingers, nothing to embarrass Perry. Just another old con went and beat up some whore, then blew his brains out. Tidy and done."

God, he hoped he was right about that.

Cal held the gun limply. "There wasn't a rape, even if she said there was. I didn't touch her that way. She's Perry's."

"Good point. I'll make sure Perry knows that."

He thought Cal was listening to him, so he kept the lie going. "I'll bullshit the whole thing until Perry believes it was the girl's fault. I'll tell him that you loved him like a son. Put that thing to your head, pull the trigger, and I will tell Perry how you died thinking of him. We'll have a good, solid funeral for you."

Cal nodded. "And you'll tell him. You'll tell Perry."

"Do it, Cal."

The gun shot didn't sound as loud as he thought it would.

Janvier couldn't move. He couldn't close his eyes. He couldn't shut out the sight of the gore dripping down the back of the chair.

Cal's bowels gave away. Janvier stumbled, finding his legs under him as he walked away from the stink, the mess, the ruin in that chair. He pulled his phone out. Dialed.

"Nine-one-one. What is your emergency?"

He was in the kitchen. "This is Janvier Reed. My uncle, I mean my girlfriend's uncle, just shot himself in the head. He's dead." He didn't know where the bathroom was and there was no time. He vomited water and bile into the sink. "God. Oh God."

"Sir, can you hear me?"

"Yes. I'm sorry." He wiped his mouth, grabbed an electric bill from on top of the microwave and read off the address. The 911 operator was patient but wanted him to stay on the phone and wanted to know if he was sure that Cal was dead.

"Yeah, his brains…" Again, he vomited into the sink. Shit, what a mess. "I'm sorry, can you get someone here?" He hung up the phone as he dry-heaved. The operator didn't need to hear that.

He was seventeen when he found his mother. He knew even before he touched her that she'd feel cold, dead. She'd left him a note with his name on the envelope. It was still in the bottom of the chest in Señor Rijos' house.

After he found his mother, he had walked the block to Nate's house. There, he sat down on the front step, unable to go any further. When Señor Rijos found him, he had to pry the unopened suicide note from Janvier's hands.

Adult Janvier Reed sat on Cal's front steps and waited as the first police car rushed to the house. He'd never read his mother's note, but he was sure she said that she loved him. Janvier looked up at the moon. She'd loved him, but she'd completely messed him up by killing herself.

Perhaps he was ready to read his mother's note now.

An hour later, he sat in the front yard on a cold garden bench under a Magnolia tree. Behind the cars, an ambulance was jammed in the driveway. Janvier watched as a stunned-looking Perry made his way through the maze of police cars with their blinding blue lights. He looked like a lost child. Janvier waved him over and Perry sat down next to him.

Perry murmured, "Did you see Julie? Donny said she was probably in 'serious condition.' What did he mean?"

"She was beaten up pretty badly."

"God, why? Why?"

The bench was small, and their shoulders touched. Perry's tremble radiated through his jacket. His voice was low, barely a whisper.

"I didn't mean for that to happen. I didn't even tell Cal about her. I didn't think he would ever do…"

Janvier pressed Perry's shoulder lightly with his shoulder. "This isn't your fault." It didn't matter if that was true or true only to a degree. Perry was shivering, and that did matter.

"Janvier, I didn't know Cal could do that. You said you didn't trust him, but…"

They fell silent as the storm door slammed open. A uniformed police officer held it open and worked at keeping her balance on the small concrete landing. The stretcher had a black body bag strapped to it. Janvier tried not to notice the way the body jiggled within that bag when they took it down the three steps.

Perry whispered. "Did you do this?"

Janvier said, "Yeah."

Perry tried to whisper, "Thank you," but choked. He tried again, but Janvier shook his head.

They sat silently as a detective walked towards them. "Mr. Ravaterra?"

Perry grabbed his arm as they got to their feet. They stood, shoulder to shoulder, together.

ACKNOWLEDGMENTS

I wish to thank my family for believing in me and tolerating me during the writing marathons. My partner, Martha, and the three wonderful young men who are my sons: James, Grant, and Andrew.

I cannot express enough appreciation for fellow writers who held my hand until they were holding Janvier's hand. With thanks: Samantha Bryant, Elizabeth Hein, Sarah Suggs, Jason Feingold, Dawn Taylor, K. Lynn, Nolah Reed, Sara Smith, and Mary Evelyn Sorrell.

I would also like to thank Elizabeth Carroll, a good friend and the author of the 'The Secret Keeper' series. She has been there right from the beginning of this book, encouraging me, arguing with me, and finally in an official capacity of content/line editing. This book would not exist without her.

ABOUT THE AUTHOR

In the late fifties through the sixties, Rebecca Leanda grew up moving. She went to school in both the eastern and western hemispheres. Young Becky often lived in areas that didn't have niceties like television, but she always had books.

So much moving left Rebecca wondering about people who grew up in one place. It also left her wondering about how to explain how difficult it is to be accepted when you aren't from "around here."

She spent the first part of her adulthood in the Virginia suburbs of the D.C area. Almost two decades ago, she moved to North Carolina. In between, she raised four beautiful children and started writing her own stories.

She and her partner ended on a farm near Hillsborough, North Carolina. Rebecca has developed a slight southern accent, but is still trying to figure out how to accept things like tomato sandwiches, Brunswick stew, and mowing a yard with a tractor.

Since moving to the farm, she has had her first bout with poison ivy and wasp stings; and determined that bluebirds like to poop on cars. Rebecca discovered that the black snake is a good snake and spiders make glorious webs on the outside of windows that have just been cleaned. And yes, stink-bugs are real.

But the stars are bright at night and she wouldn't live anywhere else, probably.